PENGUIN CLASSICS

MARTIN EDEN

Born in 1935, Andrew Sinclair took his doctorate at Harvard University and Cambridge University and became a noted social historian and novelist. He has written major works on Prohibition and on feminism in the United States and biographies of John Ford and J. P. Morgan. Mr. Sinclair spent more than two years reading all the London family papers before writing his definitive biography of Jack London, *Jack* (1977). Andrew Sinclair has also edited The Penguin Classics edition of Jack London's *The Call of the Wild, White Fang, and Other Stories.*

Martin Eden

BY

Jack London

With an Introduction by
ANDREW SINCLAIR

PENGUIN BOOKS

PENGUIN BOOKS
Published by the Penguin Group
Viking Penguin, a division of Penguin Books USA Inc.,
375 Hudson Street, New York, New York 10014, U.S.A.
Penguin Books Ltd, 27 Wrights Lane, London W8 5TZ, England
Penguin Books Australia Ltd, Ringwood, Victoria, Australia
Penguin Books Canada Ltd, 10 Alcorn Avenue, Suite 300,
Toronto, Ontario, Canada M4V 3B2
Penguin Books (N.Z.) Ltd, 182–190 Wairau Road, Auckland 10, New Zealand

Penguin Books Ltd, Registered Offices:
Harmondsworth, Middlesex, England

First published in the United States of America by
The Macmillan Company 1909
Published in Penguin Books, 1967
Reprinted in 1968, 1972, 1974
This edition published in The Penguin American Library 1984
Reprinted in Penguin Classics 1985

9 10 8

Introduction copyright © Viking Penguin Inc., 1984
All rights reserved

LIBRARY OF CONGRESS CATALOGING IN PUBLICATION DATA
London, Jack, 1876–1916.
Martin Eden.
(Penguin classics)
Bibliography: p.
I. Title. II. Series.
PS3523.O46M3   1984   818'.5209   83-17255
ISBN 0 14 03.9036 7

Printed in the United States of America
Set in Linotron Janson

CONTENTS

INTRODUCTION

Jack London was a born rebel whose personality demanded the immediate gratification of his contradictory wants. He had a dialectic of appetites without a synthesis of satisfaction. He once confessed to wanting to drive forty horses abreast with the thousand strong arms of his mind; his ambitions in writing and ranching were as excessive as his self-discipline and vigor. Yet his incessant forcing of himself led to occasional nervous collapses into morbidity and despair. Then his horses changed masters. "Satiety and possession are Death's horses," he wrote; "they run in span."

Martin Eden (1909) is London's most autobiographical novel. It describes his struggle for education and literary fame in his youth and his disillusion with success in his middle age. It mythologizes his rise from obscurity and prophesies his early death at forty. The author's passionate identification with his hero, Martin Eden, creates the power and compulsion of the book, which remains today equaled only by Knut Hamsen's *Hunger* as an archetypal study of the urge to write subordinating even the will to live.

London had a hard raising, although not as hard as did Martin Eden, who mysteriously has no parents, only a brood of vagrant brothers and slatternly sisters. London himself was born in 1876 in San Francisco, the only child of Flora Wellman, a spiritualist and music teacher from a middle-class family. His father was probably a wandering astrologer called William Henry Chaney. Shortly after the boy's birth, his mothe married a widower, John London, and her son was given his stepfather's name.

The boy grew up in Oakland and on neighboring small farms. To earn a few dollars, he worked as a newsboy and fought some of the fights Martin Eden fought with Cheese-Face. He had an early love of books and of sailing on San Francisco Bay. By the age of fifteen, he was a delinquent, gang leader, and oyster pirate. Foreseeing an early death on shore, he set off for a seven-month sealing voyage, on which he saw the bloody battle for life between men and beasts. On his return, he worked in factories before joining an army of the unemployed for a march on Washington. A thirty-day jail sentence for vagrancy made him determined to use his mind and avoid the degradation of life as a wage-slave in the Social Pit. He resolved to sell his muscle no more but to become a vendor of brains. Then began for him a frantic pursuit of knowledge.

It is at a similar point in life that London chose to introduce his hero Martin Eden. London himself, supported by his mother and by a job as a school janitor, completed high school, took the entrance examinations for the University of California at Berkeley, and attended classes there for two semesters, grasping at knowledge with the desperation of a drowning man and the arrogance of the self-taught. He met a middle-class family, the Applegarths, and fell in love with their daughter Mabel, whose ethereal beauty embodied the visions of his favorite romantic poets. Browning and Swinburne on the shelves always signified for London a touch of class.

Mabel Applegarth was the model for Ruth Morse in *Martin Eden*, observed with the ruthless hindsight of eleven years' more experience of life. The episode in the novel when Ruth is seen as a woman because black cherry juice stains her lips is based on the moment at which Jack London first saw Mabel "stripping off her immortality." As he wrote in 1900 to the second love of his life, Anna Strunsky, Mabel seemed very small a mere four years after he first knew her. "Her virtues led her nowhere. Works? She had none. Her culture was a surface smear, her deepest depth a singing shallow. Do you understand? Can I explain further? I awoke, and judged, and my puppy love was over."

During the time, however, when the young Jack London adored Mabel Applegarth, he was trying to adopt the values of her class and to leave his own. His memory of his feelings explains the marvel of the opening chapters of *Martin Eden*, when the youthful sailor rolls into the Morse household and soon feels like "God's own mad lover dying on a kiss." Eden's reverence for bourgeois standards and culture mirrors London's own rapture at his first encounter with them. When London described the novel as primarily an attack upon the bourgeoisie and all it stood for, he was not wrong; but fortunately, his artistry and awareness of his former illusions enable him to lurch with his hero through the bric-a-brac and deceits of the Morses' mansion and see all as Camelot and Parnassus.

The novel, London always insisted, was also an attack on individualism. "Being unaware of the needs of others, of the whole human collective need, Martin Eden lived only for himself, fought only for himself, and, if you please, died for himself." He died because of his lack of faith in men. London, however, claimed to have faith in men. He was a socialist and not an individualist. And so he lived.

Unfortunately, London's character was nearer Martin

Eden's than he allowed. His individualism and Nietzschean belief in the strength of the will were usually
more apparent than his faith in socialism. To reconcile
his beliefs in the survival of the fittest and in the aristocracy of the intellect with his compassion for his
fellow workers was a task as difficult as driving forty
horses abreast. Martin Eden was more consistent, living and dying an individualist, ignoring the decadent
poet Brissenden, who praised socialism as the answer
to the death wish.

After leaving Berkeley, London joined the Klondike
gold rush, a vain quest that he equated with Martin
Eden's treasure hunt in the South Seas. He returned,
married his first wife, Bess Maddern, and began to
make some literary progress. After the success of his
short Klondike stories, *The Call of the Wild* (1903) and
The Sea-Wolf (1904) gave him an international reputation almost as sudden and spectacular as Martin
Eden's. Disillusioned with fame, he retreated from
Oakland to a ranch at Glen Ellen, where he hoped to
counteract the rape of the American earth by restoring
the virgin soil and making a paradise from the land
looted by the greed of the pioneers.

By 1906, London's reaction to overwork and no-
toriety—experiences that drove Martin Eden to commit suicide—plunged him into long periods of disgust.
He summed it up in his drinking confession, the novel
John Barleycorn:

> The things I had fought for and burned my midnight
> oil for had failed me. Success—I despised it. Recog-
> nition—it was dead ashes. Society, men and women
> above the ruck and the muck of the waterfront and the
> forecastle—I was appalled by their unlovely mental
> mediocrity. Love of woman—it was like all the rest.

Money—I could sleep in only one bed at a time, and of what worth was an income of a hundred porter-houses a day when I could eat only one? Art, culture—in the face of the iron facts of biology such things were ridiculous, the exponents of such things only the more ridiculous.

The way out of disgust was love of the people and escape. In 1906, London married Charmian Kittredge, made a lecture tour of the United States preaching revolutionary socialism, and set off on a self-designed ketch called the *Snark* to sail round the world. He had bought too much land at Glen Ellen and had ruined himself building the boat. His captain was incompetent, the ketch was inefficient, and London found himself navigating the vessel with Charmian as his true "mate-woman." Only his iron determination—and the need to earn a large income to pay for the voyage and the ranch in California—kept him writing a thousand words a day in any weather.

The book he wrote on the voyage was *Martin Eden*. He was only thirty-one years of age, yet he had already achieved too much too soon. His mental energy seemed to him at times to be mental sickness. He had lamed his splendid body and began to suffer from bowel diseases. The voyage of the *Snark* was meant to reassert his physical dominance, but it ended in his physical collapse. By the time the *Snark* reached Hawaii, London had to fire his captain for allowing the sails, ropes, and decking to rot in the sun. Penniless, he had to beg an advance from his publisher to refit the ketch; he beat two thousand miles in variable winds on the Pacific Traverse to the Marquesas, where Gauguin had found his own disillusion and death. There London rented the clubhouse where his boyhood idol Robert

Louis Stevenson had stayed and set out for Melville's paradise of Happar. Tuberculosis, leprosy, and elephantiasis had decimated Melville's noble warriors. The survivors were mostly freaks and monsters.

More disillusion was to come. There was a financial panic in the United States. London's checks were being returned by the banks; the mortgages on his properties were threatened with foreclosure. His teeth, which were in terrible shape (unlike Martin Eden's), were giving him incessant pain. He booked a passage back to California on the *Mariposa* so he could finish the novel and use the proceeds to pay his debts.

London's sense of disgust and despair, his physical pain, and his pressing financial problems all help to explain why he pushed his hero through the porthole of a boat that he was taking back to California. Charmian's diary reveals London's state of mind while he was finishing *Martin Eden* on the voyage home: "Jack is sick sometimes, mentally, or he wouldn't do as he does. This reflection helps me through some hopeless, loveless times—seldom, thank God." London's disgust and self-destructive urges at that time were transferred to Martin Eden, but not fully explained. The result is that Eden's sudden suicide by drowning appears not inevitable but willful—the self-dramatization of a spoiled youth, not the necessary action of a strong man. The published work was an immediate failure with the critics and the public—but has had long-term success as the parable that London always intended it to be, the parable of an individualist who had to die, "not because of his lack of faith in God, but because of his lack of faith in men."

Had London not been in a temporary slough of disgust, he might have let Martin Eden continue his South Seas voyage as originally intended, even if in the end he was still to drown splendidly in the surf. But the book was long enough, the finish fitting, if depressing. It suited the dark side of London: preoccupied with the struggle of all life against death, the "Noseless One," he was prodigal with his own energies and physique, excessive in his eating and drinking, driven to die unwillingly at forty from a drug overdose, his body no longer capable of responding to the demands his dominant will put upon it. As a young man he had once tried suicide by drowning—and that is the end he wished for Martin Eden, an end when death no longer hurts, and at the instant of knowing the mind ceases to know.

Unlike Socrates, who only knew that he knew nothing, and spent his life inquiring, both Martin Eden and Jack London though they knew everything and therefore died from a surfeit of boredom. Satisfaction kills the cat, curiosity brings it back. "Work performed" was the ceaseless maggot in Martin Eden's mind that led him to world-weariness and self-destruction. He had worked too hard and wanted to perform no more. To the self-taught American at the turn of this century, the facile world view of Herbert Spencer comprehended all knowledge and superseded all other philosophies. The paradox was never clear to London or to his surrogate hero: If evolution and Social Darwinism explained everything, thought could evolve no further, and the Social Darwinist would become bigoted and reactionary.

Although the action of *Martin Eden* takes place primarily on land, the novel itself is dominated by the sea. At the beginning, Martin Eden heaves in, the quintessential sailor, terrified that his sway and gait and shoulders will destroy the bourgeois furniture around him. He is literally at sea in the Morses' genteel parlor. He sees an oil painting of a schooner in a storm, approaches it, and finds it only an illusion, a trick picture. He does not heed the warning that this new world will trick him. He holds the guests captive at dinner with his vehemence about life afloat and provokes in Ruth the desire to put her lily-white vampire hands about his rough neck and absorb its vigor into her frailty.

Martin Eden himself is a fluid organism, swiftly adaptable, ready to be channeled, like any flow. Ruth first shows her desire for him by leaning against him, the master of a sailboat, at the tiller; and she first shows her jealousy when he recalls a shipwreck and the love of a leper princess. It is the sailor's diseases he might have caught from port whores that make marriage with him impossible for Ruth; he has played much with pitch, Mrs. Morse thinks, and the children will be unclean. When he cannot pay for his education, Martin Eden considers returning to the sea; but as the city enfeebles him, the sea's lure becomes more dreamlike and literary, the siren call of South Sea maidens and tropical beaches. His Lucifer figure, Brissenden, urges him to go before the city rots him, but he will not. In his memories of his past, which crosscut the narrative, the images of his life in the forecastle give way to images of himself as the hoodlum gang leader, the Cheese-Face he might have become, the Cheese-Face he had to destroy in himself before he went to sea or took to books. His successful novel, worthy of Conrad, is a sea-novel called *Overdue*. Finally, when he does return to the sea as a first-class passenger on the *Mariposa*, it is to die. He has left his own class and found it impossible to join a new one. The forecastle is brutish, the petty officers truly petty, the captain a snob interested only in reputation. So he chooses to drown, quoting his favorite stanza from Swinburne, the poet whom the sailor read first in the overstuffed Morse parlor, the poet whose verse seduces him to plunge into the depths to terminate his ennui. He has had too much of living. He knows that dead men rise up never. So, like the weariest river, he winds his way safely to sea, and darkness.

Set against the theme of the sea is Moloch, the machine that eats up men and women, hope and vitality, youth and age. It is the machines of the cannery that roughen Lizzie Connolly's hands and make her, in his eyes, unfit for Martin Eden's love; Ruth's hands are soft, for she has never had to work and so is superior in culture. The magazine editors seem to run a machine that takes in manuscripts, puts them through cogs, inserts a rejection slip, and spits them out. When Martin is forced to work in a laundry with Joe, the washing machines make of him an intelligent machine, a rapidly exhausted machine, a machine that will wear out and be discarded. "Fancy starch" is the nightmare that machines make of Martin's romantic love—and the seventy miles to Oakland that Martin has to cover on his mechanical wheels. When he sets up a simple laundry machine for Maria Silva, he loses his status in her eyes; he is a manual worker, not a writer. In his fever soon afterward, he confuses the laundry and the literary machine, so that Joe starches manuscripts, while he mangles checks in the wringer. His ancient typewriter, his Blickensdorfer, is a necessity if his writing is to be read and accepted; when it is pawned, he cannot write. And lastly, when he beats the literary machine and makes a fortune, he sets up Maria in a dairy, Joe in a laundry, his brothers-in-law in commerce, so that they can make ordinary lives out of their automatic existences, while Martin, weary of work performed, goes down to the sea to rest forever.

The chief quality of the novel lies in London's recapturing of his relentless toil to gain literary fame. London first wanted to call the book *Success*, or *Stardust*; he knew the lure of fame for him and Martin Eden. He often used to belittle his own artistry and skill with words, presenting himself as a blacksmith of literature rather than a wordsmith of style and grace. "Don't loaf and invite inspiration," he advised the aspiring writer, "light out after it with a club, and if you don't get it you will nonetheless get something that looks remarkably like it." The secret was to work all the time. Martin Eden's obsessive and incessant concentration has inspired tens of thousands of young writers, even if few of them have won the recognition that Eden both desired and rejected.

The secondary quality of the novel lies in London's awareness of the difficulty of changing social classes. Martin Eden (a Biblical name suggesting struggle and innocence) adores Ruth (another Biblical name, suggesting love and waiting) and is adored by Lizzie. He should love Lizzie, who comes from his own class, and make her happy, but by the time he has become acceptable to Ruth's class, he despises it, yet cannot return to Lizzie. If London had dwelt more on the emotional aspects of the hopeless struggle to change classes rather than on the philosophical questions, if he had concentrated on the love triangle rather than on his recollections of the bohemian and radical "Crowd" at San Francisco, the one weakness of the novel would have been avoided. For the long chats about evolution and the superman and socialism have dated. The need to write autobiography overcame London's talent as a novelist, and his urge to display his hard-won erudition triumphed over his feeling for his characters. To illustrate the class war, another confrontation between

Ruth and Lizzie would have been worth more than ten sophomoric debates between Eden and Brissenden and the Oakland socialists.

Brissenden was modeled on George Sterling, the "Greek" who provided the most intense male friendship in London's life. Sterling was a minor romantic poet who admired and envied London's profligate vigor and natural genius, and, above all, his international success. Brissenden is an idealized portrait of Sterling, and his manner of speaking provokes the worst writing in the novel, the poet's mawkish effusions about beauty and corruption. Sterling did tend to write and talk like a man who had swallowed Swinburne whole and Rossetti undigested. "Beauty hurts you," Brissenden declares to Martin Eden. "It is an everlasting pain in you, a wound that does not heal, a knife of flame. Why should you palter with magazines? Let beauty be your end. Why should you mint beauty into gold?" Such gossamer gallimaufry is as much "Ephemera" as Brissenden's posthumous masterpiece, but is unfortunately preserved forever in *Martin Eden*. The thorns in the text that prick the reader are the simple truths, such as Ruth's perception of poverty as an unpleasant condition of existence, or Lizzie's piercing comment, "Something's wrong with your think-machine."

As Earle Labor has pointed out, *Martin Eden* is a *Bildungsroman*, a novel about the necessary education of a young man from a state of ignorance and innocence through the trials of knowledge to a condition of dark awareness. Rousseau and Goethe, Melville and D. H. Lawrence, Thomas Wolfe and Thomas Mann have all written novels in this tradition. As London was a self-mythologizing hero in so much of his writing, many of his fifty books contribute to a continuing *Bildungsroman*. *Martin Eden* particularly does so. Part of London's education was to escape from Sterling and the "Crowd," a group of self-conscious young writers and artists and debaters who had first met at Coppa's restaurant in San Francisco and who formed a colony at Carmel, characterized by daily hedonism and occasional suicide, abalone-diving and criticism of all but themselves. Martin Eden grows bored with the "Crowd" and chooses a watery death rather than listen to it. In a later novel, *The Valley of the Moon*, which eulogizes flight from the city to the land rather than to the sea, London parodies the false Eden of the Carmel colony, where intellectuals played at Thoreau in safe suburban woods. For London, the true Eden lay in the ranch at Glen Ellen.

First published as a book in 1909, *Martin Eden* was too early for its audience. The myth of individual success through hard work still dominated American culture. Horatio Alger inspired, whereas Jack London depressed. The revolutionary idea that hard work and success were self-defeating in an unlovely mechanical society was unpalatable, both to radicals and to Republicans. London had been liked by the left wing for his socialist views, yet Martin Eden's ambition seemed an attack on socialism, a glorification of the Nietzschean hero and man on horseback. Although London might protest that the novel was an attack on individualism, not socialism, he had made it so autobiographical that his radical readers could not distinguish him from his leading character. He might be conscious that his socialist sympathies separated him from Martin Eden, but by confusing the facts of his own rise to fame with his hero's, he risked condemnation as an apostate. There was already a contradiction between his life-style and his political professions. As Mark Twain commented, if Jack London got the kind of society he wanted, he would have to call out the militia to collect his royalties. Many of London's socialist comrades took *Martin Eden* to be the testament of the man who had deserted the cause by sailing away on the *Snark*, and by becoming a rancher. One of them wrote to him, wishing him the same fate as Martin Eden's: "When you swallow the last mouthful of salt chuck you can hold before sinking, remember that we at least protested."

To established critics, *Martin Eden* also seemed a failure. It denigrated capitalism and self-improvement and ambition without providing any alternatives. London had been known for his celebration of man's struggle for survival, his will to live in the bleakest of conditions. Now, confused with the hero of his book, London seemed to preach futility and deny the elemental and archetypal force of the message in his previous books about nature, the Klondike, and the sea. *Martin Eden* was universally condemned, and London's reputation sank, until the publication in 1910 of a vigorous, optimistic Klondike adventure story, *Burning Daylight*, which did not preach a thing, but entertained. As the reviewer in *The Bookman* declared, it was a pleasure to see London return to using his power as a storyteller, after passing through "the sad phase of unrest out of which *Martin Eden* grew—it's certainly sad to have one's emotions take such unpleasant forms."

Ironically, contemporary reviews of *Martin Eden* confirmed the disgust London felt for readers and reviewers, expressed in this passage about his hero:

His intrinsic beauty and power meant nothing to the hundreds of thousands who were acclaiming him and buying his books. He was the fad of the hour, the adventurer who had stormed Parnassus while the gods nodded. The hundreds of thousands read him and acclaimed him with the same brute non-understanding with which they had flung themselves on Brissenden's "Ephemera" and torn it to pieces—a wolf-rabble that fawned on him instead of fanging him. Fawn or fang, it was all a matter of chance.

Posterity confirmed London's disdain. If *Martin Eden* was a failure at the time because it was before its time, it proved to be the only one of his fifty books that his publishers, Macmillan, kept in print in a cloth edition for seventy years, selling a quarter of a million copies. Against its author's intention, it appealed to young writers determined to succeed by force of will and dedication, without benefit of innate talent. The novel's disillusion with bourgeois values suited the iconoclasm of the 1920s and the anticapitalism of the Depression decade of the 1930s. Its uneasy balance between the drive to succeed at all costs and the despair that follows victory seemed truthful. Only the problem of Martin Eden's suicide—paralleled by the early death of London from excess in 1916—prevented full acceptance and critical acclaim.

In the general reevaluation of London's work begun by Maxwell Geismar and Franklin Walker, *Martin Eden* has taken a significant place. Its force and appeal have survived the passage of time; its flaws and unevenness are less relevant. Always popular in France and Italy, Germany and Russia, the novel has been recently adapted into a television series that proved more successful in many European countries than even *Roots* or *Holocaust*. (CBS will screen the television series in the United States.) For Jack London was the incessant Californian pilgrim. However great his self-destructiveness, his mind ranged after the infinite possibilities of mankind. If he despaired from time to time, he also sought a new vision on a renewed earth. *Martin Eden* was his autobiographical novel. His determination and his questings make it live.

—Andrew Sinclair

SUGGESTIONS FOR FURTHER READING

BOOKS BY JACK LONDON

The Abysmal Brute. New York, 1913.

The Acorn Planter. New York, 1916.

Adventure. New York, 1911.

Before Adam. New York, 1907.

Burning Daylight. New York, 1910.

The Call of the Wild. New York, 1903.

Children of the Frost. New York, 1902.

The Cruise of the Dazzler. New York, 1902.

The Cruise of the Snark. New York, 1911.

A Daughter of the Snows. Philadelphia, 1902.

Dutch Courage and Other Stories. New York, 1922.

The Faith of Men. New York, 1904.

The Game. New York, 1905.

The God of His Fathers. New York, 1901.

Hearts of Three. New York, 1920.

The House of Pride and Other Tales of Hawaii. New York, 1912.

The Human Drift. New York, 1917.

The Iron Heel. New York, 1908.

Jerry of the Islands. New York, 1917.

John Barleycorn. New York, 1913.

The Little Lady of the Big House. New York, 1916.

Lost Face. New York, 1910.

Love of Life and Other Stories. New York, 1907.

Martin Eden. New York, 1909.

Michael, Brother of Jerry. New York, 1917.

Moon-Face and Other Stories. New York, 1906.
The Mutiny of the Elsinore. New York, 1914.
The Night-Born. New York, 1913.
On the Makaloa Mat. New York, 1919.
The People of the Abyss. New York, 1903.
The Red One. New York, 1918.
Revolution and Other Essays. New York, 1910.
The Road. New York, 1907.
The Scarlet Plague. New York, 1915.
Scorn of Women. New York, 1906.
The Sea-Wolf. New York, 1904.
Smoke Bellew. New York, 1912.
The Son of the Wolf. Boston, 1900.
A Son of the Sun. New York, 1912.
South Sea Tales. New York, 1911.
The Star Rover. New York, 1915.
The Strength of the Strong. New York, 1914.
Tales of the Fish Patrol. New York, 1905.
Theft: A Play in Four Acts. New York, 1910.
The Turtles of Tasman. New York, 1916.
The Valley of the Moon. New York, 1913.
War of the Classes. New York, 1905.
When God Laughs and Other Stories. New York, 1911.
White Fang. New York, 1906.

BOOKS BY JACK LONDON AND OTHERS

London, Jack, and Strunsky, Anna. *The Kempton–Wace Letters*. New York, 1903.

London, Jack, completed by Robert L. Fish. *The Assassination Bureau, Ltd*. New York, 1963.

CRITICISM AND BIOGRAPHY

Bridgwater, P. *Nietzsche in Anglosaxony: A Study of Nietzsche's Impact on English and American Literature*. Leicester, 1972.

Brown, D. *Soviet Attitudes Toward American Writing*. Princeton, N. J., 1962.

Foner, P. S. *Jack London: American Rebel*. New York, 1947.

Hendricks, K., and Shepard, I., eds. *Letters from Jack London*. New York, 1965.

Johnson, M. *Through the South Seas with Jack London*. New York, 1913.

Kingman, R. *A Pictorial Life of Jack London*. New York, 1979.

Labor, E. *Jack London*. New York, 1974.

London, C. K. *The Book of Jack London*, 2 vols. New York, 1921.

London, J. *Jack London and His Times: An Unconventional Biography*. Seattle, 1968.

Lynn, K. S. *The Dream of Success*. Boston, 1955.

Ownbey, R. W., ed. *Jack London: Essays in Criticism*. Layton, Utah, 1978.

Sinclair, A. *Jack: A Biography of Jack London*. New York, 1977.

Starr, Kevin. *Americans and the California Dream, 1850–1915*. New York, 1973.

Walcutt, C. C. *Jack London*. Minneapolis, 1966.

Walker, D. L., ed. *The Fiction of Jack London: A Chronological Bibliography*. El Paso, Texas, 1972.

Walker, F. *Jack London and the Klondike*. San Marino, California, 1966.

———. *The Seacoast of Bohemia: An Account of Early Carmel*. San Francisco, 1966.

ARTICLES

Calder-Marshall, A. "Introduction." *Martin Eden* (The Bodley Head Jack London). 4 vols. London, 1965.

Etulain, R. "The Lives of Jack London." *Western American Literature* 11 (1976).

Geismar, M. "Jack London: The Short Cut." In *Rebels and Ancestors: The American Novel, 1890–1915*. Boston, 1953.

Pattee, F. L. "The Prophet of the Last Frontier." In *Sidelights on American Literature*. New York, 1922.

Shivers, A. S. "The Romantic in Jack London." *Alaska Review* 1 (1963).

Walcutt, C. C. "Jack London: Blond Beasts and Supermen." In *American Literary Naturalism: A Divided Stream*. Minneapolis, 1956.

Walker, F. "Jack London: *Martin Eden*." In *The American Novel from James Fenimore Cooper to William Faulkner*, edited by W. Stegner. New York, 1965.

A NOTE ON THE TEXT

The text of *Martin Eden* is that of the first edition of the book, published by The Macmillan Company in 1909. No Collected Edition of the works of Jack London has yet been published, and London himself refused to revise his printed works. Punctuation and spelling have been slightly modernized; the author's very occasional archaisms and grammatical errors have also been corrected; for example, "bicycle shop" has been substituted for "cyclery" and "wafting" for "wafture."

Chapter One

The one opened the door with a latch-key and went
in, followed by a young fellow who awkwardly
removed his cap. He wore rough clothes that smacked
of the sea, and he was manifestly out of place in the
spacious hall in which he found himself. He did not
know what to do with his cap, and was stuffing it into
his coat pocket when the other took it from him. The
act was done quietly and naturally, and the awkward
young fellow appreciated it. "He understands," was
his thought. "He'll see me through all right."

He walked at the other's heels with a swing to his
shoulders, and his legs spread unwittingly, as if the
level floors were tilting up and sinking down to the
heave and lunge of the sea. The wide rooms seemed
too narrow for his rolling gait, and to himself he was
in terror lest his broad shoulders should collide with
the doorways or sweep the bric-a-brac from the low
mantel. He recoiled from side to side between the
various objects and multiplied the hazards that in reality lodged only in his mind. Between a grand piano
and a center-table piled high with books was space for
a half a dozen to walk abreast, yet he essayed it with
trepidation. His heavy arms hung loosely at his sides.
He did not know what to do with those arms and
hands, and when, to his excited vision, one arm seemed
liable to brush against the books on the table, he lurched
away like a frightened horse, barely missing the piano
stool. He watched the easy walk of the other in front

of him, and for the first time realized that his walk
was different from that of other men He experienced
a momentary pang of shame that he should walk so
uncouthly. The sweat burst through the skin of his
forehead in tiny beads, and he paused and mopped
his bronzed face with his handkerchief.

"Hold on, Arthur, my boy," he said, attempting to
mask his anxiety with facetious utterance. "This is too
much all at once for yours truly. Give me a chance to
get my nerve. You know I didn't want to come, an' I
guess your fam'ly ain't hankerin' to see me neither."

"That's all right," was the reassuring answer. "You
mustn't be frightened at us. We're just homely
people— Hello, there's a letter for me."

He stepped back to the table, tore open the envelope, and began to read, giving the stranger an opportunity to recover himself. And the stranger
understood and appreciated. His was the gift of sym
pathy, understanding; and beneath his alarmed exte-
rior that sympathetic process went on. He mopped
his forehead dry and glanced about him with a con·
trolled face, though in the eyes there was an expression
such as wild animals betray when they fear the trap.
He was surrounded by the unknown, apprehensive of
what might happen, ignorant of what he should do,
aware that he walked and bore himself awkwardly,
fearful that every attribute and power of him was similarly afflicted. He was keenly sensitive, hopelessly
self-conscious, and the amused glance that the other
stole privily at him over the top of the letter burned
into him like a dagger-thrust. He saw the glance, but
he gave no sign, for among the things he had learned
was discipline. Also, that dagger-thrust went to his
pride. He cursed himself for having come, and at the
same time resolved that, happen what would, having

come, he would carry it through. The lines of his face hardened, and into his eyes came a fighting light. He looked about more unconcernedly, sharply observant, every detail of the pretty interior registering itself on his brain. His eyes were wide apart; nothing in their field of vision escaped; and as they drank in the beauty before them the fighting light died out and a warm glow took its place. He was responsive to beauty, and here was cause to respond.

An oil painting caught and held him. A heavy surf thundered and burst over an outjutting rock; lowering storm-clouds covered the sky; and, outside the line of surf, a pilot-schooner, close-hauled, heeled over till every detail of her deck was visible, was surging along against a stormy sunset sky. There was beauty, and it drew him irresistibly. He forgot his awkward walk and came closer to the painting, very close. The beauty faded out of the canvas. His face expressed his be-puzzlement. He stared at what seemed a careless daub of paint, then stepped away. Immediately all the beauty flashed back into the canvas. "A trick picture," was his thought, as he dismissed it, though in the midst of the multitudinous impressions he was receiving he found time to feel a prod of indignation that so much beauty should be sacrificed to make a trick. He did not know painting. He had been brought up on chromos and lithographs that were always definite and sharp, near or far. He had seen oil paintings, it was true, in the show windows of shops, but the glass of the windows had prevented his eager eyes from approaching too near.

He glanced around at his friend reading the letter and saw the books on the table. Into his eyes leaped a wistfulness and a yearning as promptly as the yearning leaps into the eyes of a starving man at sight of food. An impulsive stride, with one lurch to right and left of the shoulders, brought him to the table, where he began affectionately handling the books. He glanced at the titles and the authors' names, read fragments of text, caressing the volumes with his eyes and hands, and, once, recognized a book he had read. For the rest, they were strange books and strange authors. He chanced upon a volume of Swinburne and began reading steadily, forgetful of where he was, his face glowing. Twice he closed the book on his forefinger to look at the name of the author. Swinburne! he would remember that name. That fellow had eyes, and he had certainly seen color and flashing light. But who was Swinburne? Was he dead a hundred years or so, like most of the poets? Or was he alive still, and writing? He turned to the title-page . . . yes, he had written other books; well, he would go to the free library the first thing in the morning and try to get hold of some of Swinburne's stuff. He went back to the text and lost himself. He did not notice that a young woman had entered the room. The first he knew was when he heard Arthur's voice saying:—

"Ruth, this is Mr. Eden."

The book was closed on his forefinger, and before he turned he was thrilling to the first new impression, which was not of the girl, but of her brother's words. Under that muscled body of his he was a mass of quivering sensibilities. At the slightest impact of the outside world upon his consciousness, his thoughts, sympathies, and emotions leapt and played like lambent flame. He was extraordinarily receptive and responsive, while his imagination, pitched high, was ever at work establishing relations of likeness and difference. "Mr. Eden," was what he had thrilled to— he who had been called "Eden," or "Martin Eden," or just "Martin," all his life. And *"Mister!"* It was certainly going some, was his internal comment. His mind seemed to turn, on the instant, into a vast camera obscura, and he saw arrayed around his consciousness endless pictures from his life, of stokeholes and fore-castles, camps and beaches, jails and boozing-kens, fever-hospitals and slum streets, wherein the thread of association was the fashion in which he had been addressed in those various situations.

And then he turned and saw the girl. The phan-tasmagoria of his brain vanished at sight of her. She was a pale, ethereal creature, with wide, spiritual blue eyes and a wealth of golden hair. He did not know how she was dressed, except that the dress was as wonderful as she. He likened her to a pale gold flower upon a slender stem. No, she was a spirit, a divinity, a goddess; such sublimated beauty was not of the earth. Or perhaps the books were right, and there were many such as she in the upper walks of life. She might well be sung by that chap Swinburne. Perhaps he had had somebody like her in mind when he painted that girl, Iseult, in the book there on the table. All this plethora of sight, and feeling, and thought occurred on the instant. There was no pause of the realities wherein he moved. He saw her hand coming out to his, and she looked him straight in the eyes as she shook hands, frankly, like a man. The women he had known did not shake hands that way. For that matter, most of them did not shake hands at all. A flood of associations, visions of various ways he had made the acquaintance of women, rushed into his mind and threatened to swamp it. But he shook them aside and looked at her. Never had he seen such a woman. The women he had known! Immediately, beside her, on either hand, ranged the women he had known. For an eternal second he stood in the midst of a portrait gallery, wherein she occupied the central place, while about her were limned many women, all to be weighed and measured by a fleeting glance, herself the unit of weight and measure. He saw the weak and sickly faces of the girls of the factories, and the simpering, boisterous girls from the south of Market. There were women of the cattle camps, and swarthy cigarette-smoking women of Old Mexico. These, in turn, were crowded out by Japanese women, doll-like, stepping mincingly on wooden clogs; by Eurasians, delicate featured, stamped with degeneracy; by full-bodied South-Sea-Island women, flower-crowned and brown-skinned. All these were blotted out by a grotesque and terrible nightmare brood—frowsy, shuffling creatures from the pavements of Whitechapel, gin-bloated hags of the stews, and all the vast hell's following of harpies, vile-mouthed and filthy, that under the guise of monstrous female form prey upon sailors, the scrapings of the ports, the scum and slime of the human pit.

"Won't you sit down, Mr. Eden?" the girl was saying. "I have been looking forward to meeting you ever since Arthur told us. It was brave of you—"

He waved his hand deprecatingly and muttered that it was nothing at all, what he had done, and that any fellow would have done it. She noticed that the hand he waved was covered with fresh abrasions, in the process of healing, and a glance at the other loose-hanging hand showed it to be in the same condition. Also, with quick, critical eye, she noted a scar on his cheek, another that peeped out from under the hair of the forehead, and a third that ran down and disappeared under the starched collar. She repressed a smile at sight of the red line that marked the chafe of the collar against the bronzed neck. He was evidently unused to stiff collars. Likewise her feminine eye took in the clothes he wore, the cheap and unaesthetic cut, the wrinkling of the coat across the shoulders, and the series of wrinkles in the sleeves that advertised bulging biceps muscles.

While he waved his hand and muttered that he had done nothing at all, he was obeying her behest by trying to get into a chair. He found time to admire the ease with which she sat down, then lurched toward a chair facing her, overwhelmed with consciousness of the awkward figure he was cutting. This was a new experience for him. All his life, up to then, he had been unaware of being either graceful or awkward. Such thoughts of self had never entered his mind. He sat down gingerly on the edge of the chair, greatly worried by his hands. They were in the way wherever he put them. Arthur was leaving the room, and Martin Eden followed his exit with longing eyes. He felt lost, alone there in the room with that pale spirit of a woman. There was no barkeeper upon whom to call for drink no small boy to send around the corner for a can of beer and by means of that social fluid start the amenities of friendship flowing.

"You have such a scar on your neck, Mr. Eden," the girl was saying. "How did it happen? I am sure it must have been some adventure."

"A Mexican with a knife, miss," he answered, moistening his parched lips and clearing his throat. "It was just a fight. After I got the knife away, he tried to bite off my nose."

Baldly as he had stated it, in his eyes was a rich vision of that hot, starry night at Salina Cruz, the white strip of beach, the lights of the sugar steamers in the harbor, the voices of the drunken sailors in the distance, the jostling stevedores, the flaming passion in the Mexican's face, the glint of the beast-eyes in the starlight, the sting of the steel in his neck, and the rush of blood, the crowd and the cries, the two bodies, his and the Mexican's, locked together, rolling over and over and tearing up the sand, and from away off somewhere the mellow tinkling of a guitar. Such was the picture, and he thrilled to the memory of it, wondering if the man could paint it who had painted the pilot-schooner on the wall. The white beach, the stars, and the lights of the sugar steamers would look great, he thought, and midway on the sand the dark group of figures that surrounded the fighters. The knife occupied a place in the picture, he decided, and would show well, with a sort of gleam, in the light of the stars. But of all this no hint had crept into his speech. "He tried to bite off my nose," he concluded.

"Oh," the girl said, in a faint, far voice, and he noticed the shock in her sensitive face.

He felt a shock himself, and a blush of embarrassment shone faintly on his sunburned cheeks, though to him it burned as hotly as when his cheeks had been exposed to the open furnace-door in the fire-room. Such sordid things as stabbing affrays were evidently not fit subjects for conversation with a lady. People in the books, in her walk of life, did not talk about such things—perhaps they did not know about them, either.

There was a brief pause in the conversation they were trying to get started. Then she asked tentatively about the scar on his cheek. Even as she asked, he realized that she was making an effort to talk his talk, and he resolved to get away from it and talk hers.

"It was just an accident," he said, putting his hand to his cheek. "One night, in a calm, with a heavy sea running, the main-boom-lift carried away, an' next the tackle. The lift was wire, an' it was threshin' around like a snake. The whole watch was tryin' to grab it, an' I rushed in an' got swatted."

"Oh," she said, this time with an accent of comprehension, though secretly his speech had been so much Greek to her and she was wondering what a *lift* was and what *swatted* meant.

"This man Swineburne," he began, attempting to put his plan into execution and pronouncing the *i* long.

"Who?"

"Swineburne," he repeated, with the same mispronunciation. "The poet."

"Swinburne," she corrected.

"Yes, that's the chap," he stammered, his cheeks hot again. "How long since he died?"

"Why, I haven't heard that he was dead." She looked at him curiously. "Where did you make his acquaintance?"

"I never clapped eyes on him," was the reply. "But I read some of his poetry out of that book there on the table just before you come in. How do you like his poetry?"

And thereat she began to talk quickly and easily upon the subject he had suggested. He felt better, and settled back slightly from the edge of the chair, holding tightly to its arms with his hands, as if it might get away from him and buck him to the floor. He had succeeded in making her talk her talk, and while she rattled on, he strove to follow her, marveling at all the knowledge that was stowed away in that pretty head of hers, and drinking in the pale beauty of her face. Follow her he did, though bothered by unfamiliar words that fell glibly from her lips and by critical phrases and thought-processes that were foreign to his mind, but that nevertheless stimulated his mind and set it tingling. Here was intellectual life, he thought, and here was beauty, warm and wonderful as he had never dreamed it could be. He forgot himself and stared at her with hungry eyes. Here was something to live for, to win to, to fight for—ay, and die for. The books were true. There were such women in the world. She was one of them. She lent wings to his imagination, and great, luminous canvases spread themselves before him, whereon loomed vague, gigantic figures of love and romance, and of heroic deeds for woman's sake—for a pale woman, a flower of gold. And through the swaying, palpitant vision, as through a fairy mirage, he stared at the real woman, sitting there and talking of literature and art. He listened as well, but he stared, unconscious of the fixity of his gaze or of the fact that all that was essentially masculine in his nature was shining in his eyes. But she, who knew little of the world of men, being a woman, was keenly aware of his burning eyes. She had never had men look at her in such fashion, and it embarrassed her. She stumbled and halted in her utterance. The thread of argument slipped from her. He frightened her, and at the same time it was strangely pleasant to be so looked upon. Her training warned her of peril and of wrong, subtle, mysterious, luring; while her instincts rang clarion-voiced through her being, impelling her to hurdle caste and place and gain to this traveler from another world, to this uncouth young fellow with lacerated hands and a line of raw red caused by the unaccustomed linen at his throat, who, all too evidently, was soiled and tainted by ungracious existence. She was clean, and her cleanness revolted; but she was woman, and she was just beginning to learn the paradox of woman.

"As I was saying—what was I saying?" She broke off abruptly and laughed merrily at her predicament.

"You was saying that this man Swinburne failed bein' a great poet because—an' that was as far as you got, miss," he prompted, while to himself he seemed suddenly hungry, and delicious little thrills crawled up and down his spine at the sound of her laughter. Like silver, he thought to himself, like tinkling silver bells; and on the instant, and for an instant, he was transported to a far land, where under pink cherry blossoms, he smoked a cigarette and listened to the bells of the peaked pagoda calling straw-sandaled devotees to worship.

"Yes, thank you," she said. "Swinburne fails, when all is said, because he is, well, indelicate. There are many of his poems that should never be read. Every line of the really great poets is filled with beautiful truth, and calls to all that is high and noble in the human. Not a line of the great poets can be spared without impoverishing the world by that much."

"I thought it was great," he said hesitatingly, "the little I read, I had no idea he was such a—a scoundrel. I guess that crops out in his other books."

"There are many lines that could be spared from the book you were reading," she said, her voice primly firm and dogmatic.

"I must 'a' missed 'em," he announced. "What I read was the real goods. It was all lighted up an' shining, an' it shun right into me an' lighted me up inside, like the sun or a searchlight. That's the way it landed on me, but I guess I ain't up much on poetry, miss."

He broke off lamely. He was confused, painfully conscious of his inarticulateness. He had felt the bigness and glow of life in what he had read, but his speech was inadequate. He could not express what he felt, and to himself he likened himself to a sailor, in a strange ship, on a dark night, groping about in the unfamiliar running rigging. Well, he decided, it was up to him to get acquainted in this new world. He had never seen anything that he couldn't get the hang of when he wanted to and it was about time for him to want to learn to talk the things that were inside of him so that she could understand. *She* was bulking large on his horizon.

"Now Longfellow—" she was saying.

"Yes, I've read 'm," he broke in impulsively, spurred on to exhibit and make the most of his little store of book knowledge, desirous of showing her that he was not wholly a stupid clod. " 'The Psalm of Life,' 'Excelsior,' an'. . . . I guess that's all."

She nodded her head and smiled, and he felt, somehow, that her smile was tolerant, pitifully tolerant. He was a fool to attempt to make a pretense that way. That Longfellow chap most likely had written countless books of poetry.

"Excuse me, miss, for buttin' in that way, I guess the real facts is that I don't know nothin' much about such things. It ain't in my class. But I'm goin' to make it in my class."

It sounded like a threat. His voice was determined, his eyes were flashing, the lines of his face had grown harsh. And to her it seemed that the angle of his jaw had changed; its pitch had become unpleasantly aggressive. At the same time a wave of intense virility seemed to surge out from him and impinge upon her.

"I think you could make it in—in your class," she finished with a laugh. "You are very strong."

Her gaze rested for a moment on the muscular neck, heavy corded, almost bull-like, bronzed by the sun, spilling over with rugged health and strength. And though he sat there, blushing and humble, again she felt drawn to him. She was surprised by a wanton thought that rushed into her mind. It seemed to her that if she could lay her two hands upon that neck that all its strength and vigor would flow out to her. She was shocked by this thought. It seemed to reveal to her an undreamed depravity in her nature. Besides, strength to her was a gross and brutish thing. Her ideal of masculine beauty had always been slender gracefulness. Yet the thought still persisted. It bewildered her that she should desire to place her hands on that sunburned neck. In truth, she was far from robust, and the need of her body and mind was for strength. But she did not know it. She knew only that no man had ever affected her before as this one had, who shocked her from moment to moment with his awful grammar.

"Yes, I ain't no invalid," he said. "When it comes down to hard-pan, I can digest scrap-iron. But just now I've got dyspepsia. Most of what you was sayin' I can't digest. Never trained that way, you see. I like books and poetry, and what time I've had I've read 'em, but I've never thought about 'em the way you have. That's why I can't talk about 'em. I'm like a navigator adrift on a strange sea without chart or compass. Now I want to get my bearin's. Mebbe you can put me right. How did you learn all this you've ben talkin'?"

"By going to school, I fancy, and by studying," she answered.

"I went to school when I was a kid," he began to object.

"Yes; but I mean high school, and lectures, and the university."

"You've gone to the university?" he demanded in frank amazement. He felt that she had become remoter from him by at least a million miles.

"I'm going there now. I'm taking special courses in English."

He did not know what "English" meant, but he

made a mental note of that item of ignorance and passed on.

"How long would I have to study before I could go to the university?" he asked.

She beamed encouragement upon his desire for knowledge, and said: "That depends upon how much studying you have already done. You have never attended high school? Of course not. But did you finish grammar school?"

"I had two years to run, when I left," he answered. "But I was always honorably promoted at school."

The next moment, angry with himself for the boast, he had gripped the arms of the chair so savagely that every finger-end was stinging. At the same moment he became aware that a woman was entering the room. He saw the girl leave her chair and trip swiftly across the floor to the newcomer. They kissed each other, and, with arms around each other's waists, they advanced toward him. That must be her mother, he thought. She was a tall, blonde woman, slender, and stately, and beautiful. Her gown was what he might expect in such a house. His eyes delighted in the graceful lines of it. She and her dress together reminded him of women on the stage. Then he remembered seeing similar grand ladies and gowns entering the London theatres while he stood and watched and the policemen shoved him back into the drizzle beyond the awning. Next his mind leaped to the Grand Hotel at Yokohama, where, too, from the sidewalk, he had seen grand ladies. Then the city and the harbor of Yokohama, in a thousand pictures, began flashing before his eyes. But he swiftly dismissed the kaleidoscope of memory, oppressed by the urgent need of the present. He knew that he must stand up to be introduced, and he struggled painfully to his feet, where he stood with trousers bagging at the knees, his arms loose-hanging and ludicrous, his face set hard for the impending ordeal.

Chapter Two

The process of getting into the dining room was a nightmare to him. Between halts and stumbles, jerks and lurches, locomotion had at times seemed impossible. But at last he had made it, and was seated alongside of Her. The array of knives and forks frightened him. They bristled with unknown perils, and he gazed at them, fascinated, till their dazzle became a background across which moved a succession of forecastle pictures, wherein he and his mates sat eating salt beef with sheath-knives and fingers, or scooping thick pea-soup out of pannikins by means of battered iron spoons. The stench of bad beef was in his nostrils, while in his ears, to the accompaniment of creaking timbers and groaning bulkheads, echoed the loud mouth-noises of the eaters. He watched them eating, and decided that they ate like pigs. Well, he would be careful here. He would make no noise. He would keep his mind upon it all the time.

He glanced around the table. Opposite him was Arthur, and Arthur's brother, Norman. They were her brothers, he reminded himself, and his heart warmed toward them. How they loved each other, the members of this family! There flashed into his mind the picture of her mother, of the kiss of greeting, and of the pair of them walking toward him with arms entwined. Not in his world were such displays of affection between parents and children made. It was a revelation of the heights of existence that were attained in the world above. It was the finest thing yet that he had seen in this small glimpse of that world. He was moved deeply by appreciation of it, and his heart was melting with sympathetic tenderness. He had starved for love all his life. His nature craved love. It was an organic demand of his being. Yet he had gone without, and hardened himself in the process. He had not known that he needed love. Nor did he know it now. He merely saw it in operation, and thrilled to it, and thought it fine, and high, and splendid.

He was glad that Mr. Morse was not there. It was difficult enough getting acquainted with her, and her mother, and her brother, Norman. Arthur he already knew somewhat. The father would have been too much for him, he felt sure. It seemed to him that he had never worked so hard in his life. The severest toil was child's play compared with this. Tiny nodules of moisture stood out on his forehead, and his shirt was wet with sweat from the exertion of doing so many unaccustomed things at once. He had to eat as he had never eaten before, to handle strange tools, to glance surreptitiously about and learn how to accomplish each new thing, to receive the flood of impressions that was pouring in upon him and being mentally annotated and classified; to be conscious of a yearning for her that perturbed him in the form of a dull, aching restlessness; to feel the prod of desire to win to the walk in life whereon she trod, and to have his mind ever and again straying off in speculation and vague plans of how to reach to her. Also, when his secret glance went across to Norman opposite him, or to any one else, to ascertain just what knife or fork was to be used in any particular occasion, that person's features were

seized upon by his mind, which automatically strove
to appraise them and to divine what they were—all
in relation to her. Then he had to talk, to hear what
was said to him and what was said back and forth,
and to answer, when it was necessary, with a tongue
prone to looseness of speech that required a constant
curb. And to add confusion to confusion, there was
the servant, an unceasing menace, that appeared noiselessly at his shoulder, a dire Sphinx that propounded
puzzles and conundrums demanding instantaneous solution. He was oppressed throughout the meal by the
thought of fingerbowls. Irrelevantly, insistently, scores
of times, he wondered when they would come on and
what they looked like. He had heard of such things,
and now, sooner or later, somewhere in the next few
minutes, he would see them, sit at table with exalted
beings who used them—ay, and he would use them
himself. And most important of all, far down and yet
always at the surface of his thought, was the problem
of how he should comport himself toward these persons. What should his attitude be? He wrestled continually and anxiously with the problem. There were
cowardly suggestions that he should make believe, assume a part; and there were still more cowardly suggestions that warned him he would fail in such course,
that his nature was not fitted to live up to it, and that
he would make a fool of himself.

It was during the first part of the dinner, struggling
to decide upon his attitude, that he was very quiet.
He did not know that his quietness was giving the lie
to Arthur's words of the day before, when that brother
of hers had announced that he was going to bring a
wild man home to dinner and for them not to be
alarmed, because they would find him an interesting
wild man. Martin Eden could not have found it in

him, just then, to believe that her brother could be guilty of such treachery—especially when he had been the means of getting this particular brother out of an unpleasant row. So he sat at table, perturbed by his own unfitness and at the same time charmed by all that went on about him. For the first time he realized that eating was something more than a utilitarian function. He was unaware of what he ate. It was merely food. He was feasting his love of beauty at this table where eating was an aesthetic function. It was an intellectual function, too. His mind was stirred. He heard words spoken that were meaningless to him, and other words that he had seen only in books and that no man or woman he had known was of large enough mental caliber to pronounce. When he heard such words dropping carelessly from the lips of the members of this marvelous family, her family, he thrilled with delight. The romance, and beauty, and high vigor of the books were coming true. He was in that rare and blissful state wherein a man sees his dreams stalk out from the crannies of fantasy and become fact.

Never had he been at such an altitude of living, and he kept himself in the background, listening, observing, and pleasuring, replying in reticent monosyllables, saying "Yes, miss," and "No, miss," to her, and "Yes, ma'am," and "No, ma'am," to her mother. He curbed the impulse, arising out of his sea-training, to say "Yes, sir," and "No, sir," to her brothers. He felt that it would be inappropriate and a confession of inferiority on his part—which would never do if he was to win to her. Also, it was a dictate of his pride. "By God!" he cried to himself, once; "I'm just as good as them, and if they do know lots that I don't, I could learn 'm a few myself, all the same!" And the next moment, when she or her mother addressed him as

"Mr. Eden," his aggressive pride was forgotten, and he was glowing and warm with delight. He was a civilized man, that was what he was, shoulder to shoulder, at dinner, with people he had read about in books. He was in the books himself, adventuring through the printed pages of bound volumes.

But while he belied Arthur's description, and appeared a gentle lamb rather than a wild man, he was racking his brains for a course of action. He was no gentle lamb, and the part of second fiddle would never do for the high-pitched dominance of his nature. He talked only when he had to, and then his speech was like his walk to the table, filled with jerks and halts as he groped in his polyglot vocabulary for words, debating over words he knew were fit but which he feared he could not pronounce, rejecting other words he knew would not be understood or would be raw and harsh. But all the time he was oppressed by the consciousness that this carefulness of diction was making a booby of him, preventing him from expressing what he had in him. Also, his love of freedom chafed against the restriction in much the same way his neck chafed against the starched fetter of a collar. Besides, he was confident that he could not keep it up. He was by nature powerful of thought and sensibility, and the creative spirit was restive and urgent. He was swiftly mastered by the concept or sensation in him that struggled in birth-throes to receive expression and form, and then he forgot himself and where he was, and the old words—the tools of speech he knew— slipped out.

Once, he declined something from the servant who interrupted and pestered at his shoulder, and he said, shortly and emphatically, "Pow!"

On the instant those at the table were keyed up and

expectant, the servant was smugly pleased, and he was wallowing in mortification. But he recovered himself quickly.

"It's the Kanaka for 'finish,' " he explained, "and it just come out naturally. It's spelt p-a-u."

He caught her curious and speculative eyes fixed on his hands, and, being in explanatory mood, he said:—

"I just come down the Coast on one of the Pacific mail steamers. She was behind time, an' around the Puget Sound ports we worked like niggers, storing cargo—mixed freight, if you know what that means. That's how the skin got knocked off."

"Oh, it wasn't that," she hastened to explain, in turn. "Your hands seemed too small for your body."

His cheeks were hot. He took it as an exposure of another of his deficiencies.

"Yes," he said depreciatingly. "They ain't big enough to stand the strain. I can hit like a mule with my arms and shoulders. They are too strong, an' when I smash a man on the jaw the hands get smashed, too."

He was not happy at what he had said. He was filled with disgust at himself. He had loosed the guard upon his tongue and talked about things that were not nice.

"It was brave of you to help Arthur the way you did—and you a stranger," she said tactfully, aware of his discomfiture though not of the reason for it.

He, in turn, realized what she had done, and in the consequent warm surge of gratefulness that over-whelmed him forgot his loose-worded tongue.

"It wasn't nothin' at all," he said. "Any guy 'ud do it for another. That bunch of hoodlums was lookin' for trouble, an' Arthur wasn't botherin' 'em none. They butted in on 'm, an' then I butted in on them an' poked a few. That's where some of the skin off my hands went, along with some of the teeth of the gang. I wouldn't 'a' missed it for anything. When I seen—"

He paused, open-mouthed, on the verge of the pit of his own depravity and utter worthlessness to breathe the same air she did. And while Arthur took up the tale, for the twentieth time, of his adventure with the drunken hoodlums on the ferry-boat and of how Martin Eden had rushed in and rescued him, that individual, with frowning brows, meditated upon the fool he had made of himself, and wrestled more determinedly with the problem of how he should conduct himself toward these people. He certainly had not succeeded so far. He wasn't of their tribe, and he couldn't talk their lingo, was the way he put it to himself. He couldn't fake being their kind. The masquerade would fail, and besides, masquerade was foreign to his nature. There was no room in him for sham or artifice. Whatever happened, he must be real. He couldn't talk their talk just yet, though in time he would. Upon that he was resolved. But in the meantime, talk he must, and it must be his own talk, toned down, of course, so as to be comprehensible to them and so as not to shock them too much. And furthermore, he wouldn't claim, not even by tacit acceptance, to be familiar with anything that was unfamiliar. In pursuance of this decision, when the two brothers, talking university shop, had used "trig" several times, Martin Eden demanded:—

"What is *trig?*"

"Trigonometry," Norman said; "a higher form of math."

"And what is *math?*" was the next question, which, somehow, brought the laugh on Norman.

"Mathematics, arithmetic," was the answer.

Martin Eden nodded. He had caught a glimpse of the apparently illimitable vistas of knowledge. What he saw took on tangibility. His abnormal power of vision made abstractions take on concrete form. In the alchemy of his brain, trigonometry and mathematics and the whole field of knowledge which they betokened were transmuted into so much landscape. The vistas he saw were vistas of green foliage and forest glades, all softly luminous or shot through with flashing lights. In the distance, detail was veiled and blurred by a purple haze, but behind this purple haze, he knew, was the glamour of the unknown, the lure of romance. It was like wine to him. Here was adventure, something to do with head and hand, a world to conquer—and straightway from the back of his consciousness rushed the thought, *conquering, to win to her, that lily-pale spirit sitting beside him.*

The glimmering vision was rent asunder and dissipated by Arthur, who, all evening, had been trying to draw his wild man out. Martin Eden remembered his decision. For the first time he became himself, consciously and deliberately at first, but soon lost in the joy of creating, in making life as he knew it appear before his listeners' eyes. He had been a member of the crew of the smuggling schooner *Halcyon* when she was captured by a revenue cutter. He saw with wide eyes, and he could tell what he saw. He brought the pulsing sea before them, and the men and the ships upon the sea. He communicated his power of vision, till they saw with his eyes what he had seen. He selected from the vast mass of detail with an artist's touch, drawing pictures of life that glowed and burned with light and color, injecting movement so that his listeners surged along with him on the flood of rough eloquence, enthusiasm, and power. At times he shocked

them with the vividness of the narrative and his terms
of speech, but beauty always followed fast upon the
heels of violence, and tragedy was relieved by humor,
by interpretations of the strange twists and quirks of
sailors' minds.

And while he talked, the girl looked at him with
startled eyes. His fire warmed her. She wondered if
she had been cold all her days. She wanted to lean
toward this burning, blazing man that was 'ike a volcano spouting forth strength, robustness, and health.
She felt that she must lean toward him, and resisted
by an effort. Then, too, there was the counter impulse
to shrink away from him. She was repelled by those
lacerated hands, grimed by toil so that the very dirt
of life was ingrained in the flesh itself, by that red
chafe of the collar and those bulging muscles. His
roughness frightened her; each roughness of speech
was an insult to her ear, each rough phase of his life
an insult to her soul. And ever and again would come
the draw of him, till she thought he must be evil to
have such power over her. All that was most firmly
established in her mind was rocking. His romance and
adventure were battering at the conventions. Before
his facile perils and ready laugh, life was no longer an
affair of serious effort and restraint, but a toy, to be
played with and turned topsy-turvy, carelessly to be
lived and pleasured in, and carelessly to be flung aside.
"Therefore, play!" was the cry that rang through her.
"Lean toward him, if so you will, and place your two
hands upon his neck!" She wanted to cry out at the
recklessness of the thought, and in vain she appraised
her own cleanness and culture and balanced all that
she was against what he was not. She glanced about
her and saw the others gazing at him with rapt attention; and she would have despaired had not she seen

horror in her mother's eyes—fascinated horror, it was true, but none the less horror. This man from outer darkness was evil. Her mother saw it, and her mother was right. She would trust her mother's judgment in this as she had always trusted it in all things. The fire of him was no longer warm and the fear of him was no longer poignant.

Later, at the piano, she played for him, and at him, aggressively, with the vague intent of emphasizing the impassableness of the gulf that separated them. Her music was a club that she swung brutally upon his head; and though it stunned him and crushed him down, it incited him. He gazed upon her in awe. In his mind, as in her own, the gulf widened; but faster than it widened, towered his ambition to win across it. But he was too complicated a plexus of sensibilities to sit staring at a gulf a whole evening, especially when there was music. He was remarkably susceptible to music. It was like strong drink, firing him to audacities of feeling,—a drug that laid hold of his imagination and went cloud-soaring through the sky. It banished sordid fact, flooded his mind with beauty, loosed romance and to its heels added wings. He did not understand the music she played. It was different from the dance-hall piano-banging and blatant brass bands he had heard. But he had caught hints of such music from the books, and he accepted her playing largely on faith, patiently waiting, at first, for the lilting measures of pronounced and simple rhythm, puzzled because those measures were not long continued. Just as he caught the swing of them and started, his imagination attuned in flight, always they vanished away in a chaotic scramble of sounds that was meaningless to him, and that dropped his imagination, an inert weight, back to earth.

Once, it entered his mind that there was a deliberate

rebuff in all this. He caught her spirit of antagonism and strove to divine the message that her hands pronounced upon the keys. Then he dismissed the thought as unworthy and impossible, and yielded himself more freely to the music. The old delightful condition began to be induced. His feet were no longer clay, and his flesh became spirit; before his eyes and behind his eyes shone a great glory; and then the scene before him vanished and he was away, rocking over the world that was to him a very dear world. The known and the unknown were commingled in the dream-pageant that thronged his vision. He entered strange ports of sun-washed lands, and trod market-places among barbaric peoples that no man had ever seen. The scent of the spice islands was in his nostrils as he had known it on warm, breathless nights at sea, or he beat up against the southeast trades through long tropic days, sinking palm-tufted coral islets in the turquoise sea benind and lifting palm-tufted coral islets in the turquoise sea anead. Swift as thought the pictures came and went. One instant he was astride a bronco and flying through the fairy-colored Painted Desert country; the next instant he was gazing down through shimmering heat into the whited sepulcher of Death Valley, or pulling an oar on a freezing ocean where great ice islands towered and glistened in the sun. He lay on a coral beach where the coconuts grew down to the mellow-sounding surf. The hulk of an ancient wreck burned with blue fires, in the light of which danced the *hula* dancers to the barbaric love-calls of the singers, who chanted to tinkling *ukuleles* and rumbling tom-toms. It was a sensuous, tropic night. In the background a volcano crater was silhouetted against the stars. Overhead drifted a pale crescent moon, and the Southern Cross burned low in the sky.

He was a harp; all life that he had known and that

was his consciousness was the strings; and the flood
of music was a wind that poured against those strings
and set them vibrating with memories and dreams.
He did not merely feel. Sensation invested itself in
form and color and radiance, and what his imagination
dared, it objectified in some sublimated and magic
way. Past, present, and future mingled; and he went
on oscillating across the broad, warm world, through
high adventure and noble deeds to Her—ay, and with
her, winning her, his arm about her, and carrying her
on in flight through the empery of his mind.

And she, glancing at him across her shoulder, saw
something of all this in his face. It was a transfigured
face, with great shining eyes that gazed beyond the
veil of sound and saw behind it the leap and pulse of
life and the gigantic phantoms of the spirit. She was
startled. The raw, stumbling lout was gone. The ill-
fitting clothes, battered hands, and sunburned face
remained; but these seemed the prison-bars through
which she saw a great soul looking forth, inarticulate
and dumb because of those feeble lips that would not
give it speech. Only for a flashing moment did she see
this, then she saw the lout returned, and she laughed
at the whim of her fancy. But the impression of that
fleeting glimpse lingered, and when the time came for
him to beat a stumbling retreat and go, she lent him
the volume of Swinburne, and another of Browning—
she was studying Browning in one of her English
courses. He seemed such a boy, as he stood blushing
and stammering his thanks, that a wave of pity, maternal in its prompting, welled up in her. She did not
remember the lout, nor the imprisoned soul, nor the
man who had stared at her in all masculineness and
delighted and frightened her. She saw before her only
a boy, who was shaking her hand with a hand so

callused that it felt like a nutmeg-grater and rasped her skin, and who was saying jerkily:—

"The greatest time of my life. You see, I ain't used to things. . . ." He looked about him helplessly. "To people and houses like this. It's all new to me, and I like it."

"I hope you'll call again," she said, as he was saying good night to her brothers.

He pulled on his cap, lurched desperately through the doorway, and was gone.

"Well, what do you think of him?" Arthur demanded.

"He is most interesting, a whiff of ozone," she answered. "How old is he?"

"Twenty—almost twenty-one. I asked him this afternoon. I didn't think he was that young."

And I am three years older, was the thought in her mind as she kissed her brothers good night.

Chapter Three

As Martin Eden went down the steps, his hand dropped into his coat pocket. It came out with a brown rice paper and a pinch of Mexican tobacco, which were deftly rolled together into a cigarette. He drew the first whiff of smoke deep into his lungs and expelled it in a long and lingering exhalation. "By God!" he said aloud, in a voice of awe and wonder. "By God!" he repeated. And yet again he murmured, "By God!" Then his hand went to his collar, which he ripped out of the shirt and stuffed into his pocket. A cold drizzle was falling, but he bared his head to it and unbuttoned his vest, swinging along in splendid unconcern. He was only dimly aware that it was raining. He was in an ecstasy, dreaming dreams and reconstructing the scenes just past.

He had met the woman at last—the woman that he had thought little about, not being given to thinking about women, but whom he had expected, in a remote way, he would sometime meet. He had sat next to her at table. He had felt her hand in his, he had looked into her eyes and caught a vision of a beautiful spirit;— but no more beautiful than the eyes through which it shone, nor than the flesh that gave it expression and form. He did not think of her flesh as flesh,—which was new to him; for of the women he had known that was the only way he thought. Her flesh was somehow different. He did not conceive of her body as a body, subject to the ills and frailties of bodies. Her body was more than the garb of her spirit. It was an emanation of her spirit, a pure and gracious crystallization of her divine essence. This feeling of the divine startled him. It shocked him from his dreams to sober thought. No word, no clue, no hint, of the divine had ever reached him before. He had never believed in the divine. He had always been irreligious, scoffing good-naturedly at the sky-pilots and their immortality of the soul. There was no life beyond, he had contended; it was here and now, then darkness everlasting. But what he had seen in her eyes was soul—immortal soul that could never die. No man he had known, nor any woman, had given him the message of immortality. But she had. She had whispered it to him the first moment she looked at him. Her face shimmered before his eyes as he walked along,—pale and serious, sweet and sensitive, smiling with pity and tenderness as only a spirit could smile, and pure as he had never dreamed purity could be. Her purity smote him like a blow It startled him. He had known good and bad, but purity, as an attribute of existence, had never entered his mind. And now, in her, he conceived purity to be the superlative of goodness and of cleanness, the sum of which constituted eternal life.

And promptly urged his ambition to grasp at eternal life. He was not fit to carry water for her—he knew that; it was a miracle of luck and a fantastic stroke that had enabled him to see her and be with her and talk with her that night. It was accidental. There was no merit in it. He did not deserve such fortune. His mood was essentially religious. He was humble and meek, filled with self-disparagement and abasement. In such frame of mind sinners come to the penitent form. He was convicted of sin. But as the meek and lowly at the penitent form catch splendid glimpses of their future lordly existence, so did he catch similar glimpses of the state he would gain to by possessing her. But this possession of her was dim and nebulous and totally different from possession as he had known it. Ambition soared on mad wings, and he saw himself climbing the heights with her, sharing thoughts with her, pleasuring in beautiful and noble things with her. It was a soul-possession he dreamed, refined beyond any grossness, a free comradeship of spirit that he could not put into definite thought. He did not think it. For that matter, he did not think at all. Sensation usurped reason, and he was quivering and palpitant with emotions he had never known, drifting deliciously on a sea of sensibility where feeling itself was exalted and spiritualized and carried beyond the summits of life.

He staggered along like a drunken man, murmuring fervently aloud: "By God! By God!"

A policeman on a street corner eyed him suspiciously, then noted his sailor roll.

"Where did you get it?" the policeman demanded.

Martin Eden came back to earth. His was a fluid organism, swiftly adjustable, capable of flowing into and filling all sorts of nooks and crannies. With the policeman's hail he was immediately his ordinary self, grasping the situation clearly.

"It's a beaut, ain't it?" he laughed back. "I didn't know I was talkin' out loud."

"You'll be singing next," was the policeman's diagnosis.

"No, I won't. Gimme a match an' I'll catch the next car home."

He lighted his cigarette, said good night, and went on. "Now wouldn't that rattle you?" he ejaculated under his breath. "That copper thought I was drunk." He smiled to himself and meditated. "I guess I was," he added; "but I didn't think a woman's face'd do it."

He caught a Telegraph Avenue car that was going to Berkeley. It was crowded with youths and young men who were singing songs and ever and again barking out college yells. He studied them curiously. They were university boys. They went to the same university that she did, were in her class socially, could know her, could see her every day if they wanted to. He wondered that they did not want to, that they had been out having a good time instead of being with her that evening, talking with her, sitting around her in a worshipful and adoring circle. His thoughts wandered on. He noticed one with narrow-slitted eyes and a loose-lipped mouth. That fellow was vicious, he decided. On shipboard he would be a sneak, a whiner, a tattler. He, Martin Eden, was a better man than that fellow. The thought cheered him. It seemed to draw him nearer to Her. He began comparing himself with the students. He grew conscious of the muscled mechanism of his body and felt confident that he was physically their master. But their heads were filled with knowledge that enabled them to talk her talk,—the thought depressed him. But what was a brain for? he demanded passionately. What they had done, he could do. They had been studying about life from the books while he had been busy living life. His brain was just as full of knowledge as theirs, though it was a different kind of knowledge. How many of them could tie a lanyard knot, or take a wheel or a lookout? His life spread out before him in a series of pictures of danger and daring, hardship and toil. He remembered his failures and scrapes in the process of learning. He was that much to the good, anyway. Later on they would have to begin living life and going through the mill as he had gone. Very well. While they were busy with that, he could be learning the other side of life from the books.

As the car crossed the zone of scattered dwellings that separated Oakland from Berkeley, he kept a lookout for a familiar, two-story building along the front of which ran the proud sign, HIGGINBOTHAM'S CASH STORE. Martin Eden got off at this corner. He stared up for a moment at the sign. It carried a message to him beyond its mere wording. A personality of smallness and egotism and petty underhandedness seemed to emanate from the letters themselves. Bernard Higginbotham had married his sister, and he knew him well. He let himself in with a latchkey and climbed the stairs to the second floor. Here lived his brother-in-law. The grocery was below. There was a smell of stale vegetables in the air. As he groped his way across the hall he stumbled over a toy-cart, left there by one of his numerous nephews and nieces, and brought up against a door with a resounding bang. "The pincher," was his thought; "too miserly to burn two cents' worth of gas and save his boarders' necks."

He fumbled for the knob and entered a lighted room,

where sat his sister and Bernard Higginbotham. She was patching a pair of his trousers, while his lean body was distributed over two chairs, his feet dangling in dilapidated carpet-slippers over the edge of the second chair. He glanced across the top of the paper he was reading, showing a pair of dark, insincere, sharp-staring eyes. Martin Eden never looked at him without experiencing a sense of repulsion. What his sister had seen in the man was beyond him. The other affected him as so much vermin, and always aroused in him an impulse to crush him under his foot. "Some day I'll beat the face off of him," was the way he often consoled himself for enduring the man's existence. The eyes, weasel-like and cruel, were looking at him complainingly.

"Well," Martin demanded. "Out with it."

"I had that door painted only last week," Mr. Higginbotham half whined, half bullied; "and you know what union wages are. You should be more careful."

Martin had intended to reply, but he was struck by the hopelessness of it. He gazed across the monstrous sordidness of soul to a chromo on the wall. It surprised him. He had always liked it, but it seemed that now he was seeing it for the first time. It was cheap, that was what it was, like everything else in this house. His mind went back to the house he had just left, and he saw, first, the paintings, and next, Her, looking at him with melting sweetness as she shook his hand at leaving. He forgot where he was and Bernard Higginbotham's existence, till that gentleman demanded:—

"Seen a ghost?"

Martin came back and looked at the beady eyes, sneering, truculent, cowardly, and there leaped into his vision, as on a screen, the same eyes when their owner was making a sale in the store below—subservient eyes, smug, and oily, and flattering.

"Yes," Martin answered. "I seen a ghost. Good night. Good night, Gertrude."

He started to leave the room, tripping over a loose seam in the slatternly carpet.

"Don't bang the door," Mr. Higginbotham cautioned him.

He felt the blood crawl in his veins, but controlled himself and closed the door softly behind him.

Mr. Higginbotham looked at his wife exultantly.

"He's been drinkin'," he proclaimed in a hoarse whisper. "I told you he would."

She nodded her head resignedly.

"His eyes was pretty shiny," she confessed, "and he didn't have no collar, though he went away with one. But mebbe he didn't have more'n a couple of glasses."

"He couldn't stand up straight," asserted her husband. "I watched him. He couldn't walk across the floor without stumblin'. You heard 'm yourself almost fall down in the hall."

"I think it was over Alice's cart," she said. "He couldn't see it in the dark."

Mr. Higginbotham's voice and wrath began to rise. All day he effaced himself in the store, reserving for the evening, with his family, the privilege of being himself.

"I tell you that precious brother of yours was drunk."

His voice was cold, sharp, and final, his lips stamping the enunciation of each word like the die of a machine. His wife sighed and remained silent. She was a large, stout woman, always dressed slatternly and always tired from the burdens of her flesh, her work, and her husband.

"He's got it in him, I tell you, from his father," Mr. Higginbotham went on accusingly. "An' he'll croak in the gutter the same way. You know that."

She nodded, sighed, and went on stitching. They were agreed that Martin had come home drunk. They did not have it in their souls to know beauty, or they would have known that those shining eyes and that glowing face betokened youth's first vision of love.

"Settin' a fine example to the children," Mr. Higginbotham snorted, suddenly, in the silence for which his wife was responsible and which he resented. Sometimes he almost wished she would oppose him more. "If he does it again, he's got to get out. Understand! I won't put up with his shinanigan—debotchin' innocent children with his boozing." Mr. Higginbotham liked the word, which was a new one in his vocabulary, recently gleaned from a newspaper column. "That's what it is, debotchin'—there ain't no other name for it."

Still his wife sighed, shook her head sorrowfully, and stitched on. Mr. Higginbotham resumed the newspaper.

"Has he paid last week's board?" he shot across the top of the newspaper.

She nodded, then added, "He still has some money."

"When is he goin' to sea again?"

"When his pay-day's spent, I guess," she answered. "He was over to San Francisco yesterday looking for a ship. But he's got money, yet, an' he's particular about the kind of ship he signs for."

"It's not for a deck-swab like him to put on airs," Mr. Higginbotham snorted. "Particular! Him!"

"He said something about a schooner that's gettin' ready to go off to some outlandish place to look for buried treasure, that he'd sail on her if his money held out."

"If he only wanted to steady down, I'd give him a job drivin' the wagon," her husband said, but with no trace of benevolence in his voice. "Tom's quit."

His wife looked alarm and interrogation.

"Quit tonight. Is goin' to work for Carruthers. They paid 'm more'n I could afford."

"I told you you'd lose 'm," she cried out. "He was worth more'n you was giving him."

"Now look here, old woman," Higginbotham bullied, "for the thousandth time I've told you to keep your nose out of the business. I won't tell you again."

"I don't care," she sniffled. "Tom was a good boy."

Her husband glared at her. This was unqualified defiance.

"If that brother of yours was worth his salt, he could take the wagon," he snorted.

"He pays his board, just the same," was the retort. "An' he's my brother, an' so long as he don't owe you money you've got no right to be jumping on him all the time. I've got some feelings, if I have been married to you for seven years."

"Did you tell 'm you'd charge him for gas if he goes on readin' in bed?" he demanded.

Mrs. Higginbotham made no reply. Her revolt faded away, her spirit wilting down into her tired flesh. Her husband was triumphant. He had her. His eyes snapped vindictively, while his ears joyed in the sniffles she emitted. He extracted great happiness from squelching her, and she squelched easily these days, though it had been different in the first years of their married life, before the brood of children and his incessant nagging had sapped her energy.

"Well, you tell 'm tomorrow, that's all," he said. "An' I just want to tell you, before I forget it, that you'd better send for Marian tomorrow to take care of the children. With Tom quit, I'll have to be out on the wagon, an' you can make up your mind to it to be down below waitin' on the counter."

"But tomorrow's wash day," she objected weakly.

"Get up early, then, an' do it first. I won't start out till ten o'clock."

He crinkled the paper viciously and resumed his reading.

Chapter Four

Martin Eden, with blood still crawling from contact with his brother-in-law, felt his way along the unlighted back hall and entered his room, a tiny cubbyhole with space for a bed, a wash-stand, and one chair. Mr. Higginbotham was too thrifty to keep a servant when his wife could do the work. Besides, the servant's room enabled them to take in two boarders instead of one. Martin placed the Swinburne and Browning on the chair, took off his coat, and sat down on the bed. A screeching of asthmatic springs greeted the weight of his body, but he did not notice them. He started to take off his shoes, but fell to staring at the white plaster wall opposite him, broken by long streaks of dirty brown where rain had leaked through the roof. On this befouled background visions began to flow and burn. He forgot his shoes and stared long, till his lips began to move and he murmured, "Ruth."

"Ruth." He had not thought a simple sound could be so beautiful. It delighted his ear, and he grew intoxicated with the repetition of it. "Ruth." It was a talisman, a magic word to conjure with. Each time he murmured it, her face shimmered before him, suffusing the foul wall with a golden radiance. This radiance did not stop at the wall. It extended on into infinity, and through its golden depths his soul went questing after hers. The best that was in him was pouring out in splendid flood. The very thought of her ennobled and purified him, made him better, and made him want to be better. This was new to him. He had never known women who had made him better. They had always had the counter effect of making him beastly. He did not know that many of them had done their best, bad as it was. Never having been conscious of himself, he did not know that he had that in his being that drew love from women and which had been the cause of their reaching out for his youth. Though they had often bothered him, he had never bothered about them; and he would never have dreamed that there were women who had been better because of him. Always in sublime carelessness had he lived, till now, and now it seemed to him that they had always reached out and dragged at him with vile hands. This was not just to them, nor to himself. But he, who for the first time was becoming conscious of himself, was in no condition to judge, and he burned with shame as he stared at the vision of his infamy.

He got up abruptly and tried to see himself in the dirty looking-glass over the wash-stand. He passed a towel over it and looked again, long and carefully. It was the first time he had ever really seen himself. His eyes were made for seeing, but up to that moment they had been filled with the ever changing panorama of the world, at which he had been too busy gazing, ever to gaze at himself. He saw the head and face of a young fellow of twenty, but, being unused to such appraisement, he did not know how to value it. Above a square-domed forehead he saw a mop of brown hair,

nut-brown, with a wave to it and hints of curls that
were a delight to any woman, making hands tingle to
stroke it and fingers tingle to pass caresses through it.
But he passed it by as without merit, in Her eyes,
and dwelt long and thoughtfully on the high, square
forehead,—striving to penetrate it and learn the quality of its content. What kind of a brain lay behind
there? was his insistent interrogation. What was it
capable of? How far would it take him? Would it take
him to her?

He wondered if there was soul in those steel-gray
eyes that were often quite blue of color and that
were strong with the briny airs of the sun-washed
deep. He wondered, also, how his eyes looked to her.
He tried to imagine himself her, gazing into those eyes
of his, but failed in the jugglery. He could successfully put himself inside other men's minds, but they
had to be men whose ways of life he knew. He did
not know her way of life. She was wonder and
mystery, and how could he guess one thought of
hers? Well, they were honest eyes, he concluded,
and in them was neither smallness nor meanness.
The brown sunburn of his face surprised him. He
had not dreamed he was so black. He rolled up his
shirtsleeve and compared the white underside of the
arm with his face. Yes, he was a white man, after
all. But the arms were sunburned, too. He twisted
his arm, rolled the biceps over with his other hand,
and gazed underneath where he was least touched
by the sun. It was very white. He laughed at his
bronzed face in the glass at the thought that it was
once as white as the underside of his arm; nor did he
dream that in the world there were few pale spirits of
women who could boast fairer or smoother skins than
he—fairer than where he had escaped the ravages of
the sun

His might have been a cnerub's mouth, had not the full, sensuous lips a trick, under stress, of drawing firmly across the teeth. At times, so tightly did they draw, the mouth became stern and harsh, even ascetic. They were the lips of a fighter and of a lover. They could taste the sweetness of life with relish, and they could put the sweetness aside and command life. The chin and jaw, strong and just hinting of square aggressiveness, helped the lips to command life. Strength balanced sensuousness and had upon it a tonic effect, compelling him to love beauty that was healthy and making him vibrate to sensations that were wholesome. And between the lips were teeth that had never known nor needed the dentist's care. They were white and strong and regular, he decided, as he looked at them. But as he looked he began to be troubled. Somewhere, stored away in the recesses of his mind and vaguely remembered, was the impression that there were people who washed their teeth every day. They were the people from up above—people in her class. She must wash her teeth every day, too. What would she think if she learned that he had never washed his teeth in all the days of his life? He resolved to get a tooth-brush and form the habit. He would begin at once, tomorrow. It was not by mere achievement that he could hope to win to her. He must make a personal reform in all things, even to tooth-washing and neck-gear, though a starched collar affected him as a renunciation of freedom.

He held up his hand, rubbing the ball of the thumb over the callused palm and gazing at the dirt that was ingrained in the flesh itself and which no brush could scrub away. How different was her palm! He thrilled deliciously at the remembrance. Like a rose-petal, he thought; cool and soft as a snowflake. He had never thought that a mere woman's hand could be so sweetly soft. He caught himself imagining the wonder of a caress from such a hand, and flushed guiltily. It was too gross a thought for her. In ways it seemed to impugn her high spirituality. She was a pale, slender spirit, exalted far beyond the flesh; but nevertheless the soft- ness of her palm persisted in his thoughts. He was used to the harsh callousness of factory girls and work- ing women. Well he knew why their hands were rough; but this hand of hers . . . It was soft because she had never used it to work with. The gulf yawned between her and him at the awesome thought of a person who did not have to work for a living. He suddenly saw the aristocracy of the people who did not labor. It towered before him on the wall, a figure in brass, arrogant and powerful. He had worked himself; his first memories seemed connected with work, and all his family had worked. There was Gertrude. When her hands were not hard from the endless housework, they were swollen and red like boiled beef, what with the washing. And there was his sister Marian. She had worked in the cannery the preceding summer and her slim, pretty hands were all scarred with the tomato- knives. Besides, the tips of two of her fingers had been left in the cutting machine at the paper-box factory the preceding winter. He remembered the hard palms of his mother as she lay in her coffin. And his father had worked to the last fading gasp; the horned growth on his hands must have been half an inch thick when he died. But Her hands were soft, and her mother's hands, and her brothers'. This last came to him as a surprise; it was tremendously indicative of the highness of their caste, of the enormous distance that stretched between her and him.

He sat back on the bed with a bitter laugh, and finished taking off his shoes. He was a fool; he had been made drunken by a woman's face and by a woman's soft, white hands. And then, suddenly, before his eyes, on the foul plaster wall appeared a vision. He stood in front of a gloomy tenement house. It was night-time, in the East End of London, and before him stood Margey, a little factory girl of fifteen. He had seen her home after the bean-feast. She lived in that gloomy tenement, a place not fit for swine. His hand was going out to hers as he said good night. She had put her lips up to be kissed, but he wasn't going to kiss her. Somehow he was afraid of her. And then her hand closed on his and pressed feverishly. He felt her calluses grind and grate on his, and a great wave of pity welled over him. He saw her yearning, hungry eyes, and her ill-fed female form which had been rushed from childhood into a frightened and ferocious ma turity; then he put his arms about her in large tolerance and stooped and kissed her on the lips. Her glad little cry rang in his ears, and he felt her clinging to him like a cat. Poor little starveling! He continued to stare at the vision of what had happened in the long ago. His flesh was crawling as it had crawled that night when she clung to him, and his heart was warm with pity. It was a gray scene, greasy gray, and the rain drizzled greasily on the pavement stones. And then a radiant glory shone on the wall, and up through the other vision, displacing it, glimmered Her pale face under its crown of golden hair, remote and inaccessible as a star.

He took the Browning and the Swinburne from the chair and kissed them. Just the same, she told me to call again, he thought. He took another look at himself in the glass, and said aloud, with great solemnity:—

"Martin Eden, the first thing tomorrow you go to the free library an' read up on etiquette. Understand!"

He turned off the gas, and the springs shrieked under his body.

"But you've got to quit cussin', Martin, old boy; you've got to quit cussin'," he said aloud.

Then he dozed off to sleep and to dream dreams that for madness and audacity rivaled those of poppy-eaters.

Chapter Five

He awoke next morning from rosy scenes of dream to a steamy atmosphere that smelled of soapsuds and dirty clothes, and that was vibrant with the jar and jangle of tormented life. As he came out of his room he heard the slosh of water, a sharp exclamation, and a resounding smack as his sister visited her irritation upon one of her numerous progeny. The squall of the child went through him like a knife. He was aware that the whole thing, the very air he breathed, was repulsive and mean. How different, he thought, from the atmosphere of beauty and repose of the house wherein Ruth dwelt. There it was all spiritual. Here it was all material, and meanly material.

"Come here, Alfred," he called to the crying child, at the same time thrusting his hand into his trousers pocket, where he carried his money loose in the same large way that he lived life in general. He put a quarter in the youngster's hand and held him in his arms a moment soothing his sobs. "Now run along and get some candy, and don't forget to give some to your brothers and sisters. Be sure and get the kind that lasts longest."

His sister lifted a flushed face from the wash-tub and looked at him.

"A nickel'd ha' ben enough," she said. "It's just like you, no idea of the value of money. The child'll eat himself sick."

"That's all right, sis," he answered jovially. "My money'll take care of itself. If you weren't so busy, I'd kiss you good morning."

He wanted to be affectionate to this sister, who was good, and who, in her way, he knew, loved him. But, somehow, she grew less herself as the years went by, and more and more baffling. It was the hard work, the many children, and the nagging of her husband, he decided, that had changed her. It came to him, in a flash of fancy, that her nature seemed taking on the attributes of stale vegetables, smelly soapsuds, and of the greasy dimes, nickels, and quarters she took in over the counter of the store.

"Go along an' get your breakfast," she said roughly, though secretly pleased. Of all her wandering brood of brothers he had always been her favorite. "I declare I *will* kiss you," she said, with a sudden stir at her heart.

With thumb and forefinger she swept the dripping suds first from one arm and then from the other. He put his arms round her massive waist and kissed her wet, steamy lips. The tears welled into her eyes—not so much from strength of feeling as from the weakness of chronic overwork. She shoved him away from her, but not before he caught a glimpse of her moist eyes.

"You'll find breakfast in the oven," she said hurriedly. "Jim ought to be up now. I had to get up early for the washing. Now get along with you and get out of the house early. It won't be nice today, what of Tom quittin' an' nobody but Bernard to drive the wagon."

Martin went into the kitchen with a sinking heart, the image of her red face and slatternly form eating its way like acid into his brain. She might love him if she only had some time, he concluded. But she was worked to death. Bernard Higginbotham was a brute to work her so hard. But he could not help but feel, on the other hand, that there had not been anything beautiful in that kiss. It was true, it was an unusual kiss. For years she had kissed him only when he returned from voyages or departed on voyages. But this kiss had tasted of soapsuds, and the lips, he had noticed, were flabby. There had been no quick, vigorous lip-pressure such as should accompany any kiss. Hers was the kiss of a tired woman who had been tired so long that she had forgotten how to kiss. He remembered her as a girl, before her marriage, when she would dance with the best, all night, after a hard day's work at the laundry, and think nothing of leaving the dance to go to another day's hard work. And then he thought of Ruth and the cool sweetness that must reside in her lips as it resided in all about her. Her kiss would be like her hand-shake or the way she looked at one, firm and frank. In imagination he dared to think of her lips on his, and so vividly did he imagine that he went dizzy at the thought and seemed to drift through clouds of rose-petals, filling his brain with their perfume.

In the kitchen he found Jim, the other boarder, eating mush very languidly, with a sick, faraway look in his eyes. Jim was a plumber's apprentice whose weak chin and hedonistic temperament, coupled with a certain nervous stupidity, promised to take him nowhere in the race for bread and butter

"Why don't you eat?" he demanded, as Martin dipped dolefully into the cold, half-cooked oatmeal mush. "Was you drunk again last night?"

Martin shook his head. He was oppressed by the

utter squalidness of it all. Ruth Morse seemed farther removed than ever.

"I was," Jim went on with a boastful, nervous giggle. "I was loaded right to the neck. Oh, she was a daisy. Billy brought me home."

Martin nodded that he heard,—it was a habit of nature with him to pay heed to whoever talked to him,—and poured a cup of lukewarm coffee.

"Goin' to the Lotus Club dance tonight?" Jim demanded. "They're goin' to have beer, an' if that Temescal bunch comes, there'll be a rough-house. I don't care, though. I'm takin' my lady friend just the same. Cripes, but I've got a taste in my mouth!"

He made a wry face and attempted to wash the taste away with coffee.

"D'ye know Julia?"

Martin shook his head.

"She's my lady friend," Jim explained, "and she's a peach. I'd introduce you to her, only you'd win her. I don't see what the girls see in you, honest I don't; but the way you win them away from the fellers is sickenin'."

"I never got any away from you," Martin answered uninterestedly. The breakfast had to be got through somehow.

"Yes, you did, too," the other asserted warmly. "There was Maggie."

"Never had anything to do with her. Never danced with her except that one night."

"Yes, an' that's just what did it," Jim cried out. "You just danced with her an' looked at her, an' it was all off. Of course you didn't mean nothin' by it, but it settled me for keeps. Wouldn't look at me again. Always askin' about you. She'd have made fast dates enough with you if you'd wanted to "

"But I didn't want to."

"Wasn't necessary. I was left at the pole." Jim looked at him admiringly. "How d'ye do it, anyway, Mart?"

"By not carin' about 'em," was the answer.

"You mean makin' b'lieve you don't care about them?" Jim queried eagerly.

Martin considered for a moment, then answered, "Perhaps that will do, but with me I guess it's different. I never have cared—much. If you can put it on, it's all right, most likely."

"You should 'a' ben up at Riley's barn last night," Jim announced inconsequently. "A lot of the fellers put on the gloves. There was a peach from West Oakland. They called 'm 'The Rat.' Slick as silk. No one could touch 'm. We was all wishin' you was there. Where was you anyway?"

"Down in Oakland," Martin replied.

"To the show?"

Martin shoved his plate away and got up.

"Comin' to the dance tonight?" the other called after him.

"No, I think not," he answered.

He went downstairs and out into the street, breathing great breaths of air. He had been suffocating in that atmosphere while the apprentice's chatter had driven him frantic. There had been times when it was all he could do to refrain from reaching over and mopping Jim's face in the mush-plate. The more he had chattered, the more remote had Ruth seemed to him. How could he, herding with such cattle, ever become worthy of her? He was appalled at the problem confronting him, weighted down by the incubus of his working-class station. Everything reached out to hold him down—his sister, his sister's house and family, Jim the apprentice, everybody he knew, every tie of life. Existence did not taste good in his mouth. Up to then he had accepted existence, as he had lived it with all about him, as a good thing. He had never questioned it, except when he read books; but then, they were only books, fairy stories of a fairer and impossible world. But now he had seen that world, possible and real, with a flower of a woman called Ruth in the midmost center of it; and thenceforth he must know bitter tastes, and longings sharp as pain, and hopelessness that tantalized because it fed on hope.

He had debated between the Berkeley Free Library and the Oakland Free Library, and decided upon the latter because Ruth lived in Oakland. Who could tell?—a library was a most likely place for her, and he might see her there. He did not know the way of libraries, and he wandered through endless rows of fiction, till the delicate-featured French-looking girl who seemed in charge, told him that the reference department was upstairs. He did not know enough to ask the man at the desk, and began his adventures in the philosophy alcove. He had heard of book philosophy, but had not imagined there had been so much written about it. The high, bulging shelves of heavy tomes humbled him and at the same time stimulated him. Here was work for the vigor of his brain. He found books on trigonometry in the mathematics section, and ran the pages, and stared at the meaningless formulas and figures. He could read English, but he saw there an alien speech. Norman and Arthur knew that speech. He had heard them talking it. And they were her brothers. He left the alcove in despair. From every side the books seemed to press upon him and crush him. He had never dreamed that the fund of human knowledge bulked so big. He was frightened. How could his brain ever master it all? Later, he remembered that there were other men, many men, who had mastered it; and he breathed a great oath, passionately, under his breath, swearing that his brain could do what theirs had done.

And so he wandered on, alternating between depression and elation as he stared at the shelves packed with wisdom. In one miscellaneous section he came upon a "Norrie's Epitome." He turned the pages reverently. In a way, it spoke a kindred speech. Both he and it were of the sea. Then he found a "Bowditch" and books by Lecky and Marshall. There it was; he would teach himself navigation. He would quit drinking, work up, and become a captain. Ruth seemed very near to him in that moment. As a captain, he could marry her (if she would have him). And if she wouldn't, well—he would live a good life among men, because of Her, and he would quit drinking anyway. Then he remembered the underwriters and the owners, the two masters a captain must serve, either of whom could and would break him and whose interests were diametrically opposed. He cast his eyes about the room and closed the lids down on a vision of ten thousand books. No; no more of the sea for him. There was power in all that wealth of books, and if he would do great things, he must do them on the land. Besides, captains were not allowed to take their wives to sea with them.

Noon came, and afternoon. He forgot to eat, and sought on for the books on etiquette; for, in addition to career, his mind was vexed by a simple and very concrete problem: *When you meet a young lady and she asks you to call, how soon can you call?* was the way he worded it to himself. But when he found the right shelf, he sought vainly for the answer. He was appalled at the

vast edifice of etiquette, and lost himself in the mazes
of visiting-card conduct between persons in polite society. He abandoned his search. He had not found
what he wanted, though he had found that it would
take all of a man's time to be polite, and that he would
have to live a preliminary life in which to learn how
to be polite.

"Did you find what you wanted?" the man at the
desk asked him as he was leaving.

"Yes, sir," he answered. "You have a fine library
here."

The man nodded. "We should be glad to see you
here often. Are you a sailor?"

"Yes, sir," he answered. "And I'll come again."

Now, how did he know that? he asked himself as
he went down the stairs.

And for the first block along the street he walked
very stiff and straight and awkwardly, until he forgot
himself in his thoughts, whereupon his rolling gait
gracefully returned to him.

Chapter Six

A terrible restlessness that was akin to hunger afflicted Martin Eden. He was famished for a sight
of the girl whose slender hands had gripped his life
with a giant's grasp. He could not steel himself to call
upon her. He was afraid that he might call too soon,
and so be guilty of an awful breach of that awful thing
called etiquette. He spent long hours in the Oakland
and Berkeley libraries, and made out application blanks
for membership for himself, his sisters Gertrude and

Marian, and Jim, the latter's consent being obtained at the expense of several glasses of beer. With four cards permitting him to draw books, he burned the gas late in the servant's room, and was charged fifty cents a week for it by Mr. Higginbotham.

The many books he read but served to whet his unrest. Every page of every book was a peep-hole into the realm of knowledge. His hunger fed upon what he read, and increased. Also, he did not know where to begin, and continually suffered from lack of preparation. The commonest references, that he could see plainly every reader was expected to know, he did not know. And the same was true of the poetry he read which maddened him with delight. He read more of Swinburne than was contained in the volume Ruth had lent him; and "Dolores" he understood thoroughly. But surely Ruth did not understand it, he concluded. How could she, living the refined life she did? Then he chanced upon Kipling's poems, and was swept away by the lilt and swing and glamour with which familiar things had been invested. He was amazed at the man's sympathy with life and at his incisive psychology. *Psychology* was a new word in Martin's vocabulary. He had bought a dictionary, which deed had decreased his supply of money and brought nearer the day on which he must sail in search of more. Also, it incensed Mr. Higginbotham, who would have preferred the money taking the form of board.

He dared not go near Ruth's neighborhood in the daytime, but night found him lurking like a thief around the Morse home, stealing glimpses at the windows and loving the very walls that sheltered her. Several times he barely escaped being caught by her brothers, and once he trailed Mr. Morse downtown and studied his face in the lighted streets, longing all the while for some quick danger of death to threaten so that he might spring in and save her father. On another night, his vigil was rewarded by a glimpse of Ruth through a second-story window. He saw only her head and shoulders, and her arms raised as she fixed her hair before a mirror. It was only for a moment, but it was a long moment to him, during which his blood turned to wine and sang through his veins. Then she pulled down the shade. But it was her room—he had learned that; and thereafter he strayed there often, hiding under a dark tree on the opposite side of the street and smoking countless cigarettes. One afternoon he saw her mother coming out of a bank, and received another proof of the enormous distance that separated Ruth from him. She was of the class that dealt with banks. He had never been inside a bank in his life, and he had an idea that such institutions were frequented only by the very rich and the very powerful.

In one way, he had undergone a moral revolution. Her cleanness and purity had reacted upon him, and he felt in his being a crying need to be clean. He must be that if he were ever to be worthy of breathing the same air with her. He washed his teeth, and scrubbed his hands with a kitchen scrub-brush till he saw a nail-brush in a drug-store window and divined its use. While purchasing it, the clerk glanced at his nails, suggested a nail-file, and so he became possessed of an additional toilet-tool. He ran across a book in the library on the care of the body, and promptly developed a penchant for a cold-water bath every morning, much to the amazement of Jim, and to the bewilderment of Mr. Higginbotham, who was not in sympathy with such high-fangled notions and who seriously de-

bated whether or not he should charge Martin extra
for the water. Another stride was in the direction of
creased trousers. Now that Martin was aroused in such
matters, he swiftly noted the difference between the
baggy knees of the trousers worn by the working class
and the straight line from knee to foot of those worn
by the men above the working class. Also, he learned
the reason why, and invaded his sister's kitchen in
search of irons and ironing-board. He had misadventures at first, hopelessly burning one pair and buying
another, which expenditure again brought nearer the
day on which he must put to sea.

But the reform went deeper than mere outward
appearance. He still smoked, but he drank no more.
Up to that time, drinking had seemed to him the
proper thing for men to do, and he had prided
himself on his strong head which enabled him to
drink most men under the table. Whenever he encountered a chance shipmate, and there were many in
San Francisco, he treated them and was treated in
turn, as of old, but he ordered for himself root beer
or ginger ale and good-naturedly endured their chaffing. And as they waxed maudlin he studied them,
watching the beast rise and master them and thanking
God that he was no longer as they. They had their
limitations to forget, and when they were drunk, their
dim, stupid spirits were even as gods, and each ruled
in his heaven of intoxicated desire. With Martin the
need for strong drink had vanished. He was drunken
in new and more profound ways—with Ruth, who
had fired him with love and with a glimpse of higher
and eternal life; with books, that had set myriad maggots of desire gnawing in his brain; and with the sense
of personal cleanliness he was achieving, that gave him
even more superb health than what he had enjoyed

and that made his whole body sing with physical well-being.

One night he went to the theater, on the blind chance that he might see her there, and from the second balcony he did see her. He saw her come down the aisle, with Arthur and a strange young man with a football mop of hair and eyeglasses, the sight of whom spurred him to instant apprehension and jealousy. He saw her take her seat in the orchestra circle, and little else than her did he see that night—a pair of slender white shoulders and a mass of pale gold hair, dim with distance. But there were others who saw, and now and again, glancing at those about him, he noted two young girls who looked back from the row in front, a dozen seats along, and who smiled at him with bold eyes. He had always been easy-going. It was not in his nature to give rebuff. In the old days he would have smiled back, and gone further and encouraged smiling. But now it was different. He did smile back, then looked away, and looked no more deliberately. But several times, forgetting the existence of the two girls, his eyes caught their smiles. He could not rethumb himself in a day, nor could he violate the intrinsic kindliness of his nature; so, at such moments, he smiled at the girls in warm human friendliness. It was nothing new to him. He knew they were reaching out their women's hands to him. But it was different now. Far down there in the orchestra circle was the one woman in all the world, so different, so terrifically different, from these two girls of his class, that he could feel for them only pity and sorrow. He had it in his heart to wish that they could possess, in some small measure, her goodness and glory. And not for the world could he hurt them because of their outreaching. He was not flattered by it; he even felt a slight shame at his lowliness that permitted it. He knew, did he belong in Ruth's class, that there would be no overtures from these girls; and with each glance of theirs he felt the fingers of his own class clutching at him to hold him down.

He left his seat before the curtain went down on the last act, intent on seeing Her as she passed out. There were always numbers of men who stood on the sidewalk outside, and he could pull his cap down over his eyes and screen himself behind some one's shoulder so that she should not see him. He emerged from the theater with the first of the crowd; but scarcely had he taken his position on the edge of the sidewalk when the two girls appeared. They were looking for him, he knew; and for the moment he could have cursed that in him which drew women. Their casual edging across the sidewalk to the curb, as they drew near, apprised him of discovery. They slowed down, and were in the thick of the crowd as they came up with him. One of them brushed against him and apparently for the first time noticed him. She was a slender, dark girl, with black, defiant eyes. But they smiled at him, and he smiled back.

"Hello," he said.

It was automatic; he had said it so often before under similar circumstances of first meetings. Besides, he could do no less. There was that large tolerance and sympathy in his nature that would permit him to do no less. The black-eyed girl smiled gratification and greeting, and showed signs of stopping, while her companion, arm linked in arm, giggled and likewise showed signs of halting. He thought quickly. It would never do for Her to come out and see him talking there with them. Quite naturally, as a matter of course, he swung in alongside the dark-eyed one and walked with her. There was no awkwardness on his part, no numb tongue. He was at home here, and he held his own royally in the badinage, bristling with slang and sharpness, that was always the preliminary to getting acquainted in these swift-moving affairs. At the corner where the main stream of people flowed onward, he started to edge out into the cross street. But the girl with the black eyes caught his arm, following him and dragging her companion after her, as she cried:—

"Hold on, Bill! What's yer rush? You're not goin' to shake us so sudden as all that?"

He halted with a laugh, and turned, facing them. Across their shoulders he could see the moving throng passing under the street lamps. Where he stood it was not so light, and, unseen, he would be able to see Her as she passed by. She would certainly pass by, for that way led home.

"What's her name?" he asked of the giggling girl, nodding at the dark-eyed one.

"You ask her," was the convulsed response.

"Well, what is it?" he demanded, turning squarely on the girl in question.

"You ain't told me yours, yet," she retorted.

"You never asked it," he smiled. "Besides, you guessed the first rattle. It's Bill, all right, all right."

"Aw, go 'long with you." She looked him in the eyes, her own sharply passionate and inviting. "What is it, honest?"

Again she looked. All the centuries of woman since sex began were eloquent in her eyes. And he measured her in a careless way, and knew, bold now, that she would begin to retreat, coyly and delicately, as he pursued, ever ready to reverse the game should he turn faint-hearted. And, too, he was human, and could feel the draw of her, while his ego could not but ap-

preciate the flattery of her kindness. Oh, he knew it
all, and knew them well, from A to Z. Good, as goodness might be measured in their particular class, hard-
working for meager wages and scorning the sale of self
for easier ways, nervously desirous for some small
pinch of happiness in the desert of existence, and facing a future that was a gamble between the ugliness
of unending toil and the black pit of more terrible
wretchedness, the way whereto being briefer though
better paid.

"Bill," he answered, nodding his head. "Sure, Pete,
Bill an' no other."

"No joshin'?" she queried.

"It ain't Bill at all," the other broke in.

"How do you know?" he demanded. "You never
laid eyes on me before."

"No need to, to know you're lyin'," was the retort.

"Straight, Bill, what is it?" the first girl asked.

"Bill'll do," he confessed.

She reached out to his arm and shook him playfully.
"I knew you was lyin', but you look good to me just
the same."

He captured the hand that invited, and felt on the
palm familiar markings and distortions.

"When'd you chuck the cannery?" he asked.

"How'd yeh know?" and "My, ain't cheh a mind-
reader!" the girls chorussed.

And while he exchanged the stupidities of stupid
minds with them, before his inner sight towered the
book-shelves of the library, filled with the wisdom of
the ages. He smiled bitterly at the incongruity of it,
and was assailed by doubts. But between inner vision
and outward pleasantry he found time to watch the
theater crowd streaming by. And then he saw Her,
under the lights, between her brother and the strange

young man with glasses, and his heart seemed to stand
still. He had waited long for this moment. He had
time to note the light, fluffy something that hid her
queenly head, the tasteful lines of her wrapped figure,
the gracefulness of her carriage and of the hand that
caught up her skirts; and then she was gone and he
was left staring at the two girls of the cannery, at their
tawdry attempts at prettiness of dress, their tragic
efforts to be clean and trim, the cheap cloth, the cheap
ribbons, and the cheap rings on the fingers. He felt a
tug at his arm, and heard a voice saying:—

"Wake up, Bill! What's the matter with you?"

"What was you sayin'?" he asked.

"Oh, nothin'," the dark girl answered, with a toss
of her head. "I was only remarkin'—"

"What?"

"Well, I was whisperin' it'd be a good idea if you
could dig up a gentleman friend—for her" (indicating
her companion), "and then, we could go off an' have
ice-cream soda somewhere, or coffee, or anything."

He was afflicted by a sudden spiritual nausea.
The transition from Ruth to this had been too
abrupt. Ranged side by side with the bold, defiant
eyes of the girl before him, he saw Ruth's clear, luminous eyes, like a saint's, gazing at him out of un-
plumbed depths of purity. And, somehow, he felt
within him a stir of power. He was better than this.
Life meant more to him than it meant to these two
girls whose thoughts did not go beyond ice-cream
and a gentleman friend. He remembered that he had
led always a secret life in his thoughts. These thoughts
he had tried to share, but never had he found a
woman capable of understanding—nor a man. He
had tried, at times, but had only puzzled his listeners.
And as his thoughts had been beyond them, so, he

argued now, he must be beyond them. He felt power move in him, and clenched his fists. If life meant more to him, then it was for him to demand more from life, but he could not demand it from such companionship as this. Those bold black eyes had nothing to offer. He knew the thoughts behind them—of ice-cream and of something else. But those saint's eyes alongside— they offered all he knew and more than he could guess. They offered books and painting, beauty and repose, and all the fine elegance of higher existence. Behind those black eyes he knew every thought process. It was like clockwork. He could watch every wheel go around. Their bid was low pleasure, narrow as the grave, that palled, and the grave was at the end of it. But the bid of the saint's eyes was mystery, and wonder unthinkable, and eternal life. He had caught glimpses of the soul in them, and glimpses of his own soul, too.

"There's only one thing wrong with the program," he said aloud. "I've got a date already."

The girl's eyes blazed her disappointment.

"To sit up with a sick friend, I suppose?" she sneered.

"No, a real honest date with—" he faltered, "with a girl."

"You're not stringin' me?" she asked earnestly.

He looked her in the eyes and answered: "It's straight, all right. But why can't we meet some other time? You ain't told me your name yet. An' where d'ye live?"

"Lizzie," she replied, softening toward him, her hand pressing his arm, while her body leaned against his. "Lizzie Connolly. And I live at Fifth an' Market."

He talked on a few minutes before saying good night. He did not go home immediately; and under the tree where he kept his vigils he looked up at a window and murmured: "That date was with you, Ruth. I kept it for you."

Chapter Seven

A week of heavy reading had passed since the evening he first met Ruth Morse, and still he dared not call. Time and again he nerved himself up to call, but under the doubts that assailed him his determination died away. He did not know the proper time to call, nor was there any one to tell him, and he was afraid of committing himself to an irretrievable blunder. Having shaken himself free from his old companions and old ways of life, and having no new companions, nothing remained for him but to read, and the long hours he devoted to it would have ruined a dozen pairs of ordinary eyes. But his eyes were strong, and they were backed by a body superbly strong. Furthermore, his mind was fallow. It had lain fallow all his life so far as the abstract thought of the books was concerned, and it was ripe for the sowing. It had never been jaded by study, and it bit hold of the knowledge in the books with sharp teeth that would not let go.

It seemed to him, by the end of the week, that he had lived centuries, so far behind were the old life and outlook. But he was baffled by lack of preparation. He attempted to read books that required years of preliminary specialization. One day he would read a book of antiquated philosophy, and the next day one that was ultra-modern, so that his head would be whirling with the conflict and contradiction of ideas. It was the same with the economists. On the one shelf at the library he found Karl Marx, Ricardo, Adam Smith, and Mill, and the abstruse formulas of the one gave no clue that the ideas of another were obsolete.

He was bewildered, and yet he wanted to know. He had become interested, in a day, in economics, industry, and politics. Passing through the City Hall Park, he had noticed a group of men, in the center of which were half a dozen, with flushed faces and raised voices, earnestly carrying on a discussion. He joined the listeners, and heard a new, alien tongue in the mouths of the philosophers of the people. One was a tramp, another was a labor agitator, a third was a law-school student, and the remainder was composed of wordy workingmen. For the first time he heard of socialism, anarchism, and single tax, and learned that there were warring social philosophies. He heard hundreds of technical words that were new to him, belonging to fields of thought that his meager reading had never touched upon. Because of this he could not follow the arguments closely, and he could only guess at and surmise the ideas wrapped up in such strange expressions. Then there was a black-eyed restaurant waiter who was a theosophist, a union baker who was an agnostic, an old man who baffled all of them with the strange philosophy that *what is is right*, and another old man who discoursed interminably about the cosmos and the father-atom and the mother-atom.

Martin Eden's head was in a state of addlement when he went away after several hours, and he hurried to the library to look up the definitions of a dozen unusual words. And when he left the library, he carried under his arm four volumes: Madam Blavatsky's "Secret Doctrine," "Progress and Poverty," "The Quintessence of Socialism," and "Warfare of Religion and Science." Unfortunately, he began on the "Secret Doctrine." Every line bristled with many-syllabled words he did not understand. He sat up in bed, and the dictionary was in front of him more often than the

book. He looked up so many new words that when
they recurred, he had forgotten their meaning and had
to look them up again. He devised the plan of writing
the definitions in a notebook, and filled page after page
with them. And still he could not understand. He read
until three in the morning, and his brain was in a
turmoil, but not one essential thought in the text had
he grasped. He looked up, and it seemed that the room
was lifting, heeling, and plunging like a ship upon the
sea. Then he hurled the "Secret Doctrine" and many
curses across the room, turned off the gas, and composed himself to sleep. Nor did he have much better
luck with the other three books. It was not that his
brain was weak or incapable; it could think these
thoughts were it not for lack of training in thinking
and lack of the thought-tools with which to think. He
guessed this, and for a while entertained the idea of
reading nothing but the dictionary until he had mastered every word in it.

Poetry, however, was his solace, and he read much
of it, finding his greatest joy in the simpler poets, who
were more understandable. He loved beauty, and there
he found beauty. Poetry, like music, stirred him profoundly, and, though he did not know it, he was preparing his mind for the heavier work that was to come.
The pages of his mind were blank, and, without effort,
much he read and liked, stanza by stanza, was impressed upon those pages, so that he was soon able to
extract great joy from chanting aloud or under his
breath the music and the beauty of the printed words
he had read. Then he stumbled upon Gayley's "Classic
Myths" and Bulfinch's "Age of Fable," side by side
on a library shelf. It was illumination, a great light in
the darkness of his ignorance, and he read poetry more
avidly than ever.

The man at the desk in the library had seen Martin there so often that he had become quite cordial, always greeting him with a smile and a nod when he entered. It was because of this that Martin did a daring thing. Drawing out some books at the desk, and while the man was stamping the cards, Martin blurted out:—

"Say, there's something I'd like to ask you."

The man smiled and paid attention.

"When you meet a young lady an' she asks you to call, how soon can you call?"

Martin felt his shirt press and cling to his shoulders, what with the sweat of the effort.

"Why I'd say any time," the man answered.

"Yes, but this is different," Martin objected. "She —I—well, you see, it's this way: maybe she won't be there. She goes to the university."

"Then call again."

"What I said ain't what I meant," Martin confessed falteringly, while he made up his mind to throw himself wholly upon the other's mercy. "I'm just a rough sort of a fellow, an' I ain't never seen anything of society. This girl is all that I ain't, an' I ain't anything that she is. You don't think I'm playin' the fool, do you?" he demanded abruptly.

"No, no; not at all, I assure you," the other protested. "Your request is not exactly in the scope of the reference department, but I shall be only too pleased to assist you."

Martin looked at him admiringly.

"If I could tear it off that way, I'd be all right," he said.

"I beg pardon?"

"I mean if I could talk easy that way, an' polite, an' all the rest."

"Oh," said the other, with comprehension.

"What is the best time to call? The afternoon?—not too close to meal-time? Or the evening? Or Sunday?"

"I'll tell you," the librarian said with a brightening face. "You call her up on the telephone and find out."

"I'll do it," he said, picking up his books and starting away.

He turned back and asked:—

"When you're speakin' to a young lady—say, for instance, Miss Lizzie Smith—do you say 'Miss Lizzie'? or 'Miss Smith'?"

"Say 'Miss Smith,' " the librarian stated authoritatively. "Say 'Miss Smith' always—until you come to know her better."

So it was that Martin Eden solved the problem.

"Come down any time; I'll be at home all afternoon," was Ruth's reply over the telephone to his stammered request as to when he could return the borrowed books.

She met him at the door herself, and her woman's eyes took in immediately the creased trousers and the certain slight but indefinable change in him for the better. Also, she was struck by his face. It was almost violent, this health of his, and it seemed to rush out of him and at her in waves of force. She felt the urge again of the desire to lean toward him for warmth, and marveled again at the effect his presence produced upon her. And he, in turn, knew again the swimming sensation of bliss when he felt the contact of her hand in greeting. The difference between them lay in that she was cool and self-possessed while his face flushed to the roots of the hair. He stumbled with his old awkwardness after her, and his shoulders swung and lurched perilously.

Once they were seated in the living room, he began

to get on easily—more easily by far than he had expected. She made it easy for him; and the gracious spirit with which she did it made him love her more madly than ever. They talked first of the borrowed books, of the Swinburne he was devoted to, and of the Browning he did not understand; and she led the conversation on from subject to subject, while she pondered the problem of how she could be of help to him. She had thought of this often since their first meeting. She wanted to help him. He made a call upon her pity and tenderness that no one had ever made before, and the pity was not so much derogatory of him as maternal in her. Her pity could not be of the common sort, when the man who drew it was so much man as to shock her with maidenly fears and set her mind and pulse thrilling with strange thoughts and feelings. The old fascination of his neck was there, and there was sweetness in the thought of laying her hands upon it. It seemed still a wanton impulse, but she had grown more used to it. She did not dream that in such guise newborn love would epitomize itself. Nor did she dream that the feeling he excited in her was love. She thought she was merely interested in him as an unusual type possessing various potential excellencies, and she even felt philanthropic about it.

She did not know she desired him; but with him it was different. He knew that he loved her, and he desired her as he had never before desired anything in his life. He had loved poetry for beauty's sake; but since he met her the gates to the vast field of love-poetry had been opened wide. She had given him understanding even more than Bulfinch and Gayley. There was a line that a week before he would not have favored with a second thought—"God's own mad lover dying on a kiss"; but now it was ever insistent in his mind. He marveled at the wonder of it and the truth; and as he gazed upon her he knew that he could die gladly upon a kiss. He felt himself God's own mad lover, and no accolade of knighthood could have given him greater pride. And at last he knew the meaning of life and why he had been born.

As he gazed at her and listened, his thoughts grew daring. He reviewed all the wild delight of the pressure of her hand in his at the door, and longed for it again. His gaze wandered often toward her lips, and he yearned for them hungrily. But there was nothing gross or earthly about this yearning. It gave him exquisite delight to watch every movement and play of those lips as they enunciated the words she spoke; yet they were not ordinary lips such as all men and women had. Their substance was not mere human clay. They were lips of pure spirit, and his desire for them seemed absolutely different from the desire that had led him to other women's lips. He could kiss her lips, rest his own physical lips upon them, but it would be with the lofty and awful fervor with which one would kiss the robe of God. He was not conscious of this transvaluation of values that had taken place in him, and was unaware that the light that shone in his eyes when he looked at her was quite the same light that shines in all men's eyes when the desire of love is upon them. He did not dream how ardent and masculine his gaze was, nor that the warm flame of it was affecting the alchemy of her spirit. Her penetrative virginity exalted and disguised his own emotions, elevating his thoughts to a star-cool chastity, and he would have been startled to learn that there was that shining out of his eyes, like warm waves, that flowed through her and kindled a kindred warmth. She was subtly perturbed by it, and more than once, though she knew not why, it disrupted her train of thought with its delicious intrusion and compelled her to grope for the remainder of ideas partly uttered. Speech was always easy with her, and these interruptions would have puzzled her had she not decided that it was because he was a remarkable type. She was very sensitive to impressions, and it was not strange, after all, that this aura of a traveler from another world should so affect her.

The problem in the background of her consciousness was how to help him, and she turned the conversation in that direction; but it was Martin who came to the point first.

"I wonder if I can get some advice from you," he began, and received an acquiescence of willingness that made his heart bound. "You remember the other time I was here I said I couldn't talk about books an' things because I didn't know how? Well, I've ben doin' a lot of thinkin' ever since. I've ben to the library a whole lot, but most of the books I've tackled have ben over my head. Mebbe I'd better begin at the beginnin'. I ain't never had no advantages. I've worked pretty hard ever since I was a kid, an' since I've ben to the library, lookin' with new eyes at books—an' lookin' at new books, too—I've just about concluded that I ain't ben reading the right kind. You know the books you find in cattle-camps an' fo'c's'ls ain't the same you've got in this house, for instance. Well, that's the sort of readin' matter I've ben accustomed to. And yet—an' I ain't just makin' a brag of it—I've ben different from the people I've herded with. Not that I'm any better than the sailors an' cow-punchers I traveled with,—I was cow-punchin' for a short time, you know,—but I always liked books, read everything I could lay hands on, an'—well, I guess I think differently from most of 'em.

"Now, to come to what I'm drivin' at. I was never inside a house like this. When I come a week ago, an' saw all this, an' you, an' your mother, an' brothers, an' everything—well, I liked it. I'd heard about such things an' read about such things in some of the books, an' when I looked around at your house, why, the books come true. But the thing I'm after is I liked it. I wanted it. I want it now. I want to breathe air like you get in this house—air that is filled with books, and pictures, and beautiful things, where people talk in low voices an' are clean, an' their thoughts are clean. The air I always breathed was mixed up with grub an' house-rent an' scrappin' an' booze an' that's all they talked about, too. Why, when you was crossin' the room to kiss your mother, I thought it was the most beautiful thing I ever seen. I've seen a whole lot of life, an' somehow I've seen a whole lot more of it than most of them that was with me. I like to see, an' I want to see more, an' I want to see it different.

"But I ain't got to the point yet. Here it is. I want to make my way to the kind of life you have in this house. There's more in life than booze, an' hard work, an' knockin' about. Now, how am I goin' to get it? Where do I take hold an' begin? I'm willin' to work my passage, you know, an' I can make most men sick when it comes to hard work. Once I get started, I'll work night an' day. Mebbe you think it's funny, me askin' you about all this. I know you're the last person in the world I ought to ask, but I don't know anybody else I could ask—unless it's Arthur. Mebbe I ought to ask him. If I was—"

His voice died away. His firmly planned intention had come to a halt on the verge of the horrible probability that he should have asked Arthur and that he had made a fool of himself. Ruth did not speak immediately. She was too absorbed in striving to reconcile the stumbling, uncouth speech and its simplicity of thought with what she saw in his face. She had never looked in eyes that expressed greater power. Here was a man who could do anything, was the message she read there, and it accorded ill with the weakness of his spoken thought. And for that matter so complex and quick was her own mind that she did not have a just appreciation of simplicity. And yet she had caught an impression of power in the very groping of this mind. It had seemed to her like a giant writhing and straining at the bonds that held him down. Her face was all sympathy when she did speak.

"What you need, you realize yourself, and it is education. You should go back and finish grammar school, and then go through the high school and university."

"But that takes money," he interrupted.

"Oh!" she cried. "I had not thought of that. But then you have relatives, somebody who could assist you?"

He shook his head.

"My father and mother are dead. I've two sisters, one married, an' the other'll get married soon, I suppose. Then I've a string of brothers,—I'm the youngest,—but they never helped nobody. They've just knocked around over the world, lookin' out for number one. The oldest died in India. Two are in South Africa now, an' another's on a whaling voyage, an' one's travelin' with a circus—he does trapeze work. An' I guess I'm just like them. I've taken care of myself since I was eleven—that's when my mother died. I've got to study by myself, I guess, an' what I want to know is where to begin."

"I should say the first thing of all would be to get

a grammar. Your grammar is—" She had intended saying "awful," but she amended it to "is not particularly good."

He flushed and sweated.

"I know I must talk a lot of slang an' words you don't understand. But then they're the only words I know—how to speak. I've got other words in my mind, picked 'em up from books, but I can't pronounce 'em, so I don't use 'em."

"It isn't what you say, so much as how you say it. You don't mind my being frank, do you? I don't want to hurt you."

"No, no," he cried, while he secretly blessed her for her kindness. "Fire away. I've got to know, an' I'd sooner know from you than anybody else."

"Well, then, you say, 'You was'; it should be, 'You were.' You say 'I seen' for 'I saw.' You use the double negative—"

"What's the double negative?" he demanded; then added humbly, "You see, I don't even understand your explanations."

"I'm afraid I didn't explain that," she smiled. "A double negative is—let me see—well, you say 'never helped nobody.' 'Never' is a negative. 'Nobody' is another negative. It is a rule that two negatives make a positive. 'Never helped nobody' means that not helping nobody, they must have helped somebody."

"That's pretty clear," he said. "I never thought of it before. But it don't mean they *must* have helped somebody, does it? Seems to me that 'never helped nobody' just naturally fails to say whether or not they helped somebody. I never thought of it before, and I'll never say it again."

She was pleased and surprised with the quickness

and surety of his mind. As soon as he had got the clue he not only understood but corrected her error.

"You'll find it all in the grammar," she went on. "There's something else I noticed in your speech. You say 'don't' when you shouldn't. 'Don't' is a contraction and stands for two words. Do you know them?"

He thought a moment, then answered, " 'Do not.' "

She nodded her head, and said, "And you use 'don't' when you mean 'does not.' "

He was puzzled over this, and did not get it so quickly.

"Give me an illustration," he asked.

"Well—" She puckered her brows and pursed up her mouth as she thought, while he looked on and decided that her expression was most adorable. " 'It don't do to be hasty.' Change 'don't' to 'do not,' and it reads, 'It do not do to be hasty,' which is perfectly absurd."

He turned it over in his mind and considered.

"Doesn't it jar on your ear?" she suggested.

"Can't say that it does," he replied judicially.

"Why didn't you say, 'Can't say that it do'?" she queried.

"That sounds wrong," he said slowly. "As for the other I can't make up my mind. I guess my ear ain't had the trainin' yours has."

"There is no such word as 'ain't,' " she said, prettily emphatic.

Martin flushed again.

"And you say 'ben' for 'been,' " she continued; " 'I come' for 'I came'; and the way you chop your endings is something dreadful."

"How do you mean?" He leaned forward, feeling that he ought to get down on his knees before so marvelous a mind. "How do I chop?"

"You don't complete the endings. 'A-n-d' spells

'and.' You pronounce it 'an'.' 'I-n-g' spells 'ing.' Sometimes you pronounce it 'ing' and sometimes you leave off the 'g.' And then you slur by dropping initial letters and diphthongs. 'T-h-e-m' spells 'them.' You pronounce it—oh, well, it is not necessary to go over all of them. What you need is the grammar. I'll get one and show you how to begin."

As she arose, there shot through his mind something that he had read in the etiquette books, and he stood up awkwardly, worrying as to whether he was doing the right thing, and fearing that she might take it as a sign that he was about to go.

"By the way, Mr. Eden," she called back, as she was leaving the room. "What is *booze?* You used it several times, you know."

"Oh, booze," he laughed. "It's slang. It means whiskey an' beer—anything that will make you drunk."

"And another thing," she laughed back. "Don't use 'you' when you are impersonal. 'You' is very personal, and your use of it just now was not precisely what you meant."

"I don't just see that."

"Why, you said just now, to me, 'whiskey and beer—anything that will make you drunk'—make *me* drunk, don't you see?"

"Well, it would, wouldn't it?"

"Yes, of course," she smiled. "But it would be nicer not to bring me into it. Substitute 'one' for 'you' and see how much better it sounds."

When she returned with the grammar, she drew a chair near his—he wondered if he should have helped her with the chair—and sat down beside him. She turned the pages of the grammar, and their heads were inclined toward each other. He could hardly follow her outlining of the work he must do, so amazed was he by her delightful propinquity. But when she began to lay down the importance of conjugation, he forgot all about her. He had never heard of conjugation, and was fascinated by the glimpse he was catching into the tie-ribs of language. He leaned closer to the page, and her hair touched his cheek. He had fainted but once in his life, and he thought he was going to faint again. He could scarcely breathe, and his heart was pounding the blood up into his throat and suffocating him. Never had she seemed so accessible as now. For the moment the great gulf that separated them was bridged. But there was no diminution in the loftiness of his feeling for her. She had not descended to him. It was he who had been caught up into the clouds and carried to her. His reverence for her, in that moment, was of the same order as religious awe and fervor. It seemed to him that he had intruded upon the holy of holies, and slowly and carefully he moved his head aside from the contact which thrilled him like an electric shock and of which she had not been aware.

Chapter Eight

Several weeks went by, during which Martin Eden studied his grammar, reviewed the books on etiquette, and read voraciously the books that caught his fancy. Of his own class he saw nothing. The girls of the Lotus Club wondered what had become of him and worried Jim with questions, and some of the fellows who put on the glove at Riley's were glad that Martin came no more. He made another discovery of treasure-trove in the library. As the grammar had shown him the tie-ribs of language, so that book showed him the tie-ribs of poetry, and he began to learn meter and construction and form, beneath the beauty he loved finding the why and wherefore of that beauty. Another modern book he found treated poetry as a representative art, treated it exhaustively, with copious illustrations from the best in literature. Never had he read fiction with such keen zest as he studied these books. And his fresh mind, untaxed for twenty years and impelled by maturity of desire, gripped hold of what he read with a virility unusual to the student mind.

When he looked back now from his vantage-ground, the old world he had known, the world of land and sea and ships, of sailor-men and harpy-women, seemed a very small world; and yet it blended in with this new world and expanded. His mind made for unity, and he was surprised when at first he began to see points of contact between the two worlds. And he was ennobled, as well, by the loftiness of thought and beauty he found in the books. This led him to believe more firmly than ever that up above him, in society like Ruth and her family, all men and women thought these thoughts and lived them. Down below where he lived was the ignoble, and he wanted to purge himself of the ignoble that had soiled all his days, and to rise to that sublimated realm where dwelt the upper classes. All his childhood and youth had been troubled by a vague unrest; he had never known what he wanted, but he had wanted something that he had hunted vainly for until he met Ruth. And now his unrest had become sharp and painful, and he knew at last, clearly and definitely, that it was beauty, and intellect, and love that he must have.

During those several weeks he saw Ruth half a dozen times, and each time was an added inspiration. She helped him with his English, corrected his pronunciation, and started him on arithmetic. But their intercourse was not all devoted to elementary study. He had seen too much of life, and his mind was too matured, to be wholly content with fractions, cube root, parsing, and analysis; and there were times when their conversation turned on other themes—the last poetry he had read, the latest poet she had studied. And when she read aloud to him her favorite passages, he ascended to the topmost heaven of delight. Never, in all the women he had heard speak, had he heard a voice like hers. The least sound of it was a stimulus to his love, and he thrilled and throbbed with every word she uttered. It was the quality of it, the repose, and the musical modulation—the soft, rich, indefinable product of culture and a gentle soul. As he listened to her, there rang in the ears of his memory the harsh cries of barbarian women and of hags, and, in lesser degrees of harshness, the strident voices of working women and of the girls of his own class. Then the chemistry of vision would begin to work, and they would troop in review across his mind, each, by contrast, multiplying Ruth's glories. Then, too, his bliss was heightened by the knowledge that her mind was comprehending what she read and was quivering with appreciation of the beauty of the written thought. She read to him much from "The Princess," and often he saw her eyes swimming with tears, so finely was her aesthetic nature strung. At such moments her own emotions elevated him till he was as a god, and, as he gazed at her and listened, he seemed gazing on the face of life and reading its deepest secrets. And then, becoming aware of the heights of exquisite sensibility he attained, he decided that this was love and that love was the greatest thing in the world. And in review would pass along the corridors of memory all previous thrills and burnings he had known,—the drunkenness of wine, the caresses of women, the rough play and give and take of physical contests,—and they seemed trivial and mean compared with this sublime ardor he now enjoyed.

The situation was obscured to Ruth. She had never had any experiences of the heart. Her only experiences in such matters were of the books, where the facts of ordinary day were translated by fancy into a fairy realm of unreality; and she little knew that this rough sailor was creeping into her heart and storing there pent forces that would some day burst forth and surge through her in waves of fire. She did not know the actual fire of love. Her knowledge of love was purely theoretical, and she conceived of it as lambent flame, gentle as the fall of dew or the ripple of quiet water, and cool as the velvet-dark of summer nights. Her idea of love was more that of placid affection, serving the loved one softly in an atmosphere, flower-scented and dim-lighted, of ethereal calm. She did not dream of the volcanic convulsions of love, its scorching heat and sterile wastes of parched ashes. She knew neither her own potencies, nor the potencies of the world; and the deeps of life were to her seas of illusion. The conjugal affection of her father and mother constituted her ideal of love-affinity and she looked forward some day to emerging, without shock or friction, into that same quiet sweetness of existence with a loved one.

So it was that she looked upon Martin Eden as a novelty, a strange individual, and she identified with novelty and strangeness the effects he produced upon her. It was only natural. In similar ways she had experienced unusual feelings when she looked at wild animals in the menagerie, or when she witnessed a storm of wind, or shuddered at the bright-ribbed lightning. There was something cosmic in such things, and there was something cosmic in him. He came to her breathing of large airs and great spaces. The blaze of tropic suns was in his face, and in his swelling, resilient muscles was the primordial vigor of life. He was marred and scarred by that mysterious world of rough men and rougher deeds, the outposts of which began beyond her horizon. He was untamed, wild, and in secret ways her vanity was touched by the fact that he came so mildly to her hand. Likewise she was stirred by the common impulse to tame the wild thing. It was an unconscious impulse, and farthest from her thoughts that her desire was to rethumb the clay of him into a likeness of her father's image, which image she believed to be the finest in the world. Nor was there any way, out of her inexperience, for her to know that the cosmic feel she caught of him was that most cosmic of things, love, which with equal power drew men and women together across the world, compelled stags to kill each other in the rutting season, and drove even the elements irresistibly to unite.

His swift development was a source of surprise and interest. She detected unguessed finenesses in him that seemed to bud, day by day, like flowers in congenial soil. She read Browning aloud to him, and was often puzzled by the strange interpretations he gave to mooted passages. It was beyond her to realize that, out of his experience of men and women and life, his interpretations were far more frequently correct than hers. His conceptions seemed naïve to her, though she was often fired by his daring flights of comprehension, whose orbit-path was so wide among the stars that she could not follow and could only sit and thrill to the impact of unguessed power. Then she played to him—no longer at him—and probed him with music that sank to depths beyond her plumb-line. His nature opened to music as a flower to the sun, and the transition was quick from his working-class ragtime and jingles to her classical display pieces that she knew nearly by heart. Yet he betrayed a democratic fondness for Wagner, and the "Tannhäuser" overture, when she had given him the clue to it, claimed him as nothing else she played. In an immediate way it personified his life. All his past was the *Venusburg* motif, while her he identified somehow with the *Pilgrims' Chorus* motif; and from the exalted state this elevated him to, he swept onward and upward into that vast shadow-realm of spirit-groping, where good and evil war eternally.

Sometimes he questioned, and induced in her mind temporary doubts as to the correctness of her own definitions and conceptions of music. But her singing he did not question. It was too wholly her, and he sat always amazed at the divine melody of her pure soprano voice. And he could not help but contrast it with the weak pipings and shrill quaverings of factory girls, ill-nourished and untrained, and with the raucous shriekings from gin-cracked throats of the women of the seaport towns. She enjoyed singing and playing to him. In truth, it was the first time she had ever had a human soul to play with, and the plastic clay of him was a delight to mold; for she thought she was molding it, and her intentions were good. Besides, it was pleasant to be with him. He did not repel her. That first repulsion had been really a fear of her undiscovered self, and the fear had gone to sleep. Though she did not know it, she had a feeling in him of proprietary right. Also, he had a tonic effect upon her. She was studying hard at the university, and it seemed to strengthen her to emerge from the dusty books and have the fresh seabreeze of his personality blow upon her. Strength! Strength was what she needed, and he gave it to her in generous measure. To come into the same room with him, or to meet him at the door, was to take heart of life. And when he had gone, she would return to her books with a keener zest and fresh store of energy.

She knew her Browning, but it had never sunk into her that it was an awkward thing to play with souls. As her interest in Martin increased, the remodeling of his life became a passion with her.

"There is Mr. Butler," she said one afternoon, when grammar and arithmetic and poetry had been put aside. "He had comparatively no advantages at first. His father had been a bank cashier, but he lingered for years, dying of consumption in Arizona, so that when he was dead, Mr. Butler, Charles Butler he was called, found himself alone in the world. His father had come from Australia, you know, and so he had no relatives in California. He went to work in a printing-office,— I have heard him tell of it many times,—and he got three dollars a week, at first. His income today is at least thirty thousand a year. How did he do it? He was honest, and faithful, and industrious, and economical. He denied himself the enjoyments that most boys indulge in. He made it a point to save so much every week, no matter what he had to do without in order to save it. Of course, he was soon earning more than three dollars a week, and as his wages increased he saved more and more.

"He worked in the daytime, and at night he went to night school. He had his eyes fixed always on the future. Later on he went to night high school. When he was only seventeen, he was earning excellent wages at setting type, but he was ambitious. He wanted a career, not a livelihood, and he was content to make immediate sacrifices for his ultimate gain. He decided upon the law, and he entered father's office as an office boy—think of that!—and got only four dollars a week. But he had learned how to be economical, and out of that four dollars he went on saving money."

She paused for breath, and to note how Martin was receiving it. His face was lighted up with interest in the youthful struggles of Mr. Butler; but there was a frown upon his face as well.

"I'd say they was pretty hard lines for a young fellow," he remarked. "Four dollars a week! How could he live on it? You can bet he didn't have any frills. Why, I pay five dollars a week for board now, an' there's nothin' excitin' about it, you can lay to that. He must have lived like a dog. The food he ate—"

"He cooked for himself," she interrupted, "on a little kerosene stove."

"The food he ate must have been worse than what a sailor gets on the worst-feedin' deep-water ships, than which there ain't much that can be possibly worse."

"But think of him now!" she cried enthusiastically. "Think of what his income affords him. His early denials are paid for a thousand-fold."

Martin looked at her sharply.

"There's one thing I'll bet you," he said, "and it is that Mr. Butler is nothin' gay-hearted now in his fat days. He fed himself like that for years an' years, on a boy's stomach, an' I bet his stomach's none too good now for it."

Her eyes dropped before his searching gaze.

"I'll bet he's got dyspepsia right now!" Martin challenged.

"Yes, he has," she confessed; "but—"

"An' I bet," Martin dashed on, "that he's solemn an' serious as an old owl, an' doesn't care a rap for a good time, for all his thirty thousand a year. An' I'll bet he's not particularly joyful at seein' others have a good time. Ain't I right?"

She nodded her head in agreement, and hastened to explain:—

"But he is not that type of man. By nature he is sober and serious. He always was that."

"You can bet he was," Martin proclaimed. "Three dollars a week, an' four dollars a week, an' a young boy cookin' for himself on an oil-burner an' layin' up money, workin' all day an' studyin' all night, just workin' an' never playin', never havin' a good time, an' never learnin' how to have a good time—of course his thirty thousand came along too late."

His sympathetic imagination was flashing upon his inner sight all the thousands of details of the boy's existence and of his narrow spiritual development into a thirty-thousand-dollar-a-year man. With the swiftness and wide-reaching of multitudinous thought Charles Butler's whole life was telescoped upon his vision.

"Do you know," he added, "I feel sorry for Mr. Butler. He was too young to know better, but he robbed himself of life for the sake of thirty thousand a year that's clean wasted upon him. Why, thirty thousand, lump sum, wouldn't buy for him right now what ten cents he was layin' up would have bought him, when he was a kid, in the way of candy an' peanuts or a seat in nigger heaven."

It was just such uniqueness of points of view that startled Ruth. Not only were they new to her, and contrary to her own beliefs, but she always felt in them germs of truth that threatened to unseat or modify her own convictions. Had she been fourteen instead of twenty-four, she might have been changed by them; but she was twenty-four, conservative by nature and upbringing, and already crystallized into the cranny of life where she had been born and formed. It was true, his bizarre judgments troubled her in the moments they were uttered, but she ascribed them to his novelty of type and strangeness of living, and they were soon forgotten. Nevertheless, while she disapproved of them, the strength of their utterance, and the flashing of eyes and earnestness of face that accompanied them, always thrilled her and drew her toward him. She would never have guessed that this man who had come from beyond her horizon, was, in such moments, flashing on beyond her horizon with wider and deeper concepts. Her own limits were the limits of her horizon; but limited minds can recognize limitations only in others. And so she felt that her outlook was very wide indeed, and that where his conflicted with hers marked his limitations; and she dreamed of helping him to see as she saw, of widening his horizon until it was identified with hers.

"But I have not finished my story," she said. "He worked, so father says, as no other office boy he ever had. Mr. Butler was always eager to work. He never was late, and he was usually at the office a few minutes before his regular time. And yet he saved his time. Every spare moment was devoted to study. He studied book-keeping and type-writing, and he paid for lessons in shorthand by dictating at night to a court reporter who needed practice. He quickly became a clerk, and he made himself invaluable. Father appreciated him and saw that he was bound to rise. It was on father's suggestion that he went to law college. He became a lawyer, and hardly was he back in the office when father took him in as junior partner. He is a great man. He refused the United States Senate several times, and father says he could become a justice of the Supreme Court any time a vacancy occurs, if he wants to. Such a life is an inspiration to all of us. It shows us that a man with will may rise superior to his environment."

"He is a great man," Martin said sincerely.

But it seemed to him there was something in the recital that jarred upon his sense of beauty and life. He could not find an adequate motive in Mr. Butler's life of pinching and privation. Had he done it for love of a woman, or for attainment of beauty, Martin would have understood. God's own mad lover should do anything for the kiss, but not for thirty thousand dollars a year. He was dissatisfied with Mr. Butler's career. There was something paltry about it, after all. Thirty thousand a year was all right, but dyspepsia and inability to be humanly happy robbed such princely income of all its value.

Much of this he strove to express to Ruth, and shocked her and made it clear that more remodeling was necessary. Hers was that common insularity of mind that makes human creatures believe that their color, creed, and politics are best and right and that other human creatures scattered over the world are less fortunately placed than they. It was the same insularity of mind that made the ancient Jew thank God he was not born a woman, and sent the modern missionary god-substituting to the ends of the earth; and it made Ruth desire to shape this man from other crannies of life into the likeness of the men who lived in her particular cranny of life.

Chapter Nine

Back from sea Martin Eden came, homing for California with a lover's desire. His store of money exhausted, he had shipped before the mast on the treasure-hunting schooner; and the Solomon Islands, after eight months of failure to find treasure, had witnessed the breaking up of the expedition. The men had been paid off in Australia, and Martin had immediately shipped on a deep-water vessel for San Francisco. Not alone had those eight months earned him enough money to stay on land for many weeks, but they had enabled him to do a great deal of studying and reading.

His was the student's mind, and behind his ability to learn was the indomitability of his nature and his love for Ruth. The grammar he had taken along he went through again and again until his unjaded brain had mastered it. He noticed the bad grammar used by his shipmates, and made a point of mentally correcting and reconstructing their crudities of speech. To his great joy he discovered that his ear was becoming sensitive and that he was developing grammatical nerves. A double negative jarred him like a discord, and often, from lack of practice, it was from his own lips that the jar came. His tongue refused to learn new tricks in a day.

After he had been through the grammar repeatedly, he took up the dictionary and added twenty words a day to his vocabulary. He found that this was no light task, and at wheel or lookout he steadily went over and over his lengthening list of pronunciations and definitions, while he invariably memorized himself to sleep. "Never did anything," "if I were," and "those things," were phrases, with many variations, that he repeated under his breath in order to accustom his tongue to the language spoken by Ruth. "And" and "ing," with the "d" and "g" pronounced emphatically, he went over thousands of times; and to his surprise he noticed that he was beginning to speak cleaner and more correct English than the officers themselves and the gentleman-adventurers in the cabin who had financed the expedition.

The captain was a fishy-eyed Norwegian who somehow had fallen into possession of a complete Shakespeare, which he never read, and Martin had washed his clothes for him and in return been permitted access to the precious volumes. For a time, so steeped was he in the plays and in the many favorite passages that impressed themselves almost without effort on his brain, that all the world seemed to shape itself into forms of Elizabethan tragedy or comedy and his very thoughts were in blank verse. It trained his ear and gave him a fine appreciation for noble English; withal it introduced into his mind much that was archaic and obsolete.

The eight months had been well spent, and, in addition to what he had learned of right speaking and high thinking, he had learned much of himself. Along with his humbleness because he knew so little, there arose a conviction of power. He felt a sharp gradation between himself and his shipmates, and was wise enough to realize that the difference lay in potentiality rather than achievement. What he could do, they could do; but within him he felt a confused ferment working that told him there was more in him than he had done. He was tortured by the exquisite beauty of the world, and wished that Ruth were there to share it with him. He decided that he would describe to her many of the bits of South Sea beauty. The creative spirit in him flamed up at the thought and urged that he recreate this beauty for a wider audience than Ruth. And then, in splendor and glory, came the great idea. He would write. He would be one of the eyes through which the world saw, one of the ears through which it heard, one of the hearts through which it felt. He would write—everything—poetry and prose, fiction and description, and plays like Shakespeare. There was career and the way to win to Ruth. The men of literature were the world's giants, and he conceived them to be far finer than the Mr. Butlers who earned thirty thousand a year and could be Supreme Court justices if they wanted to.

Once the idea had germinated, it mastered him, and the return voyage to San Francisco was like a dream. He was drunken with unguessed power and felt that he could do anything. In the midst of the great and lonely sea he gained perspective. Clearly, and for the first time, he saw Ruth and her world. It was all visualized in his mind as a concrete thing which he could take up in his two hands and turn around and about and examine. There was much that was dim and nebulous in that world, but he saw it as a whole and not in detail, and he saw, also, the way to master it. To write! The thought was fire in him. He would begin as soon as he got back. The first thing he would do would be to describe the voyage of the treasure-hunters. He would sell it to some San Francisco newspaper. He would not tell Ruth anything about it, and she would be surprised and pleased when she saw his name in print. While he wrote, he could go on studying. There were twenty-four hours in each day. He was invincible. He knew how to work, and the citadels would go down before him. He would not have to go to sea again—as a sailor; and for the instant he caught a vision of a steam yacht. There were other writers who possessed steam yachts. Of course, he cautioned himself, it would be slow succeeding at first, and for a time he would be content to earn enough money by his writing to enable him to go on studying. And then, after some time,—a very indeterminate time,—when he had learned and prepared himself, he would write the great things and his name would be on all men's lips. But greater than that, infinitely greater and greatest of all, he would have proved himself worthy of Ruth. Fame was all very well, but it was for Ruth that his splendid dream arose. He was not a fame-monger, but merely one of God's mad lovers.

Arrived in Oakland, with his snug pay-day in his pocket, he took up his old room at Bernard Higginbotham's and set to work. He did not even let Ruth know he was back. He would go and see her when he finished the article on the treasure-hunters. It was not so difficult to abstain from seeing her, because of the violent heat of creative fever that burned in him. Besides, the very article he was writing would bring her nearer to him. He did not know how long an article he should write, but he counted the words in a double-page article in the Sunday supplement of the *San Francisco Examiner*, and guided himself by that. Three days, at white heat, completed his narrative; but when he had copied it carefully, in a large scrawl that was easy to read, he learned from a rhetoric he picked up in the library that there were such things as paragraphs and quotation marks. He had never thought of such things before; and he promptly set to work writing the article over, referring continually to the pages of the rhetoric and learning more in a day about composition than the average schoolboy in a year. When he had copied the article a second time and rolled it up carefully, he read in a newspaper an item on hints to beginners, and discovered the iron law that manuscripts should never be rolled and that they should be written on one side of the paper. He had violated the law on both counts. Also, he learned from the item that first-class papers paid a minimum of ten dollars a column. So, while he copied the manuscript a third time, he consoled himself by multiplying ten columns by ten dollars. The product was always the same, one hundred dollars, and he decided that that was better than seafaring. If it hadn't been for his blunders, he would have finished the article in three days. One hundred dollars in three days! It would have taken him three months and longer on the sea to earn a similar amount. A man was a fool to go to sea when he could write, he concluded, though the money in itself meant nothing to him. Its value was in the liberty it would get him, the presentable garments it would buy him, all of which would bring him nearer, swiftly nearer, to the slender pale girl who had turned his life back upon itself and given him inspiration.

He mailed the manuscript in a flat envelope, and addressed it to the editor of the *San Francisco Examiner*. He had an idea that anything accepted by a paper was published immediately, and as he had sent the manuscript in on Friday he expected it to come out on the following Sunday. He conceived that it would be fine to let that event apprise Ruth of his return. Then, Sunday afternoon, he would call and see her. In the meantime he was occupied by another idea, which he prided himself upon as being a particularly sane, careful, and modest idea. He would write an adventure story for boys and sell it to *The Youth's Companion*. He went to the free reading-room and looked through the files of *The Youth's Companion*. Serial stories, he found, were usually published in that weekly in five installments of about three thousand words each. He discovered several serials that ran to seven installments, and decided to write one of that length.

He had been on a whaling voyage in the Arctic,

once—a voyage that was to have been for three years
and which had terminated in shipwreck at the end of
six months. While his imagination was fanciful, even
fantastic at times, he had a basic love of reality that
compelled him to write about the things he knew. He
knew whaling, and out of the real materials of his
knowledge he proceeded to manufacture the fictitious
adventures of the two boys he intended to use as joint
heroes. It was easy work, he decided on Saturday
evening. He had completed on that day the first in-
stallment of three thousand words—much to the
amusement of Jim, and to the open derision of Mr.
Higginbotham, who sneered throughout meal-time at
the "litery" person they had discovered in the family.

Martin contented himself by picturing his brother-
in-law's surprise on Sunday morning when he opened
his *Examiner* and saw the article on the treasure-hunters. Early that morning he was out himself to the front
door, nervously racing through the many-sheeted
newspaper. He went through it a second time, very
carefully, then folded it up and left it where he had
found it. He was glad he had not told any one about
his article. On second thought he concluded that he
had been wrong about the speed with which things
found their way into newspaper columns. Besides,
there had not been any news value in his article, and
most likely the editor would write to him about it
first.

After breakfast he went on with his serial. The words
flowed from his pen, though he broke off from the
writing frequently to look up definitions in the dictionary or to refer to the rhetoric. He often read or
reread a chapter at a time, during such pauses; and he
consoled himself that while he was not writing the
great things he felt to be in him, he was learning

composition, at any rate, and training himself to shape up and express his thoughts. He toiled on till dark, when he went out to the reading-room and explored magazines and weeklies until the place closed at ten o'clock. This was his program for a week. Each day he did three thousand words, and each evening he puzzled his way through the magazines, taking note of the stories, articles, and poems that editors saw fit to publish. One thing was certain: What these multitudinous writers did he could do, and only give him time and he would do what they could not do. He was cheered to read in *Book News*, in a paragraph on the payment of magazine writers, not that Rudyard Kipling received a dollar per word, but that the minimum rate paid by first-class magazines was two cents a word. *The Youth's Companion* was certainly first class, and at that rate the three thousand words he had written that day would bring him sixty dollars—two months' wages on the sea!

On Friday night he finished the serial, twenty-one thousand words long. At two cents a word, he calculated, that would bring him four hundred and twenty dollars. Not a bad week's work. It was more money than he had ever possessed at one time. He did not know how he could spend it all. He had tapped a gold mine. Where this came from he could always get more. He planned to buy some more clothes, to subscribe to many magazines, and to buy dozens of reference books that at present he was compelled to go to the library to consult. And still there was a large portion of the four hundred and twenty dollars unspent. This worried him until the thought came to him of hiring a servant for Gertrude and of buying a bicycle for Marian.

He mailed the bulky manuscript to *The Youth's Com-*

panion, and on Saturday afternoon, after having planned an article on pearl-diving, he went to see Ruth. He had telephoned, and she went herself to greet him at the door. The old familiar blaze of health rushed out from him and struck her like a blow. It seemed to enter into her body and course through her veins in a liquid glow, and to set her quivering with its imparted strength. He flushed warmly as he took her hand and looked into her blue eyes, but the fresh bronze of eight months of sun hid the flush, though it did not protect the neck from the gnawing chafe of the stiff collar. She noted the red line of it with amusement which quickly vanished as she glanced at his clothes. They really fitted him,—it was his first made-to-order suit,—and he seemed slimmer and better modeled. In addition, his cloth cap had been replaced by a soft hat, which she commanded him to put on and then complimented him on his appearance. She did not remember when she had felt so happy. This change in him was her handiwork, and she was proud of it and fired with ambition further to help him.

But the most radical change of all, and the one that pleased her most, was the change in his speech. Not only did he speak more correctly, but he spoke more easily, and there were many new words in his vocabulary. When he grew excited or enthusiastic, however, he dropped back into the old slurring and the dropping of final consonants. Also, there was an awkward hesitancy, at times, as he essayed the new words he had learned. On the other hand, along with his ease of expression, he displayed a lightness and facetiousness of thought that delighted her. It was his old spirit of humor and badinage that had made him a favorite in his own class, but which he had hitherto been unable to use in her presence through lack of words and training. He was just beginning to orientate himself and to feel that he was not wholly an intruder. But he was very tentative, fastidiously so, letting Ruth set the pace of sprightliness and fancy, keeping up with her but never daring to go beyond her.

He told her of what he had been doing, and of his plan to write for a livelihood and of going on with his studies. But he was disappointed at her lack of approval. She did not think much of his plan.

"You see," she said frankly, "writing must be a trade, like anything else. Not that I know anything about it, of course. I only bring common judgment to bear. You couldn't hope to be a blacksmith without spending three years at learning the trade—or is it five years! Now writers are so much better paid than blacksmiths that there must be ever so many more men who would like to write, who—try to write."

"But then, may not I be peculiarly constituted to write?" he queried, secretly exulting at the language he had used, his swift imagination throwing the whole scene and atmosphere upon a vast screen along with a thousand other scenes from his life—scenes that were rough and raw, gross and bestial.

The whole composite vision was achieved with the speed of light, producing no pause in the conversation, nor interrupting his calm train of thought. On the screen of his imagination he saw himself and this sweet and beautiful girl, facing each other and conversing in good English, in a room of books and paintings and tone and culture, and all illuminated by a bright light of steadfast brilliance; while ranged about and fading away to the remote edges of the screen were antithetical scenes, each scene a picture, and he the onlooker, free to look at will upon what he wished. He saw these other scenes through drifting vapors and swirls of sullen fog dissolving before shafts of red and garish light. He saw cowboys at the bar, drinking fierce whiskey, the air filled with obscenity and ribald language, and he saw himself with them, drinking and cursing with the wildest, or sitting at table with them, under smoking kerosene lamps, while the chips clicked and clattered and the cards were dealt around. He saw himself, stripped to the waist, with naked fists, fighting his great fight with Liverpool Red in the forecastle of the *Susquehanna;* and he saw the bloody deck of the *John Rogers,* that gray morning of attempted mutiny, the mate kicking in death-throes on the main-hatch, the revolver in the old man's hand spitting fire and smoke, the men with passion-wrenched faces, of brutes screaming vile blasphemies and falling about him—and then he returned to the central scene, calm and clean in the steadfast light, where Ruth sat and talked with him amid books and paintings; and he saw the grand piano upon which she would later play to him; and he heard the echoes of his own selected and correct words, "But then, may I not be peculiarly constituted to write?"

"But no matter how peculiarly constituted a man may be for blacksmithing," she was laughing, "I never heard of one becoming a blacksmith without first serving his apprenticeship."

"What would you advise?" he asked. "And don't forget that I feel in me this capacity to write—I can't explain it; I just know that it is in me."

"You must get a thorough education," was the answer, "whether or not you ultimately become a writer. This education is indispensable for whatever career you select, and it must not be slipshod or sketchy. You should go to high school."

"Yes—" he began; but she interrupted with an afterthought:—

"Of course, you could go on with your writing, too."

"I would have to," he said grimly.

"Why?" She looked at him, prettily puzzled, for she did not quite like the persistence with which he clung to his notion.

"Because, without writing there wouldn't be any high school. I must live and buy books and clothes, you know."

"I'd forgotten that," she laughed. "Why weren't you born with an income?"

"I'd rather have good health and imagination," he answered. "I can make good on the income, but the other things have to be made good for—" He almost said "you," then amended his sentence to, "have to be made good for one."

"Don't say 'make good,'" she cried, sweetly petulant. "It's slang, and it's horrid."

He flushed, and stammered, "That's right, and I only wish you'd correct me every time."

"I—I'd like to," she said haltingly. "You have so much in you that is good that I want to see you perfect."

He was clay in her hands immediately, as passionately desirous of being molded by her as she was desirous of shaping him into the image of her ideal of man. And when she pointed out the opportuneness of the time, that the entrance examinations to high school began on the following Monday, he promptly volunteered that he would take them.

Then she played and sang to him, while he gazed with hungry yearning at her, drinking in her loveliness and marveling that there should not be a hundred suitors listening there and longing for her as he listened and longed.

Chapter Ten

He stopped to dinner that evening, and, much to Ruth's satisfaction, made a favorable impression on her father. They talked about the sea as a career, a subject which Martin had at his finger-ends, and Mr. Morse remarked afterward that he seemed a very clear-headed young man. In his avoidance of slang and his search after right words, Martin was compelled to talk slowly, which enabled him to find the best thoughts that were in him. He was more at ease than that first night at dinner, nearly a year before, and his shyness and modesty even commended him to Mrs. Morse, who was pleased at his manifest improvement.

"He is the first man that ever drew passing notice from Ruth," she told her husband. "She has been so singularly backward where men are concerned that I have been worried greatly."

Mr. Morse looked at his wife curiously.

"You mean to use this young sailor to wake her up?" he questioned.

"I mean that she is not to die an old maid if I can help it," was the answer. "If this young Eden can arouse her interest in mankind in general, it will be a good thing."

"A very good thing," he commented. "But suppose,—and we must suppose, sometimes, my dear,— suppose he arouses her interest too particularly in him?"

"Impossible," Mrs. Morse laughed. "She is three years older than he, and, besides, it is impossible. Nothing will ever come of it. Trust that to me."

And so Martin's role was arranged for him, while he, led on by Arthur and Norman, was meditating an extravagance. They were going out for a ride into the hills Sunday morning on their wheels, which did not interest Martin until he learned that Ruth, too, rode a wheel and was going along. He did not ride, nor own a wheel, but if Ruth rode, it was up to him to begin, was his decision; and when he said good night, he stopped in at a bicycle shop on his way home and spent forty dollars for a wheel. It was more than a month's hard-earned wages, and it reduced his stock of money amazingly; but when he added the hundred dollars he was to receive from the *Examiner* to the four hundred and twenty dollars that was the least *The Youth's Companion* could pay him, he felt that he had reduced the perplexity the unwonted amount of money had caused him. Nor did he mind, in the course of learning to ride the wheel home, the fact that he ruined his suit of clothes. He caught the tailor by telephone that night from Mr. Higginbotham's store and ordered another suit. Then he carried the wheel up the narrow stairway that clung like a fire-escape to the rear wall of the building, and when he had moved his bed out from the wall, found there was just space enough in the small room for himself and the wheel.

Sunday he had intended to devote to studying for the high school examination, but the pearl-diving article lured him away, and he spent the day in the white-hot fever of recreating the beauty and romance that burned in him. The fact that the *Examiner* of that morning had failed to publish his treasure-hunting article did not dash his spirits. He was at too great a height for that, and having been deaf to a twice-repeated summons, he went without the heavy Sunday dinner with which Mr. Higginbotham invariably graced his table. To Mr. Higginbotham such a dinner was advertisement of his worldly achievement and prosperity, and he honored it by delivering platitudinous sermonettes upon American institutions and the opportunity said institutions gave to any hard-working man to rise—the rise, in his case, which he pointed out unfailingly, being from a grocer's clerk to the ownership of Higginbotham's Cash Store.

Martin Eden looked with a sigh at his unfinished "Pearl-diving" on Monday morning, and took the car down to Oakland to the high school. And when, days later, he applied for the results of his examinations, he learned that he had failed in everything save grammar.

"Your grammar is excellent," Professor Hilton informed him, staring at him through heavy spectacles; "but you know nothing, positively nothing, in the other branches, and your United States history is abominable—there is no other word for it, abominable. I should advise you—"

Professor Hilton paused and glared at him, unsympathetic and unimaginative as one of his own testtubes. He was professor of physics in the high school, possessor of a large family, a meager salary, and a select fund of parrot-learned knowledge.

"Yes, sir," Martin said humbly, wishing somehow that the man at the desk in the library was in Professor Hilton's place just then.

"And I should advise you to go back to the grammar school for at least two years. Good day."

Martin was not deeply affected by his failure, though he was surprised at Ruth's shocked expression when he told her Professor Hilton's advice. Her disappointment was so evident that he was sorry he had failed, but chiefly so for her sake.

"You see I was right," she said. "You know far more than any of the students entering high school, and yet you can't pass the examinations. It is because what education you have is fragmentary, sketchy. You need the discipline of study, such as only skilled teachers can give you. You must be thoroughly grounded. Professor Hilton is right, and if I were you, I'd go to night school. A year and a half of it might enable you to catch up that additional six months. Besides, that would leave you your days in which to write, or, if you could not make your living by your pen, you would have your days in which to work in some position."

But if my days are taken up with work and my nights with school, when am I going to see you?—was Martin's first thought, though he refrained from uttering it. Instead, he said:—

"It seems so babyish for me to be going to night school. But I wouldn't mind that if I thought it would pay. But I don't think it will pay. I can do the work quicker than they can teach me. It would be a loss of time—" he thought of her and his desire to have her—"and I can't afford the time. I haven't the time to spare, in fact."

"There is so much that is necessary." She looked at him gently, and he felt that he was a brute to oppose her. "Physics and chemistry—you can't do them without laboratory study; and you'll find algebra and geometry almost hopeless without instruction. You need the skilled teachers, the specialists in the art of imparting knowledge."

He was silent for a minute, casting about for the least vainglorious way in which to express himself.

"Please don't think I'm bragging," he began. "I don't intend it that way at all. But I have a feeling that I am what I may call a natural student. I can study by myself. I take to it kindly, like a duck to water. You see yourself what I did with grammar. And I've learned much of other things—you would never dream how much. And I'm only getting started. Wait till I get—" He hesitated and assured himself of the pronunciation before he said "momentum. I'm getting my first real feel of things now, I'm beginning to size up the situation—"

"Please don't say 'size up,' " she interrupted.

"To get a line on things," he hastily amended.

"That doesn't mean anything in correct English," she objected.

He floundered for a fresh start.

"What I'm driving at is that I'm beginning to get the lay of the land."

Out of pity she forebore, and he went on.

"Knowledge seems to me like a chart-room. Whenever I go into the library, I am impressed that way. The part played by teachers is to teach the student the contents of the chart-room in a systematic way. The teachers are guides to the chart-room, that's all. It's not something that they have in their own heads. They don't make it up, don't create it. It's all in the chart-room and they know their way about in it, and it's their business to show the place to strangers who might else get lost. Now I don't get lost easily. I have the bump of location. I usually know where I'm at— What's wrong now?"

"Don't say 'where I'm at.' "

"That's right," he said gratefully, "where I am. But where am I at—I mean, where am I? Oh, yes, in the chart-room. Well, some people—"

"Persons," she corrected.

"Some persons need guides, most persons do; but I think I can get along without them. I've spent a lot of time in the chart-room now, and I'm on the edge of knowing my way about, what charts I want to refer to, what coasts I want to explore. And from the way I line it up, I'll explore a whole lot more quickly by myself. The speed of a fleet, you know, is the speed of the slowest ship, and the speed of the teachers is affected the same way. They can't go any faster than the ruck of their scholars, and I can set a faster pace for myself than they set for a whole schoolroom."

" 'He travels the fastest who travels alone,' " she quoted at him.

But I'd travel faster with you just the same, was what he wanted to blurt out, as he caught a vision of a world without end of sunlit spaces and starry voids through which he drifted with her, his arm around her, her pale gold hair blowing about his face. In the same instant he was aware of the pitiful inadequacy of speech. God! If he could so frame words that she could see what he then saw! And he felt the stir in him, like a throe of yearning pain, of the desire to paint these visions that flashed unsummoned on the mirror of his mind. Ah, that was it! He caught at the hem of the secret. It was the very thing that the great writers and master-poets did. That was why they were giants. They knew how to express what they thought, and felt, and saw. Dogs asleep in the sun often whined and barked, but they were unable to tell what they saw that made them whine and bark. He had often wondered what it was. And that was all he was, a dog asleep in the sun. He saw noble and beautiful visions, but he could only whine and bark at Ruth. But he would cease sleeping in the sun. He would stand up, with open eyes, and he would struggle and toil and learn until, with eyes unblinded and tongue untied, he could share with her his visioned wealth. Other men had discovered the trick of expression, of making words obedient servitors, and of making combinations of words mean more than the sum of their separate meanings. He was stirred profoundly by the passing glimpse at the secret, and he was again caught up in the vision of sunlit spaces and starry voids—until it came to him that it was very quiet, and he saw Ruth regarding him with an amused expression and a smile in her eyes.

"I have had a great visioning," he said, and at the sound of his words in his own ears his heart gave a leap. Where had those words come from? They had adequately expressed the pause his vision had put in the conversation. It was a miracle. Never had he so loftily framed a lofty thought. But never had he attempted to frame lofty thoughts in words. That was it. That explained it. He had never tried. But Swinburne had, and Tennyson, and Kipling, and all the other poets. His mind flashed on to his "Pearl-diving." He had never dared the big things, the spirit of the beauty that was a fire in him. That article would be a different thing when he was done with it. He was appalled by the vastness of the beauty that rightfully belonged in it, and again his mind flashed and dared, and he demanded of himself why he could not chant that beauty in noble verse as the great poets did. And there was all the mysterious delight and spiritual wonder of his love for Ruth. Why could he not chant that, too, as the poets did? They had sung of love. So would he. By God!—

And in his frightened ears he heard his exclamation echoing. Carried away, he had breathed it aloud. The blood surged into his face, wave upon wave, mastering the bronze of it till the blush of shame flaunted itself from collar-rim to the roots of his hair.

"I—I—beg your pardon," he stammered. "I was thinking."

"It sounded as if you were praying," she said bravely, but she felt herself inside to be withering and shrinking. It was the first time she had heard an oath from the lips of a man she knew, and she was shocked, not merely as a matter of principle and training, but shocked in spirit by this rough blast of life in the garden of her sheltered maidenhood.

But she forgave, and with surprise at the ease of her forgiveness. Somehow it was not so difficult to forgive him anything. He had not had a chance to be as other men, and he was trying so hard, and succeeding, too. It never entered her head that there could be any other reason for her being kindly disposed toward him. She was tenderly disposed toward him, but she did not know it. She had no way of knowing it. The placid poise of twenty-four years without a single love affair did not fit her with a keen perception of her own feelings, and she who had never warmed to actual love was unaware that she was warming now.

Chapter Eleven

Martin went back to his pearl-diving article, which would have been finished sooner if it had not been broken in upon so frequently by his attempts to write poetry. His poems were love poems, inspired by Ruth, but they were never completed. Not in a day could he learn to chant in noble verse. Rhyme and meter and structure were serious enough in themselves, but there was, over and beyond them, an intangible and evasive something that he caught in all great poetry, but which he could not catch and imprison in his own. It was the elusive spirit of poetry itself that he sensed and sought after but could not capture. It seemed a glow to him, a warm and trailing vapor, ever beyond his reaching, though sometimes he was rewarded by catching at shreds of it and weaving them into phrases that echoed in his brain with haunting notes or drifted across his vision in misty wafting of unseen beauty. It was baffling. He ached with desire to express and could but gibber prosaically as everybody gibbered. He read his fragments aloud. The meter marched along on perfect feet, and the rhyme pounded a longer and equally faultless rhythm, but the glow and high exaltation that he felt within were lacking. He could not understand, and time and again, in despair, defeated and depressed, he returned to his article. Prose was certainly an easier medium.

Following the "Pearl-diving," he wrote an article on the sea as a career, another on turtle-catching, and a third on the northeast trades. Then he tried, as an experiment, a short story, and before he broke his stride he had finished six short stories and dispatched them to various magazines. He wrote prolifically, intensely, from morning till night, and late at night, except when he broke off to go to the reading-room, draw books from the library, or to call on Ruth. He was profoundly happy. Life was pitched high. He was in a fever that never broke. The joy of creation that is supposed to belong to the gods was his. All the life about him—the odors of stale vegetables and soap-suds, the slatternly form of his sister, and the jeering face of Mr. Higginbotham—was a dream. The real world was in his mind, and the stories he wrote were so many pieces of reality out of his mind.

The days were too short. There was so much he

wanted to study. He cut his sleep down to five hours and found that he could get along upon it. He tried four hours and a half, and regretfully came back to five. He could joyfully have spent all his waking hours upon any one of his pursuits. It was with regret that he ceased from writing to study, that he ceased from study to go to the library, that he tore himself away from that chart-room of knowledge or from the magazines in the reading-room that were filled with the secrets of writers who succeeded in selling their wares. It was like severing heartstrings, when he was with Ruth, to stand up and go; and he scorched through the dark streets so as to get home to his books at the least possible expense of time. And hardest of all was it to shut up the algebra or physics, put note-book and pencil aside, and close his tired eyes in sleep. He hated the thought of ceasing to live, even for so short a time, and his sole consolation was that the alarm clock was set five hours ahead. He would lose only five hours anyway, and then the jangling bell would jerk him out of unconsciousness and he would have before him another glorious day of nineteen hours.

In the meantime the weeks were passing, his money was ebbing low, and there was no money coming in. A month after he had mailed it, the adventure serial for boys was returned to him by *The Youth's Companion*. The rejection slip was so tactfully worded that he felt kindly toward the editor. But he did not feel so kindly toward the editor of the *San Francisco Examiner*. After waiting two whole weeks, Martin had written to him. A week later he wrote again. At the end of the month, he went over to San Francisco and personally called upon the editor. But he did not meet that exalted personage, thanks to a Cerberus of an office boy, of tender years and red hair, who guarded the portals.

At the end of the fifth week the manuscript came back to him, by mail, without comment. There was no rejection slip, no explanation, nothing. In the same way his other articles were tied up with the other leading San Francisco papers. When he recovered them, he sent them to the magazines in the East, from which they were returned more promptly, accompanied always by the printed rejection slips.

The short stories were returned in similar fashion. He read them over and over, and liked them so much that he could not puzzle out the cause of their rejection, until, one day, he read in a newspaper that manuscripts should always be typewritten. That explained it. Of course editors were so busy that they could not afford the time and strain of reading handwriting. Martin rented a typewriter and spent a day mastering the machine. Each day he typed what he composed, and he typed his earlier manuscripts as fast as they were returned him. He was surprised when the typed ones began to come back. His jaw seemed to become squarer, his chin more aggressive, and he bundled the manuscripts off to new editors.

The thought came to him that he was not a good judge of his own work. He tried it out on Gertrude. He read his stories aloud to her. Her eyes glistened, and she looked at him proudly as she said:—

"Ain't it grand, you writin' those sort of things."

"Yes, yes," he demanded impatiently. "But the story—how did you like it?"

"Just grand," was the reply. "Just grand, an' thrilling, too. I was all worked up."

He could see that her mind was not clear. The perplexity was strong in her good-natured face. So he waited.

"But, say, Mart," after a long pause, "how did it

end? Did that young man who spoke so highfalutin' get her?"

And, after he had explained the end, which he thought he had made artistically obvious, she would say:—

"That's what I wanted to know. Why didn't you write that way in the story?"

One thing he learned, after he had read her a number of stories, namely, that she liked happy endings.

"That story was perfectly grand," she announced, straightening up from the wash-tub with a tired sigh and wiping the sweat from her forehead with a red, steamy hand; "but it makes me sad. I want to cry. There is too many sad things in the world anyway. It makes me happy to think about happy things. Now if he'd married her, and— You don't mind, Mart?" she queried apprehensively. "I just happen to feel that way, because I'm tired, I guess. But the story was grand just the same, perfectly grand. Where are you goin' to sell it?"

"That's a horse of another color," he laughed.

"But if you *did* sell it, what do you think you'd get for it?"

"Oh, a hundred dollars. That would be the least, the way prices go."

"My! I do hope you'll sell it!"

"Easy money, eh?" Then he added proudly: "I wrote it in two days. That's fifty dollars a day."

He longed to read his stories to Ruth, but did not dare. He would wait till some were published, he decided, then she would understand what he had been working for. In the meantime he toiled on. Never had the spirit of adventure lured him more strongly than on this amazing exploration of the realm of mind. He bought the text-books on physics and chemistry, and, along with his algebra, worked out problems and demonstrations. He took the laboratory proofs on faith, and his intense power of vision enabled him to see the reactions of chemicals more understandingly than the average student saw them in the laboratory. Martin wandered on through the heavy pages, overwhelmed by the clues he was getting to the nature of things. He had accepted the world as the world, but now he was comprehending the organization of it, the play and interplay of force and matter. Spontaneous explanations of old matters were continually arising in his mind. Levers and purchases fascinated him, and his mind roved backward to hand-spikes and blocks and tackles at sea. The theory of navigation, which enabled the ships to travel unerringly their courses over the pathless ocean, was made clear to him. The mysteries of storm, and rain, and tide were revealed, and the reason for the existence of trade winds made him wonder whether he had written his article on the northeast trade too soon. At any rate he knew he could write it better now. One afternoon he went out with Arthur to the University of California, and, with bated breath and a feeling of religious awe, went through the laboratories, saw demonstrations, and listened to a physics professor lecturing to his classes.

But he did not neglect his writing. A stream of short stories flowed from his pen, and he branched out into the easier forms of verse—the kind he saw printed in the magazines—though he lost his head and wasted two weeks on a tragedy in blank verse, the swift rejection of which, by half a dozen magazines, dumfounded him. Then he discovered Henley and wrote a series of sea-poems on the model of "Hospital Sketches." They were simple poems, of light and color, and romance and adventure. "Sea Lyrics," he called them, and he judged them to be the best work he had yet done. There were thirty, and he completed them in a month, doing one a day after having done his regular day's work on fiction, which day's work was the equivalent to a week's work of the average successful writer. The toil meant nothing to him. It was not toil. He was finding speech, and all the beauty and wonder that had been pent for years behind his inarticulate lips was now pouring forth in a wild and virile flood.

He showed the "Sea Lyrics" to no one, not even to the editors. He had become distrustful of editors. But it was not distrust that prevented him from submitting the "Lyrics." They were so beautiful to him that he was impelled to save them to share with Ruth in some glorious, far-off time when he would dare to read to her what he had written. Against that time he kept them with him, reading them aloud, going over them until he knew them by heart.

He lived every moment of his waking hours, and he lived in his sleep, his subjective mind rioting through his five hours of surcease and combining the thoughts and events of the day into grotesque and impossible marvels. In reality, he never rested, and a weaker body or a less firmly poised brain would have been prostrated in a general breakdown. His late afternoon calls on Ruth were rarer now, for June was approaching, when she would take her degree and finish with the university. Bachelor of Arts!—when he thought of her degree, it seemed she fled beyond him faster than he could pursue.

One afternoon a week she gave to him, and arriving late, he usually stayed for dinner and for music afterward. Those were his red-letter days. The atmosphere of the house, in such contrast with that in which he lived, and the mere nearness to her, sent him forth each time with a firmer grip on his resolve to climb the heights. In spite of the beauty in him, and the aching desire to create, it was for her that he struggled. He was a lover first and always. All other things he subordinated to love. Greater than his adventure in the world of thought was his love-adventure. The world itself was not so amazing because of the atoms and molecules that composed it according to the propulsions of irresistible force; what made it amazing was the fact that Ruth lived in it. She was the most amazing thing he had ever known, or dreamed, or guessed.

But he was oppressed always by her remoteness. She was so far from him, and he did not know how to approach her. He had been a success with girls and women in his own class; but he had never loved any of them, while he did love her, and besides, she was not merely of another class. His very love elevated her above all classes. She was a being apart, so far apart that he did not know how to draw near to her as a lover should draw near. It was true, as he acquired knowledge and language, that he was drawing nearer, talking her speech, discovering ideas and delights in common; but this did not satisfy his lover's yearning. His lover's imagination had made her holy, too holy, too spiritualized, to have any kinship with him in the flesh. It was his own love that thrust her from him and made her seem impossible for him. Love itself denied him the one thing that it desired.

And then, one day, without warning, the gulf between them was bridged for a moment, and thereafter, though the gulf remained, it was ever narrower. They had been eating cherries—great, luscious, black cherries with a juice of the color of dark wine. And later, as she read aloud to him from "The Princess," he chanced to notice the stain of the cherries on her lips.

For the moment her divinity was shattered. She was clay, after all, mere clay, subject to the common law of clay as his clay was subject, or anybody's clay. Her lips were flesh like his, and cherries dyed them as cherries dyed his. And if so with her lips, then was it so with all of her. She was woman, all woman, just like any woman. It came upon him abruptly. It was a revelation that stunned him. It was as if he had seen the sun fall out of the sky, or had seen worshipped purity polluted.

Then he realized the significance of it, and his heart began pounding and challenging him to play the lover with this woman who was not a spirit from other worlds but a mere woman with lips a cherry could stain. He trembled at the audacity of his thought, but all his soul was singing, and reason, in a triumphant pæan, assured him he was right. Something of this change in him must have reached her, for she paused from her reading, looked up at him, and smiled. His eyes dropped from her blue eyes to her lips, and the sight of the stain maddened him. His arms all but flashed out to her and around her, in the way of his old careless life. She seemed to lean toward him, to wait, and all his will fought to hold him back.

"You were not following a word," she pouted.

Then she laughed at him, delighting in his confusion, and as he looked into her frank eyes and knew that she had divined nothing of what he felt, he became abashed. He had indeed in thought dared too far. Of all the women he had known there was no woman who would not have guessed—save her. And she had not guessed. There was the difference. She *was* different. He was appalled by his own grossness, awed by her clear innocence, and he gazed again at her across the gulf. The bridge had broken down.

But still the incident had brought him nearer. The

memory of it persisted, and in the moments when he was most cast down, he dwelt upon it eagerly. The gulf was never again so wide. He had accomplished a distance vastly greater than a bachelorship of arts, or a dozen bachelorships. She was pure, it was true, as he had never dreamed of purity; but cherries stained her lips. She was subject to the laws of the universe just as inexorably as he was. She had to eat to live, and when she got her feet wet, she caught cold. But that was not the point. If she could feel hunger and thirst, and heat and cold, then could she feel love—and love for a man. Well, he was a man. And why could he not be *the* man? "It's up to me to make good," he would murmur fervently. "I will be *the* man. I will make myself *the* man. I will make good."

Chapter Twelve

Early one evening, struggling with a sonnet that twisted all awry the beauty and thought that trailed in glow and vapor through his brain, Martin was called to the telephone.

"It's a lady's voice, a fine lady's," Mr. Higginbotham, who had called him, jeered.

Martin went to the telephone in the corner of the room, and felt a wave of warmth rush through him as he heard Ruth's voice. In his battle with the sonnet he had forgotten her existence, and at the sound of her voice his love for her smote him like a sudden blow. And such a voice!—delicate and sweet, like a strain of music heard far off and faint, or, better, like a bell of silver, a perfect tone, crystal-pure. No mere

woman had a voice like that. There was something
celestial about it, and it came from other worlds. He
could scarcely hear what it said, so ravished was he,
though he controlled his face, for he knew that Mr.
Higginbotham's ferret eyes were fixed upon him.

It was not much that Ruth wanted to say—merely
that Norman had been going to take her to a lecture
that night, but that he had a headache, and she was
so disappointed, and she had the tickets, and that if
he had no other engagement, would he be good enough
to take her?

Would he! He fought to suppress the eagerness in
his voice. It was amazing. He had always seen her in
her own house. And he had never dared to ask her to
go anywhere with him. Quite irrelevantly, still at the
telephone and talking with her, he felt an overpower-
ing desire to die for her, and visions of heroic sacrifice
shaped and dissolved in his whirling brain. He loved
her so much, so terribly, so hopelessly. In that moment of mad happiness that she should go out with
him, go to a lecture with him—with him, Martin
Eden—she soared so far above him that there seemed
nothing else for him to do than die for her. It was the
only fit way in which he could express the tremendous
and lofty emotion he felt for her. It was the sublime
abnegation of true love that comes to all lovers, and
it came to him there, at the telephone, in a whirlwind
of fire and glory; and to die for her, he felt, was to
have lived and loved well. And he was only twenty-
one, and he had never been in love before.

His hand trembled as he hung up the receiver, and
he was weak from the organ which had stirred him.
His eyes were shining like an angel's, and his face was
transfigured, purged of all earthly dross, and pure and
holy.

"Makin' dates outside, eh?" his brother-in-law sneered. "You know what that means. You'll be in the police court yet."

But Martin could not come down from the height. Not even the bestiality of the allusion could bring him back to earth. Anger and hurt were beneath him. He had seen a great vision and was as a god, and he could feel only profound and awful pity for this maggot of a man. He did not look at him, and though his eyes passed over him, he did not see him; and as in a dream he passed out of the room to dress. It was not until he had reached his own room and was tying his necktie that he became aware of a sound that lingered unpleasantly in his ears. On investigating this sound he identified it as the final snort of Bernard Higginbotham, which somehow had not penetrated to his brain before.

As Ruth's front door closed behind them and he came down the steps with her, he found himself greatly perturbed. It was not unalloyed bliss, taking her to the lecture. He did not know what he ought to do. He had seen, on the streets, with persons of her class, that the women took the men's arms. But then, again, he had seen them when they didn't; and he wondered if it was only in the evening that arms were taken, or only between husbands and wives and relatives.

Just before he reached the sidewalk, he remembered Minnie. Minnie had always been a stickler. She had called him down the second time she walked out with him, because he had gone along on the inside, and she had laid the law down to him that a gentleman always walked on the outside—when he was with a lady. And Minnie had made a practice of kicking his heels, whenever they crossed from one side of the street to the other, to remind him to get over on the outside. He wondered where she had got that item of etiquette, and whether it had filtered down from above and was all right.

It wouldn't do any harm to try it, he decided, by the time they had reached the sidewalk; and he swung behind Ruth and took up his station on the outside. Then the other problem presented itself. Should he offer her his arm? He had never offered anybody his arm in his life. The girls he had known never took the fellows' arms. For the first several times they walked freely, side by side, and after that it was arms around the waists, and heads against the fellows' shoulders where the streets were unlighted. But this was different. She wasn't that kind of a girl. He must do something.

He crooked the arm next to her—crooked it very slightly and with secret tentativeness, not invitingly, but just casually, as though he was accustomed to walk that way. And then the wonderful thing happened. He felt her hand upon his arm. Delicious thrills ran through him at the contact, and for a few sweet moments it seemed that he had left the solid earth and was flying with her through the air. But he was soon back again, perturbed by a new complication. They were crossing the street. This would put him on the inside. He should be on the outside. Should he therefore drop her arm and change over? And if he did so, would he have to repeat the maneuver the next time? And the next? There was something wrong about it, and he resolved not to caper about and play the fool. Yet he was not satisfied with his conclusion, and when he found himself on the inside, he talked quickly and earnestly, making a show of being carried away by what he was saying, so that, in case he was wrong in not changing sides, his enthusiasm would seem the cause for his carelessness.

As they crossed Broadway, he came face to face

with a new problem. In the blaze of the electric lights, he saw Lizzie Connolly and her giggly friend. Only for an instant he hesitated, then his hand went up and his hat came off. He could not be disloyal to his kind, and it was to more than Lizzie Connolly that his hat was lifted. She nodded and looked at him boldly, not with soft and gentle eyes like Ruth's, but with eyes that were handsome and hard, and that swept on past him to Ruth and itemized her face and dress and station. And he was aware that Ruth looked, too, with quick eyes that were timid and mild as a dove's, but which saw, in a look that was a flutter on and past, the working-class girl in her cheap finery and under the strange hat that all working-class girls were wearing just then.

"What a pretty girl!" Ruth said a moment later.

Martin could have blessed her, though he said:—

"I don't know. I guess it's all a matter of personal taste, but she doesn't strike me as being particularly pretty."

"Why, there isn't one woman in ten thousand with features as regular as hers. They are splendid. Her face is as clear-cut as a cameo. And her eyes are beautiful."

"Do you think so?" Martin queried absently, for to him there was only one beautiful woman in the world, and she was beside him, her hand upon his arm.

"Do I think so? If that girl had proper opportunity to dress, Mr. Eden, and if she were taught how to carry herself, you would be fairly dazzled by her, and so would all men."

"She would have to be taught how to speak," he commented, "or else most of the men wouldn't understand her. I'm sure you couldn't understand a quarter of what she said if she just spoke naturally."

"Nonsense! You are as bad as Arthur when you try to make your point."

"You forget how I talked when you first met me. I have learned a new language since then. Before that time I talked as that girl talks. Now I can manage to make myself understood sufficiently in your language to explain that you do not know that other girl's language. And do you know why she carries herself the way she does? I think about such things now, though I never used to think about them, and I am beginning to understand—much."

"But why does she?"

"She has worked long hours for years at machines. When one's body is young, it is very pliable, and hard work will mold it like putty according to the nature of the work. I can tell at a glance the trades of many workingmen I meet on the street. Look at me. Why am I rolling all about the shop? Because of the years I put in on the sea. If I'd put in the same years cow-punching, with my body young and pliable, I wouldn't be rolling now, but I'd be bow-legged. And so with that girl. You noticed that her eyes were what I might call hard. She has never been sheltered. She has had to take care of herself, and a young girl can't take care of herself and keep her eyes soft and gentle like—like yours, for example."

"I think you are right," Ruth said in a low voice. "And it is too bad. She is such a pretty girl."

He looked at her and saw her eyes luminous with pity. And then he remembered that he loved her and was lost in amazement at his fortune that permitted him to love her and to take her on his arm to a lecture.

Who are you, Martin Eden? he demanded of himself in the looking-glass, that night when he got back to his room. He gazed at himself long and curiously. Who

are you? What are you? Where do you belong? You
belong by rights to girls like Lizzie Connolly. You
belong with the legions of toil, with all that is low,
and vulgar, and unbeautiful. You belong with the oxen
and the drudges, in dirty surroundings among smells
and stenches. There are the stale vegetables now. Those
potatoes are rotting. Smell them, damn you, smell
them. And yet you dare to open the books, to listen
to beautiful music, to learn to love beautiful paintings,
to speak good English, to think thoughts that none of
your own kind thinks, to tear yourself away from the
oxen and the Lizzie Connollys and to love a pale spirit
of a woman who is a million miles beyond you and
who lives in the stars! Who are you? and what are
you? damn you! And are you going to make good?

He shook his fist at himself in the glass, and sat
down on the edge of the bed to dream for a space with
wide eyes. Then he got out notebook and algebra and
lost himself in quadratic equations, while the hours
slipped by, and the stars dimmed, and the gray of
dawn flooded against his window.

Chapter Thirteen

It was the knot of wordy socialists and working-class
philosophers that held forth in the City Hall Park
on warm afternoons that was responsible for the great
discovery. Once or twice in the month, while riding
through the park on his way to the library, Martin
dismounted from his wheel and listened to the arguments, and each time he tore himself away reluctantly.
The tone of discussion was much lower than at Mr.

Morse's table. The men were not grave and dignified. They lost their tempers easily and called one another names, while oaths and obscene allusions were frequent on their lips. Once or twice he had seen them come to blows. And yet, he knew not why, there seemed something vital about the stuff of these men's thoughts. Their logomachy was far more stimulating to his intellect than the reserved and quiet dogmatism of Mr. Morse. These men, who slaughtered English, gesticulated like lunatics, and fought one another's ideas with primitive anger, seemed somehow to be more alive than Mr. Morse and his crony, Mr. Butler.

Martin had heard Herbert Spencer quoted several times in the park, but one afternoon a disciple of Spencer's appeared, a seedy tramp with a dirty coat buttoned tightly at the throat to conceal the absence of a shirt. Battle royal was waged, amid the smoking of many cigarettes and the expectoration of much tobacco-juice, wherein the tramp successfully held his own, even when a socialist workman sneered, "There is no god but the Unknowable, and Herbert Spencer is his prophet." Martin was puzzled as to what the discussion was about, but when he rode on to the library he carried with him a new-born interest in Herbert Spencer, and because of the frequency with which the tramp had mentioned "First Principles," Martin drew out that volume.

So the great discovery began. Once before he had tried Spencer, and choosing the "Principles of Psychology" to begin with, he had failed as abjectly as he had failed with Madam Blavatsky. There had been no understanding the book, and he had returned it unread. But this night, after algebra and physics, and an attempt at a sonnet, he got into bed and opened "First Principles." Morning found him still reading. It was impossible for him to sleep. Nor did he write that day. He lay on the bed till his body grew tired, when he tried the hard floor, reading on his back, the book held in the air above him, or changing from side to side. He slept that night, and did his writing next morning, and then the book tempted him and he fell, reading all afternoon, oblivious to everything and oblivious to the fact that that was the afternoon Ruth gave to him. His first consciousness of the immediate world about him was when Bernard Higginbotham jerked open the door and demanded to know if he thought they were running a restaurant.

Martin Eden had been mastered by curiosity all his days. He wanted to know, and it was this desire that had sent him adventuring over the world. But he was now learning from Spencer that he never had known, and that he never could have known had he continued his sailing and wandering forever. He had merely skimmed over the surface of things, observing detached phenomena, accumulating fragments of facts, making superficial little generalizations—and all and everything quite unrelated in a capricious and disorderly world of whim and chance. The mechanism of the flight of birds he had watched and reasoned about with understanding; but it had never entered his head to try to explain the process whereby birds, as organic flying mechanisms, had been developed. He had never dreamed there was such a process. That birds should have come to be, was unguessed. They always had been. They just happened.

And as it was with birds, so had it been with everything. His ignorant and unprepared attempts at philosophy had been fruitless. The medieval metaphysics of Kant had given him the key to nothing, and had served the sole purpose of making him doubt his own intellectual powers. In similar manner his attempt to study evolution had been confined to a hopelessly technical volume by Romanes. He had understood nothing, and the only idea he had gathered was that evolution was a dry-as-dust theory, of a lot of little men possessed of huge and unintelligible vocabularies. And now he learned that evolution was no mere theory but an accepted process of development; that scientists no longer disagreed about it, their only differences being over the method of evolution.

And here was the man Spencer, organizing all knowledge for him, reducing everything to unity, elaborating ultimate realities, and presenting to his startled gaze a universe so concrete of realization that it was like the model of a ship such as sailors make and put into glass bottles. There was no caprice, no chance. All was law. It was in obedience to law that the bird flew, and it was in obedience to the same law that fermenting slime had writhed and squirmed and put out legs and wings and become a bird.

Martin had ascended from pitch to pitch of intellectual living, and here he was at a higher pitch than ever. All the hidden things were laying their secrets bare. He was drunken with comprehension. At night, asleep, he lived with the gods in colossal nightmare; and awake, in the day, he went around like a somnambulist, with absent stare, gazing upon the world he had just discovered. At table he failed to hear the conversation about petty and ignoble things, his eager mind seeking out and following cause and effect in everything before him. In the meat on the platter he saw the shining sun and traced its energy back through all its transformations to its source a hundred million miles away, or traced its energy ahead to the moving muscles in his arms that enabled him to cut the meat, and to the brain wherewith he willed the muscles to move to cut the meat, until, with inward gaze, he saw the same sun shining in his brain. He was entranced by illumination, and did not hear the "Bughouse," whispered by Jim, nor see the anxiety on his sister's face, nor notice the rotary motion of Bernard Higginbotham's finger, whereby he imparted the suggestion of wheels revolving in his brother-in-law's head.

What, in a way, most profoundly impressed Martin, was the correlation of knowledge—of all knowledge. He had been curious to know things, and whatever he acquired he had filed away in separate memory compartments in his brain. Thus, on the subject of sailing he had an immense store. On the subject of woman he had a fairly large store. But these two subjects had been unrelated. Between the two memory compartments there had been no connection. That, in the fabric of knowledge, there should be any connection whatever between a woman with hysterics and a schooner carrying a weather-helm or heaving to in a gale, would have struck him as ridiculous and impossible. But Herbert Spencer had shown him not only that it was not ridiculous, but that it was impossible for there to be no connection. All things were related to all other things from the farthermost star in the wastes of space to the myriads of atoms in the grain of sand under one's foot. This new concept was a perpetual amazement to Martin, and he found himself engaged continually in tracing the relationship between all things under the sun and on the other side of the sun. He drew up lists of the most incongruous things and was unhappy until he succeeded in establishing kinship between them all—kinship between love, poetry, earthquake, fire, rattlesnakes, rainbows, precious gems, monstrosities, sunsets, the roaring of lions, illuminating gas, cannibalism, beauty, murder, lovers, fulcrums, and tobacco. Thus, he unified the universe and held it up and looked at it, or wandered through its byways and alleys and jungles, not as a terrified traveler in the thick of mysteries seeking an unknown goal, but observing and charting and becoming familiar with all there was to know. And the more he knew, the more passionately he admired the universe, and life, and his own life in the midst of it all.

"You fool!" he cried at his image in the looking-glass. "You wanted to write, and you tried to write, and you had nothing in you to write about. What did you have in you?—some childish notions, a few half-baked sentiments, a lot of undigested beauty, a great black mass of ignorance, a heart filled to bursting with love, and an ambition as big as your love and as futile as your ignorance. And you wanted to write! Why, you're just on the edge of beginning to get something in you to write about. You wanted to create beauty, but how could you when you knew nothing about the nature of beauty? You wanted to write about life when you knew nothing of the essential characteristics of life. You wanted to write about the world and the scheme of existence when the world was a Chinese puzzle to you and all that you could have written would have been about what you did not know of the scheme of existence. But cheer up, Martin, my boy. You'll write yet. You know a little, a very little, and you're on the right road now to know more. Some day, if you're lucky, you may come pretty close to knowing all that may be known. Then you will write."

He brought his great discovery to Ruth, sharing with her all his joy and wonder in it. But she did not seem to be so enthusiastic over it. She tacitly accepted it and, in a way, seemed aware of it from her own studies. It did not stir her deeply, as it did him, and he would have been surprised had he not reasoned it out that it was not new and fresh to her as it was to him. Arthur and Norman, he found, believed in evolution and had read Spencer, though it did not seem to have made any vital impression upon them, while the young fellow with the glasses and the mop of hair, Will Olney, sneered disagreeably at Spencer and repeated the epigram, "There is no god but the Unknowable, and Herbert Spencer is his prophet."

But Martin forgave him the sneer, for he had begun to discover that Olney was not in love with Ruth. Later, he was dumfounded to learn from various little happenings not only that Olney did not care for Ruth, but that he had a positive dislike for her. Martin could not understand this. It was a bit of phenomena that he could not correlate with all the rest of the phenomena in the universe. But nevertheless he felt sorry for the young fellow because of the great lack in his nature that prevented him from a proper appreciation of Ruth's fineness and beauty. They rode out into the hills several Sundays on their wheels, and Martin had ample opportunity to observe the armed truce that existed between Ruth and Olney. The latter chummed with Norman, throwing Arthur and Martin into company with Ruth, for which Martin was duly grateful.

Those Sundays were great days for Martin, greatest because he was with Ruth, and great, also, because they were putting him more on a par with the young men of her class. In spite of their long years of disciplined education, he was finding himself their intellectual equal, and the hours spent with them in conversation was so much practice for him in the use of the grammar he had studied so hard. He had abandoned the etiquette books, falling back upon observation to show him the right things to do. Except when carried away by his enthusiasm, he was always on guard, keenly watchful of their actions and learning their little courtesies and refinements of conduct.

The fact that Spencer was very little read was for some time a source of surprise to Martin. "Herbert Spencer," said the man at the desk in the library, "oh, yes, a great mind." But the man did not seem to know anything of the content of that great mind. One evening, at dinner, when Mr. Butler was there, Martin turned the conversation upon Spencer. Mr. Morse bitterly arraigned the English philosopher's agnosticism, but confessed that he had not read "First Principles"; while Mr. Butler stated that he had no patience with Spencer, had never read a line of him, and had managed to get along quite well without him. Doubts arose in Martin's mind, and had he been less strongly individual he would have accepted the general opinion and given Herbert Spencer up. As it was, he found Spencer's explanation of things convincing; and, as he phrased it to himself, to give up Spencer would be equivalent to a navigator throwing the compass and chronometer overboard. So Martin went on into a thorough study of evolution, mastering more and more the subject himself, and being convinced by the corroborative testimony of a thousand independent writers. The more he studied, the more vistas he caught of fields of knowledge yet unexplored, and the regret that days were only twenty-four hours long became a chronic complaint with him.

One day, because the days were so short, he decided to give up algebra and geometry. Trigonometry he had not even attempted. Then he cut chemistry from his study list, retaining only physics.

"I am not a specialist," he said, in defense, to Ruth. "Nor am I going to try to be a specialist. There are too many special fields for any one man, in a whole lifetime, to master a tithe of them. I must pursue general knowledge. When I need the work of specialists, I shall refer to their books."

"But that is not like having the knowledge yourself," she protested.

"But it is unnecessary to have it. We profit from the work of the specialists. That's what they are for. When I came in, I noticed the chimney-sweeps at work. They're specialists, and when they get done, you will enjoy clean chimneys without knowing anything about the construction of chimneys."

"That's far-fetched, I am afraid."

She looked at him curiously, and he felt a reproach in her gaze and manner. But he was convinced of the rightness of his position.

"All thinkers on general subjects, the greatest minds in the world, in fact, rely on the specialists. Herbert Spencer did that. He generalized upon the findings of thousands of investigators. He would have had to live a thousand lives in order to do it all himself. And so with Darwin. He took advantage of all that had been learned by the florists and cattle-breeders."

"You're right, Martin," Olney said. "You know what you're after, and Ruth doesn't. She doesn't know what she is after for herself even.

"—Oh, yes," Olney rushed on, heading off her objection, "I know you call it general culture. But it doesn't matter what you study if you want general culture. You can study French, or you can study German, or cut them both out and study Esperanto, you'll get the culture tone just the same. You can study Greek or Latin, too, for the same purpose, though it will never be any use to you. It will be culture, though. Why, Ruth studied Saxon, became clever in it,—that was two years ago,—and all that she remembers of it now is 'Whaen that sweet Aprile with his schowers soote'—isn't that the way it goes?

"But it's given you the culture tone just the same," he laughed, again heading her off. "I know. We were in the same classes."

"But you speak of culture as if it should be a means to something," Ruth cried out. Her eyes were flashing, and in her cheeks were two spots of color. "Culture is the end in itself."

"But that is not what Martin wants."

"How do you know?"

"What do you want, Martin?" Olney demanded, turning squarely upon him.

Martin felt very uncomfortable, and looked entreaty at Ruth.

"Yes, what do you want?" Ruth asked. "That will settle it."

"Yes, of course, I want culture," Martin faltered. "I love beauty, and culture will give me a finer and keener appreciation of beauty."

She nodded her head and looked triumphant.

"Rot, and you know it," was Olney's comment. "Martin's after career, not culture. It just happens that culture, in his case, is incidental to career. If he wanted to be a chemist, culture would be unnecessary. Martin wants to write, but he's afraid to say so because it will put you in the wrong.

"And why does Martin want to write?" he went on. "Because he isn't rolling in wealth. Why do you fill your head with Saxon and general culture? Because you don't have to make your way in the world. Your father sees to that. He buys your clothes for you, and all the rest. What rotten good is our education, yours and mine and Arthur's and Norman's? We're soaked in general culture, and if our daddies went broke to-day, we'd be falling down tomorrow on teachers' examinations. The best job you could get, Ruth, would be a country school or music teacher in a girls' boarding-school."

"And pray what would you do?" she asked.

"Not a blessed thing. I could earn a dollar and a half a day, common labor, and I might get in as instructor in Hanley's cramming joint—I say might, mind you, and I might be chucked out at the end of the week for sheer inability."

Martin followed the discussion closely, and while he was convinced that Olney was right, he resented the rather cavalier treatment he accorded Ruth. A new conception of love formed in his mind as he listened. Reason had nothing to do with love. It mattered not whether the woman he loved reasoned correctly or incorrectly. Love was above reason. If it just happened that she did not fully appreciate his necessity for a career, that did not make her a bit less lovable. She was all lovable, and what she thought had nothing to do with her lovableness.

"What's that?" he replied to a question from Olney that broke in upon his train of thought.

"I was saying that I hoped you wouldn't be fool enough to tackle Latin."

"But Latin is more than culture," Ruth broke in. "It is equipment."

"Well, are you going to tackle it?" Olney persisted.

Martin was sore beset. He could see that Ruth was hanging eagerly upon his answer.

"I am afraid I won't have time," he said finally. "I'd like to, but I won't have time."

"You see, Martin's not seeking culture," Olney exulted. "He's trying to get somewhere, to do something."

"Oh, but it's mental training. It's mind discipline. It's what makes disciplined minds." Ruth looked expectantly at Martin, as if waiting for him to change his judgment. "You know, the football players have to train before the big game. And that is what Latin does for the thinker. It trains."

"Rot and bosh! That's what they told us when we were kids. But there is one thing they didn't tell us then. They let us find it out for ourselves afterwards." Olney paused for effect, then added, "And what they didn't tell us was that every gentleman should have studied Latin, but that no gentleman should know Latin."

"Now that's unfair," Ruth cried. "I knew you were turning the conversation just in order to get off something."

"It's clever all right," was the retort, "but it's fair, too. The only men who know their Latin are the apothecaries, the lawyers, and the Latin professors. And if Martin wants to be one of them, I miss my guess. But what's all that got to do with Herbert Spencer anyway? Martin's just discovered Spencer, and he's wild over him. Why? Because Spencer is taking him somewhere. Spencer couldn't take me anywhere, nor you. We haven't got anywhere to go. You'll get married some day, and I'll have nothing to do but keep track of the lawyers and business agents who will take care of the money my father's going to leave me."

Olney got up to go, but turned at the door and delivered a parting shot.

"You leave Martin alone, Ruth. He knows what's best for himself. Look at what he's done already. He makes me sick sometimes, sick and ashamed of myself. He knows more now about the world, and life, and man's place, and all the rest, than Arthur, or Norman, or I, or you, too, for that matter, and in spite of all our Latin, and French, and Saxon, and culture."

"But Ruth is my teacher," Martin answered chivalrously. "She is responsible for what little I have learned."

"Rats!" Olney looked at Ruth, and his expression was malicious. "I suppose you'll be telling me next that you read Spencer on her recommendation—only you didn't. And she doesn't know anything more about Darwin and evolution than I do about King Solomon's mines. What's that jawbreaker definition about something or other, of Spencer's, that you sprang on us the other day—that indefinite, incoherent homogeneity thing? Spring it on her, and see if she understands a word of it. That isn't culture, you see. Well, tra la, and if you tackle Latin, Martin, I won't have any respect for you."

And all the while, interested in the discussion, Martin had been aware of an irk in it as well. It was about studies and lessons, dealing with the rudiments of knowledge, and the school-boyish tone of it conflicted with the big things that were stirring in him—with the grip upon life that was even then crooking his fingers like eagle's talons, with the cosmic thrills that made him ache, and with the inchoate consciousness of mastery of it all. He likened himself to a poet, wrecked on the shores of a strange land, filled with power of beauty, stumbling and stammering and vainly trying to sing in the rough, barbaric tongue of his brethren in the new land. And so with him. He was alive, painfully alive, to the great universal things, and yet he was compelled to potter and grope among schoolboy topics and debate whether or not he should study Latin.

"What in hell has Latin to do with it?" he demanded before his mirror that night. "I wish dead people would stay dead. Why should I and the beauty in me be ruled by the dead? Beauty is alive and everlasting. Languages come and go. They are the dust of the dead."

And his next thought was that he had been phrasing his ideas very well, and he went to bed wondering why he could not talk in similar fashion when he was with Ruth. He was only a schoolboy, with a schoolboy's tongue, when he was in her presence.

"Give me time," he said aloud. "Only give me time."

Time! Time! Time! was his unending plaint.

Chapter Fourteen

It was not because of Olney, but in spite of Ruth, and his love for Ruth, that he finally decided not to take up Latin. His money meant time. There was so much that was more important than Latin, so many studies that clamored with imperious voices. And he must write. He must earn money. He had had no acceptances. Twoscore of manuscripts were traveling the endless round of the magazines. How did the others do it? He spent long hours in the free reading-room, going over what others had written, studying their work eagerly and critically, comparing it with his own, and wondering, wondering, about the secret trick they had discovered which enabled them to sell their work.

He was amazed at the immense amount of printed stuff that was dead. No light, no life, no color, was shot through it. There was no breath of life in it, and yet it sold, at two cents a word, twenty dollars a thousand—the newspaper clipping had said so. He was puzzled by countless short stories, written lightly and cleverly he confessed, but without vitality or reality. Life was so strange and wonderful, filled with an immensity of problems, of dreams, and of heroic toils, and yet these stories dealt only with the commonplaces of life. He felt the stress and strain of life, its fevers and sweats and wild insurgences—surely this was the stuff to write about! He wanted to glorify the leaders of forlorn hopes, the mad lovers, the giants that fought under stress and strain, amid terror and tragedy, making life crackle with the strength of their endeavor. And yet the magazine short stories seemed intent on glorifying the Mr. Butlers, the sordid dollar-chasers, and the commonplace little love affairs of commonplace little men and women. Was it because the editors of the magazines were commonplace? he demanded. Or were they afraid of life, these writers and editors and readers?

But his chief trouble was that he did not know any editors or writers. And not merely did he not know any writers, but he did not know anybody who had ever attempted to write. There was nobody to tell him, to hint to him, to give him the least word of advice. He began to doubt that editors were real men. They seemed cogs in a machine. That was what it was, a machine. He poured his soul into stories, articles, and poems, and entrusted them to the machine. He folded them just so, put the proper stamps inside the long envelope along with the manuscript, sealed the envelope, put more stamps outside, and dropped it into the mail-box. It traveled across the continent, and after a certain lapse of time the postman returned him the manuscript in another long envelope, on the outside of which were the stamps he had enclosed. There was no human editor at the other end, but a mere cunning arrangement of cogs that changed the manuscript from one envelope to another and stuck on the stamps. It was like the slot machines wherein one dropped pennies, and, with a metallic whirl of machinery had delivered to him a stick of chewing-gum or a tablet of chocolate. It depended upon which slot one dropped the penny in, whether he got chocolate or gum. And so with the editorial machine. One slot brought checks and the other brought rejection slips. So far he had found only the latter slot.

It was the rejection slips that completed the horrible machine-likeness of the process. These slips were printed in stereotyped forms and he had received hundreds of them—as many as a dozen or more on each of his earlier manuscripts. If he had received one line, one personal line, along with one rejection of all his rejections, he would have been cheered. But not one editor had given that proof of existence. And he could conclude only that there were no warm human men at the other end, only mere cogs, well oiled and running beautifully in the machine.

He was a good fighter, whole-souled and stubborn, and he would have been content to continue feeding the machine for years; but he was bleeding to death, and not years but weeks would determine the fight. Each week his board bill brought him nearer destruction, while the postage on forty manuscripts bled him almost as severely. He no longer bought books, and he economized in petty ways and sought to delay the inevitable end; though he did not know how to economize, and brought the end nearer by a week when he gave his sister Marian five dollars for a dress.

He struggled in the dark, without advice, without encouragement, and in the teeth of discouragement. Even Gertrude was beginning to look askance. At first she had tolerated with sisterly fondness what she conceived to be his foolishness; but now, out of sisterly solicitude, she grew anxious. To her it seemed that his foolishness was becoming a madness. Martin knew this and suffered more keenly from it than from the open and nagging contempt of Bernard Higginbotham. Martin had faith in himself, but he was alone in this faith. Not even Ruth had faith. She had wanted him to devote himself to study, and, though she had not openly disapproved of his writing she had never approved.

He had never offered to show her his work. A fastidious delicacy had prevented him. Besides, she had been studying heavily at the university, and he felt averse to robbing her of her time. But when she had taken her degree, she asked him herself to let her see something of what he had been doing. Martin was elated and diffident. Here was a judge. She was a bachelor of arts. She had studied literature under skilled instructors. Perhaps the editors were capable judges, too. But she would be different from them. She would not hand him a stereotyped rejection slip, nor would she inform him that lack of preference for his work did not necessarily imply lack of merit in his work. She would talk, a warm human being, in her quick, bright way, and, most important of all, she would catch glimpses of the real Martin Eden. In his work she would discern what his heart and soul were like, and she would come to understand something, a little something, of the stuff of his dreams and the strength of his power.

Martin gathered together a number of carbon copies of his short stories, hesitated a moment, then added his "Sea Lyrics." They mounted their wheels on a late June afternoon and rode for the hills. It was the second time he had been out with her alone, and as they rode along through the balmy warmth, just chilled by the sea-breeze to refreshing coolness, he was profoundly impressed by the fact that it was a very beautiful and well-ordered world and that it was good to be alive and to love. They left their wheels by the roadside and climbed to the brown top of an open knoll where the sunburnt grass breathed a harvest breath of dry sweetness and content.

"Its work is done," Martin said, as they seated themselves, she upon his coat, and he sprawling close to the warm earth. He sniffed the sweetness of the tawny grass, which entered his brain and set his thoughts whirling on from the particular to the universal. "It has achieved its reason for existence," he went on, patting the dry grass affectionately. "It quickened with ambition under the dreary downpour of last winter, fought the violent early spring, flowered, and lured the insects and the bees, scattered its seeds, squared itself with its duty and the world, and—"

"Why do you always look at things with such dreadfully practical eyes?" she interrupted.

"Because I've been studying evolution, I guess. It's only recently that I got my eyesight, if the truth were told."

"But it seems to me you lose sight of beauty by being so practical, that you destroy beauty like the boys who catch butterflies and rub the down off their beautiful wings."

He shook his head.

"Beauty has significance, but I never knew its significance before. I just accepted beauty as something meaningless, as something that was just beautiful without rhyme or reason. I did not know anything about beauty. But now I know, or, rather, am just beginning to know. This grass is more beautiful to me now that I know why it is grass, and all the hidden chemistry of sun and rain and earth that makes it become grass. Why, there is romance in the life-history of any grass, yes, and adventure, too. The very thought of it stirs me. When I think of the play of force and matter, and all the tremendous struggle of it, I feel as if I could write an epic on the grass."

"How well you talk," she said absently, and he noted that she was looking at him in a searching way.

He was all confusion and embarrassment on the instant, the blood flushing red on his neck and brow.

"I hope I am learning to talk," he stammered. "There seems to be so much in me I want to say. But it is all so big. I can't find ways to say what is really in me. Sometimes it seems to me that all the world, all life, everything, had taken up residence inside of me and was clamoring for me to be the spokesman. I feel— oh, I can't describe it—I feel the bigness of it, but when I speak, I babble like a little child. It is a great task to transmute feeling and sensation into speech, written or spoken, that will, in turn, in him who reads or listens, transmute itself back into the selfsame feel-ing and sensation. It is a lordly task. See, I bury my face in the grass, and the breath I draw in through my nostrils sets me quivering with a thousand thoughts and fancies. It is a breath of the universe I have breathed. I know song and laughter, and success and pain, and struggle and death; and I see visions that arise in my brain somehow out of the scent of the grass, and I would like to tell them to you, to the world. But how can I? My tongue is tied. I have tried, by the spoken word, just now, to describe to you the effect on me of the scent of the grass. But I have not succeeded. I have no more than hinted in awkward speech. My words seem gibberish to me. And yet I am stifled with desire to tell. Oh!—" he threw up his hands with a despairing gesture—"it is impossible! It is not understandable! It is incommunicable!"

"But you do talk well," she insisted. "Just think how you have improved in the short time I have known you. Mr. Butler is a noted public speaker. He is always asked by the State Committee to go out on stump during campaign. Yet you talked just as well as he the other night at dinner. Only he was more controlled. You get too excited; but you will get over that with practice. Why, you would make a good public speaker. You can go far—if you want to. You are masterly. You can lead men, I am sure, and there is no reason why you should not succeed at anything you set your hand to, just as you have succeeded with grammar. You would make a good lawyer. You should shine in politics. There is nothing to prevent you from making as great a success as Mr. Butler has made. And minus the dyspepsia," she added with a smile.

They talked on; she, in her gently persistent way, returning always to the need of thorough grounding in education and to the advantages of Latin as part of the foundation for any career. She drew her ideal of the successful man, and it was largely in her father's image, with a few unmistakable lines and touches of color from the image of Mr. Butler. He listened eagerly, with receptive ears, lying on his back and looking up and joying in each movement of her lips as she talked. But his brain was not receptive. There was nothing alluring in the pictures she drew, and he was aware of a dull pain of disappointment and of a sharper

ache of love for her. In all she said there was no mention of his writing, and the manuscripts he had brought
to read lay neglected on the ground.

At last, in a pause, he glanced at the sun, measured
its height above the horizon, and suggested his manuscripts by picking them up.

"I had forgotten," she said quickly. "And I am so
anxious to hear."

He read to her a story, one that he flattered himself
was among his very best. He called it "The Wine of
Life," and the wine of it, that had stolen into his brain
when he wrote it, stole into his brain now as he read
it. There was a certain magic in the original conception, and he had adorned it with more magic of phrase
and touch. All the old fire and passion with which he
had written it were reborn in him, and he was swayed
and swept away so that he was blind and deaf to the
faults of it. But it was not so with Ruth. Her trained
ear detected the weaknesses and exaggerations, the
overemphasis of the tyro, and she was instantly aware
each time the sentence-rhythm tripped and faltered.
She scarcely noted the rhythm otherwise, except when
it became too pompous, at which moments she was
disagreeably impressed with its amateurishness. That
was her final judgment on the story as a whole—
amateurish, though she did not tell him so. Instead,
when he had done, she pointed out the minor flaws
and said that she liked the story.

But he was disappointed. Her criticism was just.
He acknowledged that, but he had a feeling that he
was not sharing his work with her for the purpose of
schoolroom correction. The details did not matter.
They could take care of themselves. He could mend
them, he could learn to mend them. Out of life he
had captured something big and attempted to imprison
it in the story. It was the big thing out of life he had

read to her, not sentence-structure and semicolons. He wanted her to feel with him this big thing that was his, that he had seen with his own eyes, grappled with his own brain, and placed there on the page with his own hands in printed words. Well, he had failed, was his secret decision. Perhaps the editors were right. He had felt the big thing, but he had failed to transmute it. He concealed his disappointment, and joined so easily with her in her criticism that she did not realize that deep down in him was running a strong undercurrent of disagreement.

"This next thing I've called 'The Pot'," he said, unfolding the manuscript. "It has been refused by four or five magazines now, but still I think it is good. In fact, I don't know what to think of it, except that I've caught something there. Maybe it won't affect you as it does me. It's a short thing—only two thousand words."

"How dreadful!" she cried, when he had finished. "It is horrible, unutterably horrible!"

He noted her pale face, her eyes wide and tense, and her clenched hands, with secret satisfaction. He had succeeded. He had communicated the stuff of fancy and feeling from out of his brain. It had struck home. No matter whether she liked it or not, it had gripped her and mastered her, made her sit there and listen and forget details.

"It is life," he said, "and life is not always beautiful. And yet, perhaps because I am strangely made, I find something beautiful there. It seems to me that the beauty is tenfold enhanced because it is there—"

"But why couldn't the poor woman—" she broke in disconnectedly. Then she left the revolt of her thought unexpressed to cry out: "Oh! It is degrading! It is not nice! It is nasty!"

For the moment it seemed to him that his heart

stood still. *Nasty!* He had never dreamed it. He had not meant it. The whole sketch stood before him in letters of fire, and in such blaze of illumination he sought vainly for nastiness. Then his heart began to beat again. He was not guilty.

"Why didn't you select a nice subject?" she was saying. "We know there are nasty things in the world, but that is no reason—"

She talked on in her indignant strain, but he was not following her. He was smiling to himself as he looked up into her virginal face, so innocent, so penetratingly innocent, that its purity seemed always to enter into him, driving out of him all dross and bathing him in some ethereal effulgence that was as cool and soft and velvety as starshine. *We know there are nasty things in the world!* He cuddled to him the notion of her knowing, and chuckled over it as a love joke. The next moment, in a flashing vision of multitudinous detail, he sighted the whole sea of life's nastiness that he had known and voyaged over and through, and he forgave her for not understanding the story. It was through no fault of hers that she could not understand. He thanked God that she had been born and sheltered to such innocence. But he knew life, its foulness as well as its fairness, its greatness in spite of the slime that infested it, and by God he was going to have his say on it to the world. Saints in heaven—how could they be anything but fair and pure? No praise to them. But saints in slime—ah, that was the everlasting wonder! That was what made life worth while. To see moral grandeur rising out of cesspools of iniquity; to rise himself and first glimpse beauty, faint and far, through mud-dripping eyes; to see out of weakness, and frailty, and viciousness, and all abysmal brutishness, arising strength, and truth, and high spiritual endowment—

He caught a stray sequence of sentences she was uttering.

"The tone of it all is low. And there is so much that is high. Take 'In Memoriam.' "

He was impelled to suggest "Locksley Hall," and would have done so, had not his vision gripped him again and left him staring at her, the female of his kind, who, out of the primordial ferment, creeping and crawling up the vast ladder of life for a thousand thousand centuries, had emerged on the topmost rung, having become one Ruth, pure, and fair, and divine, and with power to make him know love, and to aspire toward purity, and to desire to taste divinity—him, Martin Eden, who, too, had come up in some amazing fashion from out of the ruck and the mire and the countless mistakes and abortions of unending creation. There was the romance, and the wonder, and the glory. There was the stuff to write, if he could only find speech. Saints in heaven!—They were only saints and could not help themselves. But he was a man.

"You have strength," he could hear her saying, "but it is untutored strength."

"Like a bull in a china shop," he suggested, and won a smile.

"And you must develop discrimination. You must consult taste, and fineness, and tone."

"I dare too much," he muttered.

She smiled approbation, and settled herself to listen to another story.

"I don't know what you'll make of this," he said apologetically. "It's a funny thing. I'm afraid I got beyond my depth in it, but my intentions were good. Don't bother about the little features of it. Just see if you catch the feel of the big thing in it. It is big, and it is true, though the chance is large that I have failed to make it intelligible."

He read, and as he read he watched her. At last he had reached her, he thought. She sat without movement, her eyes steadfast upon him, scarcely breathing, caught up and out of herself, he thought, by the witchery of the thing he had created. He had entitled the story "Adventure," and it was the apotheosis of adventure—not of the adventure of the story-books, but of real adventure, the savage taskmaster, awful of punishment and awful of reward, faithless and whimsical, demanding terrible patience and heartbreaking days and nights of toil, offering the blazing sunlight glory or dark death at the end of thirst and famine or of the long drag and monstrous delirium of rotting fever, through blood and sweat and stinging insects leading up by long chains of petty and ignoble contacts to royal culminations and lordly achievements.

It was this, all of it, and more, that he had put into his story, and it was this, he believed, that warmed her as she sat and listened. Her eyes were wide, color was in her pale cheeks, and before he finished it seemed to him that she was almost panting. Truly, she was warmed; but she was warmed, not by the story, but by him. She did not think much of the story; it was Martin's intensity of power, the old excess of strength that seemed to pour from his body and on and over her. The paradox of it was that it was the story itself that was freighted with his power, that was the channel, for the time being, through which his strength poured out to her. She was aware only of the strength, and not of the medium, and when she seemed most carried away by what he had written, in reality she had been carried away by something quite foreign to it—by a thought, terrible and perilous, that had formed itself unsummoned in her brain. She had caught herself wondering what marriage was like, and the becoming conscious of the waywardness and ardor of the thought had terrified her. It was unmaidenly. It was not like her. She had never been tormented by womanhood, and she had lived in a dreamland of Tennysonian poesy, dense even to the full significance of that delicate master's delicate allusions to the grossnesses that intrude upon the relations of queens and knights. She had been asleep, always, and now life was thundering imperatively at all her doors. Mentally she was in a panic to shoot the bolts and drop the bars into place, while wanton instincts urged her to throw wide her portals and bid the deliciously strange visitor to enter in.

Martin waited with satisfaction for her verdict. He had no doubt of what it would be, and he was astounded when he heard her say:—

"It is beautiful."

"It *is* beautiful," she repeated, with emphasis, after a pause.

Of course it was beautiful; but there was something more than mere beauty in it, something more stingingly splendid which had made beauty its handmaiden. He sprawled silently on the ground, watching the grisly form of a great doubt rising before him. He had failed. He was inarticulate. He had seen one of the greatest things in the world, and he had not expressed it.

"What did you think of the—" He hesitated, abashed at his first attempt to use a strange word. "Of the *motif?*" he asked.

"It was confused," she answered. "That is my only criticism in the large way. I followed the story, but there seemed so much else. It is too wordy. You clog the action by introducing so much extraneous material."

"That was the major *motif*," he hurriedly explained, "the big underrunning *motif*, the cosmic and universal thing. I tried to make it keep time with the story itself, which was only superficial after all. I was on the right scent, but I guess I did it badly. I did not succeed in suggesting what I was driving at. But I'll learn in time."

She did not follow him. She was a bachelor of arts, but he had gone beyond her limitations. This she did not comprehend, attributing her incomprehension to his incoherence.

"You were too voluble," she said. "But it was beautiful, in places."

He heard her voice as from far off, for he was debating whether he would read her the "Sea Lyrics." He lay in dull despair, while she watched him searchingly, pondering again upon unsummoned and wayward thoughts of marriage.

"You want to be famous?" she asked abruptly.

"Yes, a little bit," he confessed. "That is part of the adventure. It is not the being famous, but the process of becoming so, that counts. And after all, to be famous would be, for me, only a means to something else. I want to be famous very much, for that matter, and for that reason."

"For your sake," he wanted to add, and might have added had she proved enthusiastic over what he had read to her.

But she was too busy in her mind, carving out a career for him that would at least be possible, to ask what the ultimate something was which he had hinted at. There was no career for him in literature. Of that she was convinced. He had proved it today, with his amateurish and sophomoric productions. He could talk well, but he was incapable of expressing himself in a literary way. She compared Tennyson, and Browning, and her favorite prose masters with him, and to his hopeless discredit. Yet she did not tell him her whole mind. Her strange interest in him led her to temporize. His desire to write was, after all, a little weakness which he would grow out of in time. Then he would devote himself to the more serious affairs of life. And he would succeed, too. She knew that. He was so strong that he could not fail—if only he would drop writing.

"I wish you would show me all you write, Mr. Eden," she said.

He flushed with pleasure. She was interested, that much was sure. And at least she had not given him a rejection slip. She had called certain portions of his work beautiful, and that was the first encouragement he had ever received from any one.

"I will," he said passionately. "And I promise you, Miss Morse, that I will make good. I have come far, I know that; and I have far to go, and I will cover it if I have to do it on my hands and knees." He held up a bunch of manuscript. "Here are the 'Sea Lyrics.' When you get home, I'll turn them over to you to read at your leisure. And you must be sure to tell me just what you think of them. What I need, you know, above all things, is criticism. And do, please, be frank with me."

"I will be perfectly frank," she promised, with an uneasy conviction that she had not been frank with him and with a doubt if she could be quite frank with him the next time.

Chapter Fifteen

"The first battle, fought and finished," Martin said to the looking-glass ten days later. "But there will be a second battle, and a third battle, and battles to the end of time, unless—"

He had not finished the sentence, but looked about the mean little room and let his eyes dwell sadly upon a heap of returned manuscripts, still in their long envelopes, which lay in a corner on the floor. He had no stamps with which to continue them on their travels, and for a week they had been piling up. More of them would come in on the morrow, and on the next day, and the next, till they were all in. And he would be unable to start them out again. He was a month's rent behind on the typewriter, which he could not pay, having barely enough for the week's board which was due and for the employment office fees.

He sat down and regarded the table thoughtfully. There were ink stains upon it, and he suddenly discovered that he was fond of it.

"Dear old table," he said, "I've spent some happy hours with you, and you've been a pretty good friend when all is said and done. You never turned me down, never passed me out a reward-of-unmerit rejection slip, never complained about working overtime."

He dropped his arms upon the table and buried his face in them. His throat was aching, and he wanted to cry. It reminded him of his first fight, when he was six years old, when he punched away with the tears running down his cheeks while the other boy, two years his elder, had beaten and pounded him into exhaustion. He saw the ring of boys, howling like barbarians as he went down at last, writing in the throes of nausea, the blood streaming from his nose and the tears from his bruised eyes.

"Poor little shaver," he murmured. "And you're just as badly licked now. You're beaten to a pulp. You're down and out."

But the vision of that first fight still lingered under his eyelids, and as he watched he saw it dissolve and reshape into the series of fights which had followed. Six months later Cheese-Face (that was the boy) had whipped him again. But he had blacked Cheese-Face's eye that time. That was going some. He saw them all, fight after fight, himself always whipped and Cheese-Face exulting over him. But he had never run away. He felt strengthened by the memory of that. He had always stayed and taken his medicine. Cheese-Face had been a little fiend at fighting, and had never once shown mercy to him. But he had stayed! He had stayed with it!

Next, he saw a narrow alley, between ramshackle frame buildings. The end of the alley was blocked by a one-story brick building, out of which issued the rhythmic thunder of the presses, running off the first edition of the *Enquirer*. He was eleven, and Cheese-Face was thirteen, and they both carried the *Enquirer*. That was why they were there, waiting for their papers. And, of course, Cheese-Face had picked on him again, and there was another fight that was indeterminate, because at quarter to four the door of the press-room was thrown open and the gang of boys crowded in to fold their papers.

"I'll lick you tomorrow," he heard Cheese-Face promise; and he heard his own voice, piping and trembling with unshed tears, agreeing to be there on the morrow.

And he had come there the next day, hurrying from school to be there first, and beating Cheese-Face by two minutes. The other boys said he was all right, and gave him advice, pointing out his faults as a scrapper and promising him victory if he carried out their instructions. The same boys gave Cheese-Face advice, too. How they had enjoyed the fight! He paused in his recollections long enough to envy them the spectacle he and Cheese-Face had put up. Then the fight was on, and it went on, without rounds, for thirty minutes, until the press-room door was opened.

He watched the youthful apparition of himself, day after day, hurrying from school to the *Enquirer* alley. He could not walk very fast. He was stiff and lame from the incessant fighting. His forearms were black and blue from wrist to elbow, what with the countless blows he had warded off, and here and there the tortured flesh was beginning to fester. His head and arms and shoulders ached, the small of his back ached,— he ached all over, and his brain was heavy and dazed. He did not play at school. Nor did he study. Even to sit still all day at his desk, as he did, was a torment. It seemed centuries since he had begun the round of daily fights, and time stretched away into a nightmare and infinite future of daily fights. Why couldn't Cheese-Face be licked? he often thought; that would put him, Martin, out of his misery. It never entered his head to cease fighting, to allow Cheese-Face to whip him.

And so he dragged himself to the *Enquirer* alley, sick in body and soul, but learning the long patience, to confront his eternal enemy, Cheese-Face, who was just as sick as he, and just a bit willing to quit if it were not for the gang of newsboys that looked on and made pride painful and necessary. One afternoon, after twenty minutes of desperate efforts to annihilate each other according to set rules that did not permit kicking, striking below the belt, nor hitting when one was down, Cheese-Face, panting for breath and reeling, offered to call it quits. And Martin, head on arms, thrilled at the picture he caught of himself, at that moment in the afternoon of long ago, when he reeled and panted and choked with the blood that ran into his mouth and down his throat from his cut lips; when he tottered toward Cheese-Face, spitting out a mouthful of blood so that he could speak, crying out that he would never quit, though Cheese-Face could give in if he wanted to. And Cheese-Face did not give in, and the fight went on.

The next day and the next, days without end, witnessed the afternoon fight. When he put up his arms, each day, to begin, they pained exquisitely, and the first few blows, struck and received, racked his soul; after that things grew numb, and he fought on blindly, seeing as in a dream, dancing and wavering, the large features and burning, animal-like eyes of Cheese-Face. He concentrated upon that face; all else about him was a whirling void. There was nothing else in the world but that face, and he would never know rest, blessed rest, until he had beaten that face into a pulp with his bleeding knuckles, or until the bleeding knuckles that somehow belonged to that face had beaten him into a pulp. And then, one way or the other, he would have rest. But to quit,—for him, Martin, to quit,—that was impossible!

Came the day when he dragged himself into the *Enquirer* alley, and there was no Cheese-Face. Nor did Cheese-Face come. The boys congratulated him, and told him that he had licked Cheese-Face. But Martin was not satisfied. He had not licked Cheese-Face, nor had Cheese-Face licked him. The problem had not been solved. It was not until afterward that they learned that Cheese-Face's father had died suddenly that very day.

Martin skipped on through the years to the night in the nigger heaven at the Auditorium. He was seventeen and just back from sea. A row started. Somebody was bullying somebody, and Martin interfered, to be confronted by Cheese-Face's blazing eyes.

"I'll fix you after de show," his ancient enemy hissed.

Martin nodded. The nigger-heaven bouncer was making his way toward the disturbance.

"I'll meet you outside, after the last act," Martin whispered, the while his face showed undivided interest in the buck-and-wing dancing on the stage.

The bouncer glared and went away.

"Got a gang?" he asked Cheese-Face, at the end of the act.

"Sure."

"Then I got to get one," Martin announced. Between the acts he mustered his following—three fellows he knew from the nail works, a railroad fireman, and half a dozen of the Boo Gang, along with as many more from the dread Eighteen-and-Market Gang.

When the theater let out, the two gangs strung along inconspicuously on opposite sides of the street. When they came to a quiet corner, they united and held a council of war.

"Eighth Street Bridge is the place," said a red-headed fellow belonging to Cheese-Face's gang. "You kin fight in the middle, under the electric light, an' whichever way the bulls come in we kin sneak the other way."

"That's agreeable to me," Martin said, after consulting with the leaders of his own gang.

The Eighth Street Bridge, crossing an arm of San Antonio Estuary, was the length of three city blocks. In the middle of the bridge, and at each end, were electric lights. No policeman could pass those end-lights unseen. It was the safe place for the battle that revived itself under Martin's eyelids. He saw the two gangs, aggressive and sullen, rigidly keeping apart from each other and backing their respective champions; and he saw himself and Cheese-Face stripping. A short distance away lookouts were set, their task being to watch the lighted ends of the bridge. A member of the Boo Gang held Martin's coat, and shirt, and cap, ready to race with them into safety in case the police interfered. Martin watched himself go into the center, facing Cheese-Face, and he heard himself say, as he held up his hand warningly:—

"They ain't no hand-shakin' in this. Understand? They ain't nothin' but scrap. No throwin' up the sponge. This is a grudge-fight an' it's to a finish. Understand? Somebody's goin' to get licked."

Cheese-Face wanted to demur,—Martin could see that,—but Cheese-Face's old perilous pride was touched before the two gangs.

"Aw, come on," he replied. "Wot's the good of chewin' de rag about it? I'm wit' cheh to de finish."

Then they fell upon each other, like young bulls, in all the glory of youth, with naked fists, with hatred, with desire to hurt, to maim, to destroy. All the painful, thousand years' gains of man in his upward climb through creation were lost. Only the electric light remained, a milestone on the path of the great human adventure. Martin and Cheese-Face were two savages, of the stone age, of the squatting place and the tree refuge. They sank lower and lower into the muddy abyss, back into the dregs of the raw beginnings of life, striving blindly and chemically, as atoms strive, as the star-dust of the heavens strives, colliding, re-coiling, and colliding again and eternally again.

"God! We are animals! Brute-beasts!" Martin muttered aloud, as he watched the progress of the fight. It was to him, with his splendid power of vision, like gazing into a kinetoscope. He was both onlooker and participant. His long months of culture and refinement shuddered at the sight; then the present was blotted out of his consciousness and the ghosts of the past possessed him, and he was Martin Eden, just returned from sea and fighting Cheese-Face on the Eighth Street Bridge. He suffered and toiled and sweated and bled, and exulted when his naked knuckles smashed home.

They were twin whirlwinds of hatred, revolving about each other monstrously. The time passed, and the two hostile gangs became very quiet. They had never witnessed such intensity of ferocity, and they were awed by it. The two fighters were greater brutes than they. The first splendid velvet edge of youth and condition wore off, and they fought more cautiously and deliberately. There had been no advantage gained either way. "It's anybody's fight," Martin heard some one saying. Then he followed up a feint, right and left, was fiercely countered, and felt his cheek laid open to the bone. No bare knuckle had done that. He heard mutters of amazement at the ghastly damage wrought, and was drenched with his own blood. But he gave no sign. He became immensely wary, for he was wise with knowledge of the low cunning and foul vileness of his kind. He watched and waited, until he feigned a wild rush, which he stopped midway, for he had seen the glint of metal.

"Hold up yer hand!" he screamed. "Them's brass knuckles, an' you hit me with 'em!"

Both gangs surged forward, growling and snarling. In a second there would be a free-for-all fight, and he would be robbed of his vengeance. He was beside himself.

"You guys keep out!" he screamed hoarsely. "Understand? Say, d'ye understand?"

They shrank away from him. They were brutes, but he was the arch-brute, a thing of terror that towered over them and dominated them.

"This is my scrap, an' they ain't goin' to be no buttin' in. Gimme them knuckles."

Cheese-Face, sobered and a bit frightened, surrendered the foul weapon.

"You passed 'em to him, you red-head sneakin' in behind the push there," Martin went on, as he tossed the knuckles into the water. "I seen you, an' I was wonderin' what you was up to. If you try anything like that again, I'll beat cheh to death. Understand?"

They fought on, through exhaustion and beyond, to exhaustion immeasurable and inconceivable, until the crowd of brutes, its blood-lust sated, terrified by what it saw, begged them impartially to cease. And Cheese-Face, ready to drop and die, or to stay on his legs and die, a grisly monster out of whose features all likeness to Cheese-Face had been beaten, wavered and hesitated; but Martin sprang in and smashed him again and again.

Next, after a seeming century or so, with Cheese-Face weakening fast, in a mix-up of blows there was a loud snap, and Martin's right arm dropped to his side. It was a broken bone. Everybody heard it and knew; and Cheese-Face knew, rushing like a tiger in the other's extremity and raining blow on blow. Martin's gang surged forward to interfere. Dazed by the rapid succession of blows, Martin warned them back with vile and earnest curses sobbed out and groaned in ultimate desolation and despair.

He punched on, with his left hand only, and as he punched, doggedly, only half-conscious, as from a remote distance he heard murmurs of fear in the gangs, and one who said with shaking voice: "This ain't a scrap, fellows. It's murder, an' we ought to stop it."

But no one stopped it, and he was glad, punching on wearily and endlessly with his one arm, battering away at a bloody something before him that was not a face but a horror, an oscillating, hideous, gibbering, nameless thing that persisted before his wavering vision and would not go away. And he punched on and on, slower and slower, as the last shreds of vitality oozed from him, through centuries and eons and enormous lapses of time, until, in a dim way, he became aware that the nameless thing was sinking, slowly sinking down to the rough board-planking of the bridge. And the next moment he was standing over it, staggering and swaying on shaky legs, clutching at the air for support, and saying in a voice he did not recognize:—

"D'ye want any more? Say, d'ye want any more?"

He was still saying it, over and over,—demanding, entreating, threatening, to know if it wanted any more,—when he felt the fellows of his gang laying hands on him, patting him on the back and trying to put his coat on him. And then came a sudden rush of blackness and oblivion.

The tin alarm-clock on the table ticked on, but Martin Eden, his face buried on his arms, did not hear it. He heard nothing. He did not think. So absolutely had he relived life that he had fainted just as he fainted years before on the Eighth Street Bridge. For a full minute the blackness and the blankness endured. Then, like one from the dead, he sprang upright, eyes flaming, sweat pouring down his face, shouting:—

"I licked you, Cheese-Face! It took me eleven years, but I licked you!"

His knees were trembling under him, he felt faint,

and he staggered back to the bed, sinking down and sitting on the edge of it. He was still in the clutch of the past. He looked about the room, perplexed, alarmed, wondering where he was, until he caught sight of the pile of manuscripts in the corner. Then the wheels of memory slipped ahead through four years of time, and he was aware of the present, of the books he had opened and the universe he had won from their pages, of his dreams and ambitions, and of his love for a pale wraith of a girl, sensitive and sheltered and ethereal, who would die of horror did she witness but one moment of what he had just lived through—one moment of all the muck of life through which he had waded.

He arose to his feet and confronted himself in the looking-glass.

"And so you arise from the mud, Martin Eden," he said solemnly. "And you cleanse your eyes in a great brightness, and thrust your shoulders among the stars, doing what all life has done, letting the 'ape and tiger die' and wresting highest heritage from all powers that be."

He looked more closely at himself and laughed.

"A bit of hysteria and melodrama, eh?" he queried. "Well, never mind. You licked Cheese-Face, and you'll lick the editors if it takes thrice eleven years to do it in. You can't stop here. You've got to go on. It's to a finish, you know."

Chapter Sixteen

The alarm-clock went off, jerking Martin out of sleep with a suddenness that would have given headache to one with less splendid constitution. Though he slept soundly, he awoke instantly, like a cat, and he awoke eagerly, glad that the five hours of unconsciousness were gone. He hated the oblivion of sleep. There was too much to do, too much of life to live. He grudged every moment of life sleep robbed him of, and before the clock had ceased its clattering he was head and ears in the wash-basin and thrilling to the cold bite of the water.

But he did not follow his regular program. There was no unfinished story waiting his hand, no new story demanding articulation. He had studied late, and it was nearly time for breakfast. He tried to read a chapter in Fiske, but his brain was restless and he closed the book. Today witnessed the beginning of the new battle, wherein for some time there would be no writing. He was aware of a sadness akin to that with which one leaves home and family. He looked at the manuscripts in the corner. That was it. He was going away from them, his pitiful, dishonored children that were welcome nowhere. He went over and began to rummage among them, reading snatches here and there, his favorite portions. "The Pot" he honored with reading aloud, as he did "Adventure." "Joy," his latest-born, completed the day before and tossed into the corner for lack of stamps, won his keenest approbation.

"I can't understand," he murmured. "Or maybe it's the editors who can't understand. There's nothing wrong with that. They publish worse every month. Everything they publish is worse—nearly everything, anyway."

After breakfast he put the typewriter in its case and carried it down into Oakland.

"I owe a month on it," he told the clerk in the store. "But you tell the manager I'm going to work and that I'll be in in a month or so and straighten up."

He crossed on the ferry to San Francisco and made his way to an employment office. "Any kind of work, no trade," he told the agent; and was interrupted by a newcomer, dressed rather foppishly, as some workingmen dress who have instincts for finer things. The agent shook his head despondently.

"Nothin' doin', eh?" said the other. "Well, I got to get somebody today."

He turned and stared at Martin, and Martin, staring back, noted the puffed and discolored face, handsome and weak, and knew that he had been making a night of it.

"Lookin' for a job?" the other queried. "What can you do?"

"Hard labor, sailorizing, run a typewriter, no short hand, can sit on a horse, willing to do anything and tackle anything," was the answer.

The other nodded.

"Sounds good to me. My name's Dawson, Joe Dawson, an' I'm tryin' to scare up a laundryman."

"Too much for me." Martin caught an amusing glimpse of himself ironing fluffy white things that women wear. But he had taken a liking to the other, and he added: "I might do the plain washing. I learned that much at sea."

Joe Dawson thought visibly for a moment.

"Look here, let's get together an' frame it up. Willin' to listen?"

Martin nodded.

"This is a small laundry, up country, belongs to Shelly Hot Springs,—hotel, you know. Two men do the work, boss and assistant. I'm the boss. You don't work for me, but you work under me. Think you'd be willin' to learn?"

Martin paused to think. The prospect was alluring.

A few months of it, and he would have time to himself
for study. He could work hard and study hard.

"Good grub an' a room to yourself," Joe said.

That settled it. A room to himself where he could
burn the midnight oil unmolested.

"But work like hell," the other added.

Martin caressed his swelling shoulder-muscles sig-
nificantly. "That came from hard work."

"Then let's get to it." Joe held his hand to his head
for a moment. "Gee, but it's a stem-winder. Can hardly
see. I went down the line last night—everything—
everything. Here's the frame-up. The wages for two
is a hundred and board. I've ben drawin' down sixty,
the second man forty. But he knew the biz. You're
green. If I break you in, I'll be doing plenty of your
work at first. Suppose you begin at thirty, an' work
up to the forty. I'll play fair. Just as soon as you can
do your share you get the forty."

"I'll go you," Martin announced, stretching out his
hand, which the other shook. "Any advance?—for railroad ticket and extras?"

"I blew it in," was Joe's sad answer, with another
reach at his aching head. "All I got is a return ticket."

"And I'm broke—when I pay my board."

"Jump it," Joe advised.

"Can't. Owe it to my sister."

Joe whistled a long, perplexed whistle, and racked
his brains to little purpose.

"I've got the price of the drinks," he said desperately. "Come on, an' mebbe we'll cook up something."

Martin declined.

"Water-wagon?"

This time Martin nodded, and Joe lamented, "Wish
I was. But I somehow just can't," he said in exten-
uation. "After I've ben workin' like hell all week I just

got to booze up. If I didn't, I'd cut my throat or burn up the premises. But I'm glad you're on the wagon. Stay with it."

Martin knew of the enormous gulf between him and this man—the gulf the books had made; but he found no difficulty in crossing back over that gulf. He had lived all his life in the working-class world, and the *camaraderie* of labor was second nature with him. He solved the difficulty of transportation that was too much for the other's aching head. He would send his trunk up to Shelly Hot Springs on Joe's ticket. As for himself, there was his wheel. It was seventy miles, and he could ride it on Sunday and be ready for work Monday morning. In the meantime he would go home and pack up. There was no one to say good-by to. Ruth and her whole family were spending the long summer in the Sierras, at Lake Tahoe.

He arrived at Shelly Hot Springs, tired and dusty, on Sunday night. Joe greeted him exuberantly. With a wet towel bound about his aching brow, he had been at work all day.

"Part of last week's washin' mounted up, me bein' away to get you," he explained. "Your box arrived all right. It's in your room. But it's a hell of a thing to call a trunk. An' what's in it? Gold bricks?"

Joe sat on the bed while Martin unpacked. The box was a packing-case for breakfast food, and Mr. Higginbotham had charged him half a dollar for it. Two rope handles, nailed on by Martin, had technically transformed it into a trunk eligible for the baggage-car. Joe watched, with bulging eyes, a few shirts and several changes of underclothes come out of the box, followed by books, and more books.

"Books clean to the bottom?" he asked.

Martin nodded, and went on arranging the books

on a kitchen table which served in the room in place of a wash-stand.

"Gee!" Joe exploded, then waited in silence for the deduction to arise in his brain. At last it came.

"Say, you don't care for the girls—much?" he queried.

"No," was the answer. "I used to chase a lot before I tackled the books. But since then there's no time."

"And there won't be any time here. All you can do is work an' sleep."

Martin thought of his five hours' sleep a night, and smiled. The room was situated over the laundry and was in the same building with the engine that pumped water, made electricity, and ran the laundry machinery. The engineer, who occupied the adjoining room, dropped in to meet the new hand and helped Martin rig up an electric bulb, on an extension wire, so that it traveled along a stretched cord from over the table to the bed.

The next morning, at quarter-past six, Martin was routed out for a quarter-to-seven breakfast. There happened to be a bathtub for the servants in the laundry building, and he electrified Joe by taking a cold bath.

"Gee, but you're a hummer!" Joe announced, as they sat down to breakfast in a corner of the hotel kitchen.

With them was the engineer, the gardener, and the assistant gardener, and two or three men from the stable. They ate hurriedly and gloomily, with but little conversation, and as Martin ate and listened he realized how far he had travelled from their status. Their small mental caliber was depressing to him, and he was anxious to get away from them. So he bolted his breakfast, a sickly, sloppy affair, as rapidly as they, and heaved a sigh of relief when he passed out through the kitchen door.

It was a perfectly appointed, small steam laundry, wherein the most modern machinery did everything that was possible for machinery to do. Martin, after a few instructions, sorted the great heaps of soiled clothes, while Joe started the masher and made up fresh supplies of soft-soap, compounded of biting chemicals that compelled him to swathe his mouth and nostrils and eyes in bath-towels till he resembled a mummy. Finished the sorting, Martin lent a hand in wringing the clothes. This was done by dumping them into a spinning receptacle that went at a rate of a few thousand revolutions a minute, tearing the water from the clothes by centrifugal force. Then Martin began to alternate between the dryer and the wringer, between times "shaking out" socks and stockings. By the afternoon, one feeding and one stacking up, they were running socks and stockings through the mangle while the irons were heating. Then it was hot irons and underclothes till six o'clock, at which time Joe shook his head dubiously.

"Way behind," he said "Got to work after supper."

And after supper they worked until ten o'clock, under the blazing electric lights, until the last piece of underclothing was ironed and folded away in the distributing room. It was a hot California night, and though the windows were thrown wide, the room, with its red-hot ironing-stove, was a furnace. Martin and Joe, down to undershirts, bare armed, sweated and panted for air.

"Like trimming cargo in the tropics," Martin said, when they went upstairs.

"You'll do," Joe answered. "You take hold like a good fellow. If you keep up the pace, you'll be on thirty dollars only one month. The second month you'll be gettin' your forty. But don't tell me you never ironed before. I know better."

"Never ironed a rag in my life, honestly, until to-day," Martin protested.

He was surprised at his weariness when he got into his room, forgetful of the fact that he had been on his feet and working without let up for fourteen hours. He set the alarm at six, and measured back five hours to one o'clock. He could read until then. Slipping off his shoes, to ease his swollen feet, he sat down at the table with his books. He opened Fiske, where he had left off two days before, and began to read. But he found trouble with the first paragraph and began to read it through a second time. Then he awoke, in pain from his stiffened muscles and chilled by the mountain wind that had begun to blow in through the window. He looked at the clock. It marked two. He had been asleep four hours. He pulled off his clothes and crawled into bed, where he was asleep the moment after his head touched the pillow.

Tuesday was a day of similar unremitting toil. The speed with which Joe worked won Martin's admiration. Joe was a dozen of demons for work. He was keyed up to concert pitch, and there was never a moment in the long day when he was not fighting for moments. He concentrated himself upon his work and upon how to save time, pointing out to Martin where he did in five motions what could be done in three, or in three motions what could be done in two. "Elimination of waste motion," Martin phrased it as he watched and patterned after. He was a good workman himself, quick and deft, and it had always been a point of pride with him that no man should do any of his work for him or outwork him. As a result, he concentrated with a similar singleness of purpose, greedily snapping up the hints and suggestions thrown out by his working mate. He "rubbed out" collars and cuffs, rubbing the starch out from between the double thick-nesses of linen so that there would be no blisters when it came to the ironing, and doing it at a pace that elicited Joe's praise.

There was never an interval when something was not at hand to be done. Joe waited for nothing, waited on nothing, and went on the jump from task to task. They starched two hundred white shirts, with a single gathering movement seizing a shirt so that the wrist-bands, neckband, yoke, and bosom protruded beyond the circling right hand. At the same moment the left hand held up the body of the shirt so that it would not enter the starch, and at the same moment the right hand dipped into the starch—starch so hot that, in order to wring it out, their hands had to be thrust, and thrust continually, into a bucket of cold water. And that night they worked till half-past ten, dipping "fancy starch"—all the frilled and airy, delicate wear of ladies.

"Me for the tropics and no clothes," Martin laughed.

"And me out of a job," Joe answered seriously. "I don't know nothin' but laundrying."

"And you know it well."

"I ought to. Began in the Contra Costa in Oakland when I was eleven, shakin' out for the mangle. That was eighteen years ago, an' I've never done a tap of anything else. But this job is the fiercest I ever had. Ought to be one more man on it at least. We work tomorrow night. Always run the mangle Wednesday nights—collars an' cuffs."

Martin set his alarm, drew up to the table, and opened Fiske. He did not finish the first paragraph. The lines blurred and ran together and his head nod-ded. He walked up and down, batting his head sav-agely with his fists, but he could not conquer the numbness of sleep. He propped the book before him, and propped his eyelids with his fingers, and fell asleep with his eyes wide open. Then he surrendered, and, scarcely conscious of what he did, got off his clothes and into bed. He slept seven hours of heavy, animal-like sleep, and awoke by the alarm, feeling that he had not had enough.

"Doin' much readin'?" Joe asked.

Martin shook his head.

"Never mind. We got to run the mangle tonight, but Thursday we'll knock off at six. That'll give you a chance."

Martin washed woolens that day, by hand, in a large barrel, with strong soft-soap, by means of a hub from a wagon wheel, mounted on a plunger-pole that was attached to a spring-pole overhead.

"My invention," Joe said proudly. "Beats a wash-board an' your knuckles, and, besides, it saves at least fifteen minutes in the week, an' fifteen minutes ain't to be sneezed at in this shebang."

Running the collars and cuffs through the mangle was also Joe's idea. That night, while they toiled on under the electric lights, he explained it.

"Something no laundry ever does, except this one. An' I got to do it if I'm goin' to get done Saturday afternoon at three o'clock. But I know how, an' that's the difference. Got to have right heat, right pressure, and run 'em through three times. Look at that!" He held a cuff aloft. "Couldn't do it better by hand or on a tiler."

Thursday, Joe was in a rage. A bundle of extra "fancy starch" had come in.

"I'm goin' to quit," he announced. "I won't stand for it. I'm goin' to quit it cold. What's the good of me workin' like a slave all week a-savin' minutes, an' them

a-comin' an' ringin' in fancy-starch extras on me? This
is a free country, an' I'm goin' to tell that fat Dutchman
what I think of him. An' I won't tell 'm in French.
Plain United States is good enough for me. Him a-
ringin' in fancy starch extras!

"We got to work tonight," he said the next moment,
reversing his judgment and surrendering to fate.

And Martin did no reading that night. He had seen
no daily paper all week, and, strangely to him, felt no
desire to see one. He was not interested in the news.
He was too tired and jaded to be interested in anything, though he planned to leave Saturday afternoon,
if they finished at three, and ride on his wheel to
Oakland. It was seventy miles, and the same distance
back on Sunday afternoon would leave him anything
but rested for the second week's work. It would have
been easier to go on the train, but the round trip was
two dollars and a half, and he was intent on saving
money.

Chapter Seventeen

Martin learned to do many things. In the course
of the first week, in one afternoon, he and Joe
accounted for the two hundred white shirts. Joe ran
the tiler, a machine wherein a hot iron was hooked on
a steel string which furnished the pressure. By this
means he ironed the yoke, wristbands, and neckband,
setting the latter at right angles to the shirt, and put
the glossy finish on the bosom. As fast as he finished
them, he flung the shirts on a rack between him and
Martin, who caught them up and "backed" them. This

task consisted of ironing all the unstarched portions of the shirts.

It was exhausting work, carried on, hour after hour, at top speed. Out on the broad verandas of the hotel, men and women, in cool white, sipped iced drinks and kept their circulation down. But in the laundry the air was sizzling. The huge stove roared red hot and white hot, while the irons, moving over the damp cloth, sent up clouds of steam. The heat of these irons was different from that used by housewives. An iron that stood the ordinary test of a wet finger was too cold for Joe and Martin, and such test was useless. They went wholly by holding the irons close to their cheeks, gauging the heat by some secret mental process that Martin admired but could not understand. When the fresh irons proved too hot, they hooked them on iron rods and dipped them into cold water. This again required a precise and subtle judgment. A fraction of a second too long in the water and the fine and silken edge of the proper heat was lost, and Martin found time to marvel at the accuracy he developed—an automatic accuracy, founded upon criteria that were machine-like and unerring.

But there was little time in which to marvel. All Martin's consciousness was concentrated in the work. Ceaselessly active, head and hand, an intelligent machine, all that constituted him a man was devoted to furnishing that intelligence. There was no room in his brain for the universe and its mighty problems. All the broad and spacious corridors of his mind were closed and hermetically sealed. The echoing chamber of his soul was a narrow room, a conning tower, whence were directed his arm and shoulder muscles, his ten nimble fingers, and the swift-moving iron along its steaming path in broad, sweeping strokes, just so many

strokes and no more, just so far with each stroke and
not a fraction of an inch farther, rushing along interminable sleeves, sides, backs, and tails, and tossing
the finished shirts, without rumpling, upon the receiving frame. And even as his hurrying soul tossed,
it was reaching for another shirt. This went on, hour
after hour, while outside all the world swooned under
the overhead California sun. But there was no swoon-
ing in that superheated room. The cool guests on the
verandas needed clean linen.

The sweat poured from Martin. He drank enormous
quantities of water, but so great was the heat of the
day and of his exertions, that the water sluiced through
the interstices of his flesh and out at all his pores.
Always, at sea, except at rare intervals, the work he
performed had given him ample opportunity to com-
mune with himself. The master of the ship had been
lord of Martin's time; but here the manager of the
hotel was lord of Martin's thoughts as well. He had
no thoughts save for the nerve-racking, body-destroy-
ing toil. Outside of that it was impossible to think.
He did not know that he loved Ruth. She did not even
exist, for his driven soul had no time to remember
her. It was only when he crawled to bed at night, or
to breakfast in the morning, that she asserted herself
to him in fleeting memories.

"This is hell, ain't it?" Joe remarked once.

Martin nodded, but felt a rasp of irritation. The
statement had been obvious and unnecessary. They
did not talk while they worked. Conversation threw
them out of their stride, as it did this time, compelling
Martin to miss a stroke of his iron and to make two
extra motions before he caught his stride again.

On Friday morning the washer ran. Twice a week
they had to put through hotel linen,—the sheets, pil-

low-slips, spreads, table-cloths, and napkins. This finished, they buckled down to "fancy starch." It was slow work, fastidious and delicate, and Martin did not learn it so readily. Besides, he could not take chances. Mistakes were disastrous.

"See that," Joe said, holding up a filmy corset-cover that he could have crumpled from view in one hand. "Scorch that an' it's twenty dollars out of your wages."

So Martin did not scorch that, and eased down on his muscular tension, though nervous tension rose higher than ever, and he listened sympathetically to the other's blasphemies as he toiled and suffered over the beautiful things that women wear when they do not have to do their own laundrying. "Fancy starch" was Martin's nightmare, and it was Joe's, too. It was "fancy starch" that robbed them of their hard-won minutes. They toiled at it all day. At seven in the evening they broke off to run the hotel linen through the mangle. At ten o'clock, while the hotel guests slept, the two laundrymen sweated on at "fancy starch" till midnight, till one, till two. At half-past two they knocked off.

Saturday morning it was "fancy starch," and odds and ends, and at three in the afternoon the week's work was done.

"You ain't a-goin' to ride them seventy miles into Oakland on top of this?" Joe demanded, as they sat on the stairs and took a triumphant smoke.

"Got to," was the answer.

"What are you goin' for?—a girl?"

"No; to save two and a half on the railroad ticket. I want to renew some books at the library."

"Why don't you send 'em down an' up by express? That'll cost only a quarter each way."

Martin considered it.

"An' take a rest tomorrow," the other urged. "You need it. I know I do. I'm plumb tuckered out."

He looked it. Indomitable, never resting, fighting for seconds and minutes all week, circumventing delays and crushing down obstacles, a fount of resistless energy, a high-driven human motor, a demon for work, now that he had accomplished the week's task he was in a state of collapse. He was worn and haggard, and his handsome face drooped in lean exhaustion. He puffed his cigarette spiritlessly, and his voice was peculiarly dead and monotonous. All the snap and fire had gone out of him. His triumph seemed a sorry one.

"An' next week we got to do it all over again," he said sadly. "An' what's the good of it all, hey? Sometimes I wish I was a hobo. They don't work, an' they get their livin'. Gee! I wish I had a glass of beer; but I can't get up the gumption to go down to the village an' get it. You'll stay over, an' send your books down by express, or else you're a damn fool."

"But what can I do here all day Sunday?" Martin asked.

"Rest. You don't know how tired you are. Why, I'm that tired Sunday I can't even read the papers. I was sick once—typhoid. In the hospital two months an' a half. Didn't do a tap of work all that time. It was beautiful.

"It was beautiful," he repeated dreamily, a minute later.

Martin took a bath, after which he found that the head laundryman had disappeared. Most likely he had gone for the glass of beer, Martin decided, but the half-mile walk down to the village to find out seemed a long journey to him. He lay on his bed with his shoes off, trying to make up his mind. He did not reach out for a book. He was too tired to feel sleepy, and he lay, scarcely thinking, in a semi-stupor of weariness, until it was time for supper. Joe did not appear for that function, and when Martin heard the gardener remark that most likely he was ripping the slats off the bar, Martin understood. He went to bed immediately afterward, and in the morning decided that he was greatly rested. Joe being still absent, Martin procured a Sunday paper and lay down in a shady nook under the trees. The morning passed, he knew not how. He did not sleep, nobody disturbed him, and he did not finish the paper. He came back to it in the afternoon, after dinner, and fell asleep over it.

So passed Sunday, and Monday morning he was hard at work, sorting clothes, while Joe, a towel bound tightly around his head, with groans and blasphemies, was running the washer and mixing soft-soap.

"I simply can't help it," he explained. "I got to drink when Saturday night comes around."

Another week passed, a great battle that continued under the electric lights each night and that culminated on Saturday afternoon at three o'clock, when Joe tasted his moment of wilted triumph and then drifted down to the village to forget. Martin's Sunday was the same as before. He slept in the shade of the trees, toiled aimlessly through the newspaper, and spent long hours lying on his back, doing nothing, thinking nothing. He was too dazed to think, though he was aware that he did not like himself. He was self-repelled, as though he had undergone some degradation or was intrinsically foul. All that was god-like in him was blotted out. The spur of ambition was blunted; he had no vitality with which to feel the prod of it. He was dead. His soul seemed dead. He was a beast, a work-beast. He saw no beauty in the sunshine sifting down through the green leaves, nor did the azure vault of the sky whisper as of old and hint of cosmic vastness and secrets trembling to disclosure. Life was intolerably dull and stupid, and its taste was bad in his mouth. A black screen was drawn across his mirror of inner vision, and fancy lay in a darkened sick-room where entered no ray of light. He envied Joe, down in the village, rampant, tearing the slats off the bar, his brain gnawing with maggots, exulting in maudlin ways over maudlin things, fantastically and gloriously drunk and forgetful of Monday morning and the week of deadening toil to come.

A third week went by, and Martin loathed himself, and loathed life. He was oppressed by a sense of failure. There was reason for the editors refusing his stuff. He could see that clearly now, and laugh at himself and the dreams he had dreamed. Ruth returned his "Sea Lyrics" by mail. He read her letter apathetically. She did her best to say how much she liked them and that they were beautiful. But she could not lie, and she could not disguise the truth from herself. She knew they were failures, and he read her disapproval in every perfunctory and unenthusiastic line of her letter. And she was right. He was firmly convinced of it as he read the poems over. Beauty and wonder had departed from him, and as he read the poems he caught himself puzzling as to what he had had in mind when he wrote them. His audacities of phrase struck him as grotesque, his felicities of expression were monstrosities, and everything was absurd, unreal, and impossible. He would have burned the "Sea Lyrics" on the spot, had his will been strong enough to set them aflame. There was the engine-room, but the exertion of carrying them to the furnace was not worthwhile. All his exertion was used in washing other persons' clothes. He did not have any left for private affairs.

He resolved that when Sunday came he would pull himself together and answer Ruth's letter. But Saturday afternoon, after work was finished and he had taken a bath, the desire to forget overpowered him. "I guess I'll go down and see how Joe's getting on," was the way he put it to himself; and in the same moment he knew that he lied. But he did not have the energy to consider the lie. If he had had the energy, he would have refused to consider the lie, because he wanted to forget. He started for the village slowly and casually, increasing his pace in spite of himself as he neared the saloon.

"I thought you was on the water-wagon," was Joe's greeting.

Martin did not deign to offer excuses, but called for whiskey, filling his own glass brimming before he passed the bottle.

"Don't take all night about it," he said roughly.

The other was dawdling with the bottle, and Martin refused to wait for him, tossing the glass off in a gulp and refilling it.

"Now, I can wait for you," he said grimly, "but hurry up."

Joe hurried, and they drank together.

"The work did it, eh?" Joe queried.

Martin refused to discuss the matter.

"It's fair hell, I know," the other went on, "but I kind of hate to see you come off the wagon, Mart. Well, here's how!"

Martin drank on silently, biting out his orders and invitations and awing the barkeeper, an effeminate country youngster with watery blue eyes and hair parted in the middle.

"It's something scandalous the way they work us poor devils," Joe was remarking. "If I didn't bowl up,

I'd break loose an' burn down the shebang. My bowlin'
up is all that saves 'em, I can tell you that."

But Martin made no answer. A few more drinks,
and in his brain he felt the maggots of intoxication
beginning to crawl. Ah, it was living, the first breath
of life he had breathed in three weeks. His dreams
came back to him. Fancy came out of the darkened
room and lured him on, a thing of flaming brightness.
His mirror of vision was silver-clear, a flashing, dazzling palimpsest of imagery. Wonder and beauty walked
with him, hand in hand, and all power was his. He
tried to tell it to Joe, but Joe had visions of his own,
infallible schemes whereby he would escape the slavery of laundry-work and become himself the owner
of a great steam laundry.

"I tell yeh, Mart, they won't be no kids workin' in
my laundry—not on yer life. An' they won't be no
workin' a livin' soul after six P.M. You hear me talk!
They'll be machinery enough an' hands enough to do
it all in decent workin' hours, an' Mart, s'help me, I'll
make yeh superintendent of the shebang—the whole
of it, all of it. Now here's the scheme. I get on the
water-wagon an' save my money for two years—save
an' then—"

But Martin turned away, leaving him to tell it to
the barkeeper, until that worthy was called away to
furnish drinks to two farmers who, coming in, accepted Martin's invitation. Martin dispensed royal
largesse, inviting everybody up, farm-hands, a stable-
man, and the gardener's assistant from the hotel,
the barkeeper, and the furtive hobo who slid in like
a shadow and like a shadow hovered at the end of
the bar.

Chapter Eighteen

Monday morning, Joe groaned over the first truck load of clothes to the washer.

"I say," he began.

"Don't talk to me," Martin snarled.

"I'm sorry, Joe," he said at noon, when they knocked off for dinner.

Tears came into the other's eyes.

"That's all right, old man," he said. "We're in hell, an' we can't help ourselves. An', you know, I kind of like you a whole lot. That's what made it hurt. I cottoned to you from the first."

Martin shook his hand.

"Let's quit," Joe suggested. "Let's chuck it, an' go hoboin'. I ain't never tried it, but it must be dead easy. An' nothin' to do. Just think of it, nothin' to do. I was sick once, typhoid, in the hospital, an' it was beautiful. I wish I'd get sick again."

The week dragged on. The hotel was full, and extra "fancy starch" poured in upon them. They performed prodigies of valor. They fought late each night under the electric lights, bolted their meals, and even got in a half hour's work before breakfast. Martin no longer took his cold baths. Every moment was drive, drive, drive, and Joe was the masterful shepherd of moments, herding them carefully, never losing one, counting them over like a miser counting gold, working on in a frenzy, toil-mad, a feverish machine, aided ably by that other machine that thought of itself as once having been one Martin Eden, a man.

But it was only at rare moments that Martin was able to think. The house of thought was closed, its

windows boarded up, and he was its shadow caretaker.
He was a shadow. Joe was right. They were both
shadows, and this was the unending limbo of toil. Or
was it a dream? Sometimes, in the steaming, sizzling
heat, as he swung the heavy irons back and forth over
the white garments, it came to him that it was a dream.
In a short while, or maybe after a thousand years or
so, he would awake, in his little room with the ink-
stained table, and take up his writing where he had
left off the day before. Or maybe that was a dream,
too, and the awakening would be the changing of the
watches, when he would drop down out of his bunk
in the lurching forecastle and go up on deck, under
the tropic stars, and take the wheel and feel the cool
trade wind blowing through his flesh.

Came Saturday and its hollow victory at three o'clock.

"Guess I'll go down an' get a glass of beer," Joe said,
in the queer, monotonous tones that marked his weekend collapse.

Martin seemed suddenly to wake up. He opened
the kit bag and oiled his wheel, putting graphite on
the chain and adjusting the bearings. Joe was halfway
down to the saloon when Martin passed by, bending
low over the handle-bars, his legs driving the ninety-
six gear with rhythmic strength, his face set for seventy miles of road and grade and dust. He slept in
Oakland that night, and on Sunday covered the seventy miles back. And on Monday morning, weary, he
began the new week's work, but he had kept sober.

A fifth week passed, and a sixth, during which he
lived and toiled as a machine, with just a spark of
something more in him, just a glimmering bit of soul,
that compelled him, at each weekend, to scorch off
the hundred and forty miles. But this was not rest. It
was super-machinelike, and it helped to crush out the

glimmering bit of soul that was all that was left him from former life. At the end of the seventh week, without intending it, too weak to resist, he drifted down to the village with Joe and drowned life and found life until Monday morning.

Again, at the weekends, he ground out the one hundred and forty miles, obliterating the numbness of too great exertion by the numbness of still greater exertion. At the end of three months he went down a third time to the village with Joe. He forgot, and lived again, and, living, he saw, in clear illumination, the beast he was making of himself—not by the drink, but by the work. The drink was an effect, not a cause. It followed inevitably upon the work, as the night follows upon the day. Not by becoming a toil-beast could he win to the heights, was the message the whiskey whispered to him, and he nodded approbation. The whiskey was wise. It told secrets on itself.

He called for paper and pencil, and for drinks all around, and while they drank his very good health, he clung to the bar and scribbled.

"A telegram, Joe," he said. "Read it."

Joe read it with a drunken, quizzical leer. But what he read seemed to sober him. He looked at the other reproachfully, tears oozing into his eyes and down his cheeks.

"You ain't goin' back on me, Mart?" he queried hopelessly.

Martin nodded, and called one of the loungers to him to take the message to the telegraph office.

"Hold on," Joe muttered thickly. "Lemme think."

He held on to the bar, his legs wobbling under him, Martin's arm around him and supporting him, while he thought.

"Make that two laundrymen," he said abruptly. "Here, lemme fix it."

"What are you quitting for?" Martin demanded.

"Same reason as you."

"But I'm going to sea. You can't do that."

"Nope," was the answer, "but I can hobo all right, all right."

Martin looked at him searchingly for a moment, then cried:—

"By God, I think you're right! Better a hobo than a beast of toil. Why, man, you'll live. And that's more than you ever did before."

"I was in hospital, once," Joe corrected. "It was beautiful. Typhoid—did I tell you?"

While Martin changed the telegram to "two laundrymen," Joe went on:—

"I never wanted to drink when I was in hospital. Funny, ain't it? But when I've ben workin' like a slave all week, I just got to bowl up. Ever noticed that cooks drink like hell?—an' bakers, too? It's the work. They've sure got to. Here, lemme pay half of that telegram."

"I'll shake you for it," Martin offered.

"Come on, everybody drink," Joe called, as they rattled the dice and rolled them out on the damp bar.

Monday morning Joe was wild with anticipation. He did not mind his aching head, nor did he take interest in his work. Whole herds of moments stole away and were lost while their careless shepherd gazed out of the window at the sunshine and the trees.

"Just look at it!" he cried. "An' it's all mine! It's free. I can lie down under them trees an' sleep for a thousan' years if I want to. Aw, come on, Mart, let's chuck it. What's the good of waitin' another moment. That's the land of nothin' to do out there, an' I got a ticket for it—an' it ain't no return ticket, b'gosh!"

A few minutes later, filling the truck with soiled clothes for the washer, Joe spied the hotel manager's shirt. He knew its mark, and with a sudden glorious consciousness of freedom he threw it on the floor and stamped on it.

"I wish you was in it, you pig-headed Dutchman!" he shouted. "In it, an' right there where I've got you! Take that! an' that! an' that! damn you! Hold me back, somebody! Hold me back!"

Martin laughed and held him to his work. On Tuesday night the new laundrymen arrived, and the rest of the week was spent breaking them into the routine. Joe sat around and explained his system, but he did no more work.

"Not a tap," he announced. "Not a tap. They can fire me if they want to, but if they do, I'll quit. No more work in mine, thank you kindly. Me for the freight cars an' the shade under the trees. Go to it, you slaves! That's right. Slave an' sweat! Slave an' sweat! An' when you're dead, you'll rot the same as me, an' what's it matter how you live?—eh? Tell me that—what's it matter in the long run?"

On Saturday they drew their pay and came to the parting of the ways.

"They ain't no use in me askin' you to change your mind an' hit the road with me?" Joe asked hopelessly.

Martin shook hands, and Joe held on to his for a moment, as he said:—

"I'm goin' to see you again, Mart, before you an' me die. That's straight dope. I feel it in my bones. Good-by, Mart, an' be good. I like you like hell, you know."

He stood, a forlorn figure, in the middle of the road, watching until Martin turned a bend and was gone from sight.

"He's a good Indian, that boy," he muttered. "A good Indian."

Then he plodded down the road himself, to the water tank, where half a dozen empties lay on a sidetrack waiting for the up freight.

Chapter Nineteen

Ruth and her family were home again, and Martin, returned to Oakland, saw much of her. Having gained her degree, she was doing no more studying; and he, having worked all vitality out of his mind and body, was doing no writing. This gave them time for each other that they had never had before, and their intimacy ripened fast.

At first, Martin had done nothing but rest. He had slept a great deal, and spent long hours musing and thinking and doing nothing. He was like one recovering from some terrible bout of hardship. The first signs of re-awakening came when he discovered more than languid interest in the daily paper. Then he began to read again—light novels, and poetry; and after several days more he was head over heels in his long-neglected Fiske. His splendid body and health made new vitality, and he possessed all the resiliency and rebound of youth.

Ruth showed her disappointment plainly when he announced that he was going to sea for another voyage as soon as he was well rested.

"Why do you want to do that?" she asked.

"Money," was the answer. "I'll have to lay in a supply for my next attack on the editors. Money is the sinews of war, in my case—money and patience."

"But if all you wanted was money, why didn't you stay in the laundry?"

"Because the laundry was making a beast of me. Too much work of that sort drives to drink."

She stared at him with horror in her eyes.

"Do you mean—?" she quavered.

It would have been easy for him to get out of it; but his natural impulse was for frankness, and he remembered his old resolve to be frank, no matter what happened.

"Yes," he answered. "Just that. Several times."

She shivered and drew away from him.

"No man that I have ever known did that—ever did that."

"Then they never worked in the laundry at Shelly Hot Springs," he laughed bitterly. "Toil is a good thing. It is necessary for human health, so all the preachers say, and Heaven knows I've never been afraid of it. But there is such a thing as too much of a good thing, and the laundry up there is one of them. And that's why I'm going to sea one more voyage. It will be my last, I think, for when I come back, I shall break into the magazines. I am certain of it."

She was silent, unsympathetic, and he watched her moodily, realizing how impossible it was for her to understand what he had been through.

"Some day I shall write it up—'The Degradation of Toil' or the 'Psychology of Drink in the Working-class,' or something like that for a title."

Never, since the first meeting, had they seemed so far apart as that day. His confession, told in frankness, with the spirit of revolt behind, had repelled her. But she was more shocked by the repulsion itself than by the cause of it. It pointed out to her how near she had drawn to him, and once accepted, it paved the way for greater intimacy. Pity, too, was aroused, and innocent, idealistic thoughts of reform. She would save this raw young man who had come so far. She would save him from the curse of his early environment, and she would save him from himself in spite of himself. And all this affected her as a very noble state of consciousness; nor did she dream that behind it and underlying it were the jealousy and desire of love.

They rode on their wheels much in the delightful fall weather, and out in the hills they read poetry aloud, now one and now the other, noble, uplifting poetry that turned one's thoughts to higher things. Renunciation, sacrifice, patience, industry, and high endeavor were the principles she thus indirectly preached—such abstractions being objectified in her mind by her father, and Mr. Butler, and by Andrew Carnegie, who, from a poor immigrant boy had arisen to be the book-giver of the world.

All of which was appreciated and enjoyed by Martin. He followed her mental processes more clearly now, and her soul was no longer the sealed wonder it had been. He was on terms of intellectual equality with her. But the points of disagreement did not affect his love. His love was more ardent than ever, for he loved her for what she was, and even her physical frailty was an added charm in his eyes. He read of sickly Elizabeth Barrett, who for years had not placed her feet upon the ground, until that day of flame when she eloped with Browning and stood upright, upon the earth, under the open sky; and what Browning had done for her, Martin decided he could do for Ruth. But first, she must love him. The rest would be easy. He would give her strength and health. And he caught glimpses of their life, in the years to come, wherein, against a background of work and comfort and general well-being, he saw himself and Ruth reading and discussing poetry, she propped amid a multitude of cushions on the ground while she read aloud to him. This was the key to the life they would live. And always he saw that particular picture. Sometimes it was she who leaned against him while he read, one arm about her, her head upon his shoulder. Sometimes they pored together over the printed pages of beauty. Then, too, she loved nature, and with generous imagination he changed the scene of their reading—sometimes they read in closed-in valleys with precipitous walls, or in high mountain meadows, and, again, down by the gray sand-dunes with a wreath of billows at their feet, or afar on some volcanic tropic isle where waterfalls descended and became mist, reaching the sea in vapor veils that swayed and shivered to every vagrant wisp of wind. But always, in the foreground, lords of beauty and eternally reading and sharing, lay he and Ruth, and always in the background that was beyond the background of nature, dim and hazy, were work and success and money earned that made them free of the world and all its treasures.

"I should recommend my little girl to be careful," her mother warned her one day.

"I know what you mean. But it is impossible. He is not—"

Ruth was blushing, but it was the blush of maidenhood called upon for the first time to discuss the sacred things of life with a mother held equally sacred.

"Your kind." Her mother finished the sentence for her.

Ruth nodded.

"I did not want to say it, but he is not. He is rough, brutal, strong—too strong. He has not—"

She hesitated and could not go on. It was a new experience, talking over such matters with her mother. And again her mother completed her thought for her.

"He has not lived a clean life, is what you wanted to say."

Again Ruth nodded, and again a blush mantled her face.

"It is just that," she said. "It has not been his fault, but he has played much with—"

"With pitch?"

"Yes, with pitch. And he frightens me. Sometimes I am positively in terror of him, when he talks in that free and easy way of the things he has done—as if they did not matter. They do matter, don't they?"

They sat with their arms twined around each other, and in the pause her mother patted her hand and waited for her to go on.

"But I am interested in him dreadfully," she continued. "In a way he is my protégé. Then, too, he is my first boy friend—but not exactly friend; rather protégé and friend combined. Sometimes, too, when he frightens me, it seems that he is a bulldog I have taken for a plaything, like some of the 'frat' girls, and he is tugging hard, and showing his teeth, and threatening to break loose."

Again her mother waited.

"He interests me, I suppose, like the bulldog. And there is much good in him, too; but there is much in him that I would not like in—in the other way. You see, I have been thinking. He swears, he smokes, he drinks, he has fought with his fists (he has told me so, and he likes it; he says so). He is all that a man should not be—a man I would want for my—" her voice sank very low—"husband. Then he is too strong. My prince must be tall, and slender, and dark—a graceful, bewitching prince. No, there is no danger of my falling in love with Martin Eden. It would be the worst fate that could befall me."

"But it is not that that I spoke about," her mother equivocated. "Have you thought about him? He is so ineligible in every way, you know, and suppose he should come to love you?"

"But he does—already," she cried.

"It was to be expected," Mrs. Morse said gently. "How could it be otherwise with any one who knew you?"

"Olney hates me!" she exclaimed passionately. "And I hate Olney. I feel always like a cat when he is around. I feel that I must be nasty to him, and even when I don't happen to feel that way, why, he's nasty to me, anyway. But I am happy with Martin Eden. No one ever loved me before—no man, I mean, in that way. And it is sweet to be loved—that way. You know what I mean, mother dear. It is sweet to feel that you are really and truly a woman." She buried her face in her mother's lap, sobbing. "You think I am dreadful, I know, but I am honest, and I tell you just how I feel."

Mrs. Morse was strangely sad and happy. Her child-daughter, who was a bachelor of arts, was gone; but in her place was a woman-daughter. The experiment had succeeded. The strange void in Ruth's nature had been filled, and filled without danger or penalty. This rough sailor-fellow had been the instrument, and, though Ruth did not love him, he had made her conscious of her womanhood.

"His hand trembles," Ruth was confessing, her face, for shame's sake, still buried. "It is most amusing and ridiculous, but I feel sorry for him, too. And when his hands are too trembly, and his eyes too shiny, why, I lecture him about his life and the wrong way he is going about it to mend it. But he worships me, I know. His eyes and his hands do not lie. And it makes me feel grown-up, the thought of it, the very thought of it; and I feel that I am possessed of something that is by rights my own—that makes me like the other girls—and—and young women. And, then, too, I knew that I was not like them before, and I

knew that it worried you. You thought you did not
let me know that dear worry of yours, but I did, and
I wanted to—'to make good,' as Martin Eden says."

It was a holy hour for mother and daughter, and
their eyes were wet as they talked on in the twilight,
Ruth all white innocence and frankness, her mother
sympathetic, receptive, yet calmly explaining and
guiding.

"He is four years younger than you," she said. "He
has no place in the world. He has neither position nor
salary. He is impractical. Loving you, he should, in
the name of common sense, be doing something that
would give him the right to marry, instead of paltering
around with those stories of his and with childish
dreams. Martin Eden, I am afraid, will never grow
up. He does not take to responsibility and a man's
work in the world like your father did, or like all our
friends, Mr. Butler for one. Martin Eden, I am afraid,
will never be a money-earner. And this world is so
ordered that money is necessary to happiness—oh,
no, not these swollen fortunes, but enough of money
to permit of common comfort and decency. He—he
has never spoken?"

"He has not breathed a word. He has not attempted
to; but if he did, I would not let him, because, you
see, I do not love him."

"I am glad of that. I should not care to see my
daughter, my one daughter, who is so clean and pure,
love a man like him. There are noble men in the world
who are clean and true and manly. Wait for them.
You will find one some day, and you will love him
and be loved by him, and you will be happy with him
as your father and I have been happy with each other.
And there is one thing you must always carry in
mind—"

"Yes, mother."

Mrs. Morse's voice was low and sweet as she said, "And that is the children."

"I—have thought about them," Ruth confessed, remembering the wanton thoughts that had vexed her in the past, her face again red with maiden shame that she should be telling such things.

"And it is that, the children, that makes Mr. Eden impossible," Mrs. Morse went on incisively. "Their heritage must be clean, and he is, I am afraid, not clean. Your father has told me of sailors' lives, and—and you understand."

Ruth pressed her mother's hand in assent, feeling that she really did understand, though her conception was of something vague, remote, and terrible that was beyond the scope of imagination.

"You know I do nothing without telling you," she began. "—Only, sometimes you must ask me, like this time. I wanted to tell you, but I did not know how. It is false modesty, I know it is that, but you can make it easy for me. Sometimes, like this time, you must ask me, you must give me a chance.

"Why, mother, you are a woman, too!" she cried exultantly, as they stood up, catching her mother's hands and standing erect, facing her in the twilight, conscious of a strangely sweet equality between them. "I should never have thought of you in that way if we had not had this talk. I had to learn that I was a woman to know that you were one, too."

"We are women together," her mother said, drawing her to her and kissing her. "We are women together," she repeated, as they went out of the room, their arms around each other's waists, their hearts swelling with a new sense of companionship.

"Our little girl has become a woman," Mrs. Morse said proudly to her husband an hour later.

"That means," he said, after a long look at his wife, "that means she is in love."

"No, but that she is loved," was the smiling rejoinder. "The experiment has succeeded. She is awakened at last."

"Then we'll have to get rid of him." Mr. Morse spoke briskly, in matter-of-fact, businesslike tones.

But his wife shook her head. "It will not be necessary. Ruth says he is going to sea in a few days. When he comes back, she will not be here. We will send her to Aunt Clara's. And, besides, a year in the East, with the change in climate, people, ideas, and everything, is just the thing she needs."

Chapter Twenty

The desire to write was stirring in Martin once more. Stories and poems were springing into spontaneous creation in his brain, and he made notes of them against the future time when he would give them expression. But he did not write. This was his little vacation; he had resolved to devote it to rest and love, and in both matters he prospered. He was soon spilling over with vitality, and each day he saw Ruth, at the moment of meeting, she experienced the old shock of his strength and health.

"Be careful," her mother warned her once again. "I am afraid you are seeing too much of Martin Eden."

But Ruth laughed from security. She was sure of herself, and in a few days he would be off to sea. Then, by the time he returned, she would be away on her visit East. There was a magic, however, in the strength and health of Martin. He, too, had been told

of her contemplated Eastern trip, and he felt the need
for haste. Yet he did not know how to make love to
a girl like Ruth. Then, too, he was handicapped by
the possession of a great fund of experience with girls
and women who had been absolutely different from
her. They had known about love and life and flirtation,
while she knew nothing about such things. Her prodigious innocence appalled him, freezing on his lips
all ardors of speech, and convincing him, in spite of
himself, of his own unworthiness. Also he was handicapped in another way. He had himself never been
in love before. He had liked women in that turgid past
of his, and been fascinated by some of them, but he
had not known what it was to love them. He had
whistled in a masterful, careless way, and they had
come to him. They had been diversions, incidents,
part of the game men play, but a small part at most.
And now, and for the first time, he was a suppliant,
tender and timid and doubting. He did not know the
way of love, nor its speech, while he was frightened
at his loved one's clear innocence.

In the course of getting acquainted with a varied
world, whirling on through the ever changing phases
of it, he had learned a rule of conduct which was to
the effect that when one played a strange game, he
should let the other fellow play first. This had stood
him in good stead a thousand times and trained him
as an observer as well. He knew how to watch the
thing that was strange, and to wait for a weakness,
for a place of entrance, to divulge itself. It was like
sparring for an opening in fist-fighting. And when
such an opening came, he knew by long experience to
play for it and to play hard.

So he waited with Ruth and watched, desiring to
speak his love but not daring. He was afraid of shock-

ing her, and he was not sure of himself. Had he but known it, he was following the right course with her. Love came into the world before articulate speech, and in its own early youth it had learned ways and means that it had never forgotten. It was in this old, primitive way that Martin wooed Ruth. He did not know he was doing it at first, though later he divined it. The touch of his hand on hers was vastly more potent than any word he could utter, the impact of his strength on her imagination was more alluring than the printed poems and spoken passions of a thousand generations of lovers. Whatever his tongue could express would have appealed, in part, to her judgment; but the touch of hand, the fleeting contact, made its way directly to her instinct. Her judgment was as young as she, but her instincts were as old as the race and older. They had been young when love was young, and they were wiser than convention and opinion and all the new-born things. So her judgment did not act. There was no call upon it, and she did not realize the strength of the appeal Martin made from moment to moment to her love-nature. That he loved her, on the other hand was as clear as day, and she consciously delighted in beholding his love-manifestations—the glowing eyes with their tender lights, the trembling hands, and the never failing swarthy flush that flooded darkly under his sunburn. She even went farther, in a timid way inciting him, but doing it so delicately that he never suspected, and doing it half-consciously, so that she scarcely suspected herself. She thrilled with these proofs of her power that proclaimed her a woman, and she took an Eve-like delight in tormenting him and playing upon him.

Tongue-tied by inexperience and by excess of ardor, wooing unwittingly and awkwardly, Martin contin-

ued his approach by contact. The touch of his hand
was pleasant to her, and something deliciously more
than pleasant. Martin did not know it, but he did know
that it was not distasteful to her. Not that they touched
hands often, save at meeting and parting; but that in
handling the bicycles, in strapping on the books of
verse they carried into the hills, and in conning the
pages of books side by side, there were opportunities
for hand to stray against hand. And there were opportunities, too, for her hair to brush his cheek, and
for shoulder to touch shoulder, as they leaned together
over the beauty of the books. She smiled to herself at
vagrant impulses which arose from nowhere and suggested that she rumple his hair; while he desired greatly,
when they tired of reading, to rest his head in her lap
and dream with closed eyes about the future that was
to be theirs. On Sunday picnics at Shellmound Park
and Schuetzen Park, in the past, he had rested his
head on many laps, and, usually, he had slept soundly
and selfishly while the girls shaded his face from the
sun and looked down and loved him and wondered at
his lordly carelessness of their love. To rest his head
in a girl's lap had been the easiest thing in the world
until now, and now he found Ruth's lap inaccessible
and impossible. Yet it was right here, in his reticence,
that the strength of his wooing lay. It was because of
this reticence that he never alarmed her. Herself fastidious and timid, she never awakened to the perilous
trend of their intercourse. Subtly and unaware she
grew toward him and closer to him, while he, sensing
the growing closeness, longed to dare but was afraid.

Once he dared, one afternoon, when he found her
in the darkened living room with a blinding headache.

"Nothing can do it any good," she had answered
his inquiries. "And besides, I don't take headache
powders. Doctor Hall won't permit me."

"I can cure it, I think, and without drugs," was Martin's answer. "I am not sure, of course, but I'd like to try. It's simply massage. I learned the trick first from the Japanese. They are a race of masseurs, you know. Then I learned it all over again with variations from the Hawaiians. They call it *lomi-lomi*. It can accomplish most of the things drugs accomplish and a few things that drugs can't."

Scarcely had his hands touched her head when she sighed deeply.

"That is so good," she said.

She spoke once again, half an hour later, when she asked, "Aren't you tired?"

The question was perfunctory, and she knew what the answer would be. Then she lost herself in drowsy contemplation of the soothing balm of his strength. Life poured from the ends of his fingers, driving the pain before it, or so it seemed to her, until with the easement of pain, she fell asleep and he stole away.

She called him up by telephone that evening to thank him.

"I slept until dinner," she said. "You cured me completely, Mr. Eden, and I don't know how to thank you."

He was warm, and bungling of speech, and very happy, as he replied to her, and there was dancing in his mind, throughout the telephone conversation, the memory of Browning and of sickly Elizabeth Barrett. What had been done could be done again, and he, Martin Eden, could do it and would do it for Ruth Morse. He went back to his room and to the volume of Spencer's "Sociology" lying open on the bed. But he could not read. Love tormented him and overrode his will, so that, despite all determination, he found himself at the little ink-stained table. The sonnet he composed that night was the first of a love-cycle of fifty sonnets which was completed within two months. He had the "Love-sonnets from the Portuguese" in mind as he wrote, and he wrote under the best conditions for great work, at a climacteric of living, in the throes of his own sweet love-madness.

The many hours he was not with Ruth he devoted to the "Love-cycle," to reading at home, or to the public reading-rooms, where he got more closely in touch with the magazines of the day and the nature of their policy and content. The hours he spent with Ruth were maddening alike in promise and in inconclusiveness. It was a week after he cured her headache that a moonlight sail on Lake Merritt was proposed by Norman and seconded by Arthur and Olney. Martin was the only one capable of handling a boat, and he was pressed into service. Ruth sat near him in the stern, while the three young fellows lounged amidships, deep in a wordy wrangle over "frat" affairs.

The moon had not yet risen, and Ruth, gazing into the starry vault of the sky and exchanging no speech with Martin, experienced a sudden feeling of loneliness. She glanced at him. A puff of wind was heeling the boat over till the deck was awash, and he, one hand on tiller and the other on main-sheet, was luffing slightly, at the same time peering ahead to make out the near-lying north shore. He was unaware of her gaze, and she watched him intently, speculating fancifully about the strange warp of soul that led him, a young man with signal powers, to fritter away his time on the writing of stories and poems foredoomed to mediocrity and failure.

Her eyes wandered along the strong throat, dimly seen in the starlight, and over the firm-poised head, and the old desire to lay her hands upon his neck came back to her. The strength she abhorred attracted her.

Her feeling of loneliness became more pronounced, and she felt tired. Her position on the heeling boat irked her, and she remembered the headache he had cured and the soothing rest that resided in him. He was sitting beside her, quite beside her, and the boat seemed to tilt her toward him. Then arose in her the impulse to lean against him, to rest herself against his strength—a vague, half-formed impulse which, even as she considered it, mastered her and made her lean toward him. Or was it the heeling of the boat? She did not know. She never knew. She knew only that she was leaning against him and that the easement and soothing rest were very good. Perhaps it had been the boat's fault, but she made no effort to retrieve it. She leaned lightly against his shoulder, but she leaned, and she continued to lean when he shifted his position to make it more comfortable for her.

It was a madness, but she refused to consider the madness. She was no longer herself but a woman, with a woman's clinging need; and though she leaned ever so lightly, the need seemed satisfied. She was no longer tired. Martin did not speak. Had he, the spell would have been broken. But his reticence of love prolonged it. He was dazed and dizzy. He could not understand what was happening. It was too wonderful to be anything but a delirium. He conquered a mad desire to let go sheet and tiller and to clasp her in his arms. His intuition told him it was the wrong thing to do, and he was glad that sheet and tiller kept his hands occupied and fended off temptation. But he luffed the boat less delicately, spilling the wind shamelessly from the sail so as to prolong the tack to the north shore. The shore would compel him to go about, and the contact would be broken. He sailed with skill, stopping way on the boat without exciting the notice of the wranglers, and mentally forgiving his hardest voyages in that they had made this marvelous night possible, giving him mastery over sea and boat and wind so that he could sail with her beside him, her dear weight against him on his shoulder.

When the first light of the rising moon touched the sail, illuminating the boat with pearly radiance, Ruth moved away from him. And, even as she moved, she felt him move away. The impulse to avoid detection was mutual. The episode was tacitly and secretly intimate. She sat apart from him with burning cheeks, while the full force of it came home to her. She had been guilty of something she would not have her brothers see, nor Olney see. Why had she done it? She had never done anything like it in her life, and yet she had been moonlight-sailing with young men before. She had never desired to do anything like it. She was overcome with shame and with the mystery of her own burgeoning womanhood. She stole a glance at Martin, who was busy putting the boat about on the other tack, and she could have hated him for having made her do an immodest and shameful thing. And he, of all men! Perhaps her mother was right, and she was seeing too much of him. It would never happen again, she resolved, and she would see less of him in the future. She entertained a wild idea of explaining to him the first time they were alone together, of lying to him, of mentioning casually the attack of faintness that had overpowered her just before the moon came up. Then she remembered how they had drawn mutually away before the revealing moon, and she knew he would know it for a lie.

In the days that swiftly followed she was no longer herself but a strange, puzzling creature, willful over judgment and scornful of self-analysis, refusing to peer into the future or to think about herself and whither she was drifting. She was in a fever of tingling mystery, alternately frightened and charmed, and in constant bewilderment. She had one idea firmly fixed, however, which insured her security. She would not let Martin speak his love. As long as she did this, all would be well. In a few days he would be off to sea. And even if he did speak, all would be well. It could not be otherwise, for she did not love him. Of course, it would be a painful half hour for him, and an embarrassing half hour for her, because it would be her first proposal. She thrilled deliciously at the thought. She was really a woman, with a man ripe to ask for her in marriage. It was a lure to all that was fundamental in her sex. The fabric of her life, of all that constituted her, quivered and grew tremulous. The thought fluttered in her mind like a flame-attracted moth. She went so far as to imagine Martin proposing, herself putting the words into his mouth; and she rehearsed her refusal, tempering it with kindness and exhorting him to true and noble manhood. And especially he must stop smoking cigarettes. She would make a point of that. But no, she must not let him speak at all. She could stop him, and she had told her mother that she would. All flushed and burning, she regretfully dismissed the conjured situation. Her first proposal would have to be deferred to a more propitious time and a more eligible suitor.

Chapter Twenty-one

Came a beautiful fall day, warm and languid, palpitant with the hush of the changing season, a California Indian summer day, with hazy sun and

wandering wisps of breeze that did not stir the slumber
of the air. Filmy purple mists, that were not vapors
but fabrics woven of color, hid in the recesses of the
hills. San Francisco lay like a blur of smoke upon her
heights. The intervening bay was a dull sheen of mol-
ten metal, whereon sailing craft lay motionless or drifted
with the lazy tide. Far Tamalpais, barely seen in the
silver haze, bulked hugely by the Golden Gate, the
latter a pale gold pathway under the westering sun.
Beyond, the Pacific, dim and vast, was raising on its
sky-line tumbled cloud-masses that swept landward,
giving warning of the first blustering breath of winter.

The erasure of summer was at hand. Yet summer
lingered, fading and fainting among her hills, deep-
ening the purple of her valleys, spinning a shroud of
haze from waning powers and sated raptures, dying
with the calm content of having lived and lived well.
And among the hills, on their favorite knoll, Martin
and Ruth sat side by side, their heads bent over the
same pages, he reading aloud from the love-sonnets of
the woman who had loved Browning as it is given to
few men to be loved.

But the reading languished. The spell of passing
beauty all about them was too strong. The golden
year was dying as it had lived, a beautiful and unre-
pentant voluptuary, and reminiscent rapture and content freighted heavily the air. It entered into them,
dreamy and languorous, weakening the fibers of resolution, suffusing the face of morality, or of judgment, with haze and purple mist. Martin felt tender
and melting, and from time to time warm glows
passed over him. His head was very near to hers, and
when wandering phantoms of breeze stirred her hair
so that it touched his face, the printed pages swam
before his eyes.

"I don't believe you know a word of what you are reading," she said once when he had lost his place.

He looked at her with burning eyes, and was on the verge of becoming awkward, when a retort came to his lips.

"I don't believe you know either. What was the last sonnet about?"

"I don't know," she laughed frankly. "I've already forgotten. Don't let us read any more. The day is too beautiful."

"It will be our last in the hills for some time," he announced gravely. "There's a storm gathering out there on the sea-rim."

The book slipped from his hands to the ground, and they sat idly and silently, gazing out over the dreamy bay with eyes that dreamed and did not see. Ruth glanced sidewise at his neck. She did not lean toward him. She was drawn by some force outside of herself and stronger than gravitation, strong as destiny. It was only an inch to lean, and it was accomplished without volition on her part. Her shoulder touched his as lightly as a butterfly touches a flower, and just as lightly was the counter-pressure. She felt his shoulder press hers, and a tremor run through him. Then was the time for her to draw back. But she had become an automaton. Her actions had passed beyond the control of her will—she never thought of control or will in the delicious madness that was upon her. His arm began to steal behind her and around her. She waited its slow progress in a torment of delight. She waited, she knew not for what, panting, with dry, burning lips, a leaping pulse, and a fever of expectancy in all her blood. The girdling arm lifted higher and drew her toward him, drew her slowly and caressingly. She could wait no longer. With a tired sigh, and with an impulsive movement all her own, unpremeditated, spasmodic, she rested her head upon his breast. His head bent over swiftly, and, as his lips approached, hers flew to meet them.

This must be love, she thought, in the one rational moment that was vouchsafed her. If it was not love, it was too shameful. It could be nothing else than love. She loved the man whose arms were around her and whose lips were pressed to hers. She pressed more tightly to him, with a snuggling movement of her body. And a moment later, tearing herself half out of his embrace, suddenly and exultantly she reached up and placed both hands upon Martin Eden's sunburnt neck. So exquisite was the pang of love and desire fulfilled that she uttered a low moan, relaxed her hands, and lay half-swooning in his arms.

Not a word had been spoken, and not a word was spoken for a long time. Twice he bent and kissed her, and each time her lips met his shyly and her body made its happy, nestling movement. She clung to him, unable to release herself, and he sat, half supporting her in his arms, as he gazed with unseeing eyes at the blur of the great city across the bay. For once there were no visions in his brain. Only colors and lights and glows pulsed there, warm as the day and warm as his love. He bent over her. She was speaking.

"When did you love me?" she whispered.

"From the first, the very first, the first moment I laid eyes on you. I was mad for love of you then, and in all the time that has passed since then I have only grown the madder. I am maddest, now, dear. I am almost a lunatic, my head is so turned with joy."

"I am glad I am a woman, Martin—dear," she said, after a long sigh.

He crushed her in his arms again and again, and then asked:—

"And you? When did you first know?"

"Oh, I knew it all the time, almost from the first."

"And I have been as blind as a bat!" he cried, a ring of vexation in his voice. "I never dreamed it until just now, when I—when I kissed you."

"I didn't mean that." She drew herself partly away and looked at him. "I meant I knew you loved me almost from the first."

"And you?" he demanded.

"It came to me suddenly." She was speaking very slowly, her eyes warm and fluttery and melting, a soft flush on her cheeks that did not go away. "I never knew until just now when—you put your arms around me. And I never expected to marry you, Martin, not until just now. How did you make me love you?"

"I don't know," he laughed, "unless just by loving you, for I loved you hard enough to melt the heart of a stone, much less the heart of the living, breathing woman you are."

"This is so different from what I thought love would be," she announced irrelevantly.

"What did you think it would be like?"

"I didn't think it would be like this." She was looking into his eyes at the moment, but her own dropped as she continued, "You see, I didn't know what this was like."

He offered to draw her toward him again, but it was no more than a tentative muscular movement of the girdling arm, for he feared that he might be greedy. Then he felt her body yielding, and once again she was close in his arms and lips were pressed on lips.

"What will my people say?" she queried, with sudden apprehension, in one of the pauses.

"I don't know. We can find out very easily any time we are so minded."

"But if mamma objects? I am sure I am afraid to tell her."

"Let me tell her," he volunteered valiantly. "I think your mother does not like me, but I can win her around. A fellow who can win you can win anything. And if we don't—"

"Yes?"

"Why, we'll have each other. But there's no danger of not winning your mother to our marriage. She loves you too well."

"I should not like to break her heart," Ruth said pensively.

He felt like assuring her that mothers' hearts were not so easily broken, but instead he said, "And love is the greatest thing in the world."

"Do you know, Martin, you sometimes frighten me. I am frightened now, when I think of you and of what you have been. You must be very, very good to me. Remember, after all, that I am only a child. I never loved before."

"Nor I. We are both children together. And we are fortunate above most, for we have found our first love in each other."

"But that is impossible!" she cried, withdrawing herself from his arms with a swift, passionate movement. "Impossible for you. You have been a sailor, and sailors, I have heard, are—are—"

Her voice faltered and died away.

"Are addicted to having a wife in every port?" he suggested. "Is that what you mean?"

"Yes," she answered in a low voice.

"But that is not love." He spoke authoritatively. "I have been in many ports, but I never knew a passing touch of love until I saw you that first night. Do you know, when I said good night and went away, I was almost arrested."

"Arrested?"

"Yes. The policeman thought I was drunk; and I was, too—with love for you."

"But you said we were children, and I said it was impossible, for you, and we have strayed away from the point."

"I said that I never loved anybody but you," he replied. "You are my first, my very first."

"And yet you have been a sailor," she objected.

"But that doesn't prevent me from loving you the first."

"And there have been women—other women—oh!"

And to Martin Eden's supreme surprise, she burst into a storm of tears that took more kisses than one and many caresses to drive away. And all the while there was running through his head Kipling's line: *"And the Colonel's lady and Judy O'Grady are sisters under their skins."* It was true, he decided; though the novels he had read had led him to believe otherwise. His idea, for which the novels were responsible, had been that only formal proposals obtained in the upper classes. It was all right enough, down whence he had come, for youths and maidens to win each other by contact; but for the exalted personages up above on the heights to make love in similar fashion had seemed unthinkable. Yet the novels were wrong. Here was a proof of it. The same pressures and caresses, unaccompanied by speech, that were efficacious with the girls of the working class, were equally efficacious with the girls above the working class. They were all of the same flesh, after all, sisters under their skins; and he might have known as much himself had he remembered his Spencer. As he held Ruth in his arms and soothed her, he took great consolation in the thought that the Colonel's lady and Judy O'Grady were pretty much alike under their skins. It brought Ruth closer to him, made her possible. Her dear flesh was as anybody's flesh, as his flesh. There was no bar to their marriage. Class difference was the only difference, and class was extrinsic. It could be shaken off. A slave, he had read, had risen to the Roman purple. That being so, then he could rise to Ruth. Under her purity, and saintliness, and culture, and ethereal beauty of soul, she was, in things fundamentally human, just like Lizzie Connolly and all Lizzie Connollys. All that was possible of them was possible of her. She could love, and hate, maybe have hysterics; and she could certainly be jealous, as she was jealous now, uttering her last sobs in his arms.

"Besides, I am older than you," she remarked suddenly, opening her eyes and looking up at him, "three years older."

"Hush, you are only a child, and I am forty years older than you, in experience," was his answer.

In truth, they were children together, so far as love was concerned, and they were as naïve and immature in the expression of their love as a pair of children, and this despite the fact that she was crammed with a university education and that his head was full of scientific philosophy and the hard facts of life.

They sat on through the passing glory of the day, talking as lovers are prone to talk, marveling at the wonder of love and at destiny that had flung them so strangely together, and dogmatically believing that they loved to a degree never attained by lovers before. And they returned insistently, again and again, to a rehearsal of their first impressions of each other and to hopeless attempts to analyze just precisely what they felt for each other and how much there was of it.

The cloud-masses on the western horizon received the descending sun, and the circle of the sky turned to rose, while the zenith glowed with the same warm color. The rosy light was all about them, flooding over them, as she sang, "Good-by, Sweet Day." She sang softly, leaning in the cradle of his arm, her hands in his, their hearts in each other's hands.

Chapter Twenty-two

Mrs. Morse did not require a mother's intuition to read the advertisement in Ruth's face when she returned home. The flush that would not leave the cheeks told the simple story, and more eloquently did the eyes, large and bright, reflecting an unmistakable inward glory.

"What has happened?" Mrs. Morse asked, having bided her time till Ruth had gone to bed.

"You know?" Ruth queried, with trembling lips.

For reply, her mother's arm went around her, and a hand was softly caressing her hair.

"He did not speak," she blurted out. "I did not intend that it should happen, and I would never have let him speak—only he didn't speak."

"But if he did not speak, then nothing could have happened, could it?"

"But it did, just the same."

"In the name of goodness, child, what are you babbling about?" Mrs. Morse was bewildered. "I don't think I know what happened, after all. What did happen?"

Ruth looked at her mother in surprise.

"I thought you knew. Why, we're engaged, Martin and I."

Mrs. Morse laughed with incredulous vexation.

"No, he didn't speak," Ruth explained. "He just loved me, that was all. I was as surprised as you are. He didn't say a word. He just put his arm around me. And—and I was not myself. And he kissed me, and I kissed him. I couldn't help it. I just had to. And then I knew I loved him."

She paused, waiting with expectancy the benediction of her mother's kiss, but Mrs. Morse was coldly silent.

"It is a dreadful accident, I know," Ruth recommenced with a sinking voice. "And I don't know how you will ever forgive me. But I couldn't help it. I did not dream that I loved him until that moment. And you must tell father for me."

"Would it not be better not to tell your father? Let me see Martin Eden, and talk with him, and explain. He will understand and release you."

"No! no!" Ruth cried, starting up. "I do not want to be released. I love him, and love is very sweet. I am going to marry him—of course, if you will let me."

"We have other plans for you, Ruth dear, your father and I—oh, no, no; no man picked out for you, or anything like that. Our plans go no farther than your marrying some man in your own station in life, a good and honorable gentleman, whom you will select yourself, when you love him."

"But I love Martin already," was the plaintive protest.

"We would not influence your choice in any way; but you are our daughter, and we could not bear to see you make a marriage such as this. He has nothing but roughness and coarseness to offer you in exchange for all that is refined and delicate in you. He is no match for you in any way. He could not support you.

We have no foolish ideas about wealth, but comfort is another matter, and our daughter should at least marry a man who can give her that—and not a penniless adventurer, a sailor, a cowboy, a smuggler, and Heaven knows what else, who, in addition to everything, is hare-brained and irresponsible."

Ruth was silent. Every word she recognized as true.

"He wastes his time over his writing, trying to accomplish what geniuses and rare men with college educations sometimes accomplish. A man thinking of marriage should be preparing for marriage. But not he. As I have said, and I know you agree with me, he is irresponsible. And why should he not be? It is the way of sailors. He has never learned to be economical or temperate. The spendthrift years have marked him. It is not his fault, of course, but that does not alter his nature. And have you thought of the years of licentiousness he inevitably has lived? Have you thought of that, daughter? You know what marriage means."

Ruth shuddered and clung close to her mother.

"I have thought." Ruth waited a long time for the thought to frame itself. "And it is terrible. It sickens me to think of it. I told you it was a dreadful accident, my loving him; but I can't help myself. Could you help loving father? Then it is the same with me. There is something in me, in him—I never knew it was there until today—but it is there, and it makes me love him. I never thought to love him, but, you see, I do," she concluded, a certain faint triumph in her voice.

They talked long, and to little purpose, in conclusion agreeing to wait an indeterminate time without doing anything.

The same conclusion was reached, a little later that night, between Mrs. Morse and her husband, after she had made due confession of the miscarriage of her plans.

"It could hardly have come otherwise," was Mr. Morse's judgment. "This sailor-fellow has been the only man she was in touch with. Sooner or later she was going to awaken anyway; and she did awaken, and lo! here was this sailor-fellow, the only accessible man at the moment, and of course she promptly loved him, or thought she did, which amounts to the same thing."

Mrs. Morse took it upon herself to work slowly and indirectly upon Ruth, rather than to combat her. There would be plenty of time for this, for Martin was not in position to marry.

"Let her see all she wants of him," was Mr. Morse's advice. "The more she knows him, the less she'll love him, I wager. And give her plenty of contrast. Make a point of having young people at the house. Young women and young men, all sorts of young men, clever men, men who have done something or who are doing things, men of her own class, gentlemen. She can gauge him by them. They will show him up for what he is. And after all, he is a mere boy of twenty-one. Ruth is no more than a child. It is calf love with the pair of them, and they will grow out of it."

So the matter rested. Within the family it was accepted that Ruth and Martin were engaged, but no announcement was made. The family did not think it would ever be necessary. Also, it was tacitly understood that it was to be a long engagement. They did not ask Martin to go to work, nor to cease writing. They did not intend to encourage him to mend himself. And he aided and abetted them in their unfriendly designs, for going to work was farthest from his thoughts.

"I wonder if you'll like what I have done!" he said to Ruth several days later. "I've decided that boarding with my sister is too expensive, and I am going to board myself. I've rented a little room out in North Oakland, retired neighborhood and all the rest, you know, and I've bought an oil-burner on which to cook."

Ruth was overjoyed. The oil-burner especially pleased her.

"That was the way Mr. Butler began his start," she said.

Martin frowned inwardly at the citation of that worthy gentleman, and went on: "I put stamps on all my manuscripts and started them off to the editors again. Then today I moved in, and tomorrow I start to work."

"A position!" she cried, betraying the gladness of her surprise in all her body, nestling closer to him, pressing his hand, smiling. "And you never told me! What is it?"

He shook his head.

"I meant that I was going to work at my writing." Her face fell, and he went on hastily. "Don't misjudge me. I am not going in this time with any iridescent ideas. It is to be a cold, prosaic, matter-of-fact business proposition. It is better than going to sea again, and I shall earn more money than any position in Oakland can bring an unskilled man.

"You see, this vacation I have taken has given me perspective. I haven't been working the life out of my body, and I haven't been writing, at least not for publication. All I've done has been to love you and to think. I've read some, too, but it has been part of my thinking, and I have read principally magazines. I have generalized about myself, and the world, my place in it, and my chance to win to a place that will be fit for you. Also, I've been reading Spencer's 'Philosophy of Style,' and found out a lot of what was the matter with me—or my writing, rather; and for that matter with most of the writing that is published every month in the magazines.

"But the upshot of it all—of my thinking and reading and loving—is that I am going to move to Grub Street. I shall leave masterpieces alone and do hackwork—jokes, paragraphs, feature articles, humorous verse, and society verse—all the rot for which there seems so much demand. Then there are the newspaper syndicates, and the newspaper short-story syndicates, and the syndicates for the Sunday supplements. I can go ahead and hammer out the stuff they want, and earn the equivalent of a good salary by it. There are free-lances, you know, who earn as much as four or five hundred a month. I don't care to become as they; but I'll earn a good living, and have plenty of time to myself, which I wouldn't have in any position.

"Then, I'll have my spare time for study and for real work. In between the grind I'll try my hand at masterpieces, and I'll study and prepare myself for the writing of masterpieces. Why, I am amazed at the distance I have come already. When I first tried to write, I had nothing to write about except a few paltry experiences which I neither understood nor appreciated. But I had no thoughts. I really didn't. I didn't even have the words with which to think. My experiences were so many meaningless pictures. But as I began to add to my knowledge, and to my vocabulary, I saw something more in my experiences than mere pictures. I retained the pictures and I found their interpretation. That was when I began to do good work, when I wrote 'Adventure,' 'Joy,' 'The Pot,' 'The Wine of Life,' 'The Jostling Street,' the 'Love-cycle,' and the 'Sea Lyrics.' I shall write more like them, and

better; but I shall do it in my spare time. My feet are
on the solid earth, now. Hack-work and income first,
masterpieces afterward. Just to show you, I wrote half
a dozen jokes last night for the comic weeklies; and
just as I was going to bed, the thought struck me to
try my hand at a triolet—a humorous one; and inside
an hour I had written four. They ought to be worth
a dollar apiece. Four dollars right there for a few after-
thoughts on the way to bed.

"Of course it's all valueless, just so much dull and
sordid plodding; but it is no more dull and sordid than
keeping books at sixty dollars a month, adding up
endless columns of meaningless figures until one dies.
And furthermore, the hack-work keeps me in touch
with things literary and gives me time to try bigger
things."

"But what good are these bigger things, these masterpieces?" Ruth demanded. "You can't sell them."

"Oh, yes, I can," he began; but she interrupted.

"All those you named, and which you say yourself
are good—you have not sold any of them. We can't
get married on masterpieces that won't sell."

"Then we'll get married on triolets that will sell,"
he asserted stoutly, putting his arm around her and
drawing a very unresponsive sweetheart toward him.

"Listen to this," he went on in attempted gaiety.
"It's not art, but it's a dollar.

> "He came in
>   When I was out,
> To borrow some tin
> Was why he came in,
>   And he went without;
> So I was in
>   And he was out."

The merry lilt with which he had invested the jingle was at variance with the dejection that came into his face as he finished. He had drawn no smile from Ruth. She was looking at him in an earnest and troubled way.

"It may be a dollar," she said, "but it is a jester's dollar, the fee of a clown. Don't you see, Martin, the whole thing is lowering. I want the man I love and honor to be something finer and higher than a perpetrator of jokes and doggerel."

"You want him to be like—say Mr. Butler?" he suggested.

"I know you don't like Mr. Butler," she began.

"Mr. Butler's all right," he interrupted. "It's only his indigestion I find fault with. But to save me I can't see any difference between writing jokes or comic verse and running a typewriter, taking dictation, or keeping sets of books. It is all a means to an end. Your theory is for me to begin with keeping books in order to become a successful lawyer or man of business. Mine is to begin with hack-work and develop into an able author."

"There is a difference," she insisted.

"What is it?"

"Why, your good work, what you yourself call good, you can't sell. You have tried,—you know that,—but the editors won't buy it."

"Give me time, dear," he pleaded. "The hack-work is only makeshift, and I don't take it seriously. Give me two years. I shall succeed in that time, and the editors will be glad to buy my good work. I know what I am saying; I have faith in myself. I know what I have in me; I know what literature is, now; I know the average rot that is poured out by a lot of little men; and I know that at the end of two years I shall be on the highroad to success. As for business, I shall never succeed at it. I am not in sympathy with it. It strikes me as dull, and stupid, and mercenary, and tricky. Anyway I am not adapted for it. I'd never get beyond a clerkship, and how could you and I be happy on the paltry earnings of a clerk? I want the best of everything in the world for you, and the only time when I won't want it will be when there is something better. And I'm going to get it, going to get all of it. The income of a successful author makes Mr. Butler look cheap. A 'best-seller' will earn anywhere between fifty and a hundred thousand dollars—sometimes more and sometimes less; but, as a rule, pretty close to those figures."

She remained silent; her disappointment was apparent.

"Well?" he asked.

"I had hoped and planned otherwise. I had thought, and I still think, that the best thing for you would be to study shorthand—you already know typewriting—and go into father's office. You have a good mind, and I am confident you would succeed as a lawyer."

Chapter Twenty-three

That Ruth had little faith in his power as a writer, did not alter her nor diminish her in Martin's eyes. In the breathing spell of the vacation he had taken, he had spent many hours in self-analysis, and thereby learned much of himself. He had discovered that he loved beauty more than fame, and that what desire he had for fame was largely for Ruth's sake. It was for this reason that his desire for fame was strong. He wanted to be great in the world's eyes; "to make good," as he expressed it, in order that the woman he loved should be proud of him and deem him worthy.

As for himself, he loved beauty passionately, and the joy of serving her was to him sufficient wage. And more than beauty he loved Ruth. He considered love the finest thing in the world. It was love that had worked the revolution in him, changing him from an uncouth sailor to a student and an artist; therefore, to him, the finest and greatest of the three, greater than learning and artistry, was love. Already he had discovered that his brain went beyond Ruth's, just as it went beyond the brains of her brothers, or the brain of her father. In spite of every advantage of university training, and in the face of her bachelorship of arts, his power of intellect overshadowed hers, and his year or so of self-study and equipment gave him a mastery of the affairs of the world and art and life that she could never hope to possess.

All this he realized, but it did not affect his love for her, nor her love for him. Love was too fine and noble, and he was too loyal a lover for him to besmirch love with criticism. What did love have to do with Ruth's divergent views on art, right conduct, the French Revolution, or equal suffrage? They were mental processes, but love was beyond reason; it was superrational. He could not belittle love. He worshipped it. Love lay on the mountain-tops beyond the valley-land of reason. It was a sublimated condition of existence, the topmost peak of living, and it came rarely. Thanks to the school of scientific philosophers he favored, he knew the biological significance of love; but by a refined process of the same scientific reasoning he reached the conclusion that the human organism achieved its highest purpose in love, that love must not be questioned, but must be accepted as the highest guerdon of life. Thus, he considered the lover blessed over all creatures, and it was a delight to him to think of "God's own mad lover," rising above the things of earth, above wealth and judgment, public opinion and applause, rising above life itself and "dying on a kiss."

Much of this Martin had already reasoned out, and some of it he reasoned out later. In the meantime he worked, taking no recreation except when he went to see Ruth, and living like a Spartan. He paid two dollars and a half a month rent for the small room he got from his Portuguese landlady, Maria Silva, a virago and a widow, hard working and harsher tempered, rearing her large brood of children somehow, and drowning her sorrow and fatigue at irregular intervals in a gallon of the thin, sour wine that she bought from the corner grocery and saloon for fifteen cents. From detesting her and her foul tongue at first, Martin grew to admire her as he observed the brave fight she made. There were but four rooms in the little house—three, when Martin's was subtracted. One of these, the parlor, gay with an ingrain carpet and dolorous with a funeral card and a death-picture of one of her numerous departed babes, was kept strictly for company. The blinds were always down, and her barefooted tribe was never permitted to enter the sacred precinct save on state occasions. She cooked, and all ate, in the kitchen, where she likewise washed, starched, and ironed clothes on all days of the week except Sunday; for her income came largely from taking in washing from her more prosperous neighbors. Remained the bedroom, small as the one occupied by Martin, into which she and her seven little ones crowded and slept. It was an everlasting miracle to Martin how it was accomplished, and from her side of the thin partition he heard nightly every detail of the going to bed, the squalls and squabbles, the soft chattering, and the sleepy, twittering noises as of birds. Another source of income to Maria were her cows, two of them, which she milked night and morning and which gained a surreptitious livelihood from vacant lots and the grass that grew on either side of the public sidewalks, attended always by one or more of her ragged boys, whose watchful guardianship consisted chiefly in keeping their eyes out for the poundmen.

In his own small room Martin lived, slept, studied, wrote, and kept house. Before the one window, looking out on the tiny front porch, was the kitchen table that served as desk, library, and typewriting stand. The bed, against the rear wall, occupied two-thirds of the total space of the room. The table was flanked on one side by a gaudy bureau, manufactured for profit and not for service, the thin veneer of which was shed day by day. This bureau stood in the corner, and in the opposite corner, on the table's other flank, was the kitchen—the oil-stove on a dry-goods box, inside of which were dishes and cooking utensils, a shelf on the wall for provisions, and a bucket of water on the floor. Martin had to carry his water from the kitchen sink, there being no tap in his room. On days when there was much steam to his cooking, the harvest of veneer from the bureau was unusually generous. Over the bed, hoisted by a tackle to the ceiling, was his bicycle. At first he had tried to keep it in the basement; but the tribe of Silva, loosening the bearings and puncturing the tires, had driven him out. Next he attempted the tiny front porch, until a howling southeaster drenched the wheel a night long. Then he had retreated with it to his room and slung it aloft.

A small closet contained his clothes and the books he had accumulated and for which there was no room on the table or under the table. Hand in hand with reading, he had developed the habit of making notes, and so copiously did he make them that there would have been no existence for him in the confined quarters had he not rigged several clothes-lines across the room on which the notes were hung. Even so, he was crowded until navigating the room was a difficult task. He could not open the door without first closing the closet door, and *vice versa*. It was impossible for him anywhere to traverse the room in a straight line. To go from the door to the head of the bed was a zigzag course that he was never quite able to accomplish in the dark without collisions. Having settled the difficulty of the conflicting doors, he had to steer sharply to the right to avoid the kitchen. Next, he sheered to the left, to escape the foot of the bed; but this sheer, if too generous, brought him against the corner of the table. With a sudden twitch and lurch, he terminated the sheer and bore off to the right along a sort of canal, one bank of which was the bed, the other the table. When the one chair in the room was at its usual place before the table, the canal was unnavigable. When the chair was not in use, it reposed on top of the bed, though sometimes he sat on the chair when cooking, reading a book while the water boiled, and even becoming skillful enough to manage a paragraph or two while steak was frying. Also, so small was the little corner that constituted the kitchen, he was able, sitting down, to reach anything he needed. In fact, it was expedient to cook sitting down; standing up, he was too often in his own way.

In conjunction with a perfect stomach that could digest anything, he possessed knowledge of the various foods that were at the same time nutritious and cheap. Pea-soup was a common article in his diet, as well as potatoes and beans, the latter large and brown and cooked in Mexican style. Rice, cooked as American housewives never cook it and can never learn to cook it, appeared on Martin's table at least once a day. Dried fruits were less expensive than fresh, and he had usually a pot of them, cooked and ready at hand, for they took the place of butter on his bread. Occasionally he graced his table with a piece of round-steak, or with a soup-bone. Coffee, without cream or milk, he had twice a day, in the evening substituting tea; but both coffee and tea were excellently cooked.

There was need for him to be economical. His vacation had consumed nearly all he had earned in the laundry, and he was so far from his market that weeks must elapse before he could hope for the first returns from his hack-work. Except at such times as he saw Ruth, or dropped in to see his sister Gertrude, he lived a recluse, in each day accomplishing at least three days' labor of ordinary men. He slept a scant five hours, and only one with a constitution of iron could have held himself down, as Martin did, day after day, to nineteen consecutive hours of toil. He never lost a moment. On the looking-glass were lists of definitions and pronunciations; when shaving, or dressing, or combing his hair, he conned these lists over. Similar lists were on the wall over the oil-stove, and they were similarly conned while he was engaged in cooking or in washing the dishes. New lists continually displaced the old ones. Every strange or partly familiar word encountered in his reading was immediately jotted down, and later, when a sufficient number had been accumulated, were typed and pinned to the wall or looking-glass. He even carried them in his pockets, and reviewed them at odd moments on the street, or while waiting in butcher shop or grocery to be served.

He went farther in the matter. Reading the works of men who had arrived, he noted every result achieved by them, and worked out the tricks by which they had been achieved—the tricks of narrative, of exposition, of style, the points of view, the contrasts, the epigrams; and of all these he made lists for study. He did not ape. He sought principles. He drew up lists of effective and fetching mannerisms, till out of many such, culled from many writers, he was able to induce the general principle of mannerism, and, thus equipped, to cast about for new and original ones of his own, and to weigh and measure and appraise them properly. In similar manner he collected lists of strong phrases, the phrases of living language, phrases that bit like acid and scorched like flame, or that glowed and were mellow and luscious in the midst of the arid desert of common speech. He sought always for the principle that lay behind and beneath. He wanted to know how the thing was done; after that he could do it for himself. He was not content with the fair face of beauty. He dissected beauty in his crowded little bedroom laboratory, where cooking smells alternated with the outer bedlam of the Silva tribe; and, having dissected and learned the anatomy of beauty, he was nearer being able to create beauty itself.

He was so made that he could work only with understanding. He could not work blindly, in the dark, ignorant of what he was producing and trusting to chance and the star of his genius that the effect produced should be right and fine. He had no patience with chance effects. He wanted to know why and how. His was deliberate creative genius, and, before he began a story or poem, the thing itself was already alive in his brain, with the end in sight and the means of realizing that end in his conscious possession. Otherwise the effort was doomed to failure. On the other hand, he appreciated the chance effects in words and phrases that came lightly and easily into his brain, and that later stood all tests of beauty and power and developed tremendous and incommunicable connotations. Before such he bowed down and marveled, knowing that they were beyond the deliberate creation of any man. And no matter how much he dissected beauty in search of the principles that underlie beauty and make beauty possible, he was aware, always, of the innermost mystery of beauty to which he did not penetrate and to which no man had ever penetrated. He knew full well, from his Spencer, that man can never attain ultimate knowledge of anything, and that the mystery of beauty was no less than that of life—nay, more—that the fibers of beauty and life were intertwisted, and that he himself was but a bit of the same nonunderstandable fabric, twisted of sunshine and star-dust and wonder.

In fact, it was when filled with these thoughts that he wrote his essay entitled "Star-dust," in which he had his fling, not at the principles of criticism, but at the principal critics. It was brilliant, deep, philosophical, and deliciously touched with laughter. Also it was promptly rejected by the magazines as often as it was submitted. But having cleared his mind of it, he went serenely on his way. It was a habit he developed, of incubating and maturing his thought upon a subject, and of then rushing into the typewriter with it. That it did not see print was a matter of small moment with him. The writing of it was the culminating act of a long mental process, the drawing together of scattered threads of thought and the final generalizing upon all the data with which his mind was burdened. To write such an article was the conscious effort by which he freed his mind and made it ready for fresh material and problems. It was in a way akin to that common habit of men and women troubled by real or fancied grievances, who periodically and volubly break their long-suffering silence and "have their say" till the last word is said.

Chapter Twenty-four

The weeks passed. Martin ran out of money, and publishers' checks were far away as ever. All his important manuscripts had come back and been started out again, and his hack-work fared no better. His little kitchen was no longer graced with a variety of foods. Caught in the pinch with a part sack of rice and a few pounds of dried apricots, rice and apricots was his menu three times a day for five days running. Then he started to realize on his credit. The Portuguese grocer, to whom he had hitherto paid cash, called a halt when Martin's bill reached the magnificent total of three dollars and eighty-five cents.

"For you see," said the grocer, "you no catcha da work, I losa da mon'."

And Martin could reply nothing. There was no way of explaining. It was not true business principle to allow credit to a strong-bodied young fellow of the working class who was too lazy to work.

"You catcha da job, I let you have mora da grub," the grocer assured Martin. "No job, no grub. Thata da business." And then, to show that it was purely business foresight and not prejudice, "Hava da drink on da house—good friends justa da same."

So Martin drank, in his easy way, to show that he was good friends with the house, and then went supperless to bed.

The fruit store, where Martin had bought his vegetables, was run by an American whose business principles were so weak that he let Martin run a bill of five dollars before stopping his credit. The baker stopped at two dollars, and the butcher at four dollars. Martin added his debts and found that he was possessed of a total credit in all the world of fourteen dollars and eighty-five cents. He was up with his typewriter rent, but he estimated that he could get two months' credit on that, which would be eight dollars. When that occurred, he would have exhausted all possible credit.

The last purchase from the fruit store had been a sack of potatoes, and for a week he had potatoes, and nothing but potatoes, three times a day. An occasional dinner at Ruth's helped to keep strength in his body, though he found it tantalizing enough to refuse further helpings when his appetite was raging at sight of so much food spread before it. Now and again, though afflicted with secret shame, he dropped in at his sister's at meal-time and ate as much as he dared—more than he dared at the Morse table.

Day by day he worked on, and day by day the postman delivered to him rejected manuscripts. He had no money for stamps, so the manuscripts accumulated in a heap under the table. Came a day when for forty hours he had not tasted food. He could not hope for a meal at Ruth's, for she was away to San Rafael on a two weeks' visit; and for very shame's sake he could not go to his sister's. To cap misfortune, the postman, in his afternoon round, brought him five returned manuscripts. Then it was that Martin wore his overcoat down into Oakland, and came back without it, but with five dollars tinkling in his pocket. He paid a dollar each on account to the four tradesmen, and in his kitchen fried steak and onions, made coffee, and stewed a large pot of prunes. And having dined, he sat down at his table-desk and completed before midnight an essay which he entitled "The Dignity of Usury." Having typed it out, he flung it under the table, for there had been nothing left from the five dollars with which to buy stamps.

Later on he pawned his watch, and still later his wheel, reducing the amount available for food by putting stamps on all his manuscripts and sending them out. He was disappointed with his hack-work. Nobody cared to buy. He compared it with what he found in the newspapers, weeklies, and cheap magazines, and decided that his was better, far better, than the average; yet it would not sell. Then he discovered that most of the newspapers printed a great deal of what was called "plate" stuff, and he got the address of the association that furnished it. His own work that he sent in was returned, along with a stereotyped slip informing him that the staff supplied all the copy that was needed.

In one of the great juvenile periodicals he noted whole columns of incident and anecdote. Here was a chance. His paragraphs were returned, and though he tried repeatedly he never succeeded in placing one. Later on, when it no longer mattered, he learned that the associate editors and sub-editors augmented their salaries by supplying those paragraphs themselves. The comic weeklies returned his jokes and humorous verse, and the light society verse he wrote for the large magazines found no abiding-place. Then there was the newspaper storiette. He knew that he could write better ones than were published. Managing to obtain the addresses of two newspaper syndicates, he deluged them with storiettes. When he had written twenty and failed to place one of them, he ceased. And yet, from day to day, he read storiettes in the dailies and weeklies, scores and scores of storiettes, not one of which would compare with his. In his despondency, he concluded that he had no judgment whatever, that he was hypnotized by what he wrote, and that he was a self-deluded pretender.

The inhuman editorial machine ran smoothly as ever. He folded the stamps in with his manuscript, dropped it into the letter-box, and from three weeks to a month afterward the postman came up the steps and handed him the manuscript. Surely there were no live, warm editors at the other end. It was all wheels and cogs and oil-cups—a clever mechanism operated by automatons. He reached stages of despair wherein he doubted if editors existed at all. He had never received a sign of the existence of one, and from absence of judgment in rejecting all he wrote it seemed plausible that editors were myths, manufactured and maintained by office boys, typesetters, and pressmen.

The hours he spent with Ruth were the only happy ones he had, and they were not all happy. He was afflicted always with a gnawing restlessness, more tantalizing than in the old days before he possessed her love; for now that he did possess her love, the possession of her was far away as ever. He had asked for two years; time was flying, and he was achieving nothing. Again, he was always conscious of the fact that she did not approve what he was doing. She did not say so directly. Yet indirectly she let him understand it as clearly and definitely as she could have spoken it. It was not resentment with her, but disapproval; though less sweet-natured women might have resented where she was no more than disappointed. Her disappointment lay in that this man she had taken to mold, refused to be molded. To a certain extent she had found his clay plastic, then it had developed stubbornness, declining to be shaped in the image of her father or of Mr. Butler.

What was great and strong in him, she missed, or, worse yet, misunderstood. This man, whose clay was so plastic that he could live in any number of pigeonholes of human existence, she thought willful and most obstinate because she could not shape him to live in her pigeonhole, which was the only one she knew. She could not follow the flights of his mind, and when his brain got beyond her, she deemed him erratic. Nobody else's brain ever got beyond her. She could always follow her father and mother, her brothers and Olney; wherefore, when she could not follow Martin, she believed the fault lay with him. It was the old tragedy of insularity trying to serve as mentor to the universal.

"You worship at the shrine of the established," he told her once, in a discussion they had over Praps and Vanderwater. "I grant that as authorities to quote they are most excellent—the two foremost literary critics in the United States. Every school teacher in the land looks up to Vanderwater as the Dean of American criticism. Yet I read his stuff, and it seems to me the perfection of the felicitous expression of the inane. Why, he is no more than a ponderous bromide, thanks to Gelett Burgess. And Praps is no better. His 'Hemlock Mosses,' for instance, is beautifully written. Not a comma is out of place; and the tone—ah!—is lofty, so lofty. He is the best-paid critic in the United States.

Though, Heaven forbid! he's not a critic at all. They do criticism better in England.

"But the point is, they sound the popular note, and they sound it so beautifully and morally and contentedly. Their reviews remind me of a British Sunday. They are the popular mouthpieces. They back up your professors of English, and your professors of English back them up. And there isn't an original idea in any of their skulls. They know only the established,—in fact, they are the established. They are weak minded, and the established impresses itself upon them as easily as the name of the brewery is impressed on a beer bottle. And their function is to catch all the young fellows attending the university, to drive out of their minds any glimmering originality that may chance to be there, and to put upon them the stamp of the established."

"I think I am nearer the truth," she replied, "when I stand by the established, than you are, raging around like an iconoclastic South Sea Islander."

"It was the missionary who did the image breaking," he laughed. "And unfortunately, all the missionaries are off among the heathen, so there are none left at home to break those old images, Mr. Vanderwater and Mr. Praps."

"And the college professors, as well," she added.

He shook his head emphatically. "No; the science professors should live. They're really great. But it would be a good deed to break the heads of nine-tenths of the English professors—little, microscopic-minded parrots!"

Which was rather severe on the professors, but which to Ruth was blasphemy. She could not help but measure the professors, neat, scholarly, in fitting clothes, speaking in well-modulated voices, breathing of culture and refinement, with this almost indescribable young fellow whom somehow she loved, whose clothes never would fit him, whose heavy muscles told of damning toil, who grew excited when he talked, substituting abuse for calm statement and passionate utterance for cool self-possession. They at least earned good salaries and were—yes, she compelled herself to face it—were gentlemen; while he could not earn a penny, and he was not as they.

She did not weigh Martin's words nor judge his argument by them. Her conclusion that his argument was wrong was reached—unconsciously, it is true—by a comparison of externals. They, the professors, were right in their literary judgments because they were successes. Martin's literary judgments were wrong because he could not sell his wares. To use his own phrase, they made good, and he did not make good. And besides, it did not seem reasonable that he should be right—he who had stood, so short a time before, in that same living room, blushing and awkward, acknowledging his introduction, looking fearfully about him at the bric-a-brac his swinging shoulders threatened to break, asking how long since Swinburne died, and boastfully announcing that he had read "Excelsior" and the "Psalm of Life."

Unwittingly, Ruth herself proved his point that she worshipped the established. Martin followed the processes of her thoughts, but forbore to go farther. He did not love her for what she thought of Praps and Vanderwater and English professors, and he was coming to realize, with increasing conviction, that he possessed brain-areas and stretches of knowledge which she could never comprehend nor know existed.

In music she thought him unreasonable, and in the matter of opera not only unreasonable but willfully perverse.

"How did you like it?" she asked him one night, on the way home from the opera.

It was a night when he had taken her at the expense of a month's rigid economizing on food. After vainly waiting for him to speak about it, herself still tremulous and stirred by what she had just seen and heard, she had asked the question.

"I liked the overture," was his answer. "It was splendid."

"Yes, but the opera itself?"

"That was splendid too; that is, the orchestra was, though I'd have enjoyed it more if those jumping-jacks had kept quiet or gone off the stage."

Ruth was aghast.

"You don't mean Tetralani or Barillo?" she queried.

"All of them—the whole kit and crew."

"But they are great artists," she protested.

"They spoiled the music just the same, with their antics and unrealities."

"But don't you like Barillo's voice?" Ruth asked. "He is next to Caruso, they say."

"Of course I liked him, and I liked Tetralani even better. Her voice is exquisite—or at least I think so."

"But, but—" Ruth stammered. "I don't know what you mean, then. You admire their voices, yet say they spoiled the music."

"Precisely that. I'd give anything to hear them in concert, and I'd give even a bit more not to hear them when the orchestra is playing. I'm afraid I am a hopeless realist. Great singers are not great actors. To hear Barillo sing a love passage with the voice of an angel, and to hear Tetralani reply like another angel, and to hear it all accompanied by a perfect orgy of glowing and colorful music—is ravishing, most ravishing. I do not admit it. I assert it. But the whole effect is spoiled when I look at them—at Tetralani, five feet ten in her stocking feet and weighing a hundred and ninety pounds, and at Barillo, a scant five feet four, greasy-featured, with the chest of a squat, undersized black-smith, and at the pair of them, attitudinizing, clasping their breasts, flinging their arms in the air like de-mented creatures in an asylum; and when I am ex-pected to accept all this as the faithful illusion of a love-scene between a slender and beautiful princess and a handsome, romantic, young prince—why, I can't accept it, that's all. It's rot; it's absurd; it's unreal. That's what's the matter with it. It's not real. Don't tell me that anybody in this world ever made love that way. Why, if I'd made love to you in such fashion, you'd have boxed my ears."

"But you misunderstand," Ruth protested. "Every form of art has its limitations." (She was busy recalling a lecture she had heard at the university on the con-ventions of the arts.) "In painting there are only two dimensions to the canvas, yet you accept the illusion of three dimensions which the art of a painter enables him to throw into the canvas. In writing, again, the author must be omnipotent. You accept as perfectly legitimate the author's account of the secret thoughts of the heroine, and yet all the time you know that the heroine was alone when thinking these thoughts, and that neither the author nor any one else was capable of hearing them. And so with the stage, with sculp-ture, with opera, with every art form. Certain irrec-oncilable things must be accepted."

"Yes, I understood that," Martin answered. "All the arts have their conventions." (Ruth was surprised at his use of the word. It was as if he had studied at the university himself, instead of being ill-equipped from browsing at haphazard through the books in the library.) "But even the conventions must be real. Trees, painted on flat cardboard and stuck up on each side of the stage, we accept as a forest. It is a real enough convention. But, on the other hand, we would not accept a sea scene as a forest. We can't do it. It violates our senses. Nor would you, or, rather, should you, accept the ravings and writhings and agonized contortions of those two lunatics tonight as a convincing portrayal of love."

"But you don't hold yourself superior to all the judges of music?" she protested.

"No, no, not for a moment. I merely maintain my right as an individual. I have just been telling you what I think, in order to explain why the elephantine gambols of Madame Tetralani spoil the orchestra for me. The world's judges of music may all be right. But I am I, and I won't subordinate my taste to the unanimous judgment of mankind. If I don't like a thing, I don't like it, that's all; and there is no reason under the sun why I should ape a liking for it just because the majority of my fellow-creatures like it, or make believe they like it. I can't follow the fashions in the things I like or dislike."

"But music, you know, is a matter of training," Ruth argued, "and opera is even more a matter of training. May it not be—"

"That I am not trained in opera?" he dashed in.

She nodded.

"The very thing," he agreed. "And I consider I am fortunate in not having been caught when I was young. If I had, I could have wept sentimental tears tonight, and the clownish antics of that precious pair would have but enhanced the beauty of their voices and the beauty of the accompanying orchestra. You are right.

It's mostly a matter of training. And I am too old, now. I must have the real or nothing. An illusion that won't convince is a palpable lie, and that's what grand opera is to me when little Barillo throws a fit, clutches mighty Tetralani in his arms (also in a fit), and tells her how passionately he adores her."

Again Ruth measured his thoughts by comparison of externals and in accordance with her belief in the established. Who was he that he should be right and all the cultured world wrong? His words and thoughts made no impression upon her. She was too firmly intrenched in the established to have any sympathy with revolutionary ideas. She had always been used to music, and she had enjoyed opera ever since she was a child, and all her world had enjoyed it, too. Then by what right did Martin Eden emerge, as he had so recently emerged, from his ragtime and work-ing-class songs, and pass judgment on the world's mu-sic? She was vexed with him, and as she walked beside him she had a vague feeling of outrage. At the best, in her most charitable frame of mind, she considered the statement of his views to be a caprice, an erratic and uncalled-for prank. But when he took her in his arms at the door and kissed her good night in tender lover-fashion, she forgot everything in the outrush of her own love to him. And later, on a sleepless pillow, she puzzled, as she had often puzzled of late, as to how it was that she loved so strange a man, and loved him despite the disapproval of her people.

And next day Martin Eden cast hack-work aside, and at white heat hammered out an essay to which he gave the title, "The Philosophy of Illusion." A stamp started it on its travels, but it was destined to receive many stamps and to be started on many travels in the months that followed.

Chapter Twenty-five

Maria Silva was poor, and all the ways of poverty were clear to her. Poverty, to Ruth, was a word signifying a not-nice condition of existence. That was her total knowledge on the subject. She knew Martin was poor, and his condition she associated in her mind with the boyhood of Abraham Lincoln, of Mr. Butler, and of other men who had become successes. Also, while aware that poverty was anything but delectable, she had a comfortable middle-class feeling that poverty was salutary, that it was a sharp spur that urged on to success all men who were not degraded and hopeless drudges. So that her knowledge that Martin was so poor that he had pawned his watch and overcoat did not disturb her. She even considered it the hopeful side of the situation, believing that sooner or later it would arouse him and compel him to abandon his writing.

Ruth never read hunger in Martin's face, which had grown lean and had enlarged the slight hollows in the cheeks. In fact, she marked the change in his face with satisfaction. It seemed to refine him, to remove from him much of the dross of flesh and the too animal-like vigor that lured her while she detested it. Sometimes, when with him, she noted an unusual brightness in his eyes, and she admired it, for it made him appear more the poet and the scholar—the things he would have liked to be and which she would have liked him to be. But Maria Silva read a different tale in the hollow cheeks and the burning eyes, and she noted the changes in them from day to day, by them following the ebb and flow of his fortunes. She saw him leave the house with his overcoat and return without it, though the day was chill and raw, and promptly she saw his cheeks fill out slightly and the fire of hunger leave his eyes. In the same way she had seen his wheel and watch go, and after each event she had seen his vigor bloom again.

Likewise she watched his toils, and knew the measure of the midnight oil he burned. Work! She knew that he outdid her, though his work was of a different order. And she was surprised to behold that the less food he had, the harder he worked. On occasion, in a casual sort of way, when she thought hunger pinched hardest, she would send him in a loaf of new baking, awkwardly covering the act with banter to the effect that it was better than he could bake. And again, she would send one of her toddlers in to him with a great pitcher of hot soup, debating inwardly the while whether she was justified in taking it from the mouths of her own flesh and blood. Nor was Martin ungrateful, knowing as he did the lives of the poor, and that if ever in the world there was charity, this was it.

On a day when she had filled her brood with what was left in the house, Maria invested her last fifteen cents in a gallon of cheap wine. Martin, coming into her kitchen to fetch water, was invited to sit down and drink. He drank her very good health, and in return she drank his. Then she drank to prosperity in his undertakings, and he drank to the hope that James Grant would show up and pay her for his washing. James Grant was a journeyman carpenter who did not always pay his bills and who owed Maria three dollars.

Both Maria and Martin drank the sour new wine on empty stomachs, and it went swiftly to their heads. Utterly differentiated creatures that they were, they were lonely in their misery, and though the misery was tacitly ignored, it was the bond that drew them together. Maria was amazed to learn that he had been in the Azores, where she had lived until she was eleven. She was doubly amazed that he had been in the Hawaiian Islands, whither she had migrated from the Azores with her people. But her amazement passed all bounds when he told her he had been on Maui, the particular island whereon she had attained womanhood and married. Kahului, where she had first met her husband,—he, Martin, had been there twice! Yes, she remembered the sugar steamers, and he had been on them—well, well, it was a small world. And Wailuku! That place, too! Did he know the head-luna of the plantation? Yes, and had had a couple of drinks with him.

And so they reminisced and drowned their hunger in the raw, sour wine. To Martin the future did not seem so dim. Success trembled just before him. He was on the verge of clasping it. Then he studied the deep-lined face of the toil-worn woman before him, remembered her soups and loaves of new baking, and felt spring up in him the warmest gratitude and philanthropy.

"Maria," he exclaimed suddenly. "What would you like to have?"

She looked at him, bepuzzled.

"What would you like to have now, right now, if you could get it?"

"Shoe alla da roun' for da childs—seven pairs da shoe."

"You shall have them," he announced, while she nodded her head gravely. "But I mean a big wish, something big that you want."

Her eyes sparkled good-naturedly. He was choosing to make fun with her, Maria, with whom few made fun these days.

"Think hard," he cautioned, just as she was opening her mouth to speak.

"Alla right," she answered. "I thinka da hard. I lika da house, dis house—all mine, no paya da rent, seven dollar da month."

"You shall have it," he granted, "and in a short time. Now wish the great wish. Make believe I am God, and I say to you anything you want you can have. Then you wish that thing, and I listen."

Maria considered solemnly for a space.

"You no 'fraid?" she asked warningly.

"No, no," he laughed, "I'm not afraid. Go ahead."

"Most verra big," she warned again.

"All right. Fire away."

"Well, den—" She drew a big breath like a child, as she voiced to the uttermost all she cared to demand of life. "I lika da have one milka ranch—good milka ranch. Plenty cow, plenty land, plenty grass. I lika da have near San Le-an; my sister liva dere. I sella da milka in Oakland. I maka da plentee mon. Joe an' Nick no runna da cow. Dey go-a to school, Bimeby maka da good engineer, worka da railroad. Yes, I lika da milka ranch."

She paused and regarded Martin with twinkling eyes.

"You shall have it," he answered promptly.

She nodded her head and touched her lips courteously to the wine-glass and to the giver of the gift she knew would never be given. His heart was right, and in her own heart she appreciated his intention as much as if the gift had gone with it.

"No, Maria," he went on; "Nick and Joe won't have to peddle milk, and all the kids can go to school and wear shoes the whole year round. It will be a first-class milk ranch—everything complete. There will be a house to live in and a stable for the horses, and cow-barns, of course. There will be chickens, pigs, vegetables, fruit trees, and everything like that; and there will be enough cows to pay for a hired man or two. Then you won't have anything to do but take care of the children. For that matter, if you find a good man, you can marry and take it easy while he runs the ranch."

And from such largesse, dispensed from his future, Martin turned and took his one good suit of clothes to the pawnshop. His plight was desperate for him to do this, for it cut him off from Ruth. He had no second-best suit that was presentable, and though he could go to the butcher and the baker, and even on occasion to his sister's, it was beyond all daring to dream of entering the Morse home so disreputably appareled.

He toiled on, miserable and well-nigh hopeless. It began to appear to him that the second battle was lost and that he would have to go to work. In doing this he would satisfy everybody—the grocer, his sister, Ruth, and even Maria, to whom he owed a month's room rent. He was two months behind with his typewriter, and the agency was clamoring for payment or for the return of the machine. In desperation, all but ready to surrender, to make a truce with fate until he could get a fresh start, he took the civil service examinations for the Railway Mail. To his surprise, he passed first. The job was assured, though when the call would come to enter upon his duties nobody knew.

It was at this time, at the lowest ebb, that the smooth-running editorial machine broke down. A cog must have slipped or an oil-cup run dry, for the postman brought him one morning a short, thin envelope. Martin glanced at the upper left-hand corner and read the name and address of the *Transcontinental Monthly*. His heart gave a great leap, and he suddenly felt faint, the sinking feeling accompanied by a strange trembling of the knees. He staggered into his room and sat down on the bed, the envelope still unopened, and in that moment came understanding to him how people suddenly fall dead upon receipt of extraordinarily good news.

Of course this was good news. There was no manuscript in that thin envelope, therefore it was an acceptance. He knew the story in the hands of the *Transcontinental*. It was "The Ring of Bells," one of his horror stories, and it was an even five thousand words. And, since first-class magazines always paid on acceptance, there was a check inside. Two cents a word—twenty dollars a thousand; the check must be a hundred dollars. One hundred dollars! As he tore the envelope open, every item of all his debts surged in his brain—$3.85 to the grocer; butcher, $4.00 flat; baker, $2.00; fruit store, $5.00; total $14.85. Then there was room rent, $2.50; another month in advance, $2.50; two months' typewriter, $8.00; a month in advance, $4.00; total, $31.85. And finally to be added, his pledges, plus interest, with the pawnbroker—watch, $5.50; overcoat, $5.50; wheel, $7.75; suit of clothes, $5.50 (60% interest, but what did it matter?)—grand total, $56.10. He saw, as if visible in the air before him, in illuminated figures, the whole sum, and the subtraction that followed and that gave a remainder of $43.90. When he had squared every debt, redeemed every pledge, he would still have jingling in his pockets a princely $43.90. And on top of that he would have a month's rent paid in advance on the typewriter and on the room.

By this time he had drawn the single sheet of typewritten letter out and spread it open. There was no check. He peered into the envelope, held it to the light, but could not trust his eyes, and in trembling haste tore the envelope apart. There was no check. He read the letter, skimming it line by line, dashing through the editor's praise of his story to the meat of the letter, the statement why the check had not been sent. He found no such statement, but he did find that which made him suddenly wilt. The letter slid from his hand. His eyes went lack-luster, and he lay back on the pillow, pulling the blanket about him and up to his chin.

Five dollars for "The Ring of Bells"—five dollars for five thousand words! Instead of two cents a word, ten words for a cent! And the editor had praised it, too. And he would receive the check when the story was published. Then it was all poppycock, two cents a word for minimum rate and payment upon acceptance. It was a lie, and it had led him astray. He would never have attempted to write had he known that. He would have gone to work—to work for Ruth. He went back to the day he first attempted to write, and was appalled at the enormous waste of time—and all for ten words for a cent. And the other high rewards of writers, that he had read about, must be lies, too. His second-hand ideas of authorship were wrong, for here was the proof of it.

The *Transcontinental* sold for twenty-five cents, and its dignified and artistic cover proclaimed it as among the first-class magazines. It was a staid, respectable magazine, and it had been published continuously since long before he was born. Why, on the outside cover were printed every month the words of one of the world's great writers, words proclaiming the inspired mission of the *Transcontinental* by a star of literature whose first coruscations had appeared inside those self-same covers. And the high and lofty, heaven-inspired

Transcontinental paid five dollars for five thousand words! The great writer had recently died in a foreign land— in dire poverty, Martin remembered, which was not to be wondered at, considering the magnificent pay authors receive.

Well, he had taken the bait, the newspaper lies about writers and their pay, and he had wasted two years over it. But he would disgorge the bait now. Not another line would he ever write. He would do what Ruth wanted him to do, what everybody wanted him to do—get a job. The thought of going to work reminded him of Joe—Joe, tramping through the land of nothing-to-do. Martin heaved a great sigh of envy. The reaction of nineteen hours a day for many days was strong upon him. But then, Joe was not in love, had none of the responsibilities of love, and he could afford to loaf through the land of nothing-to-do. He, Martin, had something to work for, and go to work he would. He would start out early next morning to hunt a job. And he would let Ruth know, too, that he had mended his ways and was willing to go into her father's office.

Five dollars for five thousand words, ten words for a cent, the market price for art. The disappointment of it, the lie of it, the infamy of it, were uppermost in his thoughts; and under his closed eyelids, in fiery figures, burned the "$3.85" he owed the grocer. He shivered, and was aware of an aching in his bones. The small of his back ached especially. His head ached, the top of it ached, the back of it ached, the brains inside of it ached and seemed to be swelling, while the ache over his brows was intolerable. And beneath the brows, planted under his lids, was the merciless "$3.85." He opened his eyes to escape it, but the white light of the room seemed to sear the balls and forced him to close his eyes, when the "$3.85" confronted him again.

Five dollars for five thousand words, ten words for a cent—that particular thought took up its residence in his brain, and he could no more escape it than he could the "$3.85" under his eyelids. A change seemed to come over the latter, and he watched curiously, till "$2.00" burned in its stead. Ah, he thought, that was the baker. The next sum that appeared was "$2.50." It puzzled him, and he pondered it as if life and death hung on the solution. He owed somebody two dollars and a half, that was certain, but who was it? To find it was the task set him by an imperious and malignant universe, and he wandered through the endless corridors of his mind, opening all manner of lumber rooms and chambers stored with odds and ends of memories and knowledge as he vainly sought the answer. After several centuries it came to him, easily, without effort, that it was Maria. With a great relief he turned his soul to the screen of torment under his lids. He had solved the problem; now he could rest. But no, the "$2.50" faded away, and in its place burned "$8.00." Who was that? He must go the dreary round of his mind again and find out.

How long he was gone on this quest he did not know, but after what seemed an enormous lapse of time, he was called back to himself by a knock at the door, and by Maria's asking if he was sick. He replied in a muffled voice he did not recognize, saying that he was merely taking a nap. He was surprised when he noted the darkness of night in the room. He had received the letter at two in the afternoon, and he realized that he was sick.

Then the "$8.00" began to smolder under his lids again, and he returned himself to servitude. But he grew cunning. There was no need for him to wander through his mind. He had been a fool. He pulled a lever and made his mind revolve about him, a monstrous wheel of fortune, a merry-go-round of memory, a revolving sphere of wisdom. Faster and faster it revolved, until its vortex sucked him in and he was flung whirling through black chaos.

Quite naturally he found himself at a mangle, feeding starched cuffs. But as he fed he noticed figures printed on the cuffs. It was a new way of marking linen, he thought, until, looking closer, he saw "$3.85" on one of the cuffs. Then it came to him that it was the grocer's bill, and that these were his bills flying around on the drum of the mangle. A crafty idea came to him. He would throw the bills on the floor and so escape paying them. No sooner thought than done, and he crumpled the cuffs spitefully as he flung them upon an unusually dirty floor. Ever the heap grew, and though each bill was duplicated a thousand times, he found only one for two dollars and a half, which was what he owed Maria. That meant that Maria would not press for payment, and he resolved generously that it would be the only one he would pay; so he began searching through the castout heap for hers. He sought it desperately, for ages, and was still searching when the manager of the hotel entered, the fat Dutchman. His face blazed with wrath, and he shouted in stentorian tones that echoed down the universe, "I shall deduct the cost of those cuffs from your wages!" The pile of cuffs grew into a mountain, and Martin knew that he was doomed to toil for a thousand years to pay for them. Well, there was nothing left to do but kill the manager and burn down the laundry. But the big Dutchman frustrated him, seizing him by the nape of the neck and dancing him up and down. He danced him over the ironing tables, the stove, and the mangles, and out into the washroom and over the wringer and washer. Martin was danced until his teeth rattled and his head ached, and he marveled that the Dutchman was so strong.

And then he found himself before the mangle, this time receiving the cuffs an editor of a magazine was feeding from the other side. Each cuff was a check, and Martin went over them anxiously, in a fever of expectation, but they were all blanks. He stood there and received the blanks for a million years or so, never letting one go by for fear it might be filled out. At last he found it. With trembling fingers he held it to the light. It was for five dollars. "Ha! Ha!" laughed the editor across the mangle. "Well, then, I shall kill you," Martin said. He went out into the washroom to get the ax, and found Joe starching manuscripts. He tried to make him desist, then swung the ax for him. But the weapon remained poised in mid-air, for Martin found himself back in the ironing room in the midst of a snow-storm. No, it was not snow that was falling, but checks of large denomination, the smallest not less than a thousand dollars. He began to collect them and sort them out, in packages of a hundred, tying each package securely with twine.

He looked up from his task and saw Joe standing before him juggling flat-irons, starched shirts, and manuscripts. Now and again he reached out and added a bundle of checks to the flying miscellany that soared through the roof and out of sight in a tremendous circle. Martin struck at him, but he seized the ax and added it to the flying circle. Then he plucked Martin and added him. Martin went up through the roof, clutching at manuscripts, so that by the time he came down he had a large armful. But no sooner down than up again, and a second and a third time and countless times he flew around the circle. From far off he could hear a childish treble singing: "Waltz me around again, Willie, around, around, around."

He recovered the ax in the midst of the Milky Way of checks, starched shirts, and manuscripts, and prepared, when he came down, to kill Joe. But he did not come down. Instead, at two in the morning, Maria, having heard his groans through the thin partition, came into his room, to put hot flat-irons against his body and damp cloths upon his aching eyes.

Chapter Twenty-six

M artin Eden did not go out to hunt for a job in the morning. It was late afternoon before he came out of his delirium and gazed with aching eyes about the room. Mary, one of the tribe of Silva, eight years old, keeping watch, raised a screech at sight of his returning consciousness. Maria hurried into the room from the kitchen. She put her work-callused hand upon his hot forehead and felt his pulse.

"You lika da eat?" she asked.

He shook his head. Eating was farthest from his desire, and he wondered that he should ever have been hungry in his life.

"I'm sick, Maria," he said weakly. "What is it? Do you know?"

"Grip," she answered. "Two or three days you alla da right. Better you no eat now. Bimeby plenty can eat, tomorrow can eat maybe."

Martin was not used to sickness, and when Maria

and her little girl left him, he essayed to get up and dress. By a supreme exertion of will, with reeling brain and eyes that ached so that he could not keep them open, he managed to get out of bed, only to be left stranded by his senses upon the table. Half an hour later he managed to regain the bed, where he was content to lie with closed eyes and analyze his various pains and weaknesses. Maria came in several times to change the cold cloths on his forehead. Otherwise she left him in peace, too wise to vex him with chatter. This moved him to gratitude, and he murmured to himself, "Maria, you getta da milka ranch, all righta, all right."

Then he remembered his long-buried past of yesterday. It seemed a life-time since he had received that letter from the *Transcontinental*, a life-time since it was all over and done with and a new page turned. He had shot his bolt, and shot it hard, and now he was down on his back. If he hadn't starved himself, he wouldn't have been caught by La Grippe. He had been run down, and he had not had the strength to throw off the germ of disease which had invaded his system. This was what resulted.

"What does it profit a man to write a whole library and lose his own life?" he demanded aloud. "This is no place for me. No more literature in mine. Me for the counting-house and ledger, the monthly salary, and the little home with Ruth."

Two days later, having eaten an egg and two slices of toast and drunk a cup of tea, he asked for his mail, but found his eyes still hurt too much to permit him to read.

"You read for me, Maria," he said. "Never mind the big, long letters. Throw them under the table. Read me the small letters."

"No can," was the answer. "Teresa, she go to school, she can."

So Teresa Silva, aged nine, opened his letters and read them to him. He listened absently to a long dun from the typewriter people, his mind busy with ways and means of finding a job. Suddenly he was shocked back to himself.

" 'We offer you forty dollars for all serial rights in your story,' " Teresa slowly spelled out, " 'provided you allow us to make the alterations suggested.' "

"What magazine is that?" Martin shouted. "Here, give it to me!"

He could see to read, now, and he was unaware of the pain of the action. It was the *White Mouse* that was offering him forty dollars, and the story was "The Whirlpool," another of his early horror stories. He read the letter through again and again. The editor told him plainly that he had not handled the idea properly, but that it was the idea they were buying because it was original. If they could cut the story down one-third, they would take it and send him forty dollars on receipt of his answer.

He called for pen and ink, and told the editor he could cut the story down three-thirds if he wanted to, and to send the forty dollars right along.

The letter despatched to the letter-box by Teresa, Martin lay back and thought. It wasn't a lie, after all. The *White Mouse* paid on acceptance. There were three thousand words in "The Whirlpool." Cut down a third, there would be two thousand. At forty dollars that would be two cents a word. Pay on acceptance and two cents a word—the newspapers had told the truth. And he had thought the *White Mouse* a third-rater! It was evident that he did not know the magazines. He had deemed the *Transcontinental* a first-rater, and it paid a cent for ten words. He had classed the *White Mouse* as of no account, and it paid twenty times as much as the *Transcontinental* and also had paid on acceptance.

Well, there was one thing certain: when he got well, he would not go out looking for a job. There were more stories in his head as good as "The Whirlpool," and at forty dollars apiece he could earn far more than in any job or position. Just when he thought the battle lost, it was won. He had proved for his career. The way was clear. Beginning with the *White Mouse* he would add magazine after magazine to his growing list of patrons. Hack-work could be put aside. For that matter, it had been wasted time, for it had not brought him a dollar. He would devote himself to work, good work, and he would pour out the best that was in him. He wished Ruth was there to share in his joy, and when he went over the letters left lying on his bed, he found one from her. It was sweetly reproachful, wondering what had kept him away for so dreadful a length of time. He reread the letter adoringly, dwelling over her handwriting, loving each stroke of her pen, and in the end kissing her signature.

And when he answered, he told her recklessly that he had not been to see her because his best clothes were in pawn. He told her that he had been sick, but was once more nearly well, and that inside ten days or two weeks (as soon as a letter could travel to New York City and return) he would redeem his clothes and be with her.

But Ruth did not care to wait ten days or two weeks. Besides, her lover was sick. The next afternoon, accompanied by Arthur, she arrived in the Morse carriage, to the unqualified delight of the Silva tribe and of all the urchins on the street, and to the consternation of Maria. She boxed the ears of the Silvas who crowded about the visitors on the tiny front porch, and in more than usual atrocious English tried to apologize for her appearance. Sleeves rolled up from soap-flecked arms and a wet gunny-sack around her waist told of the task at which she had been caught. So flustered was she by two such grand young people asking for her lodger, that she forgot to invite them to sit down in the little parlor. To enter Martin's room, they passed through the kitchen, warm and moist and steamy from the big washing in progress. Maria, in her excitement, jammed the bedroom and bedroom-closet doors together, and for five minutes, through the partly open door, clouds of steam, smelling of soap-suds and dirt, poured into the sick chamber.

Ruth succeeded in veering right and left and right again, and in running the narrow passage between table and bed to Martin's side; but Arthur veered too wide and fetched up with clatter and bang of pots and pans in the corner where Martin did his cooking. Arthur did not linger long. Ruth occupied the only chair, and having done his duty, he went outside and stood by the gate, the center of seven marveling Silvas, who watched him as they would have watched a curiosity in a side-show. All about the carriage were gathered the children from a dozen blocks, waiting and eager for some tragic and terrible denouement. Carriages were seen on their street only for weddings and funerals. Here was neither marriage nor death; therefore, it was something transcending experience and well worth waiting for.

Martin had been wild to see Ruth. His was essentially a love-nature, and he possessed more than the average man's need for sympathy. He was starving for sympathy, which, with him, meant intelligent understanding; and he had yet to learn that Ruth's sympathy was largely sentimental and tactful, and that it proceeded from gentleness of nature rather than from understanding of the objects of her sympathy. So it was while Martin held her hand and gladly talked, that her love for him prompted her to press his hand in return, and that her eyes were moist and luminous at sight of his helplessness and of the marks suffering had stamped upon his face.

But while he told her of his two acceptances, of his despair when he received the one from the *Transcontinental*, and of the corresponding delight with which he received the one from the *White Mouse*, she did not follow him. She heard the words he uttered and understood their literal import, but she was not with him in his despair and his delight. She could not get out of herself. She was not interested in selling stories to magazines. What was important to her was matrimony. She was not aware of it, however, any more than she was aware that her desire that Martin take a position was the instinctive and preparative impulse of motherhood. She would have blushed had she been told as much in plain, set terms, and next, she might have grown indignant and asserted that her sole interest lay in the man she loved and her desire for him to make the best of himself. So, while Martin poured out his heart to her, elated with the first success his chosen work in the world had received, she paid heed to his bare words only, gazing now and again about the room, shocked by what she saw.

For the first time Ruth gazed upon the sordid face of poverty. Starving lovers had always seemed romantic to her, but she had had no idea how starving lovers lived. She had never dreamed it could be like this. Ever her gaze shifted from the room to him and

back again. The steamy smell of dirty clothes, which
had entered with her from the kitchen, was sickening.
Martin must be soaked with it, Ruth concluded, if
that awful woman washed frequently. Such was the
contagiousness of degradation. When she looked at
Martin, she seemed to see the smirch left upon him
by his surroundings. She had never seen him un-
shaven, and the three days' growth of beard on his
face was repulsive to her. Not alone did it give him
the same dark and murky aspect of the Silva house,
inside and out, but it seemed to emphasize that animal-
like strength of his which she detested. And here he
was, being confirmed in his madness by the two acceptances he took such pride in telling her about. A
little longer and he would have surrendered and gone
to work. Now he would continue on in this horrible
house, writing and starving for a few more months.

"What is that smell?" she asked suddenly.

"Some of Maria's washing smells, I imagine," was
the answer. "I am growing quite accustomed to them."

"No, no; not that. It is something else. A stale,
sickish smell."

Martin sampled the air before replying.

"I can't smell anything else, except stale tobacco
smoke," he announced.

"That's it. It is terrible. Why do you smoke so much,
Martin?"

"I don't know, except that I smoke more than usual
when I am lonely. And then, too, it's such a long-
standing habit. I learned when I was only a youngster."

"It is not a nice habit, you know," she reproved.
"It smells to heaven."

"That's the fault of the tobacco. I can afford only
the cheapest. But wait until I get that forty-dollar

check. I'll use a brand that is not offensive even to the angels. But that wasn't so bad, was it, two acceptances in three days? That forty-five dollars will pay about all my debts."

"For two years' work?" she queried.

"No, for less than a week's work. Please pass me that book over on the far corner of the table, the account book with the gray cover." He opened it and began turning over the pages rapidly. "Yes, I was right. Four days for 'The Ring of Bells,' two days for 'The Whirlpool.' That's forty-five dollars for a week's work, one hundred and eighty dollars a month. That beats any salary I can command. And, besides, I'm just beginning. A thousand dollars a month is not too much to buy for you all I want you to have. A salary of five hundred a month would be too small. That forty-five dollars is just a starter. Wait till I get my stride. Then watch my smoke."

Ruth misunderstood his slang, and reverted to cigarettes.

"You smoke more than enough as it is, and the brand of tobacco will make no difference. It is the smoking itself that is not nice, no matter what the brand may be. You are a chimney, a living volcano, a perambulating smoke-stack, and you are a perfect disgrace, Martin dear, you know you are."

She leaned toward him, entreaty in her eyes, and as he looked at her delicate face and into her pure, limpid eyes, as of old he was struck with his own unworthiness.

"I wish you wouldn't smoke any more," she whispered. "Please, for—my sake."

"All right, I won't," he cried. "I'll do anything you ask, dear love, anything; you know that."

A great temptation assailed her. In an insistent way

she had caught glimpses of the large, easy-going side of his nature, and she felt sure, if she asked him to cease attempting to write, that he would grant her wish. In the swift instant that elapsed, the words trembled on her lips. But she did not utter them. She was not quite brave enough; she did not quite dare. Instead, she leaned toward him to meet him, and in his arms murmured:—

"You know, it is really not for my sake, Martin, but for your own. I am sure smoking hurts you; and besides, it is not good to be a slave to anything, to a drug least of all."

"I shall always be your slave," he smiled.

"In which case, I shall begin issuing my commands."

She looked at him mischievously, though deep down she was already regretting that she had not preferred her largest request.

"I live but to obey, your majesty."

"Well, then, my first commandment is, Thou shalt not omit to shave every day. Look how you have scratched my cheek."

And so it ended in caresses and love-laughter. But she had made one point, and she could not expect to make more than one at a time. She felt a woman's pride in that she had made him stop smoking. Another time she would persuade him to take a position, for had he not said he would do anything she asked?

She left his side to explore the room, examining the clothes-lines of notes overhead, learning the mystery of the tackle used for suspending his wheel under the ceiling, and being saddened by the heap of manuscripts under the table which represented to her just so much wasted time. The oil-stove won her admiration, but on investigating the food shelves she found them empty.

"Why, you haven't anything to eat, you poor dear," she said with tender compassion. "You must be starving."

"I store my food in Maria's safe and in her pantry," he lied. "It keeps better there. No danger of my starving. Look at that."

She had come back to his side, and she saw him double his arm at the elbow, the biceps crawling under his shirtsleeve and swelling into a knot of muscle, heavy and hard. The sight repelled her. Sentimentally, she disliked it. But her pulse, her blood, every fiber of her, loved it and yearned for it, and, in the old, inexplicable way, she leaned toward him, not away from him. And in the moment that followed, when he crushed her in his arms, the brain of her, concerned with the superficial aspects of life, was in revolt; while the heart of her, the woman of her, concerned with life itself, exulted triumphantly. It was in moments like this that she felt to the uttermost the greatness of her love for Martin, for it was almost a swoon of delight to her to feel his strong arms about her, holding her tightly, hurting her with the grip of their fervor. At such moments she found justification for her treason to her standards, for her violation of her own high ideals, and, most of all, for her tacit disobedience to her mother and father. They did not want her to marry this man. It shocked them that she should love him. It shocked her, too, sometimes, when she was apart from him, a cool and reasoning creature. With him, she loved him—in truth, at times a vexed and worried love; but love it was, a love that was stronger than she.

"This La Grippe is nothing," he was saying. "It hurts a bit, and gives one a nasty headache, but it doesn't compare with break-bone fever."

"Have you had that, too?" she queried absently, intent on the heaven-sent justification she was finding in his arms.

And so, with absent queries, she led him on, till suddenly his words startled her.

He had had the fever in a secret colony of thirty lepers on one of the Hawaiian Islands.

"But why did you go there?" she demanded.

Such royal carelessness of body seemed criminal.

"Because I didn't know," he answered. "I never dreamed of lepers. When I deserted the schooner and landed on the beach, I headed inland for some place of hiding. For three days I lived off guavas, *ohia*-apples, and bananas, all of which grew wild in the jungle. On the fourth day I found the trail—a mere foot-trail. It led inland, and it led up. It was the way I wanted to go, and it showed signs of recent travel. At one place it ran along the crest of a ridge that was no more than a knife-edge. The trail wasn't three feet wide on the crest, and on either side the ridge fell away in precipices hundreds of feet deep. One man, with plenty of ammunition, could have held it against a hundred thousand.

"It was the only way in to the hiding-place. Three hours after I found the trail I was there, in a little mountain valley, a pocket in the midst of lava peaks. The whole place was terraced for taro-patches, fruit trees grew there, and there were eight or ten grass huts. But as soon as I saw the inhabitants I knew what I'd struck. One sight of them was enough."

"What did you do?" Ruth demanded breathlessly, listening, like any Desdemona, appalled and fascinated.

"Nothing for me to do. Their leader was a kind old fellow, pretty far gone, but he ruled like a king. He had discovered the little valley and founded the settlement—all of which was against the law. But he had guns, plenty of ammunition, and those Kanakas, trained to the shooting of wild cattle and wild pig, were dead shots. No, there wasn't any running away for Martin Eden. He stayed—for three months."

"But how did you escape?"

"I'd have been there yet, if it hadn't been for a girl there, a half-Chinese, quarter-white, and quarter-Hawaiian. She was a beauty, poor thing, and well educated. Her mother, in Honolulu, was worth a million or so. Well, this girl got me away at last. Her mother financed the settlement, you see, so the girl wasn't afraid of being punished for letting me go. But she made me swear, first, never to reveal the hiding-place; and I never have. This is the first time I have even mentioned it. The girl had just the first signs of leprosy. The fingers of her right hand were slightly twisted, and there was a small spot on her arm. That was all. I guess she is dead, now."

"But weren't you frightened? And weren't you glad to get away without catching that dreadful disease?"

"Well," he confessed, "I was a bit shivery at first; but I got used to it. I used to feel sorry for that poor girl, though. That made me forget to be afraid. She was such a beauty, in spirit as well as in appearance, and she was only slightly touched; yet she was doomed to lie there, living the life of a primitive savage and rotting slowly away. Leprosy is far more terrible than you can imagine it."

"Poor thing," Ruth murmured softly. "It's a wonder she let you get away."

"How do you mean?" Martin asked unwittingly.

"Because she must have loved you," Ruth said, still softly. "Candidly, now, didn't she?"

Martin's sunburn had been bleached by his work in

the laundry and by the indoor life he was living, while the hunger and the sickness had made his face even pale; and across this pallor flowed the slow wave of a blush. He was opening his mouth to speak, but Ruth shut him off.

"Never mind, don't answer; it's not necessary," she laughed.

But it seemed to him there was something metallic in her laughter, and that the light in her eyes was cold. On the spur of the moment it reminded him of a gale he had once experienced in the North Pacific. And for the moment the apparition of the gale rose before his eyes—a gale at night, with a clear sky and under a full moon, the huge seas glinting coldly in the moonlight. Next, he saw the girl in the leper refuge and remembered it was for love of him that she had let him go.

"She was noble," he said simply. "She gave me life."

That was all of the incident, but he heard Ruth muffle a dry sob in her throat, and noticed that she turned her face away to gaze out of the window. When she turned it back to him, it was composed, and there was no hint of the gale in her eyes.

"I'm such a silly," she said plaintively. "But I can't help it. I do so love you, Martin, I do, I do. I shall grow more catholic in time, but at present I can't help being jealous of those ghosts of the past, and you know your past is full of ghosts.

"It must be," she silenced his protest. "It could not be otherwise. And there's poor Arthur motioning me to come. He's tired waiting. And now good-by, dear.

"There's some kind of a mixture, put up by the druggists, that helps men to stop the use of tobacco," she called back from the door, "and I am going to send you some."

The door closed, but opened again.

"I do, I do," she whispered to him; and this time she was really gone.

Maria, with worshipful eyes that none the less were keen to note the texture of Ruth's garments and the cut of them (a cut unknown that produced an effect mysteriously beautiful), saw her to the carriage. The crowd of disappointed urchins stared till the carriage disappeared from view, then transferred their stare to Maria, who had abruptly become the most important person on the street. But it was one of her progeny who blasted Maria's reputation by announcing that the grand visitors had been for her lodger. After that Maria dropped back into her old obscurity and Martin began to notice the respectful manner in which he was regarded by the small fry of the neighborhood. As for Maria, Martin rose in her estimation a full hundred per cent, and had the Portuguese grocer witnessed that afternoon carriage-call he would have allowed Martin an additional three-dollars-and-eighty-five-cents' worth of credit.

Chapter Twenty-seven

The sun of Martin's good fortune rose. The day after Ruth's visit, he received a check for three dollars from a New York scandal weekly in payment for three of his triolets. Two days later a newspaper published in Chicago accepted his "Treasure Hunters," promising to pay ten dollars for it on publication. The price was small, but it was the first article he had written, his very first attempt to express his thought on the printed page. To cap everything, the adventure serial for boys, his second attempt, was accepted before the end of the week by a juvenile monthly calling itself *Youth and Age*. It was true the serial was twenty-one thousand words, and they offered to pay him sixteen dollars on publication, which was something like seventy-five cents a thousand words; but it was equally true that it was the second thing he had attempted to write and that he was himself thoroughly aware of its clumsy worthlessness.

But even his earliest efforts were not marked with the clumsiness of mediocrity. What characterized them was the clumsiness of too great strength—the clumsiness which the tyro betrays when he crushes butterflies with battering rams and hammers out vignettes with a warclub. So it was that Martin was glad to sell his early efforts for songs. He knew them for what they were, and it had not taken him long to acquire this knowledge. What he pinned his faith to was his later work. He had striven to be something more than a mere writer of magazine fiction. He had sought to equip himself with the tools of artistry. On the other hand, he had not sacrificed strength. His conscious aim had been to increase his strength by avoiding excess of strength. Nor had he departed from his love of reality. His work was realism, though he had endeavored to fuse with it the fancies and beauties of imagination. What he sought was an impassioned realism, shot through with human aspiration and faith. What he wanted was life as it was, with all its spirit-groping and soul-reaching left in.

He had discovered, in the course of his reading, two schools of fiction. One treated of man as a god, ignoring his earthly origin; the other treated of man as a clod, ignoring his heaven-sent dreams and divine possibilities. Both the god and the clod schools erred, in Martin's estimation, and erred through too great singleness of sight and purpose. There was a compromise that approximated the truth, though it flattered not the school of god, while it challenged the brute-savageness of the school of clod. It was his story, "Adventure," which had dragged with Ruth, that Martin believed had achieved his ideal of the true in fiction; and it was in an essay, "God and Clod," that he had expressed his views on the whole general subject.

But "Adventure," and all that he deemed his best work, still went begging among the editors. His early work counted for nothing in his eyes except for the money it brought, and his horror stories, two of which he had sold, he did not consider high work nor his best work. To him they were frankly imaginative and fantastic, though invested with all the glamour of the real, wherein lay their power. This investiture of the grotesque and impossible with reality, he looked upon as a trick—a skillful trick at best. Great literature could not reside in such a field. Their artistry was high, but he denied the worthwhileness of artistry when divorced from humanness. The trick had been to fling over the face of his artistry a mask of humanness, and this he had done in the half-dozen or so stories of the horror brand he had written before he emerged upon the high peaks of "Adventure," "Joy," "The Pot," and "The Wine of Life."

The three dollars he received for the triolets he used to eke out a precarious existence against the arrival of the *White Mouse* check. He cashed the first check with the suspicious Portuguese grocer, paying a dollar on account and dividing the remaining two dollars between the baker and the fruit store. Martin was not yet rich enough to afford meat, and he was on slim allowance when the *White Mouse* check arrived. He was divided on the cashing of it. He had never been in a bank in his life, much less been in one on business, and he had a naïve and childlike desire to walk into one of the big banks down in Oakland and fling down his indorsed check for forty dollars. On the other hand, practical common sense ruled that he should cash it with his grocer and thereby make an impression that would later result in an increase of credit. Reluctantly Martin yielded to the claims of the grocer, paying his bill with him in full, and receiving in change a pocketful of jingling coin. Also, he paid the other tradesmen in full, redeemed his suit and his bicycle, paid one month's rent on the typewriter, and paid Maria the overdue month for his room and a month in advance. This left him in his pocket, for emergencies, a balance of nearly three dollars.

In itself, this small sum seemed a fortune. Immediately on recovering his clothes he had gone to see Ruth, and on the way he could not refrain from jingling the little handful of silver in his pocket. He had been so long without money that, like a rescued starving man who cannot let the unconsumed food out of his sight, Martin could not keep his hand off the silver. He was not mean, nor avaricious, but the money meant more than so many dollars and cents. It stood for success, and the eagles stamped upon the coins were to him so many winged victories.

It came to him insensibly that it was a very good world. It certainly appeared more beautiful to him. For weeks it had been a very dull and somber world; but now, with nearly all debts paid, three dollars jingling in his pocket, and in his mind the consciousness of success, the sun shone bright and warm, and even a rain-squall that soaked unprepared pedestrians seemed a merry happening to him. When he starved, his thoughts had dwelt often upon the thousands he knew were starving the world over; but now that he was feasted full, the fact of the thousands starving was no longer pregnant in his brain. He forgot about them, and, being in love, remembered the countless lovers in the world. Without deliberately thinking about it, *motifs* for love-lyrics began to agitate his brain. Swept away by the creative impulse, he got off the electric car, without vexation, two blocks beyond his crossing.

He found a number of persons in the Morse home. Ruth's two girl-cousins were visiting her from San Rafael, and Mrs. Morse, under pretext of entertaining them, was pursuing her plan of surrounding Ruth with young people. The campaign had begun during Martin's enforced absence, and was already in full swing. She was making a point of having at the house men who were doing things. Thus, in addition to the cousins Dorothy and Florence, Martin encountered two university professors, one of Latin, the other of English; a young army officer just back from the Philippines, one-time schoolmate of Ruth's; a young fellow named Melville, private secretary to Joseph Perkins, head of the San Francisco Trust Company; and finally of the men, a live bank cashier, Charles Hapgood, a youngish man of thirty-five, graduate of Stanford University, member of the Nile Club and the Unity Club, and a conservative speaker for the Republican Party during campaigns—in short, a rising young man in every way. Among the women was one who painted portraits, another who was a professional musician, and still another who possessed the degree of Doctor of Sociology and who was locally famous for her social settlement work in the slums of San Francisco. But the women did not count for much in Mrs. Morse's plan. At the best, they were necessary accessories. The men who did things must be drawn to the house somehow.

"Don't get excited when you talk," Ruth admonished Martin, before the ordeal of introduction began.

He bore himself a bit stiffly at first, oppressed by a sense of his own awkwardness, especially of his shoulders, which were up to their old trick of threatening destruction to furniture and ornaments. Also, he was rendered self-conscious by the company. He had never before been in contact with such exalted beings nor with so many of them. Melville, the bank cashier, fascinated him, and he resolved to investigate him at the first opportunity. For underneath Martin's awe lurked his assertive ego, and he felt the urge to measure himself with these men and women and to find out what they had learned from the books and life which he had not learned.

Ruth's eyes roved to him frequently to see how he was getting on, and she was surprised and gladdened by the ease with which he got acquainted with her cousins. He certainly did not grow excited, while being seated removed from him the worry of his shoulders. Ruth knew them for clever girls, superficially brilliant, and she could scarcely understand their praise of Martin later that night at going to bed. But he, on the other hand, a wit in his own class, a gay quizzer and laughter-maker at dances and Sunday picnics, had found the making of fun and the breaking of good-natured lances simple enough in this environment. And on this evening success stood at his back, patting him on the shoulder and telling him that he was making good, so that he could afford to laugh and make laughter and remain unabashed.

Later, Ruth's anxiety found justification. Martin and

Professor Caldwell had got together in a conspicuous corner, and though Martin no longer wove the air with his hands, to Ruth's critical eye he permitted his own eyes to flash and glitter too frequently, talked too rapidly and warmly, grew too intense, and allowed his aroused blood to redden his cheeks too much. He lacked decorum and control, and was in decided contrast to the young professor of English with whom he talked.

But Martin was not concerned with appearances! He had been swift to note the other's trained mind and to appreciate his command of knowledge. Furthermore, Professor Caldwell did not realize Martin's concept of the average English professor. Martin wanted him to talk shop, and, though he seemed averse at first, succeeded in making him do it. For Martin did not see why a man should not talk shop.

"It's absurd and unfair," he had told Ruth weeks before, "this objection to talking shop. For what reason under the sun do men and women come together if not for the exchange of the best that is in them? And the best that is in them is what they are interested in, the thing by which they make their living, the thing they've specialized on and sat up days and nights over, and even dreamed about. Imagine Mr. Butler living up to social etiquette and enunciating his views on Paul Verlaine or the German drama or the novels of D'Annunzio. We'd be bored to death. I, for one, if I must listen to Mr. Butler, prefer to hear him talk about his law. It's the best that is in him, and life is so short that I want the best of every man and woman I meet."

"But," Ruth had objected, "there are the topics of general interest to all."

"There, you mistake," he had rushed on. "All persons in society, all cliques in society—or, rather, nearly all persons and cliques—ape their betters. Now, who are the best betters? The idlers, the wealthy idlers. They do not know, as a rule, the things known by the persons who are doing something in the world. To listen to conversation about such things would mean to be bored, wherefore the idlers decree that such things are shop and must not be talked about. Likewise they decree the things that are not shop and which may be talked about, and those things are the latest operas, latest novels, cards, billiards, cocktails, automobiles, horse shows, trout-fishing, tuna-fishing, big-game shooting, yacht sailing, and so forth—and mark you, these are the things the idlers know. In all truth, they constitute the shoptalk of the idlers. And the funniest part of it is that many of the clever people, and all the would-be clever people, allow the idlers so to impose upon them. As for me, I want the best a man's got in him, call it shop vulgarity or anything you please."

And Ruth had not understood. This attack of his on the established had seemed to her just so much willfulness of opinion.

So Martin contaminated Professor Caldwell with his own earnestness, challenging him to speak his mind. As Ruth paused beside them she heard Martin saying:—

"You surely don't pronounce such heresies in the University of California?"

Professor Caldwell shrugged his shoulders. "The honest taxpayer and the politician, you know. Sacramento gives us our appropriations and therefore we kowtow to Sacramento, and to the Board of Regents, and to the party press, or to the press of both parties."

"Yes, that's clear; but how about you?" Martin urged. "You must be a fish out of the water."

"Few like me, I imagine, in the university pond. Sometimes I am fairly sure I am out of water, and that I should belong in Paris, in Grub Street, in a hermit's cave, or in some sadly wild Bohemian crowd, drinking claret,—dago-red they call it in San Francisco,—dining in cheap restaurants in the Latin Quarter, and expressing vociferously radical views upon all creation. Really, I am frequently almost sure that I was cut out to be a radical. But then, there are so many questions on which I am not sure. I grow timid when I am face to face with my human frailty, which ever prevents me from grasping all the factors in any problem—human, vital problems, you know."

And as he talked on, Martin became aware that to his own lips had come the "Song of the Trade Wind":—

> "I am strongest at noon,
> But under the moon
> I stiffen the bunt of the sail."

He was almost humming the words, and it dawned upon him that the other reminded him of the trade-wind, of the Northeast Trade, steady, and cool, and strong. He was equable, he was to be relied upon, and withal there was a certain bafflement about him. Martin had the feeling that he never spoke his full mind, just as he had often had the feeling that the trades never blew their strongest but always held reserves of strength that were never used. Martin's trick of visioning was active as ever. His brain was a most accessible storehouse of remembered fact and fancy, and its contents seemed ever ordered and spread for his inspection. Whatever occurred in the instant present, Martin's mind immediately presented associated antithesis or similitude which ordinarily expressed themselves to him in vision. It was sheerly automatic, and his visioning was an unfailing accompaniment to the living present. Just as Ruth's face, in a momentary jealousy, had called before his eyes a forgotten moonlight gale, and as Professor Caldwell made him see again the Northeast Trade herding the white billows across the purple sea, so, from moment to moment, not disconcerting but rather identifying and classifying, new memory-visions rose before him, or spread under his eyelids, or were thrown upon the screen of his consciousness. These visions came out of the actions and sensations of the past, out of things and events and books of yesterday and last week—a countless host of apparitions that, waking or sleeping, forever thronged his mind.

So it was, as he listened to Professor Caldwell's easy flow of speech—the conversation of a clever, cultured man—that Martin kept seeing himself down all his past. He saw himself when he had been quite the hoodlum, wearing a "stiff-rim" Stetson hat and a square-cut, double-breasted coat, with a certain swagger to the shoulders and possessing the ideal of being as tough as the police permitted. He did not disguise it to himself, nor attempt to palliate it. At one time in his life he had been just a common hoodlum, the leader of a gang that worried the police and terrorized honest, working-class householders. But his ideals had changed. He glanced about him at the well-bred, well-dressed men and women, and breathed into his lungs the atmosphere of culture and refinement, and at the same moment the ghost of his early youth, in stiff-rim and square-cut, with swagger and toughness, stalked across the room. This figure, of the corner hoodlum, he saw merge into himself, sitting and talking with an actual university professor.

For, after all, he had never found his permanent abiding place. He had fitted in wherever he found himself, been a favorite always and everywhere by virtue of holding his own at work and at play and by his willingness and ability to fight for his rights and command respect. But he had never taken root. He had fitted in sufficiently to satisfy his fellows but not to satisfy himself. He had been perturbed always by a feeling of unrest, had heard always the call of something from beyond, and had wandered on through life seeking it until he found books and art and love. And here he was, in the midst of all this, the only one of all the comrades he had adventured with who could have made themselves eligible for the inside of the Morse home.

But such thoughts and visions did not prevent him from following Professor Caldwell closely. And as he followed, comprehendingly and critically, he noted the unbroken field of the other's knowledge. As for himself, from moment to moment the conversation showed him gaps and open stretches, whole subjects with which he was unfamiliar. Nevertheless, thanks to his Spencer, he saw that he possessed the outlines of the field of knowledge. It was a matter only of time, when he would fill in the outline. Then watch out, he thought—'ware shoal, everybody! He felt like sitting at the feet of the professor, worshipful and absorbent; but, as he listened, he began to discern a weakness in the other's judgments—a weakness so stray and elusive that he might not have caught it had it not been ever present. And when he did catch it, he leapt to equality at once.

Ruth came up to them a second time, just as Martin began to speak.

"I'll tell you where you are wrong, or, rather, what

weakens your judgments," he said. "You lack biology. It has no place in your scheme of things.—Oh, I mean the real interpretative biology, from the ground up, from the laboratory and the test-tube and the vitalized inorganic right on up to the widest æsthetic and sociological generalizations."

Ruth was appalled. She had sat two lecture courses under Professor Caldwell and looked up to him as the living repository of all knowledge.

"I scarcely follow you," he said dubiously.

Martin was not so sure but what he had followed him.

"Then I'll try to explain," he said. "I remember reading in Egyptian history something to the effect that understanding could not be had of Egyptian art without first studying the land question."

"Quite right," the professor nodded.

"And it seems to me," Martin continued, "that knowledge of the land question, in turn, of all questions, for that matter, cannot be had without previous knowledge of the stuff and the constitution of life. How can we understand laws and institutions, religions and customs, without understanding, not merely the nature of the creatures that made them, but the nature of the stuff out of which the creatures are made? Is literature less human than the architecture and sculpture of Egypt? Is there one thing in the known universe that is not subject to the law of evolution?— Oh, I know there is an elaborate evolution of the various arts laid down, but it seems to me to be too mechanical. The human himself is left out. The evolution of the tool, of the harp, of music and song and dance, are all beautifully elaborated; but how about the evolution of the human himself, the development of the basic and intrinsic parts that were in him before he made his first tool or gibbered his first chant? It is that which you do not consider, and which I call biology. It is biology in its largest aspects.

"I know I express myself incoherently, but I've tried to hammer out the idea. It came to me as you were talking, so I was not primed and ready to deliver it. You spoke yourself of the human frailty that prevented one from taking all the factors into consideration. And you, in turn,—or so it seems to me,—leave out the biological factor, the very stuff out of which has been spun the fabric of all the arts, the warp and the woof of all human actions and achievements."

To Ruth's amazement, Martin was not immediately crushed, and that the professor replied in the way he did struck her as forbearance for Martin's youth. Professor Caldwell sat for a full minute, silent and fingering his watch chain.

"Do you know," he said at last, "I've had that same criticism passed on me once before—by a very great man, a scientist and evolutionist, Joseph Le Conte. But he is dead, and I thought to remain undetected; and now you come along and expose me. Seriously, though—and this is confession—I think there is something in your contention—a great deal, in fact. I am too classical, not enough up-to-date in the interpretative branches of science, and I can only plead the disadvantages of my education and a temperamental slothfulness that prevents me from doing the work. I wonder if you'll believe that I've never been inside a physics or chemistry laboratory? It is true, nevertheless. Le Conte was right, and so are you, Mr. Eden, at least to an extent—how much I do not know."

Ruth drew Martin away with her on a pretext; when she had got him aside, whispering:—

"You shouldn't have monopolized Professor Caldwell that way. There may be others who want to talk with him."

"My mistake," Martin admitted contritely. "But I'd got him stirred up, and he was so interesting that I did not think. Do you know, he is the brightest, the most intellectual man I have ever talked with. And I'll tell you something else. I once thought that everybody who went to universities, or who sat in the high places in society, was just as brilliant and intelligent as he."

"He's an exception," she answered.

"I should say so. Whom do you want me to talk to now?—Oh, say, bring me up against that cashier fellow."

Martin talked for fifteen minutes with him, nor could Ruth have wished better behavior on her lover's part. Not once did his eyes flash nor his cheeks flush, while the calmness and poise with which he talked surprised her. But in Martin's estimation the whole tribe of bank cashiers fell a few hundred per cent, and for the rest of the evening he labored under the impression that bank cashiers and talkers of platitudes were synonymous phrases. The army officer he found good-natured and simple, a healthy, wholesome young fellow, content to occupy the place in life into which birth and luck had flung him. On learning that he had completed two years in the university, Martin was puzzled to know where he had stored it away. Nevertheless Martin liked him better than the platitudinous bank cashier.

"I really don't object to platitudes," he told Ruth later, "but what worries me into nervousness is the pompous, smugly complacent, superior certitude with which they are uttered and the time taken to do it. Why, I could give that man the whole history of the

Reformation in the time he took to tell me that the Union-Labor Party had fused with the Democrats. Do you know, he skins his words as a professional poker-player skins the cards that are dealt out to him. Some day I'll show you what I mean."

"I'm sorry you don't like him," was her reply. "He's a favorite of Mr. Butler's. Mr. Butler says he is safe and honest—calls him the Rock, Peter, and says that upon him any banking institution can well be built."

"I don't doubt it—from the little I saw of him and the less I heard from him; but I don't think so much of banks as I did. You don't mind my speaking my mind this way, dear?"

"No, no; it is most interesting."

"Yes," Martin went on heartily, "I'm no more than a barbarian getting my first impressions of civilization. Such impressions must be entertainingly novel to the civilized person."

"What did you think of my cousins?" Ruth queried.

"I liked them better than the other women. There's plenty of fun in them along with paucity of pretense."

"Then you did like the other women?"

He shook his head.

"That social-settlement woman is no more than a sociological poll-parrot. I swear, if you winnowed her out between the stars, like Tomlinson, there would be found in her not one original thought. As for the portrait-painter, she was a positive bore. She'd make a good wife for the cashier. And the musician woman! I don't care how nimble her fingers are, how perfect her technique, how wonderful her expression—the fact is, she knows nothing about music."

"She plays beautifully," Ruth protested.

"Yes, she's undoubtedly gymnastic in the externals of music, but the intrinsic spirit of music is unguessed by her. I asked her what music meant to her—you know I'm always curious to know that particular thing; and she did not know what it meant to her, except that she adored it, that it was the greatest of the arts, and that it meant more than life to her."

"You were making them talk shop," Ruth charged him.

"I confess it. And if they were failures on shop, imagine my sufferings if they had discoursed on other subjects. Why, I used to think that up here, where all the advantages of culture were enjoyed—" He paused for a moment, and watched the youthful shade of himself, in stiff-rim and square-cut, enter the door and swagger across the room. "As I was saying, up here I thought all men and women were brilliant and radiant. But now, from what little I've seen of them, they strike me as a pack of ninnies, most of them, and ninety per cent of the remainder as bores. Now there's Professor Caldwell—he's different. He's a man, every inch of him and every atom of his gray matter."

Ruth's face brightened.

"Tell me about him," she urged. "Not what is large and brilliant—I know those qualities; but whatever you feel is adverse. I am most curious to know."

"Perhaps I'll get myself in a pickle." Martin debated humorously for a moment. "Suppose you tell me first. Or maybe you find in him nothing less than the best."

"I attended two lecture courses under him, and I have known him for two years; that is why I am anxious for your first impression."

"Bad impression, you mean? Well, here goes. He is all the fine things you think about him, I guess. At least, he is the finest specimen of intellectual man I have met; but he is a man with a secret shame.

"Oh, no, no!" he hastened to cry. "Nothing paltry

nor vulgar. What I mean is that he strikes me as a man who has gone to the bottom of things, and is so afraid of what he saw that he makes believe to himself that he never saw it. Perhaps that's not the clearest way to express it. Here's another way. A man who has found the path to the hidden temple but has not followed it; who has, perhaps, caught glimpses of the temple and striven afterward to convince himself that it was only a mirage of foliage. Yet another way. A man who could have done things but who placed no value on the doing, and who, all the time, in his innermost heart, is regretting that he has not done them; who has secretly laughed at the rewards for doing, and yet, still more secretly, has yearned for the rewards and for the joy of doing."

"I don't read him that way," she said. "And for that matter, I don't see just what you mean."

"It is only a vague feeling on my part," Martin temporized. "I have no reason for it. It is only a feeling, and most likely it is wrong. You certainly should know him better than I."

From the evening at Ruth's Martin brought away with him strange confusions and conflicting feelings. He was disappointed in his goal, in the persons he had climbed to be with. On the other hand, he was encouraged with his success. The climb had been easier than he expected. He was superior to the climb, and (he did not, with false modesty, hide it from himself) he was superior to the beings among whom he had climbed—with the exception, of course, of Professor Caldwell. About life and the books he knew more than they, and he wondered into what nooks and crannies they had cast aside their educations. He did not know that he was himself possessed of unusual brain vigor; nor did he know that the persons who were given to probing the depths and to thinking ultimate thoughts were not to be found in the drawing rooms of the world's Morses; nor did he dream that such persons were as lonely eagles sailing solitary in the azure sky far above the earth and its swarming freight of gregarious life.

Chapter Twenty-eight

But success had lost Martin's address, and her messengers no longer came to his door. For twenty-five days, working Sundays and holidays, he toiled on "The Shame of the Sun," a long essay of some thirty thousand words. It was a deliberate attack on the mysticism of the Maeterlinck school—an attack from the citadel of positive science upon the wonder-dreamers, but an attack nevertheless that retained much of beauty and wonder of the sort compatible with ascertained fact. It was a little later that he followed up the attack with two short essays, "The Wonder-Dreamers" and "The Yardstick of the Ego." And on essays, long and short, he began to pay the traveling expenses from magazine to magazine.

During the twenty-five days spent on "The Shame of the Sun," he sold hack-work to the extent of six dollars and fifty cents. A joke had brought in fifty cents, and a second one, sold to a high-grade comic weekly, had fetched a dollar. Then two humorous poems had earned two dollars and three dollars respectively. As a result, having exhausted his credit with the tradesmen (though he had increased his credit with the grocer to five dollars), his wheel and suit of clothes went back to the pawnbroker. The typewriter people were again clamoring for money, insistently pointing out that according to the agreement rent was to be paid strictly in advance.

Encouraged by his several small sales, Martin went back to hack-work. Perhaps there was a living in it, after all. Stored away under his table were the twenty storiettes which had been rejected by the newspaper short-story syndicate. He read them over in order to find out how not to write newspaper storiettes, and so doing, reasoned out the perfect formula. He found that the newspaper storiette should never be tragic, should never end unhappily, and should never contain beauty of language, subtlety of thought, nor real delicacy of sentiment. Sentiment it must contain, plenty of it, pure and noble, of the sort that in his own early youth had brought his applause from "nigger heaven"— the "For-God-my-country-and-the-Czar" and "I-may-be-poor-but-I-am-honest" brand of sentiment.

Having learned such precautions, Martin consulted "The Duchess" for tone, and proceeded to mix according to formula. The formula consists of three parts: (1) a pair of lovers are jarred apart; (2) by some deed or event they are reunited; (3) marriage bells. The third part was an unvarying quantity, but the first and seconds parts could be varied an infinite number of times. Thus, the pair of lovers could be jarred apart by misunderstood motives, by accident of fate, by jealous rivals, by irate parents, by crafty guardians, by scheming relatives, and so forth and so forth; they could be reunited by a brave deed of the man lover, by a similar deed of the woman lover, by change of heart in one lover or the other, by forced confession of crafty guardian, scheming relative, or jealous rival, by voluntary confession of same, by discovery of some unguessed secret, by lover storming girl's heart, by lover making long and noble self-sacrifice, and so on, endlessly. It was very fetching to make the girl propose in the course of being reunited, and Martin discovered, bit by bit, other decidedly piquant and fetching ruses. But marriage bells at the end was the one thing he could take no liberties with; though the heavens rolled up as a scroll and the stars fell, the wedding bells must go on ringing just the same. In quantity, the formula prescribed twelve hundred words minimum dose, fifteen hundred words maximum dose.

Before he got very far along in the art of the storiette, Martin worked out half a dozen stock forms, which he always consulted when constructing storiettes. These forms were like the cunning tables used by mathematicians, which may be entered from top, bottom, right, and left, which entrances consist of scores of lines and dozens of columns, and from which may be drawn, without reasoning or thinking, thousands of different conclusions, all unchallengeably precise and true. Thus, in the course of half an hour with his forms, Martin could frame up a dozen or so storiettes, which he put aside and filled in at his convenience. He found that he could fill one in, after a day of serious work, in the hour before going to bed. As he later confessed to Ruth, he could almost do it in his sleep. The real work was in constructing the frames, and that was merely mechanical.

He had no doubt whatever of the efficacy of his formula, and for once he knew the editorial mind when he said positively to himself that the first two he sent off would bring checks. And checks they brought, for four dollars each, at the end of twelve days.

In the meantime he was making fresh and alarming discoveries concerning the magazines. Though the

Transcontinental had published "The Ring of Bells," no check was forthcoming. Martin needed it, and he wrote for it. An evasive answer and a request for more of his work was all he received. He had gone hungry two days waiting for the reply, and it was then that he put his wheel back in pawn. He wrote regularly, twice a week, to the *Transcontinental* for his five dollars, though it was only semi-occasionally that he elicited a reply. He did not know that the *Transcontinental* had been staggering along precariously for years, that it was a fourth-rater, or a tenth-rater, without standing, with a crazy circulation that partly rested on petty bullying and partly on patriotic appealing, and with advertisements that were scarcely more than charitable donations. Nor did he know that the *Transcontinental* was the sole livelihood of the editor and the business manager, and that they could wring their livelihood out of it only by moving to escape paying rent and by never paying any bill they could evade. Nor could he have guessed that the particular five dollars that belonged to him had been appropriated by the business manager for the painting of his house in Alameda, which painting he performed himself, on week-day afternoons, because he could not afford to pay union wages and because the first scab he had employed had had a ladder jerked out from under him and been sent to the hospital with a broken collar-bone.

The ten dollars for which Martin had sold "Treasure Hunters" to the Chicago newspaper did not come to hand. The article had been published, as he had ascertained at the file in the Central Reading-room, but no word could he get from the editor. His letters were ignored. To satisfy himself that they had been received, he registered several of them. It was nothing less than robbery, he concluded—a cold-blooded steal;

while he starved, he was pilfered of his merchandise, of his goods, the sale of which was the sole way of getting bread to eat.

Youth and Age was a weekly, and it had published two-thirds of his twenty-one-thousand-word serial when it went out of business. With it went all hopes of getting his sixteen dollars.

To cap the situation, "The Pot," which he looked upon as one of the best things he had written, was lost to him. In despair, casting about frantically among the magazines, he had sent it to *The Billow*, a society weekly in San Francisco. His chief reason for submitting it to that publication was that, having only to travel across the bay from Oakland, a quick decision could be reached. Two weeks later he was overjoyed to see, in the latest number on the news-stand, his story printed in full, illustrated, and in the place of honor. He went home with leaping pulse, wondering how much they would pay him for one of the best things he had done. Also, the celerity with which it had been accepted and published was a pleasant thought to him. That the editor had not informed him of the acceptance made the surprise more complete. After waiting a week, two weeks, and half a week longer, desperation conquered diffidence, and he wrote to the editor of *The Billow*, suggesting that possibly through some negligence of the business manager his little account had been overlooked.

Even if it isn't more than five dollars, Martin thought to himself, it will buy enough beans and pea-soup to enable me to write half a dozen like it, and possibly as good.

Back came a cool letter from the editor that at least elicited Martin's admiration.

"We thank you," it ran, "for your excellent contribution. All of us in the office enjoyed it immensely, and, as you see, it was given the place of honor and immediate publication. We earnestly hope that you liked the illustrations.

"On rereading your letter it seems to us that you are laboring under the misapprehension that we pay for unsolicited manuscripts. This is not our custom, and of course yours was unsolicited. We assumed, naturally, when we received your story, that you understood the situation. We can only deeply regret this unfortunate misunderstanding, and assure you of our unfailing regard. Again, thanking you for your kind contribution, and hoping to receive more from you in the near future, we remain, etc."

There was also a postscript to the effect that though *The Billow* carried no free list, it took great pleasure in sending him a complimentary subscription for the ensuing year.

After that experience, Martin typed at the top of the first sheet of all his manuscripts: "Submitted at your usual rate."

Some day, he consoled himself, they will be submitted at *my* usual rate.

He discovered in himself, at this period, a passion for perfection, under the sway of which he rewrote and polished "The Jostling Street," "The Wine of Life," "Joy," the "Sea Lyrics," and others of his earlier work. As of old, nineteen hours of labor a day was all too little to suit him. He wrote prodigiously, and he read prodigiously, forgetting in his toil the pangs caused by giving up his tobacco. Ruth's promised cure for the habit, flamboyantly labeled, he stowed away in the most inaccessible corner of his bureau. Especially during his stretches of famine he suffered from lack of the weed; but no matter how often he mastered the craving, it remained with him as strong as ever. He regarded it as the biggest thing he had ever achieved. Ruth's point of view was that he was doing no more than was right. She brought him the anti-tobacco remedy, purchased out of her glove money, and in a few days forgot all about it.

His machine-made storiettes, though he hated them and derided them, were successful. By means of them he redeemed all his pledges, paid most of his bills, and bought a new set of tires for his wheel. The storiettes at least kept the pot a-boiling and gave him time for ambitious work; while the one thing that upheld him was the forty dollars he had received from *The White Mouse*. He anchored his faith to that, and was confident that the really first-class magazines would pay an unknown writer at least an equal rate, if not a better one. But the thing was, how to get into the first-class magazines. His best stories, essays, and poems went begging among them, and yet, each month, he read reams of dull, prosy, inartistic stuff between all their various covers. If only one editor, he sometimes thought, would descend from his high seat of pride to write me one cheering line! No matter if my work is unusual, no matter if it is unfit, for prudential reasons, for their pages, surely there must be some sparks in it, somewhere, a few, to warm them to some sort of appreciation. And thereupon he would get out one or another of his manuscripts, such as "Adventure," and read it over and over in a vain attempt to vindicate the editorial silence.

As the sweet California spring came on, his period of plenty came to an end. For several weeks he had been worried by a strange silence on the part of the newspaper storiette syndicate. Then, one day, came back to him through the mail ten of his immaculate

machine-made storiettes. They were accompanied by
a brief letter to the effect that the syndicate was over-
stocked, and that some months would elapse before it
would be in the market again for manuscripts. Martin
had even been extravagant on the strength of those ten
storiettes. Toward the last the syndicate had been paying him five dollars each for them and accepting every
one he sent. So he had looked upon the ten as good
as sold, and he had lived accordingly, on a basis of
fifty dollars in the bank. So it was that he entered
abruptly upon a lean period, wherein he continued
selling his earlier efforts to publications that would not
pay and submitting his later work to magazines that
would not buy. Also, he resumed his trips to the pawnbroker down in Oakland. A few jokes and snatches of
humorous verse, sold to the New York weeklies, made
existence barely possible for him. It was at this time
that he wrote letters of inquiry to the several great
monthly and quarterly reviews, and learned in reply
that they rarely considered unsolicited articles, and
that most of their contents were written upon order
by well-known specialists who were authorities in their
various fields.

Chapter Twenty-nine

It was a hard summer for Martin. Manuscript readers
and editors were away on vacation, and publications
that ordinarily returned a decision in three weeks now
retained his manuscript for three months or more. The
consolation he drew from it was that a saving in postage was effected by the deadlock. Only the robber-
publications seemed to remain actively in business,

and to them Martin disposed of all his early efforts, such as "Pearl-diving," "The Sea as a Career," "Turtle-catching," and "The Northeast Trades." For these manuscripts he never received a penny. It is true, after six months' correspondence, he effected a compromise, whereby he received a safety razor for "Turtle-catching," and that *The Acropolis*, having agreed to give him five dollars cash and five yearly subscriptions for "The Northeast Trades," fulfilled the second part of the agreement.

For a sonnet on Stevenson he managed to wring two dollars out of a Boston editor who was running a magazine with a Matthew Arnold taste and a penny-dreadful purse. "The Peri and the Pearl," a clever skit of a poem of two hundred lines, just finished, white hot from his brain, won the heart of the editor of a San Francisco magazine published in the interest of a great railroad. When the editor wrote, offering him payment in transportation, Martin wrote back to inquire if the transportation was transferable. It was not, and so, being prevented from peddling it, he asked for the return of the poem. Back it came, with the editor's regrets, and Martin sent it to San Francisco again, this time to *The Hornet*, a pretentious monthly that had been fanned into a constellation of the first magnitude by the brilliant journalist who founded it. But *The Hornet's* light had begun to dim long before Martin was born. The editor promised Martin fifteen dollars for the poem, but, when it was published, seemed to forget about it. Several of his letters being ignored, Martin indicted an angry one which drew a reply. It was written by a new editor, who coolly informed Martin that he declined to be held responsible for the old editor's mistakes, and that he did not think much of "The Peri and the Pearl" anyway.

But *The Globe*, a Chicago magazine, gave Martin the

most cruel treatment of all. He had refrained from offering his "Sea Lyrics" for publication, until driven to it by starvation. After having been rejected by a dozen magazines, they had come to rest in *The Globe* office. There were thirty poems in the collection, and he was to receive a dollar apiece for them. The first month four were published, and he promptly received a check for four dollars; but when he looked over the magazine, he was appalled at the slaughter. In some cases the titles had been altered: "Finis," for instance, being changed to "The Finish," and "The Song of the Outer Reef" to "The Song of the Coral Reef." In one case, an absolutely different title, a misappropriate title, was substituted. In place of his own, "Medusa Lights," the editor had printed, "The Backward Track." But the slaughter in the body of the poems was terrifying. Martin groaned and sweated and thrust his hands through his hair. Phrases, lines, and stanzas not his own were substituted for his. He could not believe that a sane editor could be guilty of such maltreatment, and his favorite hypothesis was that his poems must have been doctored by the office boy or the stenographer. Martin wrote immediately, begging the editor to cease publishing the lyrics and to return them to him. He wrote again and again, begging, entreating, threatening, but his letters were ignored. Month by month the slaughter went on till the thirty poems were published, and month by month he received a check for those which had appeared in the current number.

Despite these various misadventures, the memory of the *White Mouse* forty-dollar check sustained him, though he was driven more and more to hack-work. He discovered a bread-and-butter field in the agricultural weeklies and trade journals, though among the religious weeklies he found he could easily starve.

At his lowest ebb, when his black suit was in pawn, he made a ten-strike—or so it seemed to him—in a prize contest arranged by the County Committee of the Republican Party. There were three branches of the contest, and he entered them all, laughing at himself bitterly the while in that he was driven to such straits to live. His poem won the first prize of ten dollars, his campaign song the second prize of five dollars, his essay on the principles of the Republican Party the first prize of twenty-five dollars. Which was very gratifying to him until he tried to collect. Something had gone wrong in the County Committee, and, though a rich banker and a state senator were members of it, the money was not forthcoming. While this affair was hanging fire, he proved that he understood the principles of the Democratic Party by winning the first prize for his essay in a similar contest. And, moreover, he received the money, twenty-five dollars. But the forty dollars won in the first contest he never received.

Driven to shifts in order to see Ruth, and deciding that the long walk from North Oakland to her house and back again consumed too much time, he kept his black suit in pawn in place of his bicycle. The latter gave him exercise, saved him hours of time for work, and enabled him to see Ruth just the same. A pair of knee duck trousers and an old sweater made him a presentable wheel costume, so that he would go with Ruth on afternoon rides. Besides, he no longer had opportunity to see much of her in her own home, where Mrs. Morse was thoroughly prosecuting her campaign of entertainment. The exalted beings he met there, and to whom he had looked up but a short time before, now bored him. They were no longer exalted. He was nervous and irritable, what of his hard times, disappointments, and close application to work, and the conversation of such people was maddening. He was not unduly egotistic. He measured the narrowness of their minds by the minds of the thinkers in the books he read. At Ruth's home he never met a large mind, with the exception of Professor Caldwell, and Caldwell he had met there only once. As for the rest, they were numskulls, ninnies, superficial, dogmatic, and ignorant. It was their ignorance that astounded him. What was the matter with them? What had they done with their educations? They had had access to the same books he had. How did it happen that they had drawn nothing from them?

He knew that the great minds, the deep and rational thinkers, existed. He had his proofs from the books, the books that had educated him beyond the Morse standard. And he knew that higher intellects than those of the Morse circle were to be found in the world. He read English society novels, wherein he caught glimpses of men and women talking politics and philosophy. And he read of salons in great cities, even in the United States, where art and intellect congregated. Foolishly, in the past, he had conceived that all well-groomed persons above the working class were persons with power of intellect and vigor of beauty. Culture and collars had gone together, to him, and he had been deceived into believing that college educations and mastery were the same things.

Well, he would fight his way on and up higher. And he would take Ruth with him. Her he dearly loved, and he was confident that she would shine anywhere. As it was clear to him that he had been handicapped by his early environment, so now he perceived that she was similarly handicapped. She had not had a chance to expand. The books on her father's shelves,

the paintings on the walls, the music on the piano—
all was just so much meretricious display. To real
literature, real painting, real music, the Morses and
their kind, were dead. And bigger than such things
was life, of which they were densely, hopelessly ignorant. In spite of their Unitarian proclivities and their
masks of conservative broadmindedness, they were
two generations behind interpretative science: their
mental processes were medieval, while their thinking
on the ultimate data of existence and of the universe
struck him as the same metaphysical method that was
as young as the youngest race, as old as the cave-man,
and older—the same that moved the first Pleistocene
ape-man to fear the dark; that moved the first hasty
Hebrew savage to incarnate Eve from Adam's rib; that
moved Descartes to build an idealistic system of the
universe out of the projections of his own puny ego;
and that moved the famous British ecclesiastic to de-
nounce evolution in satire so scathing as to win immediate applause and leave his name a notorious scrawl
on the page of history.

So Martin thought, and he thought further, till it
dawned upon him that the difference between these
lawyers, officers, business men, and bank cashiers he
had met and the members of the working class he had
known was on a par with the difference in the food
they ate, clothes they wore, neighborhoods in which
they lived. Certainly, in all of them was lacking the
something more which he found in himself and in the
books. The Morses had shown him the best their social
position could produce, and he was not impressed by
it. A pauper himself, a slave to the money-lender, he
knew himself the superior of those he met at the Morses';
and, when his one decent suit of clothes was out of
pawn, he moved among them a lord of life, quivering

with a sense of outrage akin to what a prince would suffer if condemned to live with goat-herds.

"You hate and fear the socialists," he remarked to Mr. Morse, one evening at dinner; "but why? You know neither them nor their doctrines."

The conversation had been swung in that direction by Mrs. Morse, who had been invidiously singing the praises of Mr. Hapgood. The cashier was Martin's black beast, and his temper was a trifle short where the talker of platitudes was concerned.

"Yes," he had said, "Charley Hapgood is what they call a rising young man—somebody told me as much. And it is true. He'll make the Governor's Chair before he dies, and, who knows? maybe the United States Senate."

"What makes you think so?" Mrs. Morse had inquired.

"I've heard him make a campaign speech. It was so cleverly stupid and unoriginal, and also so convincing, that the leaders cannot help but regard him as safe and sure, while his platitudes are so much like the platitudes of the average voter that—oh, well, you know you flatter any man by dressing up his own thoughts for him and presenting them to him."

"I actually think you are jealous of Mr. Hapgood," Ruth had chimed in.

"Heaven forbid!"

The look of horror on Martin's face stirred Mrs. Morse to belligerence.

"You surely don't mean to say that Mr. Hapgood is stupid?" she demanded icily.

"No more than the average Republican," was the retort, "or average Democrat, either. They are all stupid when they are not crafty, and very few of them are crafty. The only wise Republicans are the millionaires and their conscious henchmen. They know which side their bread is buttered on, and they know why."

"I am a Republican," Mr. Morse put in lightly. "Pray, how do you classify me?"

"Oh, you are an unconscious henchman."

"Henchman?"

"Why, yes. You do corporation work. You have no working-class nor criminal practice. You don't depend upon wife-beaters and pickpockets for your income. You get your livelihood from the masters of society, and whoever feeds a man is that man's master. Yes, you are a henchman. You are interested in advancing the interests of the aggregations of capital you serve."

Mr. Morse's face was a trifle red.

"I confess, sir," he said, "that you talk like a scoundrelly socialist."

Then it was that Martin made his remark:—

"You hate and fear the socialists; but why? You know neither them nor their doctrines."

"Your doctrine certainly sounds like socialism," Mr. Morse replied, while Ruth gazed anxiously from one to the other, and Mrs. Morse beamed happily at the opportunity afforded of rousing her liege lord's antagonism.

"Because I say Republicans are stupid, and hold that liberty, equality, and fraternity are exploded bubbles, does not make me a socialist," Martin said with a smile. "Because I question Jefferson and the unscientific Frenchmen who informed his mind, does not make me a socialist. Believe me, Mr. Morse, you are far nearer socialism than I who am its avowed enemy."

"Now you please to be facetious," was all the other could say.

"Not at all. I speak in all seriousness. You still believe in equality, and yet you do the work of the corporations, and the corporations, from day to day, are busily engaged in burying equality. And you call me a socialist because I deny equality, because I affirm just what you live up to. The Republicans are foes to equality, though most of them fight the battle against equality with the very word itself the slogan on their lips. In the name of equality they destroy equality. That was why I called them stupid. As for myself, I am an individualist. I believe the race is to the swift, the battle to the strong. Such is the lesson I have learned from biology, or at least think I have learned. As I said, I am an individualist, and individualism is the hereditary and eternal foe of socialism."

"But you frequent socialist meetings," Mr. Morse challenged.

"Certainly, just as spies frequent hostile camps. How else are you to learn about the enemy? Besides, I enjoy myself at their meetings. They are good fighters, and, right or wrong, they have read the books. Any one of them knows far more about sociology and all the other ologies than the average captain of industry. Yes, I have been to half a dozen of their meetings, but that doesn't make me a socialist any more than hearing Charley Hapgood orate made me a Republican."

"I can't help it," Mr. Morse said feebly, "but I still believe you incline that way."

Bless me, Martin thought to himself, he doesn't know what I was talking about. He hasn't understood a word of it. What did he do with his education, anyway?

Thus, in his development, Martin found himself face to face with economic morality, or the morality of class; and soon it became to him a grisly monster. Personally, he was an intellectual moralist, and more offending to him than platitudinous pomposity was the morality of those about him, which was a curious hotchpotch of the economic, the metaphysical, the sentimental, and the imitative.

A sample of this curious messy mixture he encountered nearer home. His sister Marian had been keeping company with an industrious young mechanic, of German extraction, who, after thoroughly learning the trade, had set up for himself in a bicycle-repair shop. Also, having got the agency for a low-grade make of wheel, he was prosperous. Marian had called on Martin in his room a short time before to announce her engagement, during which visit she had playfully inspected Martin's palm and told his fortune. On her next visit she brought Hermann von Schmidt along with her. Martin did the honors and congratulated both of them in language so easy and graceful as to affect disagreeably the peasant-mind of his sister's lover. This bad impression was further heightened by Martin's reading aloud the half-dozen stanzas of verse with which he had commemorated Marian's previous visit. It was a bit of society verse, airy and delicate, which he had named "The Palmist." He was surprised, when he finished reading it, to note no enjoyment in his sister's face. Instead, her eyes were fixed anxiously upon her betrothed, and Martin, following her gaze, saw spread on that worthy's asymmetrical features nothing but black and sullen disapproval. The incident passed over, they made an early departure, and Martin forgot all about it, though for the moment he had been puzzled that any woman, even of the working class, should not have been flattered and delighted by having poetry written about her.

Several evenings later Marian again visited him, this time alone. Nor did she waste time in coming to the point, upbraiding him sorrowfully for what he had done.

"Why, Marian," he chided, "you talk as though you were ashamed of your relatives, or of your brother at any rate."

"And I am, too," she blurted out.

Martin was bewildered by the tears of mortification he saw in her eyes. The mood, whatever it was, was genuine.

"But, Marian, why should your Hermann be jealous of my writing poetry about my own sister?"

"He ain't jealous," she sobbed. "He says it was indecent, ob—obscene."

Martin emitted a long, low whistle of incredulity, then proceeded to resurrect and read a carbon copy of "The Palmist."

"I can't see it," he said finally, proffering the manuscript to her. "Read it yourself and show me whatever strikes you as obscene—that was the word, wasn't it?"

"He says so, and he ought to know," was the answer, with a wave aside of the manuscript, accompanied by a look of loathing. "And he says you've got to tear it up. He says he won't have no wife of his with such things written about her which anybody can read. He says it's a disgrace, an' he won't stand for it."

"Now, look here, Marian, this is nothing but nonsense," Martin began; then abruptly changed his mind.

He saw before him an unhappy girl, knew the futility of attempting to convince her husband or her, and, though the whole situation was absurd and preposterous, he resolved to surrender.

"All right," he announced, tearing the manuscript into half a dozen pieces and throwing it into the wastebasket.

He contented himself with the knowledge that even then the original typewritten manuscript was reposing in the office of a New York magazine. Marian and her husband would never know, and neither himself nor they nor the world would lose if the pretty, harmless poem ever were published.

Marian, starting to reach into the waste-basket, refrained.

"Can I?" she pleaded.

He nodded his head, regarding her thoughtfully as she gathered the torn pieces of manuscript and tucked them into the pocket of her jacket—ocular evidence of the success of her mission. She reminded him of Lizzie Connolly, though there was less of fire and gorgeous flaunting life in her than in that other girl of the working class whom he had seen twice. But they were on a par, the pair of them, in dress and carriage, and he smiled with inward amusement at the caprice of his fancy which suggested the appearance of either of them in Mrs. Morse's drawing room. The amusement faded, and he was aware of a great loneliness. This sister of his and the Morse drawing room were milestones of the road he had traveled. And he had left them behind. He glanced affectionately about him at his few books. They were all the comrades left to him.

"Hello, what's that?" he demanded in startled surprise.

Marian repeated her question.

"Why don't I go to work?" He broke into a laugh that was only half-hearted. "That Hermann of yours has been talking to you."

She shook her head.

"Don't lie," he commanded, and the nod of her head affirmed his charge.

"Well, you tell that Hermann of yours to mind his

own business; that when I write poetry about the girl he's keeping company with it's his business, but that outside of that he's got no say so. Understand?

"So you don't think I'll succeed as a writer, eh?" he went on. "You think I'm no good?—that I've fallen down and am a disgrace to the family?"

"I think it would be much better if you got a job," she said firmly, and he saw she was sincere. "Hermann says—"

"Damn Hermann!" he broke out good-naturedly. "What I want to know is when you're going to get married. Also, you find out from your Hermann if he will deign to permit you to accept a wedding present from me."

He mused over the incident after she had gone, and once or twice broke out into laughter that was bitter as he saw his sister and her betrothed, all the members of his own class and the members of Ruth's class, directing their narrow little lives by narrow little formulas—herd-creatures, flocking together and patterning their lives by one another's opinions, failing of being individuals and of really living life because of the childlike formulas by which they were enslaved. He summoned them before him in apparitional procession: Bernard Higginbotham arm in arm with Mr. Butler, Hermann von Schmidt cheek by jowl with Charley Hapgood, and one by one and in pairs he judged them and dismissed them—judged them by the standards of intellect and morality he had learned from the books. Vainly he asked: Where are the great souls, the great men and women? He found them not among the careless, gross, and stupid intelligences that answered the call of vision to his narrow room. He felt a loathing for them such as Circe must have felt for her swine. When he had dismissed the last one and thought himself alone, a late-comer entered, unexpected and unsummoned. Martin watched him and saw the stiff-rim, the square-cut, double-breasted coat and the swaggering shoulders, of the youthful hoodlum who had once been he.

"You were like all the rest, young fellow," Martin sneered. "Your morality and your knowledge were just the same as theirs. You did not think and act for yourself. Your opinions, like your clothes, were ready made; your acts were shaped by popular approval. You were cock of your gang because others acclaimed you the real thing. You fought and ruled the gang, not because you liked to,—you know you really despised it,—but because the other fellows patted you on the shoulder. You licked Cheese-Face because you wouldn't give in, and you wouldn't give in partly because you were an abysmal brute and for the rest because you believed what every one about you believed, that the measure of manhood was the carnivorous ferocity displayed in injuring and marring fellow creatures' anatomies. Why, you whelp, you even won other fellows' girls away from them, not because you wanted the girls, but because in the marrow of those about you, those who set your moral pace, was the instinct of the wild stallion and the bull-seal. Well, the years have passed, and what do you think about it now?"

As if in reply, the vision underwent a swift metamorphosis. The stiff-rim and the square-cut vanished, being replaced by milder garments; the toughness went out of the face, the hardness out of the eyes; and the face, chastened and refined, was irradiated from an inner life of communion with beauty and knowledge. The apparition was very like his present self, and, as he regarded it, he noted the student-lamp by which it was illuminated, and the book over which it pored.

He glanced at the title and read, "The Science of Æsthetics." Next, he entered into the apparition, trimmed the student-lamp, and himself went on reading "The Science of Æsthetics."

Chapter Thirty

On a beautiful fall day, a day of similar Indian summer to that which had seen their love declared the year before, Martin read his "Love-cycle" to Ruth. It was in the afternoon, and, as before, they had ridden out to their favorite knoll in the hills. Now and again she had interrupted his reading with exclamations of pleasure, and now, as he laid the last sheet of manuscript with its fellows, he waited her judgment.

She delayed to speak, and at last she spoke haltingly, hesitating to frame in words the harshness of her thought.

"I think they are beautiful, very beautiful," she said; "but you can't sell them, can you? You see what I mean," she said, almost pleaded. "This writing of yours is not practical. Something is the matter—maybe it is with the market—that prevents you from earning a living by it. And please, dear, don't misunderstand me. I am flattered, and made proud, and all that—I could not be a true woman were it otherwise—that you should write these poems to me. But they do not make our marriage possible. Don't you see, Martin? Don't think me mercenary. It is love, the thought of our future with which I am burdened. A whole year has gone by since we learned we loved each other, and our wedding day is no nearer. Don't think me immodest in thus talking about our wedding, for really I have my heart, all that I am, at stake. Why don't you try to get work on a newspaper, if you are so bound up in your writing? Why not become a reporter?—for a while, at least?"

"It would spoil my style," was his answer, in a low, monotonous voice. "You have no idea how I've worked for style."

"But those storiettes," she argued. "You called them hack-work. You wrote many of them. Didn't they spoil your style?"

"No, the cases are different. The storiettes were ground out, jaded, at the end of a long day of application to style. But a reporter's work is all hack from morning till night, is the one paramount thing of life. And it is a whirlwind life, the life of the moment, with neither past nor future, and certainly without thought of any style but reportorial style, and that certainly is not literature. To become a reporter now, just as my style is taking form, crystallizing, would be to commit literary suicide. As it is, every storiette, every word of every storiette, was a violation of myself, of my self-respect, of my respect for beauty. I tell you it was sickening. I was guilty of sin. And I was secretly glad when the markets failed, even if my clothes did go into pawn. But the joy of writing the 'Love-cycle'! The creative joy in its noblest form! That was compensation for everything."

Martin did not know that Ruth was unsympathetic concerning the creative joy. She used the phrase—it was on her lips he had first heard it. She had read about it, studied about it, in the university in the course of earning her Bachelorship of Arts; but she was not original, not creative, and all manifestations of culture on her part were but harpings of the harpings of others.

"May not the editor have been right in his revision of your 'Sea Lyrics'?" she questioned. "Remember, an editor must have proved qualifications or else he would not be an editor."

"That's in line with the persistence of the established," he rejoined, his heat against the editor-folk getting the better of him. "What is, is not only right, but is the best possible. The existence of anything is sufficient vindication of its fitness to exist—to exist, mark you, as the average person unconsciously believes, not merely in present conditions, but in all conditions. It is their ignorance, of course, that makes them believe such rot—their ignorance, which is nothing more nor less than the henidical mental process described by Weininger. They think they think, and such thinkless creatures are the arbiters of the lives of the few who really think."

He paused, overcome by the consciousness that he had been talking over Ruth's head.

"I'm sure I don't know who this Weininger is," she retorted. "And you are so dreadfully general that I fail to follow you. What I was speaking of was the qualification of editors—"

"And I'll tell you," he interrupted. "The chief qualification of ninety-nine per cent of all editors is failure. They have failed as writers. Don't think they prefer the drudgery of the desk and the slavery to their circulation and to the business manager to the joy of writing. They have tried to write, and they have failed. And right there is the cursed paradox of it. Every portal to success in literature is guarded by those watchdogs, the failures in literature. The editors, sub-editors, associate editors, most of them, and the manuscript-readers for the magazines and book-publishers, most of them, nearly all of them, are men who wanted to write and who have failed. And yet they, of all creatures under the sun the most unfit, are the very creatures who decide what shall and what shall not find its way into print—they, who have proved themselves not original, who have demonstrated that they lack the divine fire, sit in judgment upon originality and genius. And after them come the reviewers, just so many more failures. Don't tell me that they have not dreamed the dream and attempted to write poetry or fiction; for they have, and they have failed. Why, the average review is more nauseating than cod-liver oil. But you know my opinion on the reviewers and the alleged critics. There are great critics, but they are as rare as comets. If I fail as a writer, I shall have proved for the career of editorship. There's bread and butter and jam, at any rate."

Ruth's mind was quick, and her disapproval of her lover's views was buttressed by the contradiction she found in his contention.

"But, Martin, if that be so, if all the doors are closed as you have shown so conclusively, how is it possible that any of the great writers ever arrived?"

"They arrived by achieving the impossible," he answered. "They did such blazing, glorious work as to burn to ashes those that opposed them. They arrived by course of miracle, by winning a thousand-to-one wager against them. They arrived because they were Carlyle's battle-scarred giants who will not be kept down. And that is what I must do; I must achieve the impossible."

"But if you fail? You must consider me as well, Martin."

"If I fail?" He regarded her for a moment as though

the thought she had uttered was unthinkable. Then intelligence illumined his eyes. "If I fail, I shall become an editor, and you will be an editor's wife."

She frowned at his facetiousness—a pretty, adorable frown that made him put his arm around her and kiss it away.

"There, that's enough," she urged, by an effort of will withdrawing herself from the fascination of his strength. "I have talked with father and mother. I never before asserted myself so against them. I demanded to be heard. I was very undutiful. They are against you, you know; but I assured them over and over of my abiding love for you, and at last father agreed that if you wanted to, you could begin right away in his office. And then, of his own accord, he said he would pay you enough at the start so that we could get married and have a little cottage somewhere. Which I think was very fine of him—don't you?"

Martin, with the dull pain of despair at his heart, mechanically reaching for the tobacco and paper (which he no longer carried) to roll a cigarette, muttered something inarticulate, and Ruth went on.

"Frankly, though, and don't let it hurt you—I tell you, to show you precisely how you stand with him —he doesn't like your radical views, and he thinks you are lazy. Of course I know you are not. I know you work hard."

How hard, even she did not know, was the thought in Martin's mind.

"Well, then," he said, "how about my views? Do you think they are so radical?"

He held her eyes and waited the answer.

"I think them, well, very disconcerting," she replied.

The question was answered for him, and so op-

pressed was he by the grayness of life that he forgot
the tentative proposition she had made for him to go
to work. And she, having gone as far as she dared,
was willing to wait the answer till she should bring
the question up again.

She had not long to wait. Martin had a question of
his own to propound to her. He wanted to ascertain
the measure of her faith in him, and within the week
each was answered. Martin precipitated it by reading
to her his "The Shame of the Sun."

"Why don't you become a reporter?" she asked when
he had finished. "You love writing so, and I am sure
you would succeed. You could rise in journalism and
make a name for yourself. There are a number of great
special correspondents. Their salaries are large, and
their field is the world. They are sent everywhere, to
the heart of Africa, like Stanley, or to interview the
Pope, or to explore unknown Tibet."

"Then you don't like my essay?" he rejoined. "You
believe that I have some show in journalism but none
in literature?"

"No, no; I do like it. It reads well. But I am afraid
it's over the heads of your readers. At least it is over
mine. It sounds beautiful, but I don't understand it.
Your scientific slang is beyond me. You are an extrem-
ist, you know, dear, and what may be intelligible to
you may not be intelligible to the rest of us."

"I imagine it's the philosophic slang that bothers
you," was all he could say.

He was flaming from the fresh reading of the ripest
thought he had expressed, and her verdict stunned
him.

"No matter how poorly it is done," he persisted,
"don't you see anything in it?—in the thought of it, I
mean?"

She shook her head.

"No, it is so different from anything I have read. I read Maeterlinck and understand him—"

"His mysticism, you understand that?" Martin flashed out.

"Yes, but this of yours, which is supposed to be an attack upon him, I don't understand. Of course, if originality counts—"

He stopped her with an impatient gesture that was not followed by speech. He became suddenly aware that she was speaking and that she had been speaking for some time.

"After all, your writing has been a toy to you," she was saying. "Surely you have played with it long enough. It is time to take up life seriously—*our* life, Martin. Hitherto you have lived solely your own."

"You want me to go to work?" he asked.

"Yes. Father has offered—"

"I understand all that," he broke in; "but what I want to know is whether or not you have lost faith in me?"

She pressed his hand mutely, her eyes dim.

"In your writing, dear," she admitted in a half-whisper.

"You've read lots of my stuff," he went on brutally. "What do you think of it? Is it utterly hopeless? How does it compare with other men's work?"

"But they sell theirs, and you—don't."

"That doesn't answer my question. Do you think that literature is not at all my vocation?"

"Then I will answer." She steeled herself to do it. "I don't think you were made to write. Forgive me, dear. You compel me to say it; and you know I know more about literature than you do."

"Yes, you are a Bachelor of Arts," he said meditatively, "and you ought to know."

"But there is more to be said," he continued, after a pause painful to both. "I know what I have in me. No one knows that so well as I. I know I shall succeed. I will not be kept down. I am afire with what I have to say in verse, and fiction, and essay. I do not ask you to have faith in that, though. I do not ask you to have faith in me, nor in my writing. What I do ask of you is to love me and have faith in love.

"A year ago I begged for two years. One of those years is yet to run. And I do believe, upon my honor and my soul, that before that year is run I shall have succeeded. You remember what you told me long ago, that I must serve my apprenticeship to writing. Well, I have served it. I have crammed it and telescoped it. With you at the end awaiting me, I have never shirked. Do you know, I have forgotten what it is to fall peacefully asleep. A few million years ago I knew what it was to sleep my fill and to awake naturally from very glut of sleep. I am awakened always now by an alarm clock. If I fall asleep early or late, I set the alarm accordingly; and this, and the putting out of the lamp, are my last conscious actions.

"When I begin to feel drowsy, I change the heavy book I am reading for a lighter one. And when I doze over that, I beat my head with my knuckles in order to drive sleep away. Somewhere I read of a man who was afraid to sleep. Kipling wrote the story. This man arranged a spur so that when unconsciousness came, his naked body pressed against the iron teeth. Well, I've done the same. I look at the time, and I resolve that not until midnight, or not until one o'clock, or two o'clock, or three o'clock, shall the spur be removed. And so it rowels me awake until the appointed time. That spur has been my bed-mate for months. I have grown so desperate that five and a half hours of sleep is an extravagance. I sleep four hours now. I am

starved for sleep. There are times when I am light-
headed from want of sleep, times when death, with
its rest and sleep, is a positive lure to me, times when
I am haunted by Longfellow's lines:—

> " 'The sea is still and deep;
>   All things within its bosom sleep;
>   A single step and all is o'er,
>   A plunge, a bubble, and no more.'

"Of course, this is sheer nonsense. It comes from
nervousness, from an overwrought mind. But the point
is: Why have I done this? For you. To shorten my
apprenticeship. To compel Success to hasten. And
my apprenticeship is now served. I know my equipment. I swear that I learn more each month than the
average college man learns in a year. I know it, I tell
you. But were my need for you to understand not so
desperate I should not tell you. It is not boasting. I
measure the results by the books. Your brothers, today, are ignorant barbarians compared with me and
the knowledge I have wrung from the books in the
hours they were sleeping. Long ago I wanted to be
famous. I care very little for fame now. What I want
is you; I am more hungry for you than for food, or
clothing, or recognition. I have a dream of laying my
head on your breast and sleeping an eon or so, and
the dream will come true ere another year is gone."

His power beat against her, wave upon wave; and
in the moment his will opposed hers most she felt
herself most strongly drawn toward him. The strength
that had always poured out from him to her was now
flowering in his impassioned voice, his flashing eyes,
and the vigor of life and intellect surging in him. And
in that moment, and for the moment, she was aware
of a rift that showed in her certitude—a rift through

which she caught sight of the real Martin Eden, splendid and invincible; and as animal-trainers have their moments of doubt, so she, for the instant, seemed to doubt her power to tame this wild spirit of a man.

"And another thing," he swept on. "You love me. But why do you love me? The thing in me that compels me to write is the very thing that draws your love. You love me because I am somehow different from the men you have known and might have loved. I was not made for the desk and counting-house, for petty business squabbling and legal jangling. Make me do such things, make me like those other men, doing the work they do, breathing the air they breathe, developing the point of view they have developed, and you have destroyed the difference, destroyed me, destroyed the thing you love. My desire to write is the most vital thing in me. Had I been a mere clod, neither would I have desired to write, nor would you have desired me for a husband."

"But you forget," she interrupted, the quick surface of her mind glimpsing a parallel. "There have been eccentric inventors, starving their families while they sought such chimeras as perpetual motion. Doubtless their wives loved them, and suffered with them and for them, not because of but in spite of their infatuation for perpetual motion."

"True," was the reply. "But there have been inventors who were not eccentric and who starved while they sought to invent practical things; and sometimes, it is recorded, they succeeded. Certainly I do not seek any impossibilities—"

"You have called it 'achieving the impossible,' " she interpolated.

"I spoke figuratively. I seek to do what men have done before me—to write and to live by my writing."

Her silence spurred him on.

"To you, then, my goal is as much a chimera as perpetual motion?" he demanded.

He read her answer in the pressure of her hand on his—the pitying mother-hand for the hurt child. And to her, just then, he was the hurt child, the infatuated man striving to achieve the impossible.

Toward the close of their talk she warned him again of the antagonism of her father and mother.

"But you love me?" he asked.

"I do! I do!" she cried.

"And I love you, not them, and nothing they do can hurt me." Triumph sounded in his voice. "For I have faith in your love, not fear of their enmity. All things may go astray in this world, but not love. Love cannot go wrong unless it be a weakling that faints and stumbles by the way."

Chapter Thirty-one

Martin had encountered his sister Gertrude by chance on Broadway—as it proved, a most propitious yet disconcerting chance. Waiting on the corner for a car, she had seen him first, and noted the eager, hungry lines of his face and the desperate, worried look of his eyes. In truth, he was desperate and worried. He had just come from a fruitless interview with the pawnbroker, from whom he had tried to wring an additional loan on his wheel. The muddy fall weather having come on, Martin had pledged his wheel some time since and retained his black suit.

"There's the black suit," the pawnbroker, who knew his every asset, had answered. "You needn't tell me you've gone and pledged it with that Jew, Lipka. Because if you have—"

The man had looked the threat, and Martin hastened to cry:—

"No, no; I've got it. But I want to wear it on a matter of business."

"All right," the mollified usurer had replied. "And I want it on a matter of business before I can let you have any more money. You don't think I'm in it for my health?"

"But it's a forty-dollar wheel, in good condition," Martin had argued. "And you've only let me have seven dollars on it. No, not even seven. Six and a quarter; you took the interest in advance."

"If you want some more, bring the suit," had been the reply that sent Martin out of the stuffy little den, so desperate at heart as to reflect it in his face and touch his sister to pity.

Scarcely had they met when the Telegraph Avenue car came along and stopped to take on a crowd of afternoon shoppers. Mrs. Higginbotham divined from the grip on her arm as he helped her on, that he was not going to follow her. She turned on the step and looked down upon him. His haggard face smote her to the heart again.

"Ain't you comin'?" she asked.

The next moment she had descended to his side.

"I'm walking—exercise, you know," he explained.

"Then I'll go along for a few blocks," she announced. "Mebbe it'll do me good. I ain't ben feelin' any too spry these last few days."

Martin glanced at her and verified her statement in her general slovenly appearance, in the unhealthy fat, in the drooping shoulders, the tired face with the sagging lines, and in the heavy fall of her feet, without elasticity—a very caricature of the walk that belongs to a free and happy body.

"You'd better stop here," he said, though she had already come to a halt at the first corner, "and take the next car."

"My goodness!—if I ain't all tired a'ready!" she panted. "But I'm just as able to walk as you in them soles. They're that thin they'll bust long before you git out to North Oakland."

"I've a better pair at home," was the answer.

"Come out to dinner tomorrow," she invited irrelevantly, "Mr. Higginbotham won't be there. He's goin' to San Leandro on business."

Martin shook his head, but he had failed to keep back the wolfish, hungry look that leapt into his eyes at the suggestion of dinner.

"You haven't a penny, Mart, and that's why you're walkin'. Exercise!" She tried to sniff contemptuously, but succeeded in producing only a sniffle. "Here, lemme see."

And, fumbling in her satchel, she pressed a five-dollar piece into his hand. "I guess I forgot your last birthday, Mart," she mumbled lamely.

Martin's hand instinctively closed on the piece of gold. In the same instant he knew he ought not to accept, and found himself struggling in the throes of indecision. That bit of gold meant food, life, and light in his body and brain, power to go on writing, and— who was to say?—maybe to write something that would bring in many pieces of gold. Clear on his vision burned the manuscripts of two essays he had just completed. He saw them under the table on top of the heap of returned manuscripts for which he had no stamps, and he saw their titles, just as he had typed them— "The High Priests of Mystery," and "The Cradle of Beauty." He had never submitted them anywhere.

They were as good as anything he had done in that line. If only he had stamps for them! Then the certitude of his ultimate success rose up in him, an able ally of hunger, and with a quick movement he slipped the coin into his pocket.

"I'll pay you back, Gertrude, a hundred times over," he gulped out, his throat painfully contracted and in his eyes a swift hint of moisture.

"Mark my words!" he cried with abrupt positiveness. "Before the year is out I'll put an even hundred of those little yellowboys into your hand. I don't ask you to believe me. All you have to do is wait and see."

Nor did she believe. Her incredulity made her uncomfortable, and failing of other expedient, she said:—

"I know you're hungry, Mart. It's sticking out all over you. Come in to meals any time. I'll send one of the children to tell you when Mr. Higginbotham ain't to be there. An' Mart—"

He waited, though he knew in his secret heart what she was about to say, so visible was her thought process to him.

"Don't you think it's about time you got a job?"

"You don't think I'll win out?" he asked.

She shook her head.

"Nobody has faith in me, Gertrude, except myself." His voice was passionately rebellious. "I've done good work already, plenty of it, and sooner or later it will sell."

"How do you know it is good?"

"Because—" He faltered as the whole vast field of literature and the history of literature stirred in his brain and pointed the futility of his attempting to convey to her the reasons for his faith. "Well, because it's better than ninety-nine per cent of what is published in the magazines."

"I wish't you'd listen to reason," she answered feebly, but with unwavering belief in the correctness of her diagnosis of what was ailing him. "I wish't you'd listen to reason," she repeated, "an' come to dinner tomorrow."

After Martin had helped her on the car, he hurried to the post-office and invested three of the five dollars in stamps; and when, later in the day, on the way to the Morse home, he stopped in at the post-office to weigh a large number of long, bulky envelopes, he affixed to them all the stamps save three of the two-cent denomination.

It proved a momentous night for Martin, for after dinner he met Russ Brissenden. How he chanced to come there, whose friend he was or what acquaintance brought him, Martin did not know. Nor had he the curiosity to inquire about him of Ruth. In short, Brissenden struck Martin as anæmic and feather-brained, and was promptly dismissed from his mind. An hour later he decided that Brissenden was a boor as well, what with the way he prowled about from one room to another, staring at the pictures or poking his nose into books and magazines he picked up from the table or drew from the shelves. Though a stranger in the house he finally isolated himself in the midst of the company, huddling into a capacious Morris chair and reading steadily from a thin volume he had drawn from his pocket. As he read, he abstractedly ran his fingers, with a caressing movement, through his hair. Martin noticed him no more that evening, except once when he observed him chaffing with great apparent success with several of the young women.

It chanced that when Martin was leaving, he over-took Brissenden already half down the walk to the street.

"Hello, is that you?" Martin said.

The other replied with an ungracious grunt, but swung alongside. Martin made no further attempt at conversation, and for several blocks unbroken silence lay upon them.

"Pompous old ass!"

The suddenness and the virulence of the exclamation startled Martin. He felt amused, and at the same time was aware of a growing dislike for the other.

"What do you go to such a place for?" was abruptly flung at him after another block of silence.

"Why do you?" Martin countered.

"Bless me, I don't know," came back. "At least this is my first indiscretion. There are twenty-four hours in each day, and I must spend them somehow. Come and have a drink."

"All right," Martin answered.

The next moment he was nonplussed by the readiness of his acceptance. At home was several hours' hack-work waiting for him before he went to bed, and after he went to bed there was a volume of Weismann waiting for him, to say nothing of Herbert Spencer's Autobiography, which was as replete for him with romance as any thrilling novel. Why should he waste any time with this man he did not like? was his thought. And yet, it was not so much the man nor the drink as was it what was associated with the drink—the bright lights, the mirrors and dazzling array of glasses, the warm and glowing faces and the resonant hum of the voices of men. That was it, it was the voices of men, optimistic men, men who breathed success and spent their money for drinks lik_ men. He was lonely, that was what was the matter with him; that was why he had snapped at the invitation as a bonita strikes at a white rag on a hook. Not since with Joe, at Shelly Hot Springs, with the one exception of the wine he took with the Portuguese grocer, had Martin had a drink at a public bar. Mental exhaustion did not produce a craving for liquor such as physical exhaustion did, and he had felt no need for it. But just now he felt desire for the drink, or, rather, for the atmosphere wherein drinks were dispensed and disposed of. Such a place was the Grotto, where Brissenden and he lounged in capacious leather chairs and drank Scotch and soda.

They talked. They talked about many things, and now Brissenden and now Martin took turn in ordering Scotch and soda. Martin, who was extremely strong-headed, marveled at the other's capacity for liquor, and ever and anon broke off to marvel at the other's conversation. He was not long in assuming that Brissenden knew everything, and in deciding that here was the second intellectual man he had met. But he noted that Brissenden had what Professor Caldwell lacked—namely, fire, the flashing insight and perception, the flaming uncontrol of genius. Living language flowed from him. His thin lips, like the dies of a machine, stamped out phrases that cut and stung; or again, pursing caressingly about the inchoate sound they articulated, the thin lips shaped soft and velvety things, mellow phrases of glow and glory, of haunting beauty, reverberant of the mystery and inscrutableness of life; and yet again the thin lips were like a bugle, from which rang the crash and tumult of cosmic strife, phrases that sounded clear as silver, that were luminous as starry spaces, that epitomized the final word of science and yet said something more—the poet's word, the transcendental truth, elusive and without words which could express, and which none the less found expression in the subtle and all but ungraspable connotations of common words. He, by some wonder of vision, saw beyond the farthest out-post of empiricism, where was no language for nar-ration, and yet, by some golden miracle of speech, investing known words with unknown significances, he conveyed to Martin's consciousness messages that were incommunicable to ordinary souls.

Martin forgot his first impression of dislike. Here was the best the books had to offer coming true. Here was an intelligence, a living man for him to look up to. "I am down in the dirt at your feet," Martin re-peated to himself again and again.

"You've studied biology," he said aloud, in signif-icant allusion.

To his surprise Brissenden shook his head.

"But you are stating truths that are substantiated only by biology," Martin insisted, and was rewarded by a blank stare. "Your conclusions are in line with the books which you must have read."

"I am glad to hear it," was the answer. "That my smattering of knowledge should enable me to short-cut my way to truth is most reassuring. As for myself, I never bother to find out if I am right or not. It is all valueless anyway. Man can never know the ultimate verities."

"You are a disciple of Spencer!" Martin cried trium-phantly.

"I haven't read him since adolescence, and all I read then was his 'Education.' "

"I wish I could gather knowledge as carelessly," Martin broke out half an hour later. He had been closely analyzing Brissenden's mental equipment. "You are a sheer dogmatist, and that's what makes it so marvelous. You state dogmatically the latest facts which science has been able to establish only by *a posteriori* reasoning. You jump at correct conclusions. You cer-

tainly short-cut with a vengeance. You feel your way
with the speed of light, by some hyperrational process,
to truth."

"Yes, that was what used to bother Father Joseph,
and Brother Dutton," Brissenden replied. "Oh, no,"
he added, "I am not anything. It was a lucky trick of
fate that sent me to a Catholic college for my education. Where did you pick up what you know?"

And while Martin told him, he was busy studying
Brissenden, ranging from his long, lean, aristocratic
face and drooping shoulders to the overcoat on a neighboring chair, its pockets sagged and bulged by the
freightage of many books. Brissenden's face and long,
slender hands were browned by the sun—excessively
browned, Martin thought. This sunburn bothered
Martin. It was patent that Brissenden was no outdoor
man. Then how had he been ravaged by the sun?
Something morbid and significant attached to that
sunburn, was Martin's thought as he returned to a
study of the face, narrow, with high cheek-bones and
cavernous hollows, and graced with as delicate and
fine an aquiline nose as Martin had ever seen. There
was nothing remarkable about the size of the eyes.
They were neither large nor small, while their color
was a nondescript brown; but in them smoldered a
fire, or, rather, lurked an expression dual and strangely
contradictory. Defiant, indomitable, even harsh to excess, they at the same time aroused pity. Martin found
himself pitying him he knew not why, though he was
soon to learn.

"Oh, I'm a lunger," Brissenden announced, off-
hand, a little later, having already stated that he came
from Arizona. "I've been down there a couple of years
living on the climate."

"Aren't you afraid to venture it up in this climate?"

"Afraid?"

There was no special emphasis in his repetition of Martin's word. But Martin saw in that ascetic face the advertisement that there was nothing of which it was afraid. The eyes had narrowed till they were eagle-like, and Martin almost caught his breath as he noted the eagle beak with its dilated nostrils, defiant, assertive, aggressive. Magnificent, was what he commented to himself, his blood thrilling at the sight. Aloud, he quoted:—

" 'Under the bludgeoning of Chance
   My head is bloody but unbowed.' "

"You like Henley," Brissenden said, his expression changing swiftly to large graciousness and tenderness. "Of course, I couldn't have expected anything else of you. Ah, Henley! A brave soul. He stands out among contemporary rhymesters—magazine rhymesters—as a gladiator stands out in the midst of a band of eunuchs."

"You don't like the magazines," Martin softly impeached.

"Do you?" was snarled back at him so savagely as to startle him.

"I—I write, or, rather, try to write, for the magazines," Martin faltered.

"That's better," was the mollified rejoinder. "You try to write, but you don't succeed. I respect and admire your failure. I know what you write. I can see it with half an eye, and there's one ingredient in it that shuts it out of the magazines. It's guts, and magazines have no use for that particular commodity. What they want is wish-wash and slush, and God knows they get it, but not from you."

"I'm not above hack-work," Martin contended.

"On the contrary—" Brissenden paused and ran an insolent eye over Martin's objective poverty, passing from the well-worn tie and the saw-edged collar to the shiny sleeves of the coat and on to the slight fray of one cuff, winding up and dwelling upon Martin's sunken cheeks. "On the contrary, hack-work is above you, so far above you that you can never hope to rise to it. Why, man, I could insult you by asking you to have something to eat."

Martin felt the heat in his face of the involuntary blood, and Brissenden laughed triumphantly.

"A full man is not insulted by such an invitation," he concluded.

"You are a devil," Martin cried irritably.

"Anyway, I didn't ask you."

"You didn't dare."

"Oh, I don't know about that. I invite you now."

Brissenden half rose from his chair as he spoke, as if with the intention of departing to the restaurant forthwith.

Martin's fists were tight-clenched, and his blood was drumming in his temples.

"Bosco! He eats 'em alive! Eats 'em alive!" Brissenden exclaimed, imitating the *spieler* of a locally famous snake-eater.

"I could certainly eat you alive," Martin said, in turn running insolent eyes over the other's disease-ravaged frame.

"Only I'm not worthy of it?"

"On the contrary," Martin considered, "because the incident is not worthy." He broke into a laugh, hearty and wholesome. "I confess you made a fool of me, Brissenden. That I am hungry and you are aware of it are only ordinary phenomena, and there's no disgrace. You see, I laugh at the conventional little moralities of the herd; then you drift by, say a sharp, true word, and immediately I am the slave of the same little moralities."

"You were insulted," Brissenden affirmed.

"I certainly was, a moment ago. The prejudice of early youth, you know. I learned such things then, and they cheapen what I have since learned. They are the skeletons in my particular closet."

"But you've got the door shut on them now?"

"I certainly have."

"Sure?"

"Sure."

"Then let's go and get something to eat."

"I'll go you," Martin answered, attempting to pay for the current Scotch and soda with the last change from his two dollars and seeing the waiter bullied by Brissenden into putting that change back on the table.

Martin pocketed it with a grimace, and felt for a moment the kindly weight of Brissenden's hand upon his shoulder.

Chapter Thirty-two

Promptly, the next afternoon, Maria was excited by Martin's second visitor. But she did not lose her head this time, for she seated Brissenden in her parlor's grandeur of respectability.

"Hope you don't mind my coming?" Brissenden began.

"No, no, not at all," Martin answered, shaking hands

and waving him to the solitary chair, himself taking to the bed. "But how did you know where I lived?"

"Called up the Morses. Miss Morse answered the 'phone. And here I am." He tugged at his coat pocket and flung a thin volume on the table. "There's a book, by a poet. Read it and keep it." And then, in reply to Martin's protest: "What have I to do with books? I had another hemorrhage this morning. Got any whiskey? No, of course not. Wait a minute."

He was off and away. Martin watched his long figure go down the outside steps, and, on turning to close the gate, noted with a pang the shoulders, which had once been broad, drawn in now over the collapsed ruin of the chest. Martin got two tumblers, and fell to reading the book of verse, Henry Vaughn Marlow's latest collection.

"No Scotch," Brissenden announced on his return. "The beggar sells nothing but American whiskey. But here's a quart of it."

"I'll send one of the youngsters for lemons, and we'll make a toddy," Martin offered.

"I wonder what a book like that will earn Marlow?" he went on, holding up the volume in question.

"Possibly fifty dollars," came the answer. "Though he's lucky if he pulls even on it, or if he can inveigle a publisher to risk bringing it out."

"Then one can't make a living out of poetry?"

Martin's tone and face alike showed his dejection.

"Certainly not. What fool expects to? Out of rhyming, yes. There's Bruce, and Virginia Spring, and Sedgwick. They do very nicely. But poetry—do you know how Vaughn Marlow makes his living?—teaching in a boys' cramming-joint down in Pennsylvania, and of all private little hells such a billet is the limit. I wouldn't trade places with him if he had fifty years of life before him. And yet his work stands out from the ruck of the contemporary versifiers as a balas ruby among carrots. And the reviews he gets! Damn them, all of them, the crass manikins!"

"Too much is written by the men who can't write about the men who do write," Martin concurred. "Why, I was appalled at the quantities of rubbish written about Stevenson and his work."

"Ghouls and harpies!" Brissenden snapped out with clicking teeth. "Yes, I know the spawn—complacently pecking at him for his Father Damien letter, analyzing him, weighing him—"

"Measuring him by the yardstick of their own miserable egos," Martin broke in.

"Yes, that's it, a good phrase,—mouthing and besliming the True, and Beautiful, and Good, and finally patting him on the back and saying, 'Good dog, Fido.' Faugh! 'The little chattering daws of men,' Richard Realf called them the night he died."

"Pecking at star-dust," Martin took up the strain warmly, "at the meteoric flight of the master-men. I once wrote a squib on them—the critics, or the reviewers, rather."

"Let's see it," Brissenden begged eagerly.

So Martin unearthed a carbon copy of "Star-dust," and during the reading of it Brissenden chuckled, rubbed his hands, and forgot to sip his toddy.

"Strikes me you're a bit of star-dust yourself, flung into a world of cowled gnomes who cannot see," was his comment at the end of it. "Of course it was snapped up by the first magazine?"

Martin ran over the pages of his manuscript book.

"It has been refused by twenty-seven of them."

Brissenden essayed a long and hearty laugh, but broke down in a fit of coughing.

"Say, you needn't tell me you haven't tackled poetry," he gasped. "Let me see some of it."

"Don't read it now," Martin pleaded. "I want to
talk with you. I'll make up a bundle and you can take
it home."

Brissenden departed with the "Love-cycle," and "The
Peri and the Pearl," returning next day to greet Martin
with:—

"I want more."

Not only did he assure Martin that he was a poet,
but Martin learned that Brissenden also was one. He
was swept off his feet by the other's work, and astounded that no attempt had been made to publish it.

"A plague on all their houses!" was Brissenden's
answer to Martin's volunteering to market his work
for him. "Love Beauty for its own sake," was his coun-
sel, "and leave the magazines alone. Back to your ships
and your sea—that's my advice to you, Martin Eden.
What do you want in these sick and rotten cities of
men? You are cutting your throat every day you waste
in them trying to prostitute beauty to the needs of
magazinedom. What was it you quoted me the other
day?—Oh, yes, 'Man, the latest of the ephemera.'
Well, what do you, the latest of the ephemera, want
with fame? If you got it, it would be poison to you.
You are too simple, too elemental, and too rational,
by my faith, to prosper on such pap. I hope you never
do sell a line to the magazines. Beauty is the only
master to serve. Serve her and damn the multitude!
Success! What in hell's success if it isn't right there in
your Stevenson sonnet, which outranks Henley's 'Apparition,' in that 'Love-cycle,' in those sea-poems?

"It is not in what you succeed in doing that you get
your joy, but in the doing of it. You can't tell me. I
know it. You know it. Beauty hurts you. It is an

everlasting pain in you, a wound that does not heal, a knife of flame. Why should you palter with magazines? Let beauty be your end. Why should you mint beauty into gold? Anyway, you can't; so there's no use in my getting excited over it. You can read the magazines for a thousand years and you won't find the value of one line of Keats. Leave fame and coin alone, sign away on a ship tomorrow, and go back to your sea."

"Not for fame, but for love," Martin laughed. "Love seems to have no place in your Cosmos; in mine, Beauty is the handmaiden of Love."

Brissenden looked at him pityingly and admiringly. "You are so young, Martin boy, so young. You will flutter high, but your wings are of the finest gauze, dusted with the fairest pigments. Do not scorch them. But of course you have scorched them already. It required some glorified petticoat to account for that 'Love-cycle,' and that's the shame of it."

"It glorifies love as well as the petticoat," Martin laughed.

"The philosophy of madness," was the retort. "So have I assured myself when wandering in hasheesh dreams. But beware. These bourgeois cities will kill you. Look at that den of traitors where I met you. Dry rot is no name for it. One can't keep his sanity in such an atmosphere. It's degrading. There's not one of them who is not degrading, man and woman, all of them animated stomachs guided by the high intellectual and artistic impulses of clams—"

He broke off suddenly and regarded Martin. Then, with a flash of divination, he saw the situation. The expression on his face turned to wondering horror.

"And you wrote that tremendous 'Love-cycle' to her—that pale, shriveled, female thing!"

The next instant Martin's right hand had shot to a throttling clutch on his throat, and he was being shaken till his teeth rattled. But Martin, looking into his eyes, saw no fear there,—naught but a curious and mocking devil. Martin remembered himself, and flung Brissenden, by the neck, sidelong upon the bed, at the same moment releasing his hold.

Brissenden panted and gasped painfully for a moment, then began to chuckle.

"You had made me eternally your debtor had you shaken out the flame," he said.

"My nerves are on a hair-trigger these days," Martin apologized. "Hope I didn't hurt you. Here, let me mix a fresh toddy."

"Ah, you young Greek!" Brissenden went on. "I wonder if you take just pride in that body of yours. You are devilish strong. You are a young panther, a lion cub. Well, well, it is you who must pay for that strength."

"What do you mean?" Martin asked curiously, passing him a glass. "Here, down this and be good."

"Because—" Brissenden sipped his toddy and smiled appreciation of it. "Because of the women. They will worry you until you die, as they have already worried you, or else I was born yesterday. Now there's no use in your choking me; I'm going to have my say. This is undoubtedly your calf love; but for Beauty's sake show better taste next time. What under heaven do you want with a daughter of the bourgeoisie? Leave them alone. Pick out some great, wanton flame of a woman, who laughs at life and jeers at death and loves one while she may. There are such women, and they will love you just as readily as any pusillanimous product of bourgeois-sheltered life."

"Pusillanimous?" Martin protested.

"Just so, pusillanimous; prattling out little moralities that have been prattled into them, and afraid to live life. They will love you, Martin, but they will love their little moralities more. What you want is the magnificent abandon of life, the great free souls, the blazing butterflies and not the little gray moths. Oh, you will grow tired of them, too, of all the female things, if you are unlucky enough to live. But you won't live. You won't go back to your ships and sea; therefore, you'll hang around these pest-holes of cities until your bones are rotten, and then you'll die."

"You can lecture me, but you can't make me talk back," Martin said. "After all, you have but the wisdom of your temperament, and the wisdom of my temperament is just as unimpeachable as yours."

They disagreed about love, and the magazines, and many things, but they liked each other, and on Martin's part it was no less than a profound liking. Day after day they were together, if for no more than the hour Brissenden spent in Martin's stuffy room. Brissenden never arrived without his quart of whiskey, and when they dined together downtown, he drank Scotch and soda throughout the meal. He invariably paid the way for both, and it was through him that Martin learned the refinements of food, drank his first champagne, and made acquaintance with Rhenish wines.

But Brissenden was always an enigma. With the face of an ascetic, he was, in all the failing blood of him, a frank voluptuary. He was unafraid to die, bitter and cynical of all the ways of living; and yet, dying, he loved life, to the last atom of it. He was possessed by a madness to live, to thrill, "to squirm my little space in the cosmic dust whence I came," as he phrased it once himself. He had tampered with drugs and done many strange things in quest of new thrills, new sensations. As he told Martin, he had once gone three days without water, had done so voluntarily, in order to experience the exquisite delight of such a thirst assuaged. Who or what he was, Martin never learned. He was a man without a past, whose future was the imminent grave and whose present was a bitter fever of living.

Chapter Thirty-three

Martin was steadily losing his battle. Economize as he would, the earnings from hack-work did not balance expenses. Thanksgiving found him with his black suit in pawn and unable to accept the Morses' invitation to dinner. Ruth was not made happy by his reason for not coming, and the corresponding effect on him was one of desperation. He told her that he would come, after all; that he would go over to San Francisco, to the *Transcontinental* office, collect the five dollars due him, and with it redeem his suit of clothes.

In the morning he borrowed ten cents from Maria. He would have borrowed it, by preference, from Brissenden, but that erratic individual had disappeared. Two weeks had passed since Martin had seen him, and he vainly cudgeled his brains for some cause of offense. The ten cents carried Martin across the ferry to San Francisco, and as he walked up Market Street he speculated upon his predicament in case he failed to collect the money. There would then be no way for him to return to Oakland, and he knew no one in San Francisco from whom to borrow another ten cents.

The door to the *Transcontinental* office was ajar, and

Martin, in the act of opening it, was brought to a sudden pause by a loud voice from within, which exclaimed:—

"But that is not the question, Mr. Ford." (Ford, Martin knew, from his correspondence, to be the editor's name.) "The question is, are you prepared to pay?—cash, and cash down, I mean? I am not interested in the prospects of the *Transcontinental* and what you expect to make it next year. What I want is to be paid for what I do. And I tell you, right now, the Christmas *Transcontinental* don't go to press till I have the money in my hand. Good day. When you get the money, come and see me."

The door jerked open, and the man flung past Martin with an angry countenance and went down the corridor, muttering curses and clenching his fists. Martin decided not to enter immediately, and lingered in the hallway for a quarter of an hour. Then he shoved the door open and walked in. It was a new experience, the first time he had been inside an editorial office. Cards evidently were not necessary in that office, for the boy carried word to an inner room that there was a man who wanted to see Mr. Ford. Returning, the boy beckoned him from halfway across the room and led him to the private office, the editorial sanctum. Martin's first impression was of the disorder and cluttered confusion of the room. Next he noticed a bewhiskered, youthful-looking man, sitting at a rolltop desk, who regarded him curiously. Martin marveled at the calm repose of his face. It was evident that the squabble with the printer had not affected his equanimity.

"I—I am Martin Eden," Martin began the conversation. ("And I want my five dollars," was what he would have liked to say.)

But this was his first editor, and under the circumstances he did not desire to scare him too abruptly. To his surprise, Mr. Ford leaped into the air with a "You don't say so!" and the next moment, with both hands, was shaking Martin's hand effusively.

"Can't say how glad I am to see you, Mr. Eden. Often wondered what you were like."

Here he held Martin off at arm's length and ran his beaming eyes over Martin's second-best suit, which was also his worst suit, and which was ragged and past repair, though the trousers showed the careful crease he had put in with Maria's flat-irons.

"I confess, though, I conceived you to be a much older man than you are. Your story, you know, showed such breadth, and vigor, such maturity and depth of thought. A masterpiece, that story—I knew it when I had read the first half-dozen lines. Let me tell you how I first read it. But no, first let me introduce you to the staff."

Still talking, Mr. Ford led him into the general office, where he introduced him to the associate editor, Mr. White, a slender, frail little man whose hand seemed strangely cold, as if he were suffering from a chill, and whose whiskers were sparse and silky.

"And Mr. Ends, Mr. Eden. Mr. Ends is our business manager, you know."

Martin found himself shaking hands with a cranky-eyed, bald-headed man, whose face looked youthful enough from what little could be seen of it, for most of it was covered by a snow-white beard, carefully trimmed—by his wife, who did it on Sundays, at which times she also shaved the back of his neck.

The three men surrounded Martin, all talking admiringly and at once, until it seemed to him that they were talking against time for a wager.

"We often wondered why you didn't call," Mr. White was saying.

"I didn't have the carfare, and I live across the Bay," Martin answered bluntly, with the idea of showing them his imperative need for the money.

Surely, he thought to himself, my glad rags in themselves are eloquent advertisement of my need. Time and again, whenever opportunity offered, he hinted about the purpose of his business. But his admirers' ears were deaf. They sang his praises, told him what they had thought of his story at first sight, what they subsequently thought, what their wives and families thought; but not one hint did they breathe of intention to pay him for it.

"Did I tell you how I first read your story?" Mr. Ford said. "Of course I didn't. I was coming west from New York, and when the train stopped at Ogden, the train-boy on the new run brought aboard the current number of the *Transcontinental*."

My God! Martin thought; you can travel in a Pullman while I starve for the paltry five dollars you owe me. A wave of anger rushed over him. The wrong done him by the *Transcontinental* loomed colossal, for strong upon him were all the dreary months of vain yearning, of hunger and privation, and his present hunger awoke and gnawed at him, reminding him that he had eaten nothing since the day before, and little enough then. For the moment he saw red. These creatures were not even robbers. They were sneak-thieves. By lies and broken promises they had tricked him out of his story. Well, he would show them. And a great resolve surged into his will to the effect that he would not leave the office until he got his money. He remembered, if he did not get it, that there was no way for him to go back to Oakland. He controlled himself with an effort, but not before the wolfish expression of his face had awed and perturbed them.

They became more voluble than ever. Mr. Ford

started anew to tell how he had first read "The Ring of Bells," and Mr. Ends at the same time was striving to repeat his niece's appreciation of "The Ring of Bells," said niece being a school-teacher in Alameda.

"I'll tell you what I came for," Martin said finally. "To be paid for that story all of you like so well. Five dollars, I believe, is what you promised me would be paid on publication."

Mr. Ford, with an expression on his mobile features of immediate and happy acquiescence, started to reach for his pocket, then turned suddenly to Mr. Ends, and said that he had left his money home. That Mr. Ends resented this, was patent; and Martin saw the twitch of his arm as if to protect his trousers pocket. Martin knew that the money was there.

"I am sorry," said Mr. Ends, "but I paid the printer not an hour ago, and he took my ready change. It was careless of me to be so short; but the bill was not yet due, and the printer's request, as a favor, to make an immediate advance was quite unexpected."

Both men looked expectantly at Mr. White, but that gentleman laughed and shrugged his shoulders. His conscience was clean at any rate. He had come into the *Transcontinental* to learn magazine literature, instead of which he had principally learned finance. The *Transcontinental* owed him four months' salary, and he knew that the printer must be appeased before the associate editor.

"It's rather absurd, Mr. Eden, to have caught us in this shape," Mr. Ford preambled airily. "All carelessness, I assure you. But I'll tell you what we'll do. We'll mail you a check the first thing in the morning. You have Mr. Eden's address, haven't you, Mr. Ends?"

Yes, Mr. Ends had the address, and the check would be mailed the first thing in the morning. Martin's knowledge of banks and checks was hazy, but he could see no reason why they should not give him the check on this day just as well as on the next.

"Then it is understood, Mr. Eden, that we'll mail you the check tomorrow?" Mr. Ford said.

"I need the money today," Martin answered stolidly.

"The unfortunate circumstances—if you had chanced here any other day," Mr. Ford began suavely, only to be interrupted by Mr. Ends, whose cranky eyes justified themselves in his shortness of temper.

"Mr. Ford has already explained the situation," he said with asperity. "And so have I. The check will be mailed—"

"I also have explained," Martin broke in, "and I have explained that I want the money today."

He had felt his pulse quicken a trifle at the business manager's brusqueness, and upon him he kept an alert eye, for it was in that gentleman's trousers pocket that he divined the *Transcontinental*'s ready cash was reposing.

"It is too bad—" Mr. Ford began.

But at that moment, with an impatient movement, Mr. Ends turned as if about to leave the room. At the same instant Martin sprang for him, clutching him by the throat with one hand in such fashion that Mr. Ends' snow-white beard, still maintaining its immaculate trimness, pointed ceilingward at an angle of forty-five degrees. To the horror of Mr. White and Mr. Ford, they saw their business manager shaken like an Astrakhan rug.

"Dig up, you venerable discourager of rising young talent!" Martin exhorted. "Dig up, or I'll shake it out of you, even if it's all in nickels." Then, to the two affrighted onlookers: "Keep away! If you interfere, somebody's liable to get hurt."

Mr. Ends was choking, and it was not until the grip

on his throat was eased that he was able to signify his acquiescence in the digging-up program. All together, after repeated digs, his trousers pocket yielded four dollars and fifteen cents.

"Inside out with it," Martin commanded.

An additional ten cents fell out. Martin counted the result of his raid a second time to make sure.

"You next!" he shouted at Mr. Ford. "I want seventy-five cents more."

Mr. Ford did not wait, but ransacked his pockets, with the result of sixty cents.

"Sure that is all?" Martin demanded menacingly, possessing himself of it. "What have you got in your vest pockets?"

In token of his good faith, Mr. Ford turned two of his pockets inside out. A strip of cardboard fell to the floor from one of them. He recovered it and was in the act of returning it, when Martin cried:—

"What's that?—A ferry ticket? Here, give it to me. It's worth ten cents. I'll credit you with it. I've now got four dollars and ninety-five cents, including the ticket. Five cents is still due me."

He looked fiercely at Mr. White, and found that fragile creature in the act of handing him a nickel.

"Thank you," Martin said, addressing them collectively. "I wish you a good day."

"Robber!" Mr. Ends snarled after him.

"Sneak-thief!" Martin retorted, slamming the door as he passed out.

Martin was elated—so elated that when he recollected that *The Hornet* owed him fifteen dollars for "The Peri and the Pearl," he decided forthwith to go and collect it. But *The Hornet* was run by a set of clean-shaven, strapping young men, frank buccaneers who robbed everything and everybody, not excepting one another. After some breakage of the office furniture, the editor (an ex-college athlete), ably assisted by the business manager, an advertising agent, and the porter, succeeded in removing Martin from the office and in accelerating, by initial impulse, his descent of the first flight of stairs.

"Come again, Mr. Eden; glad to see you any time," they laughed down at him from the landing above.

Martin grinned as he picked himself up.

"Phew!" he murmured back. "The *Transcontinental* crowd were nanny-goats, but you fellows are a lot of prize-fighters."

More laughter greeted this.

"I must say, Mr. Eden," the editor of *The Hornet* called down, "that for a poet you can go some yourself. Where did you learn that right cross—if I may ask?"

"Where you learned that half-Nelson," Martin answered. "Anyway, you're going to have a black eye."

"I hope your neck doesn't stiffen up," the editor wished solicitously. "What do you say we all go out and have a drink on it—not the neck, of course, but the little rough-house?"

"I'll go you if I lose," Martin accepted.

And robbers and robbed drank together, amicably agreeing that the battle was to the strong, and that the fifteen dollars for "The Peri and the Pearl" belonged by right to *The Hornet*'s editorial staff.

Chapter Thirty-four

Arthur remained at the gate while Ruth climbed Maria's front steps. She heard the rapid click of the typewriter, and when Martin let her in, found him on the last page of a manuscript. She had come to make certain whether or not he would be at their table for Thanksgiving dinner; but before she could broach the subject Martin plunged into the one with which he was full.

"Here, let me read you this," he cried, separating the carbon copies and running the pages of manuscript into shape. "It's my latest, and different from anything I've done. It is so altogether different that I am almost afraid of it, and yet I've a sneaking idea it is good. You be judge. It's an Hawaiian story. I've called it 'Wiki-Wiki.' "

His face was bright with the creative glow, though she shivered in the cold room and had been struck by the coldness of his hands at greeting. She listened closely while he read, and though he from time to time had seen only disapprobation in her face, at the close he asked:—

"Frankly, what do you think of it?"

"I—I don't know," she answered. "Will it—do you think it will sell?"

"I'm afraid not," was the confession. "It's too strong for the magazines. But it's true, on my word it's true."

"But why do you persist in writing such things when you know they won't sell?" she went on inexorably. "The reason for your writing is to make a living, isn't it?"

"Yes, that's right; but the miserable story got away with me. I couldn't help writing it. It demanded to be written."

"But that character, that Wiki-Wiki, why do you make him talk so roughly? Surely it will offend your readers, and surely that is why the editors are justified in refusing your work."

"Because the real Wiki-Wiki would have talked that way."

"But it is not good taste."

"It is life," he replied bluntly. "It is real. It is true. And I must write life as I see it."

She made no answer, and for an awkward moment they sat silent. It was because he loved her that he did not quite understand her, and she could not understand him because he was so large that he bulked beyond her horizon.

"Well, I've collected from the *Transcontinental*," he said in an effort to shift the conversation to a more comfortable subject. The picture of the bewhiskered trio, as he had last seen them, mulcted of four dollars and ninety cents and a ferry ticket, made him chuckle.

"Then you'll come!" she cried joyously. "That was what I came to find out."

"Come?" he muttered absently. "Where?"

"Why, to dinner tomorrow. You know you said you'd recover your suit if you got that money."

"I forgot all about it," he said humbly. "You see, this morning the poundman got Maria's two cows and the baby calf, and—well, it happened that Maria didn't have any money, and so I had to recover her cows for her. That's where the *Transcontinental* fiver went— 'The Ring of Bells' went into the poundman's pocket."

"Then you won't come?"

He looked down at his clothing.

"I can't."

Tears of disappointment and reproach glistened in her blue eyes, but she said nothing.

"Next Thanksgiving you'll have dinner with me in Delmonico's," he said cheerily, "or in London, or Paris, or anywhere you wish. I know it."

"I saw in the paper a few days ago," she announced abruptly, "that there had been several local appointments to the Railway Mail. You passed first, didn't you?"

He was compelled to admit that the call had come

for him, but that he had declined it. "I was so sure—I am so sure—of myself," he concluded. "A year from now I'll be earning more than a dozen men in the Railway Mail. You wait and see."

"Oh," was all she said, when he finished. She stood up, pulling at her gloves. "I must go, Martin. Arthur is waiting for me."

He took her in his arms and kissed her, but she proved a passive sweetheart. There was no tenseness in her body, her arms did not go around him, and her lips met his without their wonted pressure.

She was angry with him, he concluded, as he returned from the gate. But why? It was unfortunate that the poundman had gobbled Maria's cows. But it was only a stroke of fate. Nobody could be blamed for it. Nor did it enter his head that he could have done aught otherwise than what he had done. Well, yes, he was to blame a little, was his next thought, for having refused the call to the Railway Mail. And she had not liked "Wiki-Wiki."

He turned at the head of the steps to meet the letter-carrier on his afternoon round. The ever recurrent fever of expectancy assailed Martin as he took the bundle of long envelopes. One was not long. It was short and thin, and outside was printed the address of *The New York Outview*. He paused in the act of tearing the envelope open. It could not be an acceptance. He had no manuscripts with that publication. Perhaps—his heart almost stood still at the wild thought—perhaps they were ordering an article from him; but the next instant he dismissed the surmise as hopelessly impossible.

It was a short, formal letter, signed by the office editor, merely informing him that an anonymous letter which they had received was enclosed, and that he could rest assured the *Outview*'s staff never under any circumstances gave consideration to anonymous correspondence.

The enclosed letter Martin found to be crudely printed by hand. It was a hotchpotch of illiterate abuse of Martin, and of assertion that the "so-called Martin Eden" who was selling stories to magazines was no writer at all, and that in reality he was stealing stories from old magazines, typing them, and sending them out as his own. The envelope was postmarked "San Leandro." Martin did not require a second thought to discover the author. Higginbotham's grammar, Higginbotham's colloquialisms, Higginbotham's mental quirks and processes, were apparent throughout. Martin saw in every line, not the fine Italian hand, but the coarse grocer's fist, of his brother-in-law.

But why? he vainly questioned. What injury had he done Bernard Higginbotham? The thing was so unreasonable, so wanton. There was no explaining it. In the course of the week a dozen similar letters were forwarded to Martin by the editors of various Eastern magazines. The editors were behaving handsomely, Martin concluded. He was wholly unknown to them, yet some of them had even been sympathetic. It was evident that they detested anonymity. He saw that the malicious attempt to hurt him had failed. In fact, if anything came of it, it was bound to be good, for at least his name had been called to the attention of a number of editors. Sometime, perhaps, reading a submitted manuscript of his, they might remember him as the fellow about whom they had received an anonymous letter. And who was to say that such a remembrance might not sway the balance of their judgment just a trifle in his favor?

It was about this time that Martin took a great slump

in Maria's estimation. He found her in the kitchen one morning, groaning with pain, tears of weakness running down her cheeks, vainly endeavoring to put through a large ironing. He promptly diagnosed her affliction as La Grippe, dosed her with hot whiskey (the remnants in the bottles for which Brissenden was responsible), and ordered her to bed. But Maria was refractory. The ironing had to be done, she protested, and delivered that night, or else there would be no food on the morrow for the seven small and hungry Silvas.

To her astonishment (and it was something that she never ceased from relating to her dying day), she saw Martin Eden seize an iron from the stove and throw a fancy shirt-waist on the ironing-board. It was Kate Flanagan's best Sunday waist, than whom there was no more exacting and fastidiously dressed woman in Maria's world. Also, Miss Flanagan had sent special instruction that said waist must be delivered by that night. As every one knew, she was keeping company with John Collins, the blacksmith, and, as Maria knew privily, Miss Flanagan and Mr. Collins were going next day to Golden Gate Park. Vain was Maria's attempt to rescue the garment. Martin guided her tottering footsteps to a chair, from where she watched him with bulging eyes. In a quarter of the time it would have taken her she saw the shirt-waist safely ironed, and ironed as well as she could have done it, as Martin made her grant.

"I could work faster," he explained, "if your irons were only hotter."

To her, the irons he swung were much hotter than she ever dared to use.

"Your sprinkling is all wrong," he complained next. "Here, let me teach you how to sprinkle. Pressure is what's wanted. Sprinkle under pressure if you want to iron fast."

He procured a packing-case from the woodpile in the cellar, fitted a cover to it, and raided the scrap-iron the Silva tribe was collecting for the junkman. With fresh-sprinkled garments in the box, covered with the board and pressed by the iron, the device was complete and in operation.

"Now you watch me, Maria," he said, stripping off to his undershirt and gripping an iron that was what he called "really hot."

"An' when he feenish da iron' he washa da wools," as she described it afterward. "He say, 'Maria, you are da greata fool. I showa you how to washa da wools,' an' he showa me, too. Ten minutes he maka da machine—one barrel, one wheel-hub, two poles, justa like dat."

Martin had learned the contrivance from Joe at the Shelly Hot Springs. The old wheel-hub, fixed on the end of the upright pole, constituted the plunger. Making this, in turn, fast to the spring-pole attached to the kitchen rafters, so that the hub played upon the woollens in the barrel, he was able, with one hand, thoroughly to pound them.

"No more Maria washa da wools," her story always ended. "I maka da kids worka da pole an' da hub an' da barrel. Him da smarta man, Mister Eden."

Nevertheless, by his masterly operation and improvement of her kitchen-laundry, he fell an immense distance in her regard. The glamour of romance with which her imagination had invested him faded away in the cold light of fact that he was an ex-laundryman. All his books, and his grand friends who visited him in carriages or with countless bottles of whiskey, went for naught. He was, after all, a mere workingman, a member of her own class and caste. He was more human and approachable, but he was no longer mystery.

Martin's alienation from his family continued. Following upon Mr. Higginbotham's unprovoked attack, Mr. Hermann von Schmidt showed his hand. The fortunate sale of several storiettes, some humorous verse, and a few jokes gave Martin a temporary splurge of prosperity. Not only did he partially pay up his bills, but he had sufficient balance left to redeem his black suit and wheel. The latter, by virtue of a twisted crank-hanger, required repairing, and, as a matter of friendliness with his future brother-in-law, he sent it to Von Schmidt's shop.

The afternoon of the same day Martin was pleased by the wheel being delivered by a small boy. Von Schmidt was also inclined to be friendly, was Martin's conclusion from this unusual favor. Repaired wheels usually had to be called for. But when he examined the wheel, he discovered no repairs had been made. A little later in the day he telephoned his sister's betrothed, and learned that that person didn't want anything to do with him in "any shape, manner, or form."

"Hermann von Schmidt," Martin answered cheerfully, "I've a good mind to come over and punch that Dutch nose of yours."

"You come to my shop," came the reply, "an' I'll send for the police. An' I'll put you through, too. Oh, I know you, but you can't make no rough-house with me. I don't want nothin' to do with the likes of you. You're a loafer, that's what, an' I ain't asleep. You ain't goin' to do no spongin' off me just because I'm marryin' your sister. Why don't you go to work an' earn an honest livin', eh? Answer me that."

Martin's philosophy asserted itself, dissipating his

anger, and he hung up the receiver with a long whistle of incredulous amusement. But after the amusement came the reaction, and he was oppressed by his loneliness. Nobody understood him, nobody seemed to have any use for him, except Brissenden, and Brissenden had disappeared, God alone knew where.

Twilight was falling as Martin left the fruit store and turned homeward, his marketing on his arm. At the corner an electric car had stopped, and at sight of a lean, familiar figure alighting, his heart leapt with joy. It was Brissenden, and in the fleeting glimpse, ere the car started up, Martin noted the overcoat pockets, one bulging with books, the other bulging with a quart bottle of whiskey.

Chapter Thirty-five

Brissenden gave no explanation of his long absence, nor did Martin pry into it. He was content to see his friend's cadaverous face opposite him through the steam rising from a tumbler of toddy.

"I, too, have not been idle," Brissenden proclaimed, after hearing Martin's account of the work he had accomplished.

He pulled a manuscript from his inside coat pocket and passed it to Martin, who looked at the title and glanced up curiously.

"Yes, that's it," Brissenden laughed. "Pretty good title, eh? 'Ephemera'—it is the one word. And you're responsible for it, what with your *man*, who is always the erected, the vitalized inorganic, the latest of the ephemera, the creature of temperature strutting his little space on the thermometer. It got into my head and I had to write it to get rid of it. Tell me what you think of it."

Martin's face, flushed at first, paled as he read on. It was perfect art. Form triumphed over substance, if triumph it could be called where the last conceivable atom of substance had found expression in so perfect construction as to make Martin's head swim with delight, to put passionate tears into his eyes, and to send chills creeping up and down his back. It was a long poem of six or seven hundred lines, and it was a fantastic, amazing, unearthly thing. It was terrific, impossible; and yet there it was, scrawled in black ink across the sheets of paper. It dealt with man and his soul-gropings in their ultimate terms, plumbing the abysses of space for the testimony of remotest suns and rainbow spectrums. It was a mad orgy of imagination, wassailing in the skull of a dying man who half sobbed under his breath and was quick with the wild flutter of fading heart-beats. The poem swung in majestic rhythm to the cool tumult of interstellar conflict, to the onset of starry hosts, to the impact of cold suns and the flaming up of nebulae in the darkened void; and through it all, unceasing and faint, like a silver shuttle, ran the frail, piping voice of man, a querulous chirp amid the screaming of planets and the crash of systems.

"There is nothing like it in literature," Martin said, when at last he was able to speak. "It's wonderful!— wonderful! It has gone to my head. I am drunken with it. That great, infinitesimal question—I can't shake it out of my thoughts. That questing, eternal, ever recurring, thin little wailing voice of man is still ringing in my ears. It is like the dead-march of a gnat amid the trumpeting of elephants and the roaring of lions.

It is insatiable with microscopic desire. I know I'm making a fool of myself, but the thing has obsessed me. You are—I don't know what you are—you are wonderful, that's all. But how do you do it? How do you do it?"

Martin paused from his rhapsody, only to break out afresh.

"I shall never write again. I am a dauber in clay. You have shown me the work of the real artificer-artisan. Genius! This is something more than genius. It transcends genius. It is truth gone mad. It is true, man, every line of it. I wonder if you realize that, you dogmatist. Science cannot give you the lie. It is the truth of the sneer, stamped out from the black iron of the Cosmos and interwoven with mighty rhythms of sound into a fabric of splendor and beauty. And now I won't say another word. I am overwhelmed, crushed. Yes, I will, too. Let me market it for you."

Brissenden grinned. "There's not a magazine in Christendom that would dare to publish it—you know that."

"I know nothing of the sort. I know there's not a magazine in Christendom that wouldn't jump at it. They don't get things like that every day. That's no mere poem of the year. It's the poem of the century."

"I'd like to take you up on the proposition."

"Now don't get cynical," Martin exhorted. "The magazine editors are not wholly fatuous. I know that. And I'll close with you on the bet. I'll wager anything you want that 'Ephemera' is accepted either on the first or second offering."

"There's just one thing that prevents me from taking you." Brissenden waited a moment. "The thing is big— the biggest I've ever done. I know that. It's my swan song. I am almighty proud of it. I worship it. It's better than whiskey. It is what I dreamed of—the great and perfect thing—when I was a simple young man, with sweet illusions and clean ideals. And I've got it, now, in my last grasp, and I'll not have it pawed over and soiled by a lot of swine. No, I won't take the bet. It's mine. I made it, and I've shared it with you."

"But think of the rest of the world," Martin protested. "The function of beauty is joy-making."

"It's my beauty."

"Don't be selfish."

"I'm not selfish." Brissenden grinned soberly in the way he had when pleased by the thing his thin lips were about to shape. "I'm as unselfish as a famished hog."

In vain Martin strove to shake him from his decision. Martin told him that his hatred of the magazines was rabid, fanatical, and that his conduct was a thousand times more despicable than that of the youth who burned the temple of Diana at Ephesus. Under the storm of denunciation Brissenden complacently sipped his toddy and affirmed that everything the other said was quite true, with the exception of the magazine editors. His hatred of them knew no bounds, and he excelled Martin in denunciation when he turned upon them.

"I wish you'd type it for me," he said. "You know how a thousand times better than any stenographer. And now I want to give you some advice." He drew a bulky manuscript from his outside coat pocket. "Here's your 'Shame of the Sun.' I've read it not once, but twice and three times—the highest compliment I can pay you. After what you've said about 'Ephemera' I must be silent. But this I will say: when 'The Shame of the Sun' is published, it will make a hit. It will start a controversy that will be worth thousands to you just in advertising."

Martin laughed. "I suppose your next advice will be to submit it to the magazines."

"By all means no—that is, if you want to see it in print. Offer it to the first-class houses. Some publisher's reader may be mad enough or drunk enough to report favorably on it. You've read the books. The meat of them has been transmuted in the alembic of Martin Eden's mind and poured into 'The Shame of the Sun,' and one day Martin Eden will be famous, and not the least of his fame will rest upon that work. So you must get a publisher for it—the sooner the better."

Brissenden went home late that night; and just as he mounted the first step of the car, he swung suddenly back on Martin and thrust into his hand a small, tightly crumpled wad of paper.

"Here, take this," he said. "I was out to the races today, and I had the right dope."

The bell clanged and the car pulled out, leaving Martin wondering as to the nature of the crinkly, greasy wad he clutched in his hand. Back in his room he unrolled it and found a hundred-dollar bill.

He did not scruple to use it. He knew his friend had always plenty of money, and he knew also, with profound certitude, that his success would enable him to repay it. In the morning he paid every bill, gave Maria three months' advance on the room, and redeemed every pledge at the pawnshop. Next he bought Marian's wedding present, and simpler presents, suitable to Christmas, for Ruth and Gertrude. And finally, on the balance remaining to him, he herded the whole Silva tribe down into Oakland. He was a winter late in redeeming his promise, but redeemed it was, for the last, least Silva got a pair of shoes, as well as Maria herself. Also, there were horns, and dolls, and toys of various sorts, and parcels and bundles of candies and nuts that filled the arms of all the Silvas to overflowing.

It was with this extraordinary procession trooping at his and Maria's heels into a confectioner's in quest of the biggest candycane ever made, that he encountered Ruth and her mother. Mrs. Morse was shocked. Even Ruth was hurt, for she had some regard for appearances, and her lover, cheek by jowl with Maria, at the head of that army of Portuguese ragamuffins, was not a pretty sight. But it was not that which hurt so much as what she took to be his lack of pride and self-respect. Further, and keenest of all, she read into the incident the impossibility of his living down his working-class origin. There was stigma enough in the fact of it, but shamelessly to flaunt it in the face of the world—her world—was going too far. Though her engagement to Martin had been kept secret, their long intimacy had not been unproductive of gossip; and in the shop, glancing covertly at her lover and his following, had been several of her acquaintances. She lacked the easy largeness of Martin and could not rise superior to her environment. She had been hurt to the quick, and her sensitive nature was quivering with the shame of it. So it was, when Martin arrived later in the day, that he kept her present in his breast-pocket, deferring the giving of it to a more propitious occasion. Ruth in tears—passionate, angry tears—was a revelation to him. The spectacle of her suffering convinced him that he had been a brute, yet in the soul of him he could not see how nor why. It never entered his head to be ashamed of those he knew, and to take the Silvas out to a Christmas treat could in no way, so it seemed to him, show lack of consideration for Ruth. On the other hand, he did see Ruth's point of view, after she had explained it; and he looked upon it as a feminine weakness, such as afflicted all women and the best of women.

Chapter Thirty-six

"Come on,—I'll show you the real dirt," Brissenden said to him, one evening in January.

They had dined together in San Francisco, and were at the Ferry Building, returning to Oakland, when the whim came to him to show Martin the "real dirt." He turned and fled across the waterfront, a meager shadow in a flapping overcoat, with Martin straining to keep up with him. At a wholesale liquor store he bought two gallon-demijohns of old port, and with one in each hand boarded a Mission Street car, Martin at his heels burdened with several quart-bottles of whiskey.

If Ruth could see me now, was his thought, while he wondered as to what constituted the real dirt.

"Maybe nobody will be there," Brissenden said, when they dismounted and plunged off to the right into the heart of the working-class ghetto, south of Market Street. "In which case you'll miss what you've been looking for so long."

"And what the deuce is that?" Martin asked.

"Men, intelligent men, and not the gibbering nonentities I found you consorting with in that trader's den. You read the books and you found yourself all alone. Well, I'm going to show you tonight some other men who've read the books, so that you won't be lonely any more.

"Not that I bother my head about their everlasting discussions," he said at the end of a block. "I'm not interested in book philosophy. But you'll find these fellows intelligences and not bourgeois swine. But watch out, they'll talk an arm off of you on any subject under the sun.

"Hope Norton's there," he panted a little later, resisting Martin's effort to relieve him of the two demijohns. "Norton's an idealist—a Harvard man. Prodigious memory. Idealism led him to philosophic anarchy, and his family threw him off. Father's a railroad president and many times millionaire, but the son's starving in 'Frisco, editing an anarchist sheet for twenty-five a month."

Martin was little acquainted in San Francisco, and not at all south of Market; so he had no idea of where he was being led.

"Go ahead," he said, "tell me about them beforehand. What do they do for a living? How do they happen to be here?"

"Hope Hamilton's there." Brissenden paused and rested his hands. "Strawn-Hamilton's his name—hyphenated, you know—comes of old Southern stock. He's a tramp—laziest man I ever knew, though he's clerking, or trying to, in a socialist cooperative store for six dollars a week. But he's a confirmed hobo. Tramped into town. I've seen him sit all day on a bench and never a bite pass his lips, and in the evening, when I invited him to dinner—restaurant two blocks away—have him say, 'Too much trouble, old man. Buy me a package of cigarettes instead.' He was a Spencerian like you till Kreis turned him to materialistic monism. I'll start him on monism if I can. Norton's another monist—only he affirms naught but spirit. He can give Kreis and Hamilton all they want, too."

"Who is Kreis?" Martin asked.

"His rooms we're going to. One time professor—fired from university—usual story. A mind like a steel trap. Makes his living any old way. I know he's been a street fakir when he was down. Unscrupulous. Rob a corpse of a shroud—anything. Difference between him and the bourgeoisie is that he robs without illusion. He'll talk Nietzsche, or Schopenhauer, or Kant, or anything, but the only thing in this world, not excepting Mary, that he really cares for, is his monism. Haeckel is his little tin god. The only way to insult him is to take a slap at Haeckel.

"Here's the hang-out." Brissenden rested his demijohn at the upstairs entrance, preliminary to the climb. It was the usual two-story corner building, with a saloon and grocery underneath. "The gang lives here—got the whole upstairs to themselves. But Kreis is the only one who has two rooms. Come on."

No lights burned in the upper hall, but Brissenden threaded the utter blackness like a familiar ghost. He stopped to speak to Martin.

"There's one fellow—Stevens—a theosophist. Makes a pretty tangle when he gets going. Just now he's dishwasher in a restaurant. Likes a good cigar. I've seen him eat in a ten-cent hash-house and pay fifty cents for the cigar he smoked afterward. I've got a couple in my pocket for him, if he shows up.

"And there's another fellow—Parry—an Australian, a statistician and a sporting encyclopeadia. Ask him the grain output of Paraguay for 1903, or the English importation of sheetings into China for 1890, or at what weight Jimmy Britt fought Battling Nelson, or who was welterweight champion of the United States in '68, and you'll get the correct answer with the automatic celerity of a slot-machine. And there's Andy, a stone-mason, has ideas on everything, a good chess-player; and another fellow, Harry, a baker, red hot socialist and strong union man. By the way, you remember the Cooks' and Waiters' strike—Hamilton was the chap who organized that union and precipitated the strike—planned it all out in advance, right here in Kreis's rooms. Did it just for the fun of it, but was too lazy to stay by the union. Yet he could have risen high if he wanted to. There's no end to the possibilities in that man—if he weren't so insuperably lazy."

Brissenden advanced through the darkness till a thread of light marked the threshold of a door. A knock and an answer opened it, and Martin found himself shaking hands with Kreis, a handsome brunette man, with dazzling white teeth, a drooping black mustache, and large, flashing black eyes. Mary, a matronly young blonde, was washing dishes in the little back room that served for kitchen and dining room. The front room served as bedchamber and living room. Overhead was the week's washing, hanging in festoons so low that Martin did not see at first the two men talking in a corner. They hailed Brissenden and his demijohns with acclamation, and, on being introduced, Martin learned they were Andy and Parry. He joined them and listened attentively to the description of a prizefight Parry had seen the night before; while Brissenden, in his glory, plunged into the manufacture of a toddy and the serving of wine and whiskey-and-sodas. At his command, "Bring in the clan," Andy departed to go the round of the rooms for the lodgers.

"We're lucky that most of them are here," Brissenden whispered to Martin. "There's Norton and Hamilton; come on and meet them. Stevens isn't around, I hear. I'm going to get them started on monism if I can. Wait till they get a few jolts in them and they'll warm up."

At first the conversation was desultory. Nevertheless Martin could not fail to appreciate the keen play of their minds. They were men with opinions, though the opinions often clashed, and, though they were witty and clever, they were not superficial. He swiftly saw, no matter upon what they talked, that each man applied the correlation of knowledge and had also a deep-seated and unified conception of society and the Cosmos. Nobody manufactured their opinions for them; they were all rebels of one variety or another, and their lips were strangers to platitudes. Never had Martin, at the Morses', heard so amazing a range of topics discussed. There seemed no limit save time to the things they were alive to. The talk wandered from Mrs. Humphry Ward's new book to Shaw's latest play, through the future of the drama to reminiscences of Mansfield. They appreciated or sneered at the morning editorials, jumped from labor conditions in New Zealand to Henry James and Brander Matthews, passed on to the German designs in the Far East and the economic aspect of the Yellow Peril, wrangled over the German elections and Bebel's last speech, and settled down to local politics, the latest plans and scandals in the union labor party administration, and the wires that were pulled to bring about the Coast Seamen's strike. Martin was struck by the inside knowledge they possessed. They knew what was never printed in the newspapers—the wires and strings and the hidden hands that made the puppets dance. To Martin's surprise, the girl, Mary, joined in the conversation, displaying an intelligence he had never encountered in the few women he had met. They talked together on Swinburne and Rossetti, after which she led him beyond his depth into the by-paths of French literature. His revenge came when she defended Maeterlinck and he brought into action the carefully-thought-out thesis of "The Shame of the Sun."

Several other men had dropped in, and the air was thick with tobacco smoke, when Brissenden waved the red flag.

"Here's fresh meat for your axe, Kreis," he said, "a rose-white youth with the ardor of a lover for Herbert Spencer. Make a Haeckelite of him—if you can."

Kreis seemed to wake up and flash like some metallic, magnetic thing, while Norton looked at Martin sympathetically, with a sweet, girlish smile, as much as to say that he would be amply protected.

Kreis began directly on Martin, but step by step Norton interfered, until he and Kreis were off and away in a personal battle. Martin listened and fain would have rubbed his eyes. It was impossible that this should be, much less in the labor ghetto south of Market. The books were alive in these men. They talked with fire and enthusiasm, the intellectual stimulant stirring them as he had seen drink and anger stir other men. What he heard was no longer the philosophy of the dry, printed word, written by half-mythical demigods like Kant and Spencer. It was living philosophy, with warm, red blood, incarnated in these two men till its very features worked with excitement. Now and again other men joined in, and all followed the discussion with cigarettes going out in their hands and with alert, intent faces.

Idealism had never attracted Martin, but the exposition it now received at the hands of Norton was a revelation. The logical plausibility of it, that made an appeal to his intellect, seemed missed by Kreis and Hamilton, who sneered at Norton as a metaphysician, and who, in turn, sneered back at them as metaphysicians. *Phenomenon* and *noumenon* were bandied back and forth. They charged him with attempting to explain consciousness by itself. He charged them with word-jugglery, with reasoning from words to theory instead of from facts to theory. At this they were aghast. It was the cardinal tenet of their mode of reasoning to start with facts and to give names to the facts.

When Norton wandered into the intricacies of Kant, Kreis reminded him that all good little German philosophies when they died went to Oxford. A little later Norton reminded them of Hamilton's Law of Parsimony, the application of which they immediately claimed for every reasoning process of theirs. And Martin hugged his knees and exulted in it all. But Norton was no Spencerian, and he, too, strove for Martin's philosophic soul, talking as much at him as to his two opponents.

"You know Berkeley has never been answered," he said, looking directly at Martin. "Herbert Spencer came the nearest, which was not very near. Even the staunchest of Spencer's followers will not go farther. I was reading an essay of Saleeby's the other day, and the best Saleeby could say was that Herbert Spencer *nearly* succeeded in answering Berkeley."

"You know what Hume said?" Hamilton asked. Norton nodded, but Hamilton gave it for the benefit of the rest. "He said that Berkeley's arguments admit of no answer and produce no conviction."

"In his, Hume's, mind," was the reply. "And Hume's mind was the same as yours, with this difference: he was wise enough to admit there was no answering Berkeley."

Norton was sensitive and excitable, though he never lost his head, while Kreis and Hamilton were like a pair of cold-blooded savages, seeking out tender places to prod and poke. As the evening grew late, Norton, smarting under the repeated charges of being a metaphysician, clutching his chair to keep from jumping to his feet, his gray eyes snapping and his girlish face grown harsh and sure, made a grand attack upon their position.

"All right, you Haeckelites, I may reason like a medicine man, but, pray, how do you reason? You have nothing to stand on, you unscientific dogmatists with your positive science which you are always lugging about into places it has no right to be. Long before the school of materialistic monism arose, the ground was removed so that there could be no foundation. Locke was the man, John Locke. Two hundred years ago—more than that, even—in his 'Essay Concerning the Human Understanding,' he proved the non-existence of innate ideas. The best of it is that that is precisely what you claim. Tonight, again and again, you have asserted the non-existence of innate ideas.

"And what does that mean? It means that you can never know ultimate reality. Your brains are empty when you are born. Appearances, or phenomena, are all the content your minds can receive from your five senses. Then noumena, which are not in your minds when you are born, have no way of getting in—"

"I deny—" Kreis started to interrupt.

"You wait till I'm done," Norton shouted. "You can know only that much of the play and interplay of force and matter as impinges in one way or another on your senses. You see, I am willing to admit, for the sake of the argument, that matter exists; and what I am about to do is to efface you by your own argument. I can't do it any other way, for you are both congenitally unable to understand a philosophic abstraction.

"And now, what do you know of matter, according to your own positive science? You know it only by its phenomena, its appearances. You are aware only of its changes, or of such changes in it as cause changes in your consciousness. Positive science deals only with phenomena, yet you are foolish enough to strive to be ontologists and to deal with noumena. Yet, by the very definition of positive science, science is concerned only with appearances. As somebody has said, phenomenal knowledge cannot transcend phenomena.

"You cannot answer Berkeley, even if you have annihilated Kant, and yet, perforce, you assume that Berkeley is wrong when you affirm that science proves the non-existence of God, or, as much to the point, the existence of matter.—You know I granted the reality of matter only in order to make myself intelligible to your understanding. Be positive scientists, if you please; but ontology has no place in positive science, so leave it alone. Spencer is right in his agnosticism, but if Spencer—"

But it was time to catch the last ferry-boat for Oakland, and Brissenden and Martin slipped out, leaving Norton still talking and Kreis and Hamilton waiting to pounce on him like a pair of hounds as soon as he finished.

"You have given me a glimpse of fairyland," Martin said on the ferry-boat. "It makes life worthwhile to meet people like that. My mind is all worked up. I never appreciated idealism before. Yet I can't accept it. I know that I shall always be a realist. I am so made, I guess. But I'd like to have made a reply to Kreis and Hamilton, and I think I'd have had a word or two for Norton. I didn't see that Spencer was damaged any. I'm as excited as a child on its first visit to the circus. I see I must read up some more. I'm going to get hold of Saleeby. I still think Spencer is unassailable, and next time I'm going to take a hand myself."

But Brissenden, breathing painfully, had dropped off to sleep, his chin buried in a scarf and resting on his sunken chest, his body wrapped in the long overcoat and shaking to the vibration of the propellers.

Chapter Thirty-seven

The first thing Martin did next morning was to go counter both to Brissenden's advice and command. "The Shame of the Sun" he wrapped and mailed to *The Acropolis*. He believed he could find magazine publication for it, and he felt that recognition by the magazines would commend him to the book-publishing houses. "Ephemera" he likewise wrapped and mailed to a magazine. Despite Brissenden's prejudice against the magazines, which was a pronounced mania with him, Martin decided that the great poem should see print. He did not intend, however, to publish it without the other's permission. His plan was to get it accepted by one of the high magazines, and, thus armed, again to wrestle with Brissenden for consent.

Martin began, that morning, a story which he had sketched out a number of weeks before and which ever since had been worrying him with its insistent clamor to be created. Apparently it was to be a rattling sea story, a tale of twentieth-century adventure and romance, handling real characters, in a real world, under real conditions. But beneath the swing and go of the story was to be something else—something that the superficial reader would never discern and which, on the other hand, would not diminish in any way the interest and enjoyment for such a reader. It was this, and not the mere story, that impelled Martin to write it. For that matter, it was always the great, universal motif that suggested plots to him. After having found such a motif, he cast about for the particular persons and particular location in time and space wherewith and wherein to utter the universal thing. "Overdue" was the title he had decided for it, and its length he believed would not be more than sixty thousand words—a bagatelle for him with his splendid vigor of production. On this first day he took hold of it with conscious delight in the mastery of his tools. He no longer worried for fear that the sharp, cutting edges should slip and mar his work. The long months of intense application and study had brought their reward. He could now devote himself with sure hand to the larger phases of the thing he shaped; and as he worked, hour after hour, he felt, as never before, the sure and cosmic grasp with which he held life and the affairs of life. "Overdue" would tell a story that would be true of its particular characters and its particular events; but it would tell, too, he was confident, great vital things that would be true of all time, and all sea, and all life—thanks to Herbert Spencer, he thought, leaning back for a moment from the table. Ay, thanks to Herbert Spencer and to the master-key of life, evolution, which Spencer had placed in his hands.

He was conscious that it was great stuff he was writing. "It will go! It will go!" was the refrain that kept sounding in his ears. Of course it would go. At last he was turning out the thing at which the magazines would jump. The whole story worked out before him in lightning flashes. He broke off from it long enough to write a paragraph in his notebook. This would be the last paragraph in "Overdue"; but so thoroughly was the whole book already composed in his brain that he could write, weeks before he had arrived at the end, the end itself. He compared the tale, as yet unwritten, with the tales of the sea-writers, and he felt it to be immeasurably superior. "There's only one man who could touch it," he murmured aloud, "and that's Conrad. And it ought to make even him

sit up and shake hands with me, and say, 'Well done,
Martin, my boy.' "

He toiled on all day, recollecting, at the last moment, that he was to have dinner at the Morses'. Thanks
to Brissenden, his black suit was out of pawn and he
was again eligible for dinner parties. Downtown he
stopped off long enough to run into the library and
search for Saleeby's books. He drew out "The Cycle
of Life," and on the car turned to the essay Norton
had mentioned on Spencer. As Martin read, he grew
angry. His face flushed, his jaw set, and unconsciously
his hand clenched, unclenched, and clenched again as
if he were taking fresh grips upon some hateful thing
out of which he was squeezing the life. When he left
the car, he strode along the sidewalk as a wrathful man
will stride, and he rang the Morse bell with such viciousness that it roused him to consciousness of his
condition, so that he entered in good nature, smiling
with amusement at himself. No sooner, however, was
he inside than a great depression descended upon him.
He fell from the height where he had been upborne
all day on the wings of inspiration. "Bourgeois," "trader's den"—Brissenden's epithets repeated themselves
in his mind. But what of that? he demanded angrily.
He was marrying Ruth, not her family.

It seemed to him that he had never seen Ruth more
beautiful, more spiritual and ethereal and at the same
time more healthy. There was color in her cheeks, and
her eyes drew him again and again—the eyes in which
he had first read immortality. He had forgotten immortality of late, and the trend of his scientific reading
had been away from it; but here, in Ruth's eyes, he
read an argument without words that transcended all
worded arguments. He saw that in her eyes before
which all discussion fled away, for he saw love there.

And in his own eyes was love; and love was unanswerable. Such was his passionate doctrine.

The half hour he had with her, before they went in to dinner, left him supremely happy and supremely satisfied with life. Nevertheless, at table, the inevitable reaction and exhaustion consequent upon the hard day seized hold of him. He was aware that his eyes were tired and that he was irritable. He remembered it was at this table, at which he now sneered and was so often bored, that he had first eaten with civilized beings in what he had imagined was an atmosphere of high culture and refinement. He caught a glimpse of that pathetic figure of him, so long ago, a self-conscious savage, sprouting sweat at every pore in an agony of apprehension, puzzled by the bewildering minutiae of eating-implements, tortured by the ogre of a servant, striving at a leap to live at such dizzy social altitude, and deciding in the end to be frankly himself, pretending no knowledge and no polish he did not possess.

He glanced at Ruth for reassurance, much in the same manner that a passenger, with sudden panic thought of possible shipwreck, will strive to locate the life preservers. Well, that much had come out of it—love and Ruth. All the rest had failed to stand the test of the books. But Ruth and love had stood the test; for them he found a biological sanction. Love was the most exalted expression of life. Nature had been busy designing him, as she had been busy with all normal men, for the purpose of loving. She had spent ten thousand centuries—ay, a hundred thousand and a million centuries—upon the task, and he was the best she could do. She had made love the strongest thing in him, increased its power a myriad per cent with her gift of imagination, and sent him forth into the ephemera to thrill and melt and mate. His hand sought Ruth's hand beside him hidden by the table, and a warm pressure was given and received. She looked at him a swift instant, and her eyes were radiant and melting. So were his in the thrill that pervaded him; nor did he realize how much that was radiant and melting in her eyes had been aroused by what she had seen in his.

Across the table from him, cater-cornered, at Mr. Morse's right, sat Judge Blount, a local superior court judge. Martin had met him a number of times and had failed to like him. He and Ruth's father were discussing labor union politics, the local situation, and socialism, and Mr. Morse was endeavoring to twit Martin on the latter topic. At last Judge Blount looked across the table with benignant and fatherly pity. Martin smiled to himself.

"You'll grow out of it, young man," he said soothingly. "Time is the best cure for such youthful distempers." He turned to Mr. Morse. "I do not believe discussion is good in such cases. It makes the patient obstinate."

"That is true," the other assented gravely. "But it is well to warn the patient occasionally of his condition."

Martin laughed merrily, but it was with an effort. The day had been too long, the day's effort too intense, and he was deep in the throes of the reaction.

"Undoubtedly you are both excellent doctors," he said, "but if you care a whit for the opinion of the patient, let him tell you that you are poor diagnosticians. In fact, you are both suffering from the disease you think you find in me. As for me, I am immune. The socialist philosophy that riots half-baked in your veins has passed me by."

"Clever, clever," murmured the judge. "An excellent ruse in controversy, to reverse positions."

"Out of your mouth." Martin's eyes were sparkling, but he kept control of himself. "You see, Judge, I've heard your campaign speeches. By some henidical process—henidical, by the way, is a favorite word of mine which nobody understands—by some henidical process you persuade yourself that you believe in the competitive system and the survival of the strong, and at the same time you indorse with might and main all sorts of measures to shear the strength from the strong."

"My young man—"

"Remember, I've heard your campaign speeches," Martin warned. "It's on record, your position on interstate commerce regulation, on regulation of the railway trust and Standard Oil, on the conservation of the forests, on a thousand and one restrictive measures that are nothing else than socialistic."

"Do you mean to tell me that you do not believe in regulating these various outrageous exercises of power?"

"That's not the point. I mean to tell you that you are a poor diagnostician. I mean to tell you that I am not suffering from the microbe of socialism. I mean to tell you that it is you who are suffering from the emasculating ravages of that same microbe. As for me, I am an inveterate opponent of socialism just as I am an inveterate opponent of your own mongrel democracy that is nothing else than pseudo-socialism masquerading under a garb of words that will not stand the test of the dictionary.

"I am a reactionary—so complete a reactionary that my position is incomprehensible to you who live in a veiled lie of social organization and whose sight is not keen enough to pierce the veil. You make believe that you believe in the survival of the strong and the rule of the strong. I believe. That is the difference. When I was a trifle younger,—a few months younger,—I believed the same thing. You see, the ideas of you and yours had impressed me. But merchants and traders are cowardly rulers at best; they grunt and grub all their days in the trough of money-getting, and I have swung back to aristocracy, if you please. I am the only individualist in this room. I look to the state for nothing. I look only to the strong man, the man on horseback, to save the state from its own rotten futility.

"Nietzsche was right. I won't take the time to tell you who Nietzsche was, but he was right. The world belongs to the strong—to the strong who are noble as well and who do not wallow in the swine-trough of trade and exchange. The world belongs to the true noblemen, to the great blond beasts, to the non-compromisers, to the 'yes-sayers.' And they will eat you up, you socialists who are afraid of socialism and who think yourselves individualists. Your slave-morality of the meek and lowly will never save you.— Oh, it's all Greek, I know, and I won't bother you any more with it. But remember one thing. There aren't half a dozen individualists in Oakland, but Martin Eden is one of them."

He signified that he was done with the discussion, and turned to Ruth.

"I'm wrought up today," he said in an undertone. "All I want to do is to love, not talk."

He ignored Mr. Morse, who said:—

"I am unconvinced. All socialists are Jesuits. That is the way to tell them."

"We'll make a good Republican out of you yet," said Judge Blount.

"The man on horseback will arrive before that time," Martin retorted with good humor, and returned to Ruth.

But Mr. Morse was not content. He did not like the laziness and the disinclination for sober, legitimate work of this prospective son-in-law of his, for whose ideas he had no respect and of whose nature he had no understanding. So he turned the conversation to Herbert Spencer. Judge Blount ably seconded him, and Martin, whose ears had pricked at the first mention of the philosopher's name, listened to the judge enunciate a grave and complacent diatribe against Spencer. From time to time Mr. Morse glanced at Martin, as much as to say, "There, my boy, you see."

"Chattering daws," Martin muttered under his breath and went on talking with Ruth and Arthur.

But the long day and the "real dirt" of the night before were telling upon him; and, besides, still burning in his mind was what had made him angry when he read it on the car.

"What is the matter?" Ruth asked suddenly, alarmed by the effort he was making to contain himself.

"There is no god but the Unknowable, and Herbert Spencer is its prophet," Judge Blount was saying at that moment.

Martin turned upon him.

"A cheap judgment," he remarked quietly. "I heard it first in the City Hall Park, on the lips of a workingman who ought to have known better. I have heard it often since, and each time the claptrap of it nauseates me. You ought to be ashamed of yourself. To hear that great and noble man's name upon your lips is like finding a dew-drop in a cesspool. You are disgusting."

It was like a thunderbolt. Judge Blount glared at him with apoplectic countenance, and silence reigned. Mr. Morse was secretly pleased. He could see that his daughter was shocked. It was what he wanted to do—to bring out the innate ruffianism of this man he did not like.

Ruth's hand sought Martin's beseechingly under the table, but his blood was up. He was inflamed by the intellectual pretense and fraud of those who sat in the high places. A Superior Court Judge! It was only several years before that he had looked up from the mire at such glorious entities and deemed them gods.

Judge Blount recovered himself and attempted to go on, addressing himself to Martin with an assumption of politeness that the latter understood was for the benefit of the ladies. Even this added to his anger. Was there no honesty in the world?

"You can't discuss Spencer with me," he cried. "You do not know any more about Spencer than do his own countrymen. But it is no fault of yours, I grant. It is just a phase of the contemptible ignorance of the times. I ran across a sample of it on my way here this evening. I was reading an essay by Saleeby on Spencer. You should read it. It is accessible to all men. You can buy it in any bookstore or draw it from the public library. You would feel ashamed of your paucity of abuse and ignorance of that noble man compared with what Saleeby has collected on the subject. It is a record of shame that would shame your shame.

" 'The philosopher of the half-educated,' he was called by an academic philosopher who was not worthy to pollute the atmosphere he breathed. I don't think you have read ten pages of Spencer, but there have been critics, assumably more intelligent than you, who have read no more than you of Spencer, who publicly challenged his followers to adduce one single idea from all his writings—from Herbert Spencer's writings. The man who has impressed the stamp of his genius over the whole field of scientific research and modern thought; the father of psychology; the man who revolutionized pedagogy, so that today the child of the French peasant is taught the three R's according to principles laid down by him. And the little gnats of men sting his memory when they get their very bread and butter from the technical application of his ideas. What little of worth resides in their brains is largely due to him. It is certain that had he never lived, most of what is correct in their parrot-learned knowledge would be absent.

"And yet a man like Principal Fairbanks of Oxford—a man who sits in an even higher place than you, Judge Blount—has said that Spencer will be dismissed by posterity as a poet and dreamer rather than a thinker. Yappers and blatherskites, the whole brood of them! ' "First Principles" is not wholly destitute of a certain literary power,' said one of them. And others of them have said that he was an industrious plodder rather than an original thinker. Yappers and blatherskites! Yappers and blatherskites!"

Martin ceased abruptly, in a dead silence. Everybody in Ruth's family looked up to Judge Blount as a man of power and achievement, and they were horrified at Martin's outbreak. The remainder of the dinner passed like a funeral, the judge and Mr. Morse confining their talk to each other, and the rest of the conversation being extremely desultory. Then afterward, when Ruth and Martin were alone, there was a scene.

"You are unbearable," she wept.

But his anger still smoldered, and he kept muttering, "The beasts! The beasts!"

When she averred he had insulted the judge, he retorted:—

"By telling the truth about him?"

"I don't care whether it was true or not," she insisted. "There are certain bounds of decency, and you had no license to insult anybody."

"Then where did Judge Blount get the license to

assault truth?" Martin demanded. "Surely to assault truth is a more serious misdemeanor than to insult a pygmy personality such as the judge's. He did worse than that. He blackened the name of a great, noble man who is dead. Oh, the beasts! The beasts!"

His complex anger flamed afresh, and Ruth was in terror of him. Never had she seen him so angry, and it was all mystified and unreasonable to her comprehension. And yet, through her very terror ran the fibers of fascination that had drawn and that still drew her to him—that had compelled her to lean towards him, and, in that mad culminating moment, lay her hands upon his neck. She was hurt and outraged by what had taken place, and yet she lay in his arms and quivered while he went on muttering, "The beasts! The beasts!" And she still lay there when he said: "I'll not bother your table again, dear. They do not like me, and it is wrong of me to thrust my objectionable presence upon them. Besides, they are just as objectionable to me. Faugh! They are sickening. And to think of it, I dreamed in my innocence that the persons who sat in the high places, who lived in fine houses and had educations and bank accounts, were worthwhile!"

Chapter Thirty-eight

"Come on, let's go down to the local."

So spoke Brissenden, faint from a hemorrhage of half an hour before—the second hemorrhage in three days. The perennial whiskey glass was in his hands, and he drained it with shaking fingers.

"What do I want with socialism?" Martin demanded.

"Outsiders are allowed five-minute speeches," the sick man urged. "Get up and spout. Tell them why you don't want socialism. Tell them what you think about them and their ghetto ethics. Slam Nietzsche into them and get walloped for your pains. Make a scrap of it. It will do them good. Discussion is what they want, and what you want, too. You see, I'd like to see you a socialist before I'm gone. It will give you a sanction for your existence. It is the one thing that will save you in the time of disappointment that is coming to you."

"I never can puzzle out why you, of all men, are a socialist," Martin pondered. "You detest the crowd so. Surely there is nothing in the canaille to recommend it to your æsthetic soul." He pointed an accusing finger at the whiskey glass which the other was refilling. "Socialism doesn't seem to save you."

"I'm very sick," was the answer. "With you it is different. You have health and much to live for, and you must be handcuffed to life somehow. As for me, you wonder why I am a socialist. I'll tell you. It is because socialism is inevitable; because the present rotten and irrational system cannot endure; because the day is past for your man on horseback. The slaves won't stand for it. They are too many, and willy-nilly they'll drag down the would-be equestrian before ever he gets astride. You can't get away from them, and you'll have to swallow the whole slave-morality. It's not a nice mess, I'll allow. But it's been a-brewing and swallow it you must. You are antediluvian anyway, with your Nietzsche ideas. The past is past, and the man who says history repeats itself is a liar. Of course I don't like the crowd, but what's a poor chap to do?

We can't have the man on horseback, and anything is preferable to the timid swine that now rule. But come on, anyway. I'm loaded to the guards now, and if I sit there any longer, I'll get drunk. And you know the doctor says—damn the doctor! I'll fool him yet."

It was Sunday night, and they found the small hall packed by the Oakland socialists, chiefly members of the working class. The speaker, a clever Jew, won Martin's admiration at the same time that he aroused his antagonism. The man's stooped and narrow shoulders and weazened chest proclaimed him the true child of the crowded ghetto, and strong on Martin was the age-long struggle of the feeble, wretched slaves against the lordly handful of men who had ruled over them and would rule over them to the end of time. To Martin this withered wisp of a creature was a symbol. He was the figure that stood forth representative of the whole miserable mass of weaklings and inefficients who perished according to biological law on the ragged confines of life. They were the unfit. In spite of their cunning philosophy and of their antlike proclivities for cooperation, Nature rejected them for the exceptional man. Out of the plentiful spawn of life she flung from her prolific hand she selected only the best. It was by the same method that men, aping her, bred race-horses and cucumbers. Doubtless, a creator of a Cosmos could have devised a better method; but creatures of this particular Cosmos must put up with this particular method. Of course, they could squirm as they perished, as the socialists squirmed, as the speaker on the platform and the perspiring crowd were squirming even now as they counseled together for some new device with which to minimize the penalties of living and outwit the Cosmos.

So Martin thought, and so he spoke when Brissenden urged him to give them hell. He obeyed the mandate, walking up to the platform, as was the custom, and addressing the chairman. He began in a low voice, haltingly, forming into order the ideas which had surged in his brain while the Jew was speaking. In such meetings five minutes was the time allotted to each speaker; but when Martin's five minutes were up, he was in full stride, his attack upon their doctrines but half completed. He had caught their interest, and the audience urged the chairman by acclamation to extend Martin's time. They appreciated him as a foeman worthy of their intellect, and they listened intently, following every word. He spoke with fire and conviction, mincing no words in his attack upon the slaves and their morality and tactics and frankly alluding to his hearers as the slaves in question. He quoted Spencer and Malthus, and enunciated the biological law of development.

"And so," he concluded, in a swift résumé, "no state composed of the slave-types can endure. The old law of development still holds. In the struggle for existence, as I have shown, the strong and the progeny of the strong tend to survive, while the weak and the progeny of the weak are crushed and tend to perish. The result is that the strong and the progeny of the strong survive, and, so long as the struggle obtains, the strength of each generation increases. That is development. But you slaves—it is too bad to be slaves, I grant—but you slaves dream of a society where the law of development will be annulled, where no weaklings and inefficients will perish, where every inefficient will have as much as he wants to eat as many times a day as he desires, and where all will marry and have progeny—the weak as well as the strong. What will be the result? No longer will the strength and life-value of each generation increase. On the contrary, it will diminish. There is the Nemesis of your slave philosophy. Your society of slaves—of, by, and for slaves—must inevitably weaken and go to pieces as the life which composes it weakens and goes to pieces.

"Remember, I am enunciating biology and not sentimental ethics. No state of slaves can stand—"

"How about the United States?" a man yelled from the audience.

"And how about it?" Martin retorted. "The thirteen colonies threw off their rulers and formed the Republic so-called. The slaves were their own masters. There were no more masters of the sword. But you couldn't get along without masters of some sort, and there arose a new set of masters—not the great, virile, noble men, but the shrewd and spidery traders and money-lenders. And they enslaved you over again—but not frankly, as the true, noble men would do with weight of their own right arms, but secretly, by spidery machinations and by wheedling and cajolery and lies. They have purchased your slave judges, they have debauched your slave legislatures, and they have forced to worse horrors than chattel slavery your slave boys and girls. Two million of your children are toiling today in this trader-oligarchy of the United States. Ten millions of you slaves are not properly sheltered nor properly fed.

"But to return. I have shown that no society of slaves can endure, because, in its very nature, such society must annul the law of development. No sooner can a slave society be organized than deterioration sets in. It is easy for you to talk of annulling the law of development, but where is the new law of development that will maintain your strength? Formulate it. Is it already formulated? Then state it."

Martin took his seat amidst an uproar of voices. A score of men were on their feet clamoring for recognition from the chair. And one by one, encouraged by vociferous applause, speaking with fire and enthusiasm and excited gestures, they replied to the attack. It was a wild night—but it was wild intellectually, a battle of ideas. Some strayed from the point, but most of the speakers replied directly to Martin. They shook him with lines of thought that were new to him; and gave him insights, not into new biological laws, but into new applications of the old laws. They were too earnest to be always polite, and more than once the chairman rapped and pounded for order.

It chanced that a cub reporter sat in the audience, detailed there on a day dull of news and impressed by the urgent need of journalism for sensation. He was not a bright cub reporter. He was merely facile and glib. He was too dense to follow the discussion. In fact, he had a comfortable feeling that he was vastly superior to these wordy maniacs of the working class. Also, he had a great respect for those who sat in the high places and dictated the policies of nations and newspapers. Further, he had an ideal, namely, of achieving that excellence of the perfect reporter who is able to make something—even a great deal—out of nothing.

He did not know what all the talk was about. It was not necessary. Words like *revolution* gave him his cue. Like a paleontologist, able to reconstruct an entire skeleton from one fossil bone, he was able to reconstruct a whole speech from the one word *revolution*. He did it that night, and he did it well; and since Martin had made the biggest stir, he put it all into his mouth and made him the arch-anarch of the show, transforming his reactionary individualism into the most

lurid, red-shirt socialist utterance. The cub reporter
was an artist, and it was a large brush with which he
laid on the local color—wild-eyed long-haired men,
neurasthenic and degenerate types of men, voices shaken
with passion, clenched fists raised on high, and all
projected against a background of oaths, yells, and the
throaty rumbling of angry men.

Chapter Thirty-nine

O ver the coffee, in his little room, Martin read next
morning's paper. It was a novel experience to find
himself head-lined, on the first page at that; and he
was surprised to learn that he was the most notorious
leader of the Oakland socialists. He ran over the violent speech the cub reporter had constructed for him,
and, though at first he was angered by the fabrication,
in the end he tossed the paper aside with a laugh.

"Either the man was drunk or criminally malicious,"
he said that afternoon, from his perch on the bed,
when Brissenden had arrived and dropped limply into
the one chair.

"But what do you care?" Brissenden asked. "Surely
you don't desire the approval of the bourgeois swine
that read the newspapers?"

Martin thought for a while, then said:—

"No, I really don't care for their approval, not a
whit. On the other hand, it's very likely to make my
relations with Ruth's family a trifle awkward. Her
father always contended I was a socialist, and this
miserable stuff will clinch his belief. Not that I care
for his opinion—but what's the odds? I want to read

you what I've been doing today. It's 'Overdue,' of course, and I'm just about halfway through."

He was reading aloud when Maria thrust open the door and ushered in a young man in a natty suit who glanced briskly about him, noting the oil-burner and the kitchen in the corner before his gaze wandered on to Martin.

"Sit down," Brissenden said.

Martin made room for the young man on the bed and waited for him to broach his business.

"I heard you speak last night, Mr. Eden, and I've come to interview you," he began.

Brissenden burst out in a hearty laugh.

"A brother socialist?" the reporter asked, with a quick glance at Brissenden that appraised the color-value of that cadaverous and dying man.

"And he wrote that report," Martin said softly. "Why, he is only a boy!"

"Why don't you poke him?" Brissenden asked. "I'd give a thousand dollars to have my lungs back for five minutes."

The cub reporter was a trifle perplexed by this talking over him and around him and at him. But he had been commended for his brilliant description of the socialist meeting and had further been detailed to get a personal interview with Martin Eden, the leader of the organized menace to society.

"You do not object to having your picture taken, Mr. Eden?" he said. "I've a staff photographer outside, you see, and he says it will be better to take you right away before the sun gets lower. Then we can have the interview afterward."

"A photographer," Brissenden said meditatively. "Poke him, Martin! Poke him!"

"I guess I'm getting old," was the answer. "I know

I ought, but I really haven't the heart. It doesn't seem to matter."

"For his mother's sake," Brissenden urged.

"It's worth considering," Martin replied, "but it doesn't seem worth while enough to rouse sufficient energy in me. You see, it does take energy to give a fellow a poking. Besides, what does it matter?"

"That's right—that's the way to take it," the cub announced airily, though he had already begun to glance anxiously at the door.

"But it wasn't true, not a word of what he wrote," Martin went on, confining his attention to Brissenden.

"It was just in a general way a description, you understand," the cub ventured, "and besides, it's good advertising. That's what counts. It was a favor to you."

"It's good advertising, Martin, old boy," Brissenden repeated solemnly.

"And it was a favor to me—think of that!" was Martin's contribution.

"Let me see—where were you born, Mr. Eden?" the cub asked, assuming an air of expectant attention.

"He doesn't take notes," said Brissenden. "He remembers it all."

"That is sufficient for me." The cub was trying not to look worried. "No decent reporter needs to bother with notes."

"That was sufficient—for last night." But Brissenden was not a disciple of quietism, and he changed his attitude abruptly.

"Martin, if you don't poke him, I'll do it myself, if I fall dead on the floor the next moment."

"How will a spanking do?" Martin asked.

Brissenden considered judicially, and nodded his head.

The next instant Martin was seated on the edge of the bed with the cub face downward across his knees.

"Now don't bite," Martin warned, "or else I'll have to punch your face. It would be a pity, for it is such a pretty face."

His uplifted hand descended, and thereafter rose and fell in a swift and steady rhythm. The cub struggled and cursed and squirmed, but did not offer to bite. Brissenden looked on gravely, though once he grew excited and gripped the whiskey bottle, pleading, "Here, just let me swat him once."

"Sorry my hand played out," Martin said, when at last he desisted. "It is quite numb."

He uprighted the cub and perched him on the bed.

"I'll have you arrested for this," he snarled, tears of boyish indignation running down his flushed cheeks. "I'll make you sweat for this. You'll see."

"The pretty thing," Martin remarked. "He doesn't realize that he has entered upon the downward path. It is not honest, it is not square, it is not manly, to tell lies about one's fellow-creatures the way he has done, and he doesn't know it."

"He has to come to us to be told," Brissenden filled in a pause.

"Yes, to me whom he has maligned and injured. My grocery will undoubtedly refuse me credit now. The worst of it is that the poor boy will keep on this way until he deteriorates into a first-class newspaper man and also a first-class scoundrel."

"But there is yet time," quoth Brissenden. "Who knows but what you may prove the humble instrument to save him. Why didn't you let me swat him just once? I'd like to have had a hand in it."

"I'll have you arrested, the pair of you, you b-b-big brutes," sobbed the erring soul.

"No, his mouth is too pretty and too weak." Martin shook his head lugubriously. "I'm afraid I've numbed my hand in vain. The young man cannot reform. He will become eventually a very great and successful newspaper man. He has no conscience. That alone will make him great."

With that the cub passed out the door in trepidation to the last for fear that Brissenden would hit him in the back with the bottle he still clutched.

In the next morning's paper Martin learned a great deal more about himself that was new to him. "We are the sworn enemies of society," he found himself quoted as saying in a column interview. "No, we are not anarchists but socialists." When the reporter pointed out to him that there seemed little difference between the two schools, Martin had shrugged his shoulders in silent affirmation. His face was described as bilaterally asymmetrical, and various other signs of degeneration were described. Especially notable were his thuglike hands and the fiery gleams in his blood-shot eyes.

He learned, also, that he spoke nightly to the workmen in the City Hall Park, and that among the anarchists and agitators that there inflamed the minds of the people he drew the largest audiences and made the most revolutionary speeches. The cub painted a highlight picture of his poor little room, its oil-stove and the one chair, and of the death's-head tramp who kept him company and who looked as if he had just emerged from twenty years of solitary confinement in some fortress dungeon.

The cub had been industrious. He had scurried around and nosed out Martin's family history and procured a photograph of Higginbotham's Cash Store with Bernard Higginbotham himself standing out in front. That gentleman was depicted as an intelligent, dignified business man who had no patience with his brother-in-law's socialistic views, and no patience with the brother-in-law, either, whom he was quoted as characterizing as a lazy good-for-nothing who wouldn't take a job when it was offered to him and who would go to jail yet. Hermann von Schmidt, Marian's husband, had likewise been interviewed. He had called Martin the black sheep of the family and repudiated him. "He tried to sponge off of me, but I put a stop to that good and quick," Von Schmidt had said to the reporter. "He knows better than to come bumming around here. A man who won't work is no good, take that from me."

This time Martin was genuinely angry. Brissenden looked upon the affair as a good joke, but he could not console Martin, who knew that it would be no easy task to explain to Ruth. As for her father, he knew that he must be overjoyed with what had happened and that he would make the most of it to break off the engagement. How much he would make of it he was soon to realize. The afternoon mail brought a letter from Ruth. Martin opened it with a premonition of disaster, and read it standing at the open door when he had received it from the postman. As he read, mechanically his hand sought his pocket for the tobacco and brown paper of his old cigarette days. He was not aware that the pocket was empty or that he had even reached for the materials with which to roll a cigarette.

It was not a passionate letter. There were no touches of anger in it. But all the way through, from the first sentence to the last, was sounded the note of hurt and disappointment. She had expected better of him. She had thought he had got over his youthful wildness, that her love for him had been sufficiently worthwhile to enable him to live seriously and decently. And now her father and mother had taken a firm stand and commanded that the engagement be broken. That they were justified in this she could not but admit. Their relation could never be a happy one. It had been unfortunate from the first. But one regret she voiced in the whole letter, and it was a bitter one to Martin. "If only you had settled down to some position and attempted to make something of yourself," she wrote. "But it was not to be. Your past life had been too wild and irregular. I can understand that you are not to be blamed. You could act only according to your nature and your early training. So I do not blame you, Martin. Please remember that. It was simply a mistake. As father and mother have contended, we were not made for each other, and we should both be happy because it was discovered not too late." . . . "There is no use trying to see me," she said toward the last. "It would be an unhappy meeting for both of us, as well as for my mother. I feel, as it is, that I have caused her great pain and worry. I shall have to do much living to atone for it."

He read it through to the end, carefully, a second time, then sat down and replied. He outlined the remarks he had uttered at the socialist meeting, pointing out that they were in all ways the converse of what the newspaper had put in his mouth. Toward the end of the letter he was God's own lover pleading passionately for love. "Please answer," he said, "and in your answer you have to tell me but one thing. Do you love me? That is all—the answer to that one question."

But no answer came the next day, nor the next. "Overdue" lay untouched upon the table, and each day the heap of returned manuscripts under the table grew larger. For the first time Martin's glorious sleep was interrupted by insomnia, and he tossed through long, restless nights. Three times he called at the Morse home, but was turned away by the servant who answered the bell. Brissenden lay sick in his hotel, too feeble to stir out, and, though Martin was with him often, he did not worry him with his troubles.

For Martin's troubles were many. The aftermath of the cub reporter's deed was even wider than Martin had anticipated. The Portuguese grocer refused him further credit, while the greengrocer, who was an American and proud of it, had called him a traitor to his country and refused further dealings with him—carrying his patriotism to such a degree that he canceled Martin's account and forbade him ever to attempt to pay it. The talk in the neighborhood reflected the same feeling, and indignation against Martin ran high. No one would have anything to do with a socialist traitor. Poor Maria was dubious and frightened, but she remained loyal. The children of the neighborhood recovered from the awe of the grand carriage which once had visited Martin, and from safe distances they called him "hobo" and "bum." The Silva tribe, however, staunchly defended him, fighting more than one pitched battle for his honor, and black eyes and bloody noses became quite the order of the day and added to Maria's perplexities and troubles.

Once, Martin met Gertrude on the street, down in Oakland, and learned what he knew could not be otherwise—that Bernard Higginbotham was furious with him for having dragged the family into public disgrace, and that he had forbidden him the house.

"Why don't you go away, Martin?" Gertrude had begged. "Go away and get a job somewhere and steady down. Afterwards, when this all blows over, you can come back."

Martin shook his head, but gave no explanations.

How could he explain? He was appalled at the awful intellectual chasm that yawned between him and his people. He could never cross it and explain to them his position,—the Nietzschean position, in regard to socialism. There were not words enough in the English language, nor in any language, to make his attitude and conduct intelligible to them. Their highest concept of right conduct, in his case, was to get a job. That was their first word and their last. It constituted their whole lexicon of ideas. Get a job! Go to work! Poor, stupid slaves, he thought, while his sister talked. Small wonder the world belonged to the strong. The slaves were obsessed by their own slavery. A job was to them a golden fetish before which they fell down and worshipped.

He shook his head again, when Gertrude offered him money, though he knew that within the day he would have to make a trip to the pawnbroker.

"Don't come near Bernard now," she admonished him. "After a few months, when he is cooled down, if you want to, you can get the job of drivin' delivery-wagon for him. Any time you want me, just send for me an' I'll come. Don't forget."

She went away weeping audibly, and he felt a pang of sorrow shoot through him at sight of her heavy body and uncouth gait. As he watched her go, the Nietzschean edifice seemed to shake and totter. The slave-class in the abstract was all very well, but it was not wholly satisfactory when it was brought home to his own family. And yet, if there was ever a slave trampled by the strong, that slave was his sister Gertrude. He grinned savagely at the paradox. A fine Nietzsche-man he was, to allow his intellectual concepts to be shaken by the first sentiment or emotion that strayed along—ay, to be shaken by the slave-morality itself, for that was what his pity for his sister really was. The true noble men were above pity and compassion. Pity and compassion had been generated in the subterranean barracoons of the slaves and were no more than the agony and sweat of the crowded miserables and weaklings.

Chapter Forty

"Overdue" still continued to lie forgotten on the table. Every manuscript that he had had out now lay under the table. Only one manuscript he kept going, and that was Brissenden's "Ephemera." His bicycle and black suit were again in pawn, and the typewriter people were once more worrying about the rent. But such things no longer bothered him. He was seeking a new orientation, and until that was found his life must stand still.

After several weeks, what he had been waiting for happened. He met Ruth on the street. It was true, she was accompanied by her brother, Norman, and it was true that they tried to ignore him and that Norman attempted to wave him aside.

"If you interfere with my sister I'll call an officer," Norman threatened. "She does not wish to speak with you, and your insistence is insult."

"If you persist, you'll have to call that officer, and then you'll get your name in the papers," Martin answered grimly. "And now, get out of my way and get the officer if you want to. I'm going to talk with Ruth.

"I want to have it from your own lips," he said to her.

She was pale and trembling, but she held up and looked inquiringly.

"The question I asked in my letter," he prompted.

Norman made an impatient movement, but Martin checked him with a swift look.

She shook her head.

"Is all this of your own free will?" he demanded.

"It is." She spoke in a low, firm voice and with deliberation. "It is of my own free will. You have disgraced me so that I am ashamed to meet my friends. They are all talking about me, I know. That is all I can tell you. You have made me very unhappy, and I never wish to see you again."

"Friends! Gossip! Newspaper misreports! Surely such things are not stronger than love! I can only believe that you never loved me."

A blush drove the pallor from her face.

"After what has passed?" she said faintly. "Martin, you do not know what you are saying. I am not common."

"You see, she doesn't want to have anything to do with you," Norman blurted out, starting on with her.

Martin stood aside and let them pass, fumbling unconsciously in his coat pocket for the tobacco and brown papers that were not there.

It was a long walk to North Oakland, but it was not until he went up the steps and entered his room that he knew he had walked it. He found himself sitting on the edge of the bed and staring about him like an awakened somnambulist. He noticed "Overdue" lying on the table and drew up his chair and reached for his pen. There was in his nature a logical compulsion toward completeness. Here was something undone. It had been deferred against the completion of something else. Now that something else had been finished, and he would apply himself to this task until it was finished. What he would do next he did not know. All that he did know was that a climacteric in his life had been attained. A period had been reached, and he was rounding it off in workmanlike fashion. He was not curious about the future. He would soon enough find out what it held in store for him. Whatever it was, it did not matter. Nothing seemed to matter.

For five days he toiled on at "Overdue," going nowhere, seeing nobody, and eating meagerly. On the morning of the sixth day the postman brought him a thin letter from the editor of *The Parthenon*. A glance told him that "Ephemera" was accepted. "We have submitted the poem to Mr. Cartwright Bruce," the editor went on to say, "and he has reported so favorably upon it that we cannot let it go. As an earnest of our pleasure in publishing the poem, let me tell you that we have set it for the August number, our July number being already made up. Kindly extend our pleasure and our thanks to Mr. Brissenden. Please send by return mail his photograph and biographical data. If our honorarium is unsatisfactory, kindly telegraph us at once and state what you consider a fair price."

Since the honorarium they had offered was three hundred and fifty dollars, Martin thought it not worth while to telegraph. Then, too, there was Brissenden's consent to be gained. Well, he had been right, after all. Here was one magazine editor who knew real poetry when he saw it. And the price was splendid, even though it was for the poem of a century. As for Cartwright Bruce, Martin knew that he was the one critic for whose opinions Brissenden had any respect.

Martin rode downtown on an electric car, and as

he watched the houses and cross-streets slipping by he was aware of a regret that he was not more elated over his friend's success and over his own signal victory. The one critic in the United States had pronounced favorably on the poem, while his own contention that good stuff could find its way into the magazines had proved correct. But enthusiasm had lost its spring in him, and he found that he was more anxious to see Brissenden than he was to carry the good news. The acceptance of *The Parthenon* had recalled to him that during his five days' devotion to "Overdue" he had not heard from Brissenden nor even thought about him. For the first time Martin realized the daze he had been in, and he felt shame for having forgotten his friend. But even the shame did not burn very sharply. He was numb to emotions of any sort save the artistic ones concerned in the writing of "Overdue." So far as other affairs were concerned, he had been in a trance. For that matter, he was still in a trance. All this life through which the electric car whirred seemed remote and unreal, and he would have experienced little interest and less shock if the great stone steeple of the church he passed had suddenly crumbled to mortar-dust upon his head.

At the hotel he hurried up to Brissenden's room, and hurried down again. The room was empty. All luggage was gone.

"Did Mr. Brissenden leave any address?" he asked the clerk, who looked at him curiously for a moment.

"Haven't you heard?" he asked.

Martin shook his head.

"Why, the papers were full of it. He was found dead in bed. Suicide. Shot himself through the head."

"Is he buried yet?" Martin seemed to hear his voice, like some one else's voice, from a long way off, asking the question.

"No. The body was shipped East after the inquest. Lawyers engaged by his people saw to the arrangements."

"They were quick about it, I must say," Martin commented.

"Oh, I don't know. It happened five days ago."

"Five days ago?"

"Yes, five days ago."

"Oh," Martin said as he turned and went out.

At the corner he stepped into the Western Union and sent a telegram to *The Parthenon*, advising them to proceed with the publication of the poem. He had in his pocket but five cents with which to pay his carfare home, so he sent the message collect.

Once in his room, he resumed his writing. The days and nights came and went, and he sat at his table and wrote on. He went nowhere, save to the pawnbroker, took no exercise, and ate methodically when he was hungry and had something to cook, and just as methodically went without when he had nothing to cook. Composed as the story was, in advance, chapter by chapter, he nevertheless saw and developed an opening that increased the power of it, though it necessitated twenty thousand additional words. It was not that there was any vital need that the thing should be well done, but that his artistic canons compelled him to do it well. He worked on in the daze, strangely detached from the world around him, feeling like a familiar ghost among these literary trappings of his former life. He remembered that some one had said that a ghost was the spirit of a man who was dead and who did not have sense enough to know it; and he paused for the moment to wonder if he were really dead and unaware of it.

Came the day when "Overdue" was finished. The agent of the typewriter firm had come for the machine, and he sat on the bed while Martin, on the one chair, typed the last pages of the final chapter. "Finis," he wrote, in capitals, at the end, and to him it was indeed finis. He watched the typewriter carried out the door with a feeling of relief, then went over and lay down on the bed. He was faint from hunger. Food had not passed his lips in thirty-six hours, but he did not think about it. He lay on his back, with closed eyes, and did not think at all, while the daze or stupor slowly welled up, saturating his consciousness. Half in delirium, he began muttering aloud the lines of an anonymous poem Brissenden had been fond of quoting to him. Maria, listening anxiously outside his door, was perturbed by his monotonous utterance. The words in themselves were not significant to her, but the fact that he was saying them was. "I have done," was the burden of the poem.

> " 'I have done—
> Put by the lute.
> Song and singing soon are over
> As the airy shades that hover
> In among the purple clover.
> I have done—
> Put by the lute.
> Once I sang as early thrushes
> Sing among the dewy bushes;
> Now I'm mute.
> I am like a weary linnet,
> For my throat has no song in it;
> I have had my singing minute.
> I have done.
> Put by the lute.' "

Maria could stand it no longer, and hurried away to the stove, where she filled a quart-bowl with soup, putting into it the lion's share of chopped meat and vegetables which her ladle scraped from the bottom of the pot. Martin roused himself and sat up and began to eat, between spoonfuls reassuring Maria that he had not been talking in his sleep and that he did not have any fever.

After she left him he sat drearily, with drooping shoulders, on the edge of the bed, gazing about him with lack-luster eyes that saw nothing until the torn wrapper of a magazine, which had come in the morning's mail and which lay unopened, shot a gleam of light into his darkened brain. It is *The Parthenon*, he thought, the August *Parthenon*, and it must contain "Ephemera." If only Brissenden were here to see!

He was turning the pages of the magazine, when suddenly he stopped. "Ephemera" had been featured, with gorgeous head-piece and Beardsley-like margin decorations. On one side of the head-piece was Brissenden's photograph, on the other side was the photograph of Sir John Value, the British Ambassador. A preliminary editorial note quoted Sir John Value as saying that there were no poets in America, and the publication of "Ephemera" was *The Parthenon*'s, "There, take that, Sir John Value!" Cartwright Bruce was described as the greatest critic in America, and he was quoted as saying that "Ephemera" was the greatest poem ever written in America. And finally, the editor's foreword ended with: "We have not yet made up our minds entirely as to the merits of 'Ephemera'; perhaps we shall never be able to do so. But we have read it often, wondering at the words and their arrangement, wondering where Mr. Brissenden got them, and how he could fasten them together." Then followed the poem.

"Pretty good thing you died, Briss, old man," Martin murmured, letting the magazine slip between his knees to the floor.

The cheapness and vulgarity of it was nauseating, and Martin noted apathetically that he was not nauseated very much. He wished he could get angry, but did not have energy enough to try. He was too numb. His blood was too congealed to accelerate to the swift tidal flow of indignation. After all, what did it matter? It was on a par with all the rest that Brissenden had condemned in bourgeois society.

"Poor Briss," Martin communed, "he would never have forgiven me."

Rousing himself with an effort, he possessed himself of a box which had once contained typewriter paper. Going through its contents, he drew forth eleven poems which his friend had written. These he tore lengthwise and crosswise and dropped into the waste basket. He did it languidly, and, when he had finished, sat on the edge of the bed staring blankly before him.

How long he sat there he did not know, until, suddenly, across his sightless vision he saw form a long horizontal line of white. It was curious. But as he watched it grow in definiteness he saw that it was a coral reef smoking in the white Pacific surges. Next, in the line of breakers, he made out a small canoe, an outrigger canoe. In the stern he saw a young bronzed god in scarlet hip-cloth dipping a flashing paddle. He recognized him. He was Moti, the youngest son of Tati, the chief, and this was Tahiti, and beyond that smoking reef lay the sweet land of Papara and the chief's grass house by the river's mouth. It was the end of the day, and Moti was coming home from the fishing. He was waiting for the rush of a big breaker whereon to jump the reef. Then he saw himself, sitting forward in the canoe as he had often sat in the past, dipping a paddle that waited Moti's word to dig in like mad when the turquoise wall of the great breaker rose behind them. Next, he was no longer an onlooker but was himself in the canoe, Moti was crying out, they were both thrusting hard with their paddles, racing on the steep face of the flying turquoise. Under the bow the water was hissing as from a steam jet, the air was filled with driven spray, there was a rush and rumble and long-echoing roar, and the canoe floated on the placid water of the lagoon. Moti laughed and shook the salt water from his eyes, and together they paddled in to the pounded-coral beach where Tati's grass walls through the cocoanut-palms showed golden in the setting sun.

The picture faded, and before his eyes stretched the disorder of his squalid room. He strove in vain to see Tahiti again. He knew there was singing among the trees and that the maidens were dancing in the moonlight, but he could not see them. He could see only the littered writing-table, the empty space where the typewriter had stood, and the unwashed window-pane. He closed his eyes with a groan, and slept.

Chapter Forty-one

He slept heavily all night, and did not stir until aroused by the postman on his morning round. Martin felt tired and passive and went through his letters aimlessly. One thin envelope, from a robber magazine, contained a check for twenty-two dollars. He had been dunning for it for a year and a half. He noted its amount apathetically. The old-time thrill at receiving a publisher's check was gone. Unlike his earlier checks, this one was not pregnant with promise of great things to come. To him it was a check for twenty-two dollars, that was all, and it would buy him something to eat.

Another check was in the same mail, sent from a New York weekly in payment for some humorous verse which had been accepted months before. It was for ten dollars. An idea came to him, which he calmly considered. He did not know what he was going to do, and he felt in no hurry to do anything. In the meantime he must live. Also he owed numerous debts. Would it not be a paying investment to put stamps on the huge pile of manuscripts under the table and start them on their travels again? One or two of them might be accepted. That would help him to live. He decided on the investment, and, after he had cashed the checks at the bank down in Oakland, he bought ten dollars' worth of postage stamps. The thought of going home to cook breakfast in his stuffy little room was repulsive to him. For the first time he refused to consider his debts. He knew that in his room he could manufacture a substantial breakfast at a cost of from fifteen to twenty cents. But, instead, he went into the Forum Café and ordered a breakfast that cost two dollars. He tipped the waiter a quarter, and spent fifty cents for a package of Egyptian cigarettes. It was the first time he had smoked since Ruth had asked him to stop. But he could see now no reason why he should not, and besides, he wanted to smoke. And what did the money matter? For five cents he could have bought a package of Durham and brown papers and rolled forty cigarettes— but what of it? Money had no meaning to him now except what it would immediately buy. He was chartless and rudderless, and he had no port to make, while drifting involved the least living, and it was living that hurt.

The days slipped along, and he slept eight hours regularly every night. Though now, while waiting for more checks, he ate in the Japanese restaurants where meals were served for ten cents, his wasted body filled out, as did the hollows in his cheeks. He no longer abused himself with short sleep, overwork, and over-study. He wrote nothing, and the books were closed. He walked much, out in the hills, and loafed long hours in the quiet parks. He had no friends nor acquaintances, nor did he make any. He had no inclination. He was waiting for some impulse, from he knew not where, to put his stopped life into motion again. In the meantime his life remained run down, planless, and empty and idle.

Once he made a trip to San Francisco to look up the "real dirt." But at the last moment, as he stepped into the upstairs entrance, he recoiled and turned and fled through the swarming ghetto. He was frightened at the thought of hearing philosophy discussed, and he fled furtively, for fear that some one of the "real dirt" might chance along and recognize him.

Sometimes he glanced over the magazines and news-papers to see how "Ephemera" was being maltreated. It had made a hit. But what a hit! Everybody had read it, and everybody was discussing whether or not it was really poetry. The local papers had taken it up, and daily there appeared columns of learned criti-cisms, facetious editorials, and serious letters from subscribers. Helen Della Delmar (proclaimed with a flourish of trumpets and rolling of tomtoms to be the greatest woman poet in the United States) denied Bris-senden a seat beside her on Pegasus and wrote volu-minous letters to the public, proving that he was no poet.

The Parthenon came out in its next number patting

itself on the back for the stir it had made, sneering at Sir John Value, and exploiting Brissenden's death with ruthless commercialism. A newspaper with a sworn circulation of half a million published an original and spontaneous poem by Helen Della Delmar, in which she gibed and sneered at Brissenden. Also, she was guilty of a second poem, in which she parodied him.

Martin had many times to be glad that Brissenden was dead. He had hated the crowd so, and here all that was finest and most sacred of him had been thrown to the crowd. Daily the vivisection of Beauty went on. Every nincompoop in the land rushed into free print, floating their wizened little egos into the public eye on the surge of Brissenden's greatness. Quoth one paper: "We have received a letter from a gentleman who wrote a poem just like it, only better, some time ago." Another paper, in deadly seriousness, reproving Helen Della Delmar for her parody, said: "But un-questionably Miss Delmar wrote it in a moment of badinage and not quite with the respect that one great poet should show to another and perhaps to the great-est. However, whether Miss Delmar be jealous or not of the man who invented 'Ephemera,' it is certain that she, like thousands of others, is fascinated by his work, and that the day may come when she will try to write lines like his."

Ministers began to preach sermons against "Ephem-era," and one, who too stoutly stood for much of its content, was expelled for heresy. The great poem con-tributed to the gaiety of the world. The comic verse-writers and the cartoonists took hold of it with scream-ing laughter, and in the personal columns of society weeklies jokes were perpetrated on it to the effect that Charley Frensham told Archie Jennings, in confi-dence, that five lines of "Ephemera" would drive a

man to beat a cripple, and that ten lines would send
him to the bottom of the river.

Martin did not laugh; nor did he grit his teeth in
anger. The effect produced upon him was one of great
sadness. In the crash of his whole world, with love on
the pinnacle, the crash of magazinedom and the dear
public was a small crash indeed. Brissenden had been
wholly right in his judgment of the magazines, and
he, Martin, had spent arduous and futile years in order
to find it out for himself. The magazines were all
Brissenden had said they were and more. Well, he was
done, he solaced himself. He had hitched his wagon
to a star and been landed in a pestiferous marsh. The
visions of Tahiti—clean, sweet Tahiti—were coming
to him more frequently. And there were the low Pau-
motus, and the high Marquesas; he saw himself often,
now, on board trading schooners or frail little cutters,
slipping out at dawn through the reef at Papeete and
beginning the long beat through the pearl-atolls to
Nukahiva and the Bay of Taiohæ, where Tamari, he
knew, would kill a pig in honor of his coming, and
where Tamari's flower-garlanded daughters would seize
his hands and with song and laughter garland him with
flowers. The South Seas were calling, and he knew
that sooner or later he would answer the call.

In the meantime he drifted, resting and recuperating
after the long traverse he had made through the realm
of knowledge. When *The Parthenon* check of three
hundred and fifty dollars was forwarded to him, he
turned it over to the local lawyer who had attended
to Brissenden's affairs for his family. Martin took a
receipt for the check, and at the same time gave a note
for the hundred dollars Brissenden had let him have.

The time was not long when Martin ceased patron-
izing the Japanese restaurants. At the very moment

when he had abandoned the fight, the tide turned. But it had turned too late. Without a thrill he opened a thin envelope from *The Millennium*, scanned the face of a check that represented three hundred dollars, and noted that it was the payment on acceptance for "Adventure." Every debt he owed in the world, including the pawnshop with its usurious interest, amounted to less than a hundred dollars. And when he had paid everything, and lifted the hundred-dollar note with Brissenden's lawyer, he still had over a hundred dollars in pocket. He ordered a suit of clothes from the tailor and ate his meals in the best cafés in town. He still slept in his little room at Maria's, but the sight of his new clothes caused the neighborhood children to cease from calling him "hobo" and "tramp" from the roofs of woodsheds and over back fences.

"Wiki-Wiki," his Hawaiian short story, was bought by *Warren's Monthly* for two hundred and fifty dollars. *The Northern Review* took his essay, "The Cradle of Beauty," and *Mackintosh's Magazine* took "The Palmist"—the poem he had written to Marian. The editors and readers were back from their summer vacations, and manuscripts were being handled quickly. But Martin could not puzzle out what strange whim animated them to this general acceptance of the things they had persistently rejected for two years. Nothing of his had been published. He was not known anywhere outside of Oakland, and in Oakland, with the few who thought they knew him, he was notorious as a red-shirt and a socialist. So there was no explaining this sudden acceptability of his wares. It was sheer jugglery of fate.

After it had been refused by a number of magazines, he had taken Brissenden's rejected advice and started "The Shame of the Sun" on the round of publishers. After several refusals, Singletree, Darnley & Co. accepted it, promising fall publication. When Martin asked for an advance on royalties, they wrote that such was not their custom, that books of that nature rarely paid for themselves, and that they doubted if his book would sell a thousand copies. Martin figured what the book would earn him on such a sale. Retailed at a dollar, on a royalty of fifteen per cent, it would bring him one hundred and fifty dollars. He decided that if he had it to do over again he would confine himself to fiction. "Adventure," one-fourth as long, had brought him twice as much from *The Millennium*. That newspaper paragraph he had read so long ago had been true, after all. The first-class magazines did not pay on acceptance, and they paid well. Not two cents a word, but four cents a word, had *The Millennium* paid him. And, furthermore, they bought good stuff, too, for were they not buying his? This last thought he accompanied with a grin.

He wrote to Singletree, Darnley & Co., offering to sell out his rights in "The Shame of the Sun" for a hundred dollars, but they did not care to take the risk. In the meantime he was not in need of money, for several of his later stories had been accepted and paid for. He actually opened a bank account, where, without a debt in the world, he had several hundred dollars to his credit. "Overdue," after having been declined by a number of magazines, came to rest at the Meredith-Lowell Company. Martin remembered the five dollars Gertrude had given him, and his resolve to return it to her a hundred times over; so he wrote for an advance on royalties of five hundred dollars. To his surprise a check for that amount, accompanied by a contract, came by return mail. He cashed the check into five-dollar gold pieces and telephoned Gertrude that he wanted to see her.

She arrived at the house panting and short of breath

from the haste she had made. Apprehensive of trouble, she had stuffed the few dollars she possessed into her hand-satchel; and so sure was she that disaster had overtaken her brother, that she stumbled forward, sobbing, into his arms, at the same time thrusting the satchel mutely at him.

"I'd have come myself," he said. "But I didn't want a row with Mr. Higginbotham, and that is what would have surely happened."

"He'll be all right after a time," she assured him, while she wondered what the trouble was that Martin was in. "But you'd best get a job first an' steady down. Bernard does like to see a man at honest work. That stuff in the newspapers broke 'm all up. I never saw 'm so mad before."

"I'm not going to get a job," Martin said with a smile. "And you can tell him so from me. I don't need a job, and there's the proof of it."

He emptied the hundred gold pieces into her lap in a glinting, tinkling stream.

"You remember that fiver you gave me the time I didn't have carfare? Well, there it is, with ninety-nine brothers of different ages but all of the same size."

If Gertrude had been frightened when she arrived, she was now in a panic of fear. Her fear was such that it was certitude. She was not suspicious. She was convinced. She looked at Martin in horror, and her heavy limbs shrank under the golden stream as though it were burning her.

"It's yours," he laughed.

She burst into tears, and began to moan, "My poor boy, my poor boy!"

He was puzzled for a moment. Then he divined the cause of her agitation and handed her the Meredith-Lowell letter which had accompanied the check. She stumbled through it, pausing now and again to wipe her eyes, and when she had finished, said:—

"An' does it mean that you come by the money honestly?"

"More honestly than if I'd won it in a lottery. I earned it."

Slowly faith came back to her, and she reread the letter carefully. It took him long to explain to her the nature of the transaction which had put the money into his possession, and longer still to get her to understand that the money was really hers and that he did not need it.

"I'll put it in the bank for you," she said finally.

"You'll do nothing of the sort. It's yours, to do with as you please, and if you won't take it, I'll give it to Maria. She'll know what to do with it. I'd suggest, though, that you hire a servant and take a good long rest."

"I'm goin' to tell Bernard all about it," she announced, when she was leaving.

Martin winced, then grinned.

"Yes, do," he said. "And then, maybe, he'll invite me to dinner again."

"Yes, he will—I'm sure he will!" she exclaimed fervently, as she drew him to her and kissed and hugged him.

Chapter Forty-two

One day Martin became aware that he was lonely. He was healthy and strong, and had nothing to do. The cessation from writing and studying, the death of Brissenden, and the estrangement from Ruth had made a big hole in his life; and his life refused to be pinned down to good living in cafés and the smoking of Egyptian cigarettes. It was true the South Seas were calling to him, but he had a feeling that the game was not yet played out in the United States. Two books were soon to be published, and he had more books that might find publication. Money could be made out of them, and he would wait and take a sackful of it into the South Seas. He knew a valley and a bay in the Marquesas that he could buy for a thousand Chili dollars. The valley ran from the horseshoe, landlocked bay to the tops of the dizzy, cloud-capped peaks and contained perhaps ten thousand acres. It was filled with tropical fruits, wild chickens, and wild pigs, with an occasional herd of wild cattle, while high up among the peaks were herds of wild goats harried by packs of wild dogs. The whole place was wild. Not a human lived in it. And he could buy it and the bay for a thousand Chili dollars.

The bay, as he remembered it, was magnificent, with water deep enough to accommodate the largest vessel afloat, and so safe that the South Pacific Directory recommended it as the best careening place for ships for hundreds of miles around. He would buy a schooner—one of those yacht-like, coppered crafts that sailed like witches—and go trading copra and pearling among the islands. He would make the valley and the bay his headquarters. He would build a patriarchal grass house like Tati's, and have it and the valley and the schooner filled with dark-skinned servitors. He would entertain there the factor of Taiohæ, captains of wandering traders, and all the best of the South Pacific riffraff. He would keep open house and entertain like a prince. And he would forget the books he had opened and the world that had proved an illusion.

To do all this he must wait in California to fill the sack with money. Already it was beginning to flow in. If one of the books made a strike, it might enable him to sell the whole heap of manuscripts. Also he could collect the stories and the poems into books, and make sure of the valley and the bay and the schooner. He would never write again. Upon that he was resolved. But in the meantime, awaiting the publication of the books, he must do something more than live dazed and stupid in the sort of uncaring trance into which he had fallen.

He noted, one Sunday morning, that the Bricklayers' Picnic took place that day at Shell Mound Park, and to Shell Mound Park he went. He had been to the working-class picnics too often in his earlier life not to know what they were like, and as he entered the park he experienced a recrudescence of all the old sensations. After all, they were his kind, these working people. He had been born among them, he had lived among them, and though he had strayed for a time, it was well to come back among them.

"If it ain't Mart!" he heard some one say, and the next moment a hearty hand was on his shoulder. "Where you ben all the time? Off to sea? Come on an' have a drink."

It was the old crowd in which he found himself— the old crowd, with here and there a gap, and here and there a new face. The fellows were not bricklayers, but, as in the old days, they attended all Sunday picnics for the dancing, and the fighting, and the fun. Martin drank with them, and began to feel really human once more. He was a fool to have ever left them, he thought; and he was very certain that his sum of happiness would have been greater had he remained with them and let alone the books and the people who sat in the high places. Yet the beer seemed not so good as of yore. It didn't taste as it used to taste. Brissenden had spoiled him for steam beer, he concluded, and wondered if, after all, the books had spoiled him for companionship with these friends of his youth. He resolved that he would not be so spoiled, and he went on to the dancing pavilion. Jimmy, the plumber, he met there, in the company of a tall, blonde girl who promptly forsook him for Martin.

"Gee, it's like old times," Jimmy explained to the gang that gave him the laugh as Martin and the blonde whirled away in a waltz. "An' I don't give a rap. I'm too damned glad to see 'm back. Watch 'm waltz, eh? It's like silk. Who'd blame any girl?"

But Martin restored the blonde to Jimmy, and the three of them, with half a dozen friends, watched the revolving couples and laughed and joked with one another. Everybody was glad to see Martin back. No book of his had been published; he carried no fictitious value in their eyes. They liked him for himself. He felt like a prince returned from exile, and his lonely heart burgeoned in the geniality in which it bathed. He made a mad day of it, and was at his best. Also, he had money in his pockets, and, as in the old days when he returned from sea with a pay-day, he made the money fly.

Once, on the dancing-floor, he saw Lizzie Connolly go by in the arms of a young workingman; and, later, when he made the round of the pavilion, he came upon her sitting by a refreshment table. Surprise and greetings over, he led her away into the grounds, where they could talk without shouting down the music. From the instant he spoke to her, she was his. He

knew it. She showed it in the proud humility of her
eyes, in every caressing movement of her proudly carried body, and in the way she hung upon his speech.
She was not the young girl as he had known her. She
was a woman, now, and Martin noted that her wild,
defiant beauty had improved, losing none of its wildness, while the defiance and the fire seemed more in
control. "A beauty, a perfect beauty," he murmured
admiringly under his breath. And he knew she was
his, that all he had to do was to say "Come," and she
would go with him over the world wherever he led.

Even as the thought flashed through his brain he
received a heavy blow on the side of his head that
nearly knocked him down. It was a man's fist, directed
by a man so angry and in such haste that the fist had
missed the jaw for which it was aimed. Martin turned
as he staggered, and saw the fist coming at him in a
wild swing. Quite as a matter of course he ducked,
and the fist flew harmlessly past, pivoting the man
who had driven it. Martin hooked with his left, landing
on the pivoting man with the weight of his body behind the blow. The man went to the ground sidewise,
leaped to his feet, and made a mad rush. Martin saw
ois passion-distorted face and wondered what could
be the cause of the fellow's anger. But while he wondered, he shot in a straight left, the weight of his body
behind the blow. The man went over backward and
fell in a crumpled heap. Jimmy and others of the gang
were running toward them.

Martin was thrilling all over. This was the old days
with a vengeance, with their dancing, and their fighting, and their fun. While he kept a wary eye on his
antagonist, he glanced at Lizzie. Usually the girls
screamed when the fellows got to scrapping, but she
had not screamed. She was looking on with bated

breath, leaning slightly forward, so keen was her interest, one hand pressed to her breast, her cheek flushed, and in her eyes a great and amazed admiration.

The man had gained his feet and was struggling to escape the restraining arms that were laid on him.

"She was waitin' for me to come back!" he was proclaiming to all and sundry. "She was waitin' for me to come back, an' then that fresh guy comes buttin' in. Let go o' me, I tell yeh. I'm goin' to fix 'm."

"What's eatin' yer?" Jimmy was demanding, as he helped hold the young fellow back. "That guy's Mart Eden. He's nifty with his mits, lemme tell you that, an' he'll eat you alive if you monkey with 'm."

"He can't steal her on me that way," the other interjected.

"He licked the Flyin' Dutchman, an' you know *him*," Jimmy went on expostulating. "An' he did it in five rounds. You couldn't last a minute against him. See?"

This information seemed to have a mollifying effect, and the irate young man favored Martin with a measuring stare.

"He don't look it," he sneered; but the sneer was without passion.

"That's what the Flyin' Dutchman thought," Jimmy assured him. "Come on, now, let's get outa this. There's lots of other girls. Come on."

The young fellow allowed himself to be led away toward the pavilion, and the gang followed after him.

"Who is he?" Martin asked Lizzie. "And what's it all about, anyway?"

Already the zest of combat, which of old had been so keen and lasting, had died down, and he discovered that he was self-analytical, too much so to live, single heart and single hand, so primitive an existence.

Lizzie tossed her head.

"Oh, he's nobody," she said. "He's just been keepin' company with me.

"I had to, you see," she explained after a pause. "I was gettin' pretty lonesome. But I never forgot." Her voice sank lower, and she looked straight before her. "I'd throw 'm down for you any time."

Martin, looking at her averted face, knowing that all he had to do was to reach out his hand and pluck her, fell to pondering whether, after all, there was any real worth in refined, grammatical English, and, so, forgot to reply to her.

"You put it all over him," she said tentatively, with a laugh.

"He's a husky young fellow, though," he admitted generously. "If they hadn't taken him away, he might have given me my hands full."

"Who was that lady friend I seen you with that night?" she asked abruptly.

"Oh, just a lady friend," was his answer.

"It was a long time ago," she murmured contemplatively. "It seems like a thousand years."

But Martin went no further into the matter. He led the conversation off into other channels. They had lunch in the restaurant, where he ordered wine and expensive delicacies and afterward he danced with her and with no one but her, till she was tired. He was a good dancer, and she whirled around and around with him in a heaven of delight, her head against his shoulder, wishing that it could last forever. Later in the afternoon they strayed off among the trees, where, in the good old fashion, she sat down while he sprawled on his back, his head in her lap. He lay and dozed, while she fondled his hair, looked down on his closed eyes, and loved him without reserve. Looking up suddenly, he read the tender advertisement in her face.

Her eyes fluttered down, then they opened and looked into his with soft defiance.

"I've kept straight all these years," she said, her voice so low that it was almost a whisper.

In his heart Martin knew that it was the miraculous truth. And at his heart pleaded a great temptation. It was in his power to make her happy. Denied happiness himself, why should he deny happiness to her? He could marry her and take her down with him to dwell in the grass-walled castle in the Marquesas. The desire to do it was strong, but stronger still was the imperative command of his nature not to do it. In spite of himself he was still faithful to Love. The old days of license and easy living were gone. He could not bring them back, nor could he go back to them. He was changed—how changed he had not realized until now.

"I am not a marrying man, Lizzie," he said lightly.

The hand caressing his hair paused perceptibly, then went on with the same gentle stroke. He noticed her face harden, but it was with the hardness of resolution, for still the soft color was in her cheeks and she was all glowing and melting.

"I did not mean that—" she began, then faltered. "Or anyway I don't care.

"I don't care," she repeated. "I'm proud to be your friend. I'd do anything for you. I'm made that way, I guess."

Martin sat up. He took her hand in his. He did it deliberately, with warmth but without passion; and such warmth chilled her.

"Don't let's talk about it," she said.

"You are a great and noble woman," he said. "And it is I who should be proud to know you. And I am, I am. You are a ray of light to me in a very dark world, and I've got to be straight with you, just as straight as you have been."

"I don't care whether you're straight with me or not. You could do anything with me. You could throw me in the dirt an' walk on me. An' you're the only man in the world that can," she added with a defiant flash. "I ain't taken care of myself ever since I was a kid for nothin'."

"And it's just because of that that I'm not going to," he said gently. "You are so big and generous that you challenge me to equal generousness. I'm not marrying, and I'm not—well, loving without marrying, though I've done my share of that in the past. I'm sorry I came here today and met you. But it can't be helped now, and I never expected it would turn out this way.

"But look here, Lizzie. I can't begin to tell you how much I like you. I do more than like you. I admire and respect you. You are magnificent, and you are magnificently good. But what's the use of words? Yet there's something I'd like to do. You've had a hard life; let me make it easy for you." (A joyous light welled into her eyes, then faded out again.) "I'm pretty sure of getting hold of some money soon—lots of it."

In that moment he abandoned the idea of the valley and the bay, the grass-walled castle and the trim, white schooner. After all, what did it matter? He could go away, as he had done so often, before the mast, on any ship bound anywhere.

"I'd like to turn it over to you. There must be something you want—to go to school or business college. You might like to study and be a stenographer. I could fix it for you. Or maybe your father and mother are living—I could set them up in a grocery store or something. Anything you want, just name it, and I can fix it for you."

She made no reply, but sat, gazing straight before her, dry-eyed and motionless, but with an ache in the throat which Martin divined so strongly that it made his own throat ache. He regretted that he had spoken. It seemed so tawdry what he had offered her—mere money—compared with what she offered him. He offered her an extraneous thing with which he could part without a pang, while she offered him herself, along with disgrace and shame, and sin, and all her hopes of heaven.

"Don't let's talk about it," she said with a catch in her voice that she changed to a cough. She stood up. "Come on, let's go home. I'm all tired out."

The day was done, and the merrymakers had nearly all departed. But as Martin and Lizzie emerged from the trees they found the gang waiting for them. Martin knew immediately the meaning of it. Trouble was brewing. The gang was his bodyguard. They passed out through the gates of the park with, straggling in the rear, a second gang, the friends that Lizzie's young man had collected to avenge the loss of his lady. Several constables and special police officers, anticipating trouble, trailed along to prevent it, and herded the two gangs separately aboard the train for San Francisco. Martin told Jimmy that he would get off at Sixteenth Street Station and catch the electric car into Oakland. Lizzie was very quiet and without interest in what was impending. The train pulled in to Sixteenth Street Station, and the waiting electric car could be seen, the conductor of which was impatiently clanging the gong.

"There she is," Jimmy counseled. "Make a run for it, an' we'll hold 'em back. Now you go! Hit her up!"

The hostile gang was temporarily disconcerted by the maneuver, then it dashed from the train in pursuit. The staid and sober Oakland folk who sat upon the car scarcely noted the young fellow and the girl who ran for it and found a seat in front on the outside. They did not connect the couple with Jimmy, who sprang on the steps, crying to the motorman:—

"Slam on the juice, old man, and beat it outa here!"

The next moment Jimmy whirled about, and the passengers saw him land his fist on the face of a running man who was trying to board the car. But fists were landing on faces the whole length of the car. Thus, Jimmy and his gang, strung out on the long, lower steps, met the attacking gang. The car started with a great clanging of its gong, and, as Jimmy's gang drove off the last assailants, they, too, jumped off to finish the job. The car dashed on, leaving the flurry of combat far behind, and its dumfounded passengers never dreamed that the quiet young man and the pretty working-girl sitting in the corner on the outside seat had been the cause of the row.

Martin had enjoyed the fight, with a recrudescence of the old fighting thrills. But they quickly died away, and he was oppressed by a great sadness. He felt very old—centuries older than those careless, carefree young companions of his other days. He had traveled far, too far to go back. Their mode of life, which had once been his, was now distasteful to him. He was disappointed in it all. He had developed into an alien. As the steam beer had tasted raw, so their companionship seemed raw to him. He was too far removed. Too many thousands of opened books yawned between them and him. He had exiled himself. He had travelled in the vast realm of intellect until he could no longer return home. On the other hand, he was human, and his gregarious need for companionship remained unsatisfied. He had found no new home. As the gang could not understand him, as his own family could not understand him, as the bourgeoisie could not understand him, so this girl beside him, whom he honored high, could not understand him nor the honor he paid her. His sadness was not untouched with bitterness as he thought it over.

"Make it up with him," he advised Lizzie, at parting, as they stood in front of the workingman's shack in which she lived, near Sixth and Market. He referred to the young fellow whose place he had usurped that day.

"I can't—now," she said.

"Oh, go on," he said jovially. "All you have to do is whistle and he'll come running."

"I didn't mean that," she said simply.

And he knew what she had meant.

She leaned toward him as he was about to say good night. But she leaned not imperatively, not seductively, but wistfully and humbly. He was touched to the heart. His large tolerance rose up in him. He put his arms around her, and kissed her, and knew that upon his own lips rested as true a kiss as man ever received.

"My God!" she sobbed. "I could die for you. I could die for you."

She tore herself from him suddenly and ran up the steps. He felt a quick moisture in his eyes.

"Martin Eden," he communed. "You're not a brute, and you're a damn poor Nietzscheman. You'd marry her if you could and fill her quivering heart full with happiness. But you can't, you can't. And it's a damn shame.

" 'A poor old tramp explains his poor old ulcers,' " he muttered, remembering his Henley. " 'Life is, I think, a blunder and a shame.' It is—a blunder and a shame."

Chapter Forty-three

"The Shame of the Sun" was published in October. As Martin cut the cords of the express package and the half-dozen complimentary copies from the publishers spilled out on the table, a heavy sadness fell upon him. He thought of the wild delight that would have been his had this happened a few short months before, and he contrasted that delight that should have been with his present uncaring coldness. His book, his first book, and his pulse had not gone up a fraction of a beat, and he was only sad. It meant little to him now. The most it meant was that it might bring some money, and little enough did he care for money.

He carried a copy out into the kitchen and presented it to Maria.

"I did it," he explained, in order to clear up her bewilderment. "I wrote it in the room there, and I guess some few quarts of your vegetable soup went into the making of it. Keep it. It's yours. Just to remember me by, you know."

He was not bragging, not showing off. His sole motive was to make her happy, to make her proud of him, to justify her long faith in him. She put the book in the front room on top of the family Bible. A sacred thing was this book her lodger had made, a fetish of friendship. It softened the blow of his having been a laundryman, and though she could not understand a line of it, she knew that every line of it was great. She was a simple, practical, hard-working woman, but she possessed faith in large endowment.

Just as emotionlessly as he had received "The Shame of the Sun" did he read the reviews of it that came in weekly from the clipping bureau. The book was making a hit, that was evident. It meant more gold in the money sack. He could fix up Lizzie, redeem all his promises, and still have enough left to build his grass-walled castle.

Singletree, Darnley & Co. had cautiously brought

out an edition of fifteen hundred copies, but the first reviews had started a second edition of twice the size through the presses; and ere this was delivered a third edition of five thousand had been ordered. A London firm made arrangements by cable for an English edition, and hot-footed upon this came the news of French, German, and Scandinavian translations in progress. The attack upon the Maeterlinck school could not have been made at a more opportune moment. A fierce controversy was precipitated. Saleeby and Haeckel indorsed and defended "The Shame of the Sun," for once finding themselves on the same side of a question. Crookes and Wallace ranged up on the opposing side, while Sir Oliver Lodge attempted to formulate a compromise that would jibe with his particular cosmic theories. Maeterlinck's followers rallied round the standard of mysticism. Chesterton set the whole world laughing with a series of alleged non-partisan essays on the subject, and the whole affair, controversy and controversialists, was well-nigh swept into the pit by a thundering broadside from George Bernard Shaw. Needless to say the arena was crowded with hosts of lesser lights, and the dust and sweat and din became terrific.

"It is a most marvelous happening," Singletree, Darnley & Co. wrote Martin, "a critical philosophic essay selling like a novel. You could not have chosen your subject better, and all contributory factors have been unwarrantedly propitious. We need scarcely to assure you that we are making hay while the sun shines. Over forty thousand copies have already been sold in the United States and Canada, and a new edition of twenty thousand is on the presses. We are overworked, trying to supply the demand. Nevertheless we have helped to create that demand. We have already spent five thousand dollars in advertising. The book is bound to be a record-breaker.

"Please find herewith a contract in duplicate for your next book which we have taken the liberty of forwarding to you. You will please note that we have increased your royalties to twenty per cent, which is about as high as a conservative publishing house dares go. If our offer is agreeable to you, please fill in the proper blank space with the title of your book. We make no stipulations concerning its nature. Any book on any subject. If you have one already written, so much the better. Now is the time to strike. The iron could not be hotter.

"On receipt of signed contract we shall be pleased to make you an advance on royalties of five thousand dollars. You see, we have faith in you, and we are going in on this thing big. We should like, also, to discuss with you the drawing up of a contract for a term of years, say ten, during which we shall have the exclusive right of publishing in book form all that you produce. But more of this anon."

Martin laid down the letter and worked a problem in mental arithmetic, finding the product of fifteen cents times sixty thousand to be nine thousand dollars. He signed the new contract, inserting "The Smoke of Joy" in the blank space, and mailed it back to the publishers along with the twenty storiettes he had written in the days before he discovered the formula for the newspaper storiette. And promptly as the United States mail could deliver and return, came Singletree, Darnley & Co.'s check for five thousand dollars.

"I want you to come downtown with me, Maria, this afternoon about two o'clock," Martin said, the morning the check arrived. "Or, better, meet me at

Fourteenth and Broadway at two o'clock. I'll be looking out for you."

At the appointed time she was there; but *shoes* was the only clue to the mystery her mind had been capable of evolving, and she suffered a distinct shock of disappointment when Martin walked her right by a shoe-store and dived into a real estate office. What happened thereupon resided forever after in her memory as a dream. Fine gentlemen smiled at her benevolently as they talked with Martin and one another; a typewriter clicked; signatures were affixed to an imposing document; her own landlord was there, too, and affixed his signature; and when all was over and she was outside on the sidewalk, her landlord spoke to her, saying, "Well, Maria, you won't have to pay me no seven dollars and a half this month."

Maria was too stunned for speech.

"Or next month, or the next, or the next," her landlord said.

She thanked him incoherently, as if for a favor. And it was not until she had returned home to North Oakland and conferred with her own kind, and had the Portuguese grocer investigate, that she really knew that she was the owner of the little house in which she had lived and for which she had paid rent so long.

"Why don't you trade with me no more?" the Portuguese grocer asked Martin that evening, stepping out to hail him when he got off the car; and Martin explained that he wasn't doing his own cooking any more, and then went in and had a drink of wine on the house. He noted it was the best wine the grocer had in stock.

"Maria," Martin announced that night, "I'm going to leave you. And you're going to leave here yourself soon. Then you can rent the house and be a landlord yourself. You've a brother in San Leandro or Haywards, and he's in the milk business. I want you to send all your washing back unwashed—understand?—unwashed, and to go out to San Leandro tomorrow, or Haywards, or wherever it is, and see that brother of yours. Tell him to come to see me. I'll be stopping at the Metropole down in Oakland. He'll know a good milk-ranch when he sees one."

And so it was that Maria became a landlord and the sole owner of a dairy, with two hired men to do the work for her and a bank account that steadily increased despite the fact that her whole brood wore shoes and went to school. Few persons ever meet the fairy princes they dream about; but Maria, who worked hard and whose head was hard, never dreaming about fairy princes, entertained hers in the guise of an ex-laundryman.

In the meantime the world had begun to ask: "Who is this Martin Eden?" He had declined to give any biographical data to his publishers, but the newspapers were not to be denied. Oakland was his own town, and the reporters nosed out scores of individuals who could supply information. All that he was and was not, all that he had done and most of what he had not done, was spread out for the delectation of the public, accompanied by snapshots and photographs—the latter procured from the local photographer who had once taken Martin's picture and who promptly copyrighted it and put it on the market. At first, so great was his disgust with the magazines and all bourgeois society, Martin fought against publicity; but in the end, because it was easier than not to, he surrendered. He found that he could not refuse himself to the special writers who traveled long distances to see him. Then again, each day was so many hours long, and, since he no longer was occupied with writing and studying, those hours had to be occupied somehow; so he yielded to what was to him a whim, permitted interviews, gave his opinions on literature and philosophy, and even accepted invitations of the bourgeoisie. He had settled down into a strange and comfortable state of mind. He no longer cared. He forgave everybody, even the cub reporter who had painted him red and to whom he now granted a full page with specially posed photographs.

He saw Lizzie occasionally, and it was patent that she regretted the greatness that had come to him. It widened the space between them. Perhaps it was with the hope of narrowing it that she yielded to his persuasions to go to night school and business college and to have herself gowned by a wonderful dressmaker who charged outrageous prices. She improved visibly from day to day, until Martin wondered if he was doing right, for he knew that all her compliance and endeavor was for his sake. She was trying to make herself of worth in his eyes—of the sort of worth he seemed to value. Yet he gave her no hope, treating her in brotherly fashion and rarely seeing her.

"Overdue" was rushed upon the market by the Meredith-Lowell Company in the height of his popularity, and being fiction, in point of sales it made even a bigger strike than "The Shame of the Sun." Week after week his was the credit of the unprecedented performance of having two books at the head of the list of bestsellers. Not only did the story take with the fiction-readers, but those who read "The Shame of the Sun" with avidity were likewise attracted to the sea-story by the cosmic grasp of mastery with which he had handled it. First, he had attacked the literature of mysticism, and had done it exceeding well; and, next, he had successfully supplied the very literature he had exposited, thus proving himself to be that rare genius, a critic and a creator in one.

Money poured in on him, fame poured in on him; he flashed, comet-like, through the world of literature, and he was more amused than interested by the stir he was making. One thing was puzzling him, a little thing that would have puzzled the world had it known. But the world would have puzzled over his bepuzzlement rather than over the little thing that to him loomed gigantic. Judge Blount invited him to dinner. That was the little thing, or the beginning of the little thing, that was soon to become the big thing. He had insulted Judge Blount, treated him abominably, and Judge Blount, meeting him on the street, invited him to dinner. Martin bethought himself of the numerous occasions on which he had met Judge Blount at the Morses' and when Judge Blount had not invited him to dinner. Why had he not invited him to dinner then? he asked himself. He had not changed. He was the same Martin Eden. What made the difference? The fact that the stuff he had written had appeared inside the covers of books? But it was work performed. It was not something he had done since. It was achievement accomplished at the very time Judge Blount was sharing this general view and sneering at his Spencer and his intellect. Therefore it was not for any real value, but for a purely fictitious value that Judge Blount invited him to dinner.

Martin grinned and accepted the invitation, marveling the while at his complacence. And at the dinner, where, with their womenkind, were half a dozen of those that sat in high places, and where Martin found himself quite the lion, Judge Blount, warmly seconded by Judge Hanwell, urged privately that Martin should permit his name to be put up for the Styx—the ultra-select club to which belonged, not the mere men of wealth, but the men of attainment. And Martin declined, and was more puzzled than ever.

He was kept busy disposing of his heap of manuscripts. He was overwhelmed by requests from editors. It had been discovered that he was a stylist, with meat under his style. *The Northern Review*, after publishing "The Cradle of Beauty," had written him for half a dozen similar essays, which would have been supplied out of the heap, had not *Burton's Magazine*, in a speculative mood, offered him five hundred dollars each for five essays. He wrote back that he would supply the demand, but at a thousand dollars an essay. He remembered that all these manuscripts had been refused by the very magazines that were now clamoring for them. And their refusals had been cold-blooded, automatic, stereotyped. They had made him sweat, and now he intended to make them sweat. *Burton's Magazine* paid his price for five essays, and the remaining four, at the same rate, were snapped up by *Mackintosh's Monthly*, *The Northern Review* being too poor to stand the pace. Thus went out to the world "The High Priests of Mystery," "The Wonder-Dreamers," "The Yardstick of the Ego," "Philosophy of Illusion," "God and Clod," "Art and Biology," "Critics and Test-tubes," "Star-dust," and "The Dignity of Usury,"—to raise storms and rumblings and mutterings that were many a day in dying down.

Editors wrote to him telling him to name his own terms, which he did, but it was always for work performed. He refused resolutely to pledge himself to any new thing. The thought of again setting pen to paper maddened him. He had seen Brissenden torn to pieces by the crowd, and despite the fact that him the crowd acclaimed, he could not get over the shock nor gather any respect for the crowd. His very popularity seemed a disgrace and a treason to Brissenden. It made him wince, but he made up his mind to go on and fill the money-bag.

He received letters from editors like the following: "About a year ago we were unfortunate enough to refuse your collection of love-poems. We were greatly impressed by them at the time, but certain arrangements already entered into prevented our taking them. If you still have them, and if you will be kind enough to forward them, we shall be glad to publish the entire collection on your own terms. We are also prepared to make a most advantageous offer for bringing them out in book form."

Martin recollected his blank-verse tragedy, and sent it instead. He read it over before mailing, and was particularly impressed by its sophomoric amateurishness and general worthlessness. But he sent it; and it was published, to the everlasting regret of the editor. The public was indignant and incredulous. It was too far a cry from Martin Eden's high standard to that serious bosh. It was asserted that he had never written it, that the magazine had faked it very clumsily, or that Martin Eden was emulating the elder Dumas and at the height of success was hiring his writing done for him. But when he explained that the tragedy was an early effort of his literary childhood, and that the magazine had refused to be happy unless it got it, a great laugh went up at the magazine's expense and a change in the editorship followed. The tragedy was never brought out in book form, though Martin pocketed the advance royalties that had been paid.

Coleman's Weekly sent Martin a lengthy telegram, costing nearly three hundred dollars, offering him a

thousand dollars an article for twenty articles. He was
to travel over the United States, with all expenses paid,
and select whatever topics interested him. The body
of the telegram was devoted to hypothetical topics in
order to show him the freedom of range that was to
be his. The only restriction placed upon him was that
he must confine himself to the United States. Martin
sent his inability to accept and his regrets by wire
"collect."

"Wiki-Wiki," published in *Warren's Monthly*, was an
instantaneous success. It was brought out forward in
a wide-margined, beautifully decorated volume that
struck the holiday trade and sold like wildfire. The
critics were unanimous in the belief that it would take
its place with those two classics by two great writers,
"The Bottle Imp" and "The Magic Skin."

The public, however, received the "Smoke of Joy"
collection rather dubiously and coldly. The audacity
and unconventionality of the storiettes was a shock to
bourgeois morality and prejudice; but when Paris went
mad over the immediate translation that was made,
the American and English reading public followed suit
and bought so many copies that Martin compelled the
conservative house of Singletree, Darnley & Co. to
pay a flat royalty of twenty-five per cent for a third
book, and thirty per cent flat for a fourth. These two
volumes comprised all the short stories he had written
and which had received, or were receiving, serial publication. "The Ring of Bells" and his horror stories
constituted one collection; the other collection was
composed of "Adventure," "The Pot," "The Wine of
Life," "The Whirlpool," "The Jostling Street," and
four other stories. The Lowell-Meredith Company
captured the collection of all his essays, and the Max-
millian Company got his "Sea Lyrics" and the "Love-

cycle," the latter receiving serial publication in the *Ladies' Home Companion* after the payment of an extortionate price.

Martin heaved a sigh of relief when he had disposed of the last manuscript. The grass-walled castle and the white, coppered schooner were very near to him. Well, at any rate he had discovered Brissenden's contention that nothing of merit found its way into the magazines. His own success demonstrated that Brissenden had been wrong. And yet, somehow, he had a feeling that Brissenden had been right, after all. "The Shame of the Sun" had been the cause of his success more than the stuff he had written. That stuff had been merely incidental. It had been rejected right and left by the magazines. The publication of "The Shame of the Sun" had started a controversy and precipitated the landslide in his favor. Had there been no "Shame of the Sun" there would have been no landslide, and had there been no miracle in the go of "The Shame of the Sun" there would have been no landslide. Singletree, Darnley & Co. attested that miracle. They had brought out a first edition of fifteen hundred copies and been dubious of selling it. They were experienced publishers and no one had been more astounded than they at the success which had followed. To them it had been in truth a miracle. They never got over it, and every letter they wrote him reflected their reverent awe of that first mysterious happening. They did not attempt to explain it. There was no explaining it. It had happened. In the face of all experience to the contrary, it had happened.

So it was, reasoning thus, that Martin questioned the validity of his popularity. It was the bourgeoisie that bought his books and poured its gold into his money-sack, and from what little he knew of the bourgeoisie it was not clear to him how it could possibly appreciate or comprehend what he had written. His intrinsic beauty and power meant nothing to the hundreds of thousands who were acclaiming him and buying his books. He was the fad of the hour, the adventurer who had stormed Parnassus while the gods nodded. The hundreds of thousands read him and acclaimed him with the same brute non-understanding with which they had flung themselves on Brissenden's "Ephemera" and torn it to pieces—a wolf-rabble that fawned on him instead of fanging him. Fawn or fang, it was all a matter of chance. One thing he knew with absolute certitude: "Ephemera" was infinitely greater than anything he had done. It was infinitely greater than anything he had in him. It was a poem of centuries. Then the tribute the mob paid him was a sorry tribute indeed, for that same mob had wallowed "Ephemera" into the mire. He sighed heavily and with satisfaction. He was glad the last manuscript was sold and that he would soon be done with it all.

Chapter Forty-four

Mr. Morse met Martin in the office of the Hotel Metropole. Whether he had happened there just casually, intent on other affairs, or whether he had come there for the direct purpose of inviting him to dinner, Martin never could quite make up his mind, though he inclined toward the second hypothesis. At any rate, invited to dinner he was by Mr. Morse—Ruth's father, who had forbidden him the house and broken off the engagement.

Martin was not angry. He was not even on his dignity. He tolerated Mr. Morse, wondering the while how it felt to eat such humble pie. He did not decline the invitation. Instead, he put it off with vagueness and indefiniteness and inquired after the family, particularly after Mrs. Morse and Ruth. He spoke her name without hesitancy, naturally, though secretly surprised that he had had no inward quiver, no old, familiar increase of pulse and warm surge of blood.

He had many invitations to dinner, some of which he accepted. Persons got themselves introduced to him in order to invite him to dinner. And he went on puzzling over the little thing that was becoming a great thing. Bernard Higginbotham invited him to dinner. He puzzled the harder. He remembered the days of his desperate starvation when no one invited him to dinner. That was the time he needed dinners, and went weak and faint for lack of them and lost weight from sheer famine. That was the paradox of it. When he wanted dinners, no one gave them to him, and now that he could buy a hundred thousand dinners and was losing his appetite, dinners were thrust upon him right and left. But why? There was no justice in it, no merit on his part. He was no different. All the work he had done was even at that time work performed. Mr. and Mrs. Morse had condemned him for an idler and a shirk and through Ruth had urged that he take a clerk's position in an office. Furthermore, they had been aware of his work performed. Manuscript after manuscript of his had been turned over to them by Ruth. They had read them. It was the very same work that had put his name in all the papers, and it was his name being in all the papers that led them to invite him.

One thing was certain: the Morses had not cared to

have him for himself or for his work. Therefore they could not want him now for himself or for his work, but for the fame that was his, because he was somebody amongst men, and—why not?—because he had a hundred thousand dollars or so. That was the way bourgeois society valued a man, and who was he to expect it otherwise? But he was proud. He disdained such valuation. He desired to be valued for himself, or for his work, which, after all, was an expression of himself. That was the way Lizzie valued him. The work, with her, did not even count. She valued him, himself. That was the way Jimmy, the plumber, and all the old gang valued him. That had been proved often enough in the days when he ran with them; it had been proved that Sunday at Shell Mound Park. His work could go hang. What they liked, and were willing to scrap for, was just Mart Eden, one of the bunch and a pretty good guy.

Then there was Ruth. She had liked him for himself, that was indisputable. And yet, much as she had liked him she had liked the bourgeois standard of valuation more. She had opposed his writing, and principally, it seemed to him, because it did not earn money. That had been her criticism of his "Love-cycle." She, too, had urged him to get a job. It was true, she refined it to "position," but it meant the same thing, and in his own mind the old nomenclature stuck. He had read her all that he wrote—poems, stories, essays— "Wiki-Wiki," "The Shame of the Sun," everything. And she had always and consistently urged him to get a job, to go to work—good God! as if he hadn't been working, robbing sleep, exhausting life, in order to be worthy of her.

So the little thing grew bigger. He was healthy and normal, ate regularly, slept long hours, and yet the growing little thing was becoming an obsession. *Work performed.* The phrase haunted his brain. He sat opposite Bernard Higginbotham at a heavy Sunday dinner over Higginbotham's Cash Store, and it was all he could do to restrain himself from shouting:—

"It was work performed! And now you feed me, when then you let me starve, forbade me your house, and damned me because I wouldn't get a job. And the work was already done, all done. And now, when I speak, you check the thought unuttered on your lips and hang on my lips and pay respectful attention to whatever I choose to say. I tell you your party is rotten and filled with grafters, and instead of flying into a rage you hum and haw and admit there is a great deal in what I say. And why? Because I'm famous; because I've a lot of money. Not because I'm Martin Eden, a pretty good fellow and not particularly a fool. I could tell you the moon is made of green cheese and you would subscribe to the notion, at least you would not repudiate it, because I've got dollars, mountains of them. And it was all done long ago; it was work performed, I tell you, when you spat upon me as the dirt under your feet."

But Martin did not shout out. The thought gnawed in his brain, an unceasing torment, while he smiled and succeeded in being tolerant. As he grew silent, Bernard Higginbotham got the reins and did the talking. He was a success himself, and proud of it. He was self-made. No one had helped him. He owed no man. He was fulfilling his duty as a citizen and bringing up a large family. And there was Higginbotham's Cash Store, that monument of his own industry and ability. He loved Higginbotham's Cash Store as some men loved their wives. He opened up his heart to Martin, showed with what keenness and with what enormous planning he had made the store. And he had plans for it, ambitious plans. The neighborhood was growing up fast. The store was really too small. If he had more room, he would be able to put in a score of labor-saving and money-saving improvements. And he would do it yet. He was straining every effort for the day when he could buy the adjoining lot and put up another two-story frame building. The upstairs he could rent, and the whole ground-floor of both buildings would be Higginbotham's Cash Store. His eyes glistened when he spoke of the new sign that would stretch clear across both buildings.

Martin forgot to listen. The refrain of "Work performed," in his own brain, was drowning the other's clatter. The refrain maddened him, and he tried to escape from it.

"How much did you say it would cost?" he asked suddenly.

His brother-in-law paused in the middle of an expatiation on the business opportunities of the neighborhood. He hadn't said how much it would cost. But he knew. He had figured it out a score of times.

"At the way lumber is now," he said, "four thousand could do it."

"Including the sign?"

"I didn't count on that. It'd just have to come, onc't the buildin' was there."

"And the ground?"

"Three thousand more."

He leaned forward, licking his lips, nervously spreading and closing his fingers, while he watched Martin write a check. When it was passed over to him, he glanced at the amount—seven thousand dollars.

"I—I can't afford to pay more than six per cent," he said huskily.

Martin wanted to laugh, but, instead, demanded:—

"How much would that be?"

"Lemme see. Six per cent—six times seven—four hundred an' twenty."

"That would be thirty-five dollars a month, wouldn't it?"

Higginbotham nodded.

"Then, if you've no objection, we'll arrange it this way." Martin glanced at Gertrude. "You can have the principal to keep for yourself, if you'll use the thirty-five dollars a month for cooking and washing and scrubbing. The seven thousand is yours if you'll guarantee that Gertrude does no more drudgery. Is it a go?"

Mr. Higginbotham swallowed hard. That his wife should do no more housework was an affront to his thrifty soul. The magnificent present was the coating of a pill, a bitter pill. That his wife should not work! It gagged him.

"All right, then," Martin said. "I'll pay the thirty-five a month, and—"

He reached across the table for the check. But Bernard Higginbotham got his hand on it first, crying:—

"I accept! I accept!"

When Martin got on the electric car, he was very sick and tired. He looked up at the assertive sign.

"The swine," he groaned. "The swine, the swine.'

When *Mackintosh's Magazine* published "The Palmist," featuring it with decorations by Berthier and with two pictures by Wenn, Hermann von Schmidt forgot that he had called the verses obscene. He announced that his wife had inspired the poem, saw to it that the news reached the ears of a reporter, and submitted to an interview by a staff writer who was accompanied by a staff photographer and a staff artist. The result was a full page in a Sunday supplement, filled with photographs and idealized drawings of Marian, with many intimate details of Martin Eden and his family, and with the full text of "The Palmist" in large type, and republished by special permission of *Mackintosh's Magazine*. It caused quite a stir in the neighborhood, and good housewives were proud to have the acquaintance of the great writer's sister, while those who had not made haste to cultivate it. Hermann von Schmidt chuckled in his little repair shop and decided to order a new lathe. "Better than advertising," he told Marian, "and it costs nothing."

"We'd better have him to dinner," she suggested.

And to dinner Martin came, making himself agreeable with the fat wholesale butcher and his fatter wife—important folk, they, likely to be of use to a rising young man like Hermann von Schmidt. No less a bait, however, had been required to draw them to his house than his great brother-in-law. Another man at table who had swallowed the same bait was the superintendent of the Pacific Coast agencies for the Asa Bicycle Company. Him Von Schmidt desired to please and propitiate because from him could be obtained the Oakland agency for the bicycle. So Hermann von Schmidt found it a goodly asset to have Martin for a brother-in-law, but in his heart of hearts he couldn't understand where it all came in. In the silent watches of the night, while his wife slept, he had floundered through Martin's books and poems, and decided that the world was a fool to buy them.

And in his heart of hearts Martin understood the situation only too well, as he leaned back and gloated at Von Schmidt's head, in fancy punching it well-nigh off of him, sending blow after blow home just right— the chuckle-headed Dutchman! One thing he did like about him, however. Poor as he was, and determined to rise as he was, he nevertheless hired one servant to take the heavy work off of Marian's hands. Martin talked with the superintendent of the Asa agencies, and after dinner he drew him aside with Hermann, whom he backed financially for the best bicycle store with fittings in Oakland. He went further, and in a private talk with Hermann told him to keep his eyes open for an automobile agency and garage, for there was no reason that he should not be able to run both establishments successfully.

With tears in her eyes and her arms around his neck, Marian, at parting, told Martin how much she loved him and always had loved him. It was true, there was a perceptible halt midway in her assertion, which she glossed over with more tears and kisses and incoherent stammerings, and which Martin inferred to be her appeal for forgiveness for the time she had lacked faith in him and insisted on his getting a job.

"He can't never keep his money, that's sure," Hermann von Schmidt confided to his wife. "He got mad when I spoke of interest, an' he said damn the principal and if I mentioned it again, he'd punch my Dutch head off. That's what he said—my Dutch head. But he's all right, even if he ain't no business man. He's given me my chance, an' he's all right."

Invitations to dinner poured in on Martin; and the more they poured, the more he puzzled. He sat, the guest of honor, at an Arden Club banquet, with men of note whom he had heard about and read about all his life; and they told him how, when they had read "The Ring of Bells" in the *Transcontinental*, and "The Peri and the Pearl" in *The Hornet*, they had immediately picked him for a winner. My God! and I was hungry and in rags, he thought to himself. Why didn't you give me a dinner then? Then was the time. It was work performed. If you are feeding me now for work performed, why did you not feed me then when I needed it? Not one word in "The Ring of Bells," nor in "The Peri and the Pearl" has been changed. No; you're not feeding me now for work performed. You are feeding me because everybody else is feeding me and because it is an honor to feed me. You are feeding me now because you are herd animals; because you are part of the mob; because the one blind, automatic thought in the mob-mind just now is to feed me. And where does Martin Eden and the work Martin Eden performed come in in all this? he asked himself plaintively, then arose to respond cleverly and wittily to a clever and witty toast.

So it went. Wherever he happened to be—at the Press Club, at the Redwood Club, at pink teas and literary gatherings—always were remembered "The Ring of Bells" and "The Peri and the Pearl" when they were first published. And always was Martin's maddening and unuttered demand: Why didn't you feed me then? It was work performed. "The Ring of Bells" and "The Peri and the Pearl" are not changed one iota. They were just as artistic, just as worthwhile, then as now. But you are not feeding me for their sake, nor for the sake of anything else I have written. You're feeding me because it is the style of feeding just now, because the whole mob is crazy with the idea of feeding Martin Eden.

And often, at such times, he would abruptly see slouch in among the company a young hoodlum in square-cut coat and under a stiff-rim Stetson hat. It happened to him at the Gallina Society in Oakland one afternoon. As he rose from his chair and stepped forward across the platform, he saw stalk through the wide door at the rear of the great room the young hoodlum with the square-cut coat and stiff-rim hat. Five hundred fashionably gowned women turned their heads, so intent and steadfast was Martin's gaze, to see what he was seeing. But they saw only the empty center aisle. He saw the young tough lurching down that aisle and wondered if he would remove the stiff-rim which never yet had he seen him without. Straight down the aisle he came, and up the platform. Martin could have wept over that youthful shade of himself, when he thought of all that lay before him. Across the platform he swaggered, right up to Martin, and into the foreground of Martin's consciousness disappeared. The five hundred women applauded softly with gloved hands, seeking to encourage the bashful great man who was their guest. And Martin shook the vision from his brain, smiled, and began to speak.

The Superintendent of Schools, good old man, stopped Martin on the street and remembered him, recalling seances in his office when Martin was expelled from school for fighting.

"I read your 'Ring of Bells' in one of the magazines quite a time ago," he said. "It was as good as Poe. Splendid, I said at the time, splendid!"

Yes, and twice in the months that followed you passed me on the street and did not know me, Martin almost said aloud. Each time I was hungry and heading for the pawnbroker. Yet it was work performed. You did not know me then. Why do you know me now?

"I was remarking to my wife only the other day," the other was saying, "wouldn't it be a good idea to have you out to dinner sometime? And she quite agreed with me. Yes, she quite agreed with me."

"Dinner?" Martin said so sharply that it was almost a snarl.

"Why, yes, yes, dinner, you know—just pot luck with us, with your old superintendent, you rascal," he uttered nervously, poking Martin in an attempt at jocular fellowship.

Martin went down the street in a daze. He stopped at the corner and looked about him vacantly.

"Well, I'll be damned!" he murmured at last. "The old fellow was afraid of me."

Chapter Forty-five

Kreis came to Martin one day—Kreis, of the "real dirt"; and Martin turned to him with relief, to receive the glowing details of a scheme sufficiently wild-catty to interest him as a fictionist rather than an investor. Kreis paused long enough in the midst of his exposition to tell him that in most of his "Shame of the Sun" he had been a chump.

"But I didn't come here to spout philosophy," Kreis went on. "What I want to know is whether or not you will put a thousand dollars in on this deal?"

"No, I'm not chump enough for that, at any rate," Martin answered. "But I'll tell you what I will do. You gave me the greatest night of my life. You gave me what money cannot buy. Now I've got money, and it means nothing to me. I'd like to turn over to you a thousand dollars of what I don't value for what you gave me that night and which was beyond price. You need the money. I've got more than I need. You want it. You came for it. There's no use scheming it out of me. Take it."

Kreis betrayed no surprise. He folded the check away in his pocket.

"At that rate I'd like the contract of providing you with many such nights," he said.

"Too late." Martin shook his head. "That night was the one night for me. I was in paradise. It's commonplace with you, I know. But it wasn't to me. I shall never live at such a pitch again. I'm done with philosophy. I want never to hear another word of it."

"The first dollar I ever made in my life out of my philosophy," Kreis remarked, as he paused in the doorway. "And then the market broke."

Mrs. Morse drove by Martin on the street one day, and smiled and nodded. He smiled back and lifted his hat. The episode did not affect him. A month before it might have disgusted him, or made him curious and set him to speculating about her state of consciousness at that moment. But now it was not provocative of a second thought. He forgot about it the next moment. He forgot about it as he would have forgotten the Central Bank Building or the City Hall after having walked past them. Yet his mind was preternaturally active. His thoughts went ever around and around in a circle. The center of that circle was "work performed": it ate at his brain like a deathless maggot. He awoke to it in the morning. It tormented his dreams at night. Every affair of life around him that penetrated through his senses immediately related itself to "work performed." He drove along the path of relentless logic to the conclusion that he was nobody, nothing. Mart Eden, the hoodlum, and Mart Eden, the sailor, had been real, had been he; but Martin Eden! the famous writer, did not exist. Martin Eden, the famous writer, was a vapor that had arisen in the mob-mind and by the mob-mind had been thrust into the corporeal being of Mart Eden, the hoodlum and sailor. But it couldn't fool him. He was not that sun-myth that the mob was worshipping and sacrificing dinners to. He knew better.

He read the magazines about himself, and pored over portraits of himself published therein until he was unable to associate his identity with those portraits. He was the fellow who had lived and thrilled and loved; who had been easy-going and tolerant of the frailties of life; who had served in the forecastle, wandered in strange lands, and led his gang in the old fighting days. He was the fellow who had been stunned at first by the thousands of books in the free library, and who had afterward learned his way among them and mastered them; he was the fellow who had burned the midnight oil and bedded with a spur and written books himself. But the one thing he was not was that colossal appetite that all the mob was bent upon feeding.

There were things, however, in the magazines that amused him. All the magazines were claiming him. *Warren's Monthly* advertised to its subscribers that it was always on the quest after new writers, and that, among others, it had introduced Martin Eden to the reading public. *The White Mouse* claimed him; so did *The Northern Review* and *Mackintosh's Magazine*, until silenced by *The Globe*, which pointed triumphantly to its files where the mangled "Sea Lyrics" lay buried. *Youth and Age*, which had come to life again after having escaped paying its bills, put in a prior claim, which nobody but farmers' children ever read. The *Transcontinental* made a dignified and convincing statement of how it first discovered Martin Eden, which was warmly disputed by *The Hornet*, with the exhibit of "The Peri and the Pearl." The modest claim of Singletree, Darnley & Co. was lost in the din. Besides, that publishing firm did not own a magazine wherewith to make its claim less modest.

The newspapers calculated Martin's royalties. In some way the magnificent offers certain magazines had made him leaked out, and Oakland ministers called upon him in a friendly way, while professional begging letters began to clutter his mail. But worse than all this were the women. His photographs were published broadcast, and special writers exploited his strong, bronzed face, his scars, his heavy shoulders, his clear, quiet eyes, and the slight hollows in his cheeks like an ascetic's. At this last he remembered his wild youth and smiled. Often, among the women he met, he would see now one, now another, looking at him, appraising him, selecting him. He laughed to himself. He remembered Brissenden's warning and laughed again. The women would never destroy him, that much was certain. He had gone past that stage.

Once, walking with Lizzie toward night school, she caught a glance directed toward him by a well-gowned, handsome woman of the bourgeoisie. The glance was a trifle too long, a shade too considerative. Lizzie knew it for what it was, and her body tensed angrily. Martin noticed, noticed the cause of it, told her how used he was becoming to it and that he did not care anyway.

"You ought to care," she answered with blazing eyes. "You're sick. That's what's the matter."

"Never healthier in my life. I weigh five pounds more than I ever did."

"It ain't your body. It's your head. Something's wrong with your think-machine. Even I can see that, an' I ain't nobody."

He walked on beside her, reflecting.

"I'd give anything to see you get over it," she broke

out impulsively. "You ought to care when women look at you that way, a man like you. It's not natural. It's all right enough for sissy-boys. But you ain't made that way. So help me, I'd be willing an' glad if the right woman came along an' made you care."

When he left Lizzie at night school, he returned to the Metropole.

Once in his rooms, he dropped into a Morris chair and sat staring straight before him. He did not doze. Nor did he think. His mind was a blank, save for the intervals when unsummoned memory pictures took form and color and radiance just under his eyelids. He saw these pictures, but he was scarcely conscious of them—no more so than if they had been dreams. Yet he was not asleep. Once, he roused himself and glanced at his watch. It was just eight o'clock. He had nothing to do, and it was too early for bed. Then his mind went blank again, and the pictures began to form and vanish under his eyelids. There was nothing distinctive about the pictures. They were always masses of leaves and shrub-like branches shot through with hot sunshine.

A knock at the door aroused him. He was not asleep, and his mind immediately connected the knock with a telegram, or letter, or perhaps one of the servants bringing back clean clothes from the laundry. He was thinking about Joe and wondering where he was, as he said, "Come in."

He was still thinking about Joe, and did not turn toward the door. He heard it close softly. There was a long silence. He forgot that there had been a knock at the door, and was still staring blankly before him when he heard a woman's sob. It was involuntary, spasmodic, checked, and stifled—he noted that as he turned about. The next instant he was on his feet.

"Ruth!" he said, amazed and bewildered.

Her face was white and strained. She stood just inside the door, one hand against it for support, the other pressed to her side. She extended both hands toward him piteously, and started forward to meet him. As he caught her hands and led her to the Morris chair he noticed how cold they were. He drew up another chair and sat down on the broad arm of it. He was too confused to speak. In his own mind his affair with Ruth was closed and sealed. He felt much in the same way that he would have felt had the Shelly Hot Springs Laundry suddenly invaded the Hotel Metropole with a whole week's washing ready for him to pitch into. Several times he was about to speak, and each time he hesitated.

"No one knows I am here," Ruth said in a faint voice, with an appealing smile.

"What did you say?" he asked.

He was surprised at the sound of his own voice.

She repeated her words.

"Oh," he said, then wondered what more he could possibly say.

"I saw you come in, and I waited a few minutes."

"Oh," he said again.

He had never been so tongue-tied in his life. Positively he did not have an idea in his head. He felt stupid and awkward, but for the life of him he could think of nothing to say. It would have been easier had the intrusion been the Shelly Hot Springs laundry. He could have rolled up his sleeves and gone to work.

"And then you came in," he said finally.

She nodded, with a slightly arch expression, and loosened the scarf at her throat.

"I saw you first from across the street when you were with that girl."

"Oh, yes," he said simply. "I took her down to night school."

"Well, aren't you glad to see me?" she said at the end of another silence.

"Yes, yes." He spoke hastily. "But wasn't it rash of you to come here?"

"I slipped in. Nobody knows I am here. I wanted to see you. I came to tell you I have been very foolish. I came because I could no longer stay away, because my heart compelled me to come, because—because I wanted to come."

She came forward, out of her chair and over to him. She rested her hand on his shoulder a moment, breathing quickly, and then slipped into his arms. And in his large, easy way, desirous of not inflicting hurt, knowing that to repulse this offer of herself was to inflict the most grievous hurt a woman could receive, he folded his arms around her and held her close. But there was no warmth in the embrace, no caress in the contact. She had come into his arms, and he held her, that was all. She nestled against him, and then, with a change of position, her hands crept up and rested upon his neck. But his flesh was not fire beneath those hands, and he felt awkward and uncomfortable.

"What makes you tremble so?" he asked. "Is it a chill? Shall I light the grate?"

He made a movement to disengage himself, but she clung more closely to him, shivering violently.

"It is merely nervousness," she said with chattering teeth. "I'll control myself in a minute. There, I am better already."

Slowly her shivering died away. He continued to hold her, but he was no longer puzzled. He knew now for what she had come.

"My mother wanted me to marry Charley Hapgood," she announced.

"Charley Hapgood, that fellow who speaks always in platitudes?" Martin groaned. Then he added, "And now, I suppose, your mother wants you to marry me."

He did not put it in the form of a question. He stated it as a certitude, and before his eyes began to dance the rows of figures of his royalties.

"She will not object, I know that much," Ruth said.

"She considers me quite eligible?"

Ruth nodded.

"And yet I am not a bit more eligible now than I was when she broke our engagement," he meditated. "I haven't changed any. I'm the same Martin Eden, though for that matter I'm a bit worse—I smoke now. Don't you smell my breath?"

In reply she pressed her open fingers against his lips, placed them graciously and playfully, and in expectancy of the kiss that of old had always been a consequence. But there was no caressing answer of Martin's lips. He waited until the fingers were removed and then went on.

"I am not changed. I haven't got a job. I'm not looking for a job. Furthermore, I am not going to look for a job. And I still believe that Herbert Spencer is a great and noble man and that Judge Blount is an unmitigated ass. I had dinner with him the other night, so I ought to know."

"But you didn't accept father's invitation," she chided.

"So you know about that? Who sent him? Your mother?"

She remained silent.

"Then she did send him. I thought so. And now I suppose she has sent you."

"No one knows that I am here," she protested. "Do you think my mother would permit this?"

"She'd permit you to marry me, that's certain."

She gave a sharp cry. "Oh, Martin, don't be cruel.

You have not kissed me once. You are as unresponsive as a stone. And think what I have dared to do." She looked about her with a shiver, though half the look was curiosity. "Just think of where I am."

"*I could die for you! I could die for you!*"—Lizzie's words were ringing in his ears.

"Why didn't you dare it before?" he asked harshly. "When I hadn't a job? When I was starving? When I was just as I am now, as a man, as an artist, the same Martin Eden? That's the question I've been propounding to myself for many a day—not concerning you merely, but concerning everybody. You see I have not changed, though my sudden apparent appreciation in value compels me constantly to reassure myself on that point. I've got the same flesh on my bones, the same ten fingers and toes. I am the same. I have not developed any new strength nor virtue. My brain is the same old brain. I haven't made even one new generalization on literature or philosophy. I am personally of the same value that I was when nobody wanted me. And what is puzzling me is why they want me now. Surely they don't want me for myself, for myself is the same old self they did not want. Then they must want me for something else, for something that is outside of me, for something that is not I! Shall I tell you what that something is? It is for the recognition I have received. That recognition is not I. It resides in the minds of others. Then again for the money I have earned and am earning. But that money is not I. It resides in banks and in the pockets of Tom, Dick, and Harry. And is it for that, for the recognition and the money, that you now want me?"

"You are breaking my heart," she sobbed. "You know I love you, that I am here because I love you."

"I am afraid you don't see my point," he said gently.

"What I mean is: if you love me, how does it happen that you love me now so much more than you did when your love was weak enough to deny me?"

"Forget and forgive," she cried passionately. "I loved you all the time, remember that, and I am here, now, in your arms."

"I'm afraid I am a shrewd merchant, peering into the scales, trying to weigh your love and find out what manner of thing it is."

She withdrew herself from his arms, sat upright, and looked at him long and searchingly. She was about to speak, then faltered and changed her mind.

"You see, it appears this way to me," he went on. "When I was all that I am now, nobody out of my own class seemed to care for me. When my books were all written, no one who had read the manuscripts seemed to care for them. In point of fact, because of the stuff I had written they seemed to care even less for me. In writing the stuff it seemed that I had committed acts that were, to say the least, derogatory. 'Get a job,' everybody said."

She made a movement of dissent.

"Yes, yes," he said, "except in your case you told me to get a position. The homely word *job*, like much that I have written, offends you. It is brutal. But I assure you it was no less brutal to me when everybody I knew recommended it to me as they would recommend right conduct to an immoral creature. But to return. The publication of what I had written, and the public notice I received, wrought a change in the fiber of your love. Martin Eden, with his work all performed, you would not marry. Your love for him was not strong enough to enable you to marry him. But your love is now strong enough, and I cannot avoid the conclusion that its strength arises from the publication and the public notice. In your case I do not mention royalties, though I am certain that they apply to the change wrought in your mother and father. Of course, all this is not flattering to me. But worst of all, it makes me question love, sacred love. Is love so gross a thing that it must feed upon publication and public notice? It would seem so. I have sat and thought upon it till my head went around."

"Poor, dear head." She reached up a hand and passed the fingers soothingly through his hair. "Let it go around no more. Let us begin anew, now. I loved you all the time. I know that I was weak in yielding to my mother's will. I should not have done so. Yet I have heard you speak so often with broad charity of the fallibility and frailty of humankind. Extend that charity to me. I acted mistakenly. Forgive me."

"Oh, I do forgive," he said impatiently. "It is easy to forgive where there is really nothing to forgive. Nothing that you have done requires forgiveness. One acts according to one's lights, and more than that one cannot do. As well might I ask you to forgive me for my not getting a job."

"I meant well," she protested. "You know that. I could not have loved you and not meant well."

"True; but you would have destroyed me out of your well-meaning.

"Yes, yes," he shut off her attempted objection. "You would have destroyed my writing and my career. Realism is imperative to my nature, and the bourgeois spirit hates realism. The bourgeoisie is cowardly. It is afraid of life. And all your effort was to make me afraid of life. You would have formalized me. You would have compressed me into a two-by-four pigeonhole of life, where all life's values are unreal, and false, and vulgar." He felt her stir protestingly. "Vulgarity—a hearty vulgarity, I'll admit—is the basis of bourgeois refinement and culture. As I say, you wanted to formalize me, to make me over into one of your own class, with your class-ideals, class-values, and class-prejudices." He shook his head sadly. "And you do not understand, even now, what I am saying. My words do not mean to you what I endeavor to make them mean. What I say is so much fantasy to you. Yet to me it is vital reality. At the best you are a trifle puzzled and amused that this raw boy, crawling up out of the mire of the abyss, should pass judgment upon your class and call it vulgar."

She leaned her head wearily against his shoulder, and her body shivered with recurrent nervousness. He waited for a time for her to speak, and then went on.

"And now you want to renew our love. You want us to be married. You want me. And yet, listen—if my books had not been noticed, I'd nevertheless have been just what I am now. And you would have stayed away. It is all those damned books—"

"Don't swear," she interrupted.

Her reproof startled him. He broke into a harsh laugh.

"That's it," he said, "at a high moment, when what seems your life's happiness is at stake, you are afraid of life in the same old way—afraid of life and a healthy oath."

She was stung by his words into realization of the puerility of her act, and yet she felt that he had magnified it unduly and was consequently resentful. They sat in silence for a long time, she thinking desperately and he pondering upon his love which had departed. He knew, now, that he had not really loved her. It was an idealized Ruth he had loved, an ethereal creature of his own creating, the bright and luminous spirit of his love-poems. The real bourgeois Ruth, with all the bourgeois failings and with the hopeless cramp of the bourgeois psychology in her mind, he had never loved.

She suddenly began to speak.

"I know that much you have said is so. I have been afraid of life. I did not love you well enough. I have learned to love better. I love you for what you are, for what you were, for the ways even by which you have become. I love you for the ways wherein you differ from what you call my class, for your beliefs which I do not understand but which I know I can come to understand. I shall devote myself to understanding them. And even your smoking and your swearing—they are part of you and I will love you for them, too. I can still learn. In the last ten minutes I have learned much. That I have dared to come here is a token of what I have already learned. Oh, Martin!—"

She was sobbing and nestling close against him.

For the first time his arms folded her gently and with sympathy, and she acknowledged it with a happy movement and a brightening face.

"It is too late," he said. He remembered Lizzie's words. "I am a sick man—oh, not my body. It is my soul, my brain. I seem to have lost all values. I care for nothing. If you had been this way a few months ago, it would have been different. It is too late, now."

"It is not too late," she cried. "I will show you. I will prove to you that my love has grown, that it is greater to me than my class and all that is dearest to me. All that is dearest to the bourgeoisie I will flout. I am no longer afraid of life. I will leave my father and mother, and let my name become a byword with my friends. I will come to you here and now, in free love if you will, and I will be proud and glad to be with you. If I have been a traitor to love, I will now, for love's sake, be a traitor to all that made that earlier treason."

She stood before him, with shining eyes.

"I am waiting, Martin," she whispered, "waiting for you to accept me. Look at me."

It was splendid, he thought, looking at her. She had redeemed herself for all that she had lacked, rising up at last, true woman, superior to the iron rule of bourgeois convention. It was splendid, magnificent, desperate. And yet, what was the matter with him? He was not thrilled nor stirred by what she had done. It was splendid and magnificent only intellectually. In what should have been a moment of fire, he coldly appraised her. His heart was untouched. He was unaware of any desire for her. Again he remembered Lizzie's words.

"I am sick, very sick," he said with a despairing gesture. "How sick I did not know till now. Something has gone out of me. I have always been unafraid of life, but I never dreamed of being sated with life. Life has so filled me that I am empty of any desire for anything. If there were room, I should want you, now. You see how sick I am."

He leaned his head back and closed his eyes; and like a child, crying, that forgets its grief in watching the sunlight percolate through the tear-dimmed films over the pupils, so Martin forgot his sickness, the presence of Ruth, everything, in watching the masses of vegetation, shot through hotly with sunshine that took form and blazed against the background of his eyelids. It was not restful, that green foliage. The sunlight was too raw and glaring. It hurt him to look at it, and yet he looked, he knew not why

He was brought back to himself by the rattle of the door-knob. Ruth was at the door.

"How shall I get out?" she questioned tearfully. "I am afraid."

"Oh, forgive me," he cried, springing to his feet. "I'm not myself, you know. I forgot you were here." He put his hand to his head. "You see, I'm not just right. I'll take you home. We can go out by the servants' entrance. No one will see us. Pull down that veil and everything will be all right."

She clung to his arm through the dim-lighted passages and down the narrow stairs.

"I am safe now," she said, when they emerged on the sidewalk, at the same time starting to take her hand from his arm.

"No, no, I'll see you home," he answered.

"No, please don't," she objected. "It is unnecessary."

Again she started to remove her hand. He felt a momentary curiosity. Now that she was out of danger she was afraid. She was in almost a panic to be quit of him. He could see no reason for it and attributed it to her nervousness. So he restrained her withdrawing hand and started to walk on with her. Halfway down the block, he saw a man in a long overcoat shrink back into a doorway. He shot a glance in as he passed by, and, despite the high turned-up collar, he was certain that he recognized Ruth's brother, Norman.

During the walk Ruth and Martin held little conversation. She was stunned. He was apathetic. Once, he mentioned that he was going away, back to the South Seas, and, once, she asked him to forgive her having come to him. And that was all. The parting at her door was conventional. They shook hands, said

good night, and he lifted his hat. The door swung
shut, and he lighted a cigarette and turned back for
his hotel. When he came to the doorway into which
he had seen Norman shrink, he stopped and looked
in in a speculative humor.

"She lied," he said aloud. "She made believe to me
that she had dared greatly, and all the while she knew
the brother that brought her was waiting to take her
back." He burst into laughter. "Oh, these bourgeois!
When I was broke, I was not fit to be seen with his
sister. When I have a bank account, he brings her to
me."

As he swung on his heel to go on, a tramp, going
in the same direction, begged him over his shoulder.

"Say, mister, can you give me a quarter to get a
bed?" were the words.

But it was the voice that made Martin turn around.
The next instant he had Joe by the hand.

"D'ye remember that time we parted at the Hot
Springs?" the other was saying. "I said then we'd meet
again. I felt it in my bones. An' here we are."

"You're looking good," Martin said admiringly, "and
you've put on weight."

"I sure have." Joe's face was beaming. "I never knew
what it was to live till I hit hoboin'. I'm thirty pounds
heavier an' feel tiptop all the time. Why, I was worked
to skin an' bone in them old days. Hoboin' sure agrees
with me."

"But you're looking for a bed just the same," Martin
chided, "and it's a cold night."

"Huh? Lookin' for a bed?" Joe shot a hand into his
hip pocket and brought it out filled with small change.
"That beats hard graft," he exulted. "You just looked
good; that's why I battered you."

Martin laughed and gave in.

"You've several full-sized drunks right there," he insinuated.

Joe slid the money back into his pocket.

"Not in mine," he announced. "No gettin' oryide for me, though there ain't nothin' to stop me except I don't want to. I've ben drunk once since I seen you last, an' then it was unexpected, bein' on an empty stomach. When I work like a beast, I drink like a beast. When I live like a man, I drink like a man—a jolt now an' again when I feel like it, an' that's all."

Martin arranged to meet him next day, and went on to the hotel. He paused in the office to look up steamer sailings. The *Mariposa* sailed for Tahiti in five days.

"Telephone over tomorrow and reserve a stateroom for me," he told the clerk. "No deck-stateroom, but down below, on the weather-side,—the port-side, remember that, the port-side. You'd better write it down."

Once in his room he got into bed and slipped off to sleep as gently as a child. The occurrences of the evening had made no impression on him. His mind was dead to impressions. The glow of warmth with which he met Joe had been most fleeting. The succeeding minute he had been bothered by the ex-laundryman's presence and by the compulsion of conversation. That in five more days he sailed for his loved South Seas meant nothing to him. So he closed his eyes and slept normally and comfortably for eight uninterrupted hours. He was not restless. He did not change his position, nor did he dream. Sleep had become to him oblivion, and each day that he awoke, he awoke with regret. Life worried and bored him, and time was a vexation.

Chapter Forty-six

"Say, Joe," was his greeting to his old-time work-ing-mate next morning, "there's a Frenchman out on Twenty-eighth Street. He's made a pot of money and he's going back to France. It's a dandy, well-appointed, small steam laundry. There's a start for you if you want to settle down. Here, take this; buy some clothes with it and be at this man's office by ten o'clock. He looked up the laundry for me, and he'll take you out and show you around. If you like it, and think it is worth the price—twelve thousand—let me know and it is yours. Now run along. I'm busy. I'll see you later."

"Now look here, Mart," the other said slowly, with kindling anger, "I come here this mornin' to see you. Savve? I didn't come here to get no laundry. I come here for a talk for old friends' sake, and you shove a laundry at me. I tell you what you can do. You can take that laundry an' go to hell."

He was starting to fling out of the room when Martin caught him by the shoulder and whirled him around.

"Now look here, Joe," he said; "if you act that way, I'll punch your head. And for old friends' sake I'll punch it hard. Savve?—you will, will you?"

Joe had clinched and attempted to throw him, and he was twisting and writhing out of the advantage of the other's hold. They reeled about the room, locked in each other's arms, and came down with a crash across the splintered wreckage of a wicker chair. Joe was underneath, with arms spread out and held and with Martin's knee on his chest. He was panting and gasping for breath when Martin released him

"Now we'll talk a moment," Martin said. "You can't get fresh with me. I want that laundry business finished first of all. Then you can come back and we'll talk for old sake's sake. I told you I was busy. Look at that."

A servant had just come in with the morning mail, a great mass of letters and magazines.

"How can I wade through that and talk with you? You go and fix up that laundry, and then we'll get together."

"All right," Joe admitted reluctantly. "I thought you was turnin' me down, but I guess I was mistaken. But you can't lick me, Mart, in a stand-up fight. I've got the reach on you."

"We'll put on the gloves sometime and see," Martin said with a smile.

"Sure, as soon as I get that laundry going." Joe extended his arm. "You see that reach? It'll make you go a few."

Martin heaved a sigh of relief when the door closed behind the laundryman. He was becoming anti-social. Daily he found it a severer strain to be decent with people. Their presence perturbed him, and the effort of conversation irritated him. They made him restless, and no sooner was he in contact with them than he was casting about for excuses to get rid of them.

He did not proceed to attack his mail, and for a half hour he lolled in his chair, doing nothing, while no more than vague, half-formed thoughts occasionally filtered through his intelligence, or rather, at wide intervals, themselves constituted the flickering of his intelligence.

He roused himself and began glancing through his mail There were a dozen requests for autographs— he knew them at sight; there were professional begging letters; and there were letters from cranks, ranging from the man with a working model of perpetual motion, and the man who demonstrated that the surface of the earth was the inside of a hollow sphere, to the man seeking financial aid to purchase the Peninsula of Lower California for the purpose of communist colonization. There were letters from women seeking to know him, and over one such he smiled, for enclosed was her receipt for pew-rent, sent as evidence of her good faith and as proof of her respectability.

Editors and publishers contributed to the daily heap of letters, the former on their knees for his manuscripts, the latter on their knees for his books—his poor disdained manuscripts that had kept all he possessed in pawn for so many dreary months in order to find them in postage. There were unexpected checks for English serial rights and for advance payments on foreign translations. His English agent announced the sale of German translation rights in three of his books, and informed him that Swedish editions, from which he could expect nothing because Sweden was not a party to the Berne Convention, were already on the market. Then there was a nominal request for his permission for a Russian translation, that country being likewise outside the Berne Convention.

He turned to the huge bundle of clippings which had come in from his press bureau, and read about himself and his vogue, which had become a furore. All his creative output had been flung to the public in one magnificent sweep. That seemed to account for it. He had taken the public off its feet, the way Kipling had, that time when he lay near to death and all the mob, animated by a mob-mind thought, began suddenly to read him. Martin remembered how that same world-mob, having read him and acclaimed him and not understood him in the least, had, abruptly, a few months later, flung itself upon him and torn him to pieces. Martin grinned at the thought. Who was he that he should not be similarly treated in a few more months? Well, he would fool the mob. He would be away, in the South Seas, building his grass house, trading for pearls and copra, jumping reefs in frail outriggers, catching sharks and bonitas, hunting wild goats among the cliffs of the valley that lay next to the valley of Taiohæ.

In the moment of that thought the desperateness of his situation dawned upon him. He saw, clear eyed, that he was in the Valley of the Shadow. All the life that was in him was fading, fainting, making toward death. He realized how much he slept, and how much he desired to sleep. Of old, he had hated sleep. It had robbed him of precious moments of living. Four hours of sleep in the twenty-four had meant being robbed of four hours of life. How he had grudged sleep! Now it was life he grudged. Life was not good; its taste in his mouth was without tang, and bitter. This was his peril. Life that did not yearn toward life was in fair way toward ceasing. Some remote instinct for preservation stirred in him, and he knew he must get away. He glanced about the room, and the thought of packing was burdensome. Perhaps it would be better to leave that to the last. In the meantime he might be getting an outfit.

He put on his hat and went out, stopping in at a gun-store, where he spent the remainder of the morning buying automatic rifles, ammunition, and fishing tackle. Fashions changed in trading, and he knew he would have to wait till he reached Tahiti before ordering his trade-goods. They could come up from Australia, anyway. This solution was a source of pleasure. He had avoided doing something, and the doing of anything just now was unpleasant. He went back to the hotel gladly, with a feeling of satisfaction in that the comfortable Morris chair was waiting for him; and he groaned inwardly, on entering his room, at sight of Joe in the Morris chair.

Joe was delighted with the laundry. Everything was settled, and he would enter into possession next day. Martin lay on the bed, with closed eyes, while the other talked on. Martin's thoughts were far away—so far away that he was rarely aware that he was thinking. It was only by an effort that he occasionally responded. And yet this was Joe, whom he had always liked. But Joe was too keen with life. The boisterous impact of it on Martin's jaded mind was a hurt. It was an aching probe to his tired sensitiveness. When Joe reminded him that sometime in the future they were going to put on the gloves together, he could almost have screamed.

"Remember, Joe, you're to run the laundry according to those old rules you used to lay down at Shelly Hot Springs," he said. "No overworking. No working at night. And no children at the mangles. No children anywhere. And a fair wage."

Joe nodded and pulled out a notebook.

"Look at here. I was workin' out them rules before breakfast this A.M. What d'ye think of them?"

He read them aloud, and Martin approved, worrying at the same time as to when Joe would take himself off.

It was late afternoon when he awoke. Slowly the fact of life came back to him. He glanced about the room. Joe had evidently stolen away after he had dozed off. That was considerate of Joe, he thought. Then he closed his eyes and slept again.

In the days that followed Joe was too busy organizing and taking hold of the laundry to bother him much; and it was not until the day before sailing that the newspapers made the announcement that he had taken passage on the *Mariposa*. Once, when the instinct of preservation fluttered, he went to a doctor and underwent a searching physical examination. Nothing could be found the matter with him. His heart and lungs were pronounced magnificent. Every organ, so far as the doctor could know, was normal and was working normally.

"There is nothing the matter with you, Mr. Eden," he said, "positively nothing the matter with you. You are in the pink of condition. Candidly, I envy you your health. It is superb. Look at that chest. There, and in your stomach, lies the secret of your remarkable constitution. Physically, you are a man in a thousand—in ten thousand. Barring accidents, you should live to be a hundred."

And Martin knew that Lizzie's diagnosis had been correct. Physically he was all right. It was his "think-machine" that had gone wrong, and there was no cure for that except to get away to the South Seas. The trouble was that now, on the verge of departure, he had no desire to go. The South Seas charmed him no more than did bourgeois civilization. There was no zest in the thought of departure, while the act of departure appalled him as a weariness of the flesh. He would have felt better if he were already on board and gone.

The last day was a sore trial. Having read of his sailing in the morning papers, Bernard Higginbotham, Gertrude, and all the family came to say good-by, as did Hermann von Schmidt and Marian. Then there was business to be transacted, bills to be paid, and everlasting reporters to be endured. He said good-by to Lizzie Connolly, abruptly, at the entrance to night school, and hurried away. At the hotel he found Joe, too busy all day with the laundry to have come to him earlier. It was the last straw, but Martin gripped the arms of his chair and talked and listened for half an hour.

"You know, Joe," he said, "that you are not tied down to that laundry. There are no strings on it. You can sell it any time and blow the money. Any time you get sick of it and want to hit the road, just pull out. Do what will make you the happiest."

Joe shook his head.

"No more road in mine, thank you kindly. Hoboin's all right, exceptin' for one thing—the girls. I can't help it, but I'm a ladies' man. I can't get along without 'em, and you've got to get along without 'em when you're hoboin'. The times I've passed by houses where dances an' parties was goin' on, an' heard the women laugh, an' saw their white dresses and smiling faces through the windows— Gee! I tell you them moments was plain hell. I like dancin' an' picnics, an' walking in the moonlight, an' all the rest too well. Me for the laundry, and a good front, with big iron dollars clinkin' in my jeans. I seen a girl already, just yesterday, and, d'ye know, I'm feelin' already I'd just as soon marry her as not. I've ben whistlin' all day at the thought of it. She's a beaut, with the kindest eyes and softest voice you ever heard. Me for her, you can stack on that. Say, why don't you get married with all this money to burn? You could get the finest girl in the land."

Martin shook his head with a smile, but in his secret heart he was wondering why any man wanted to marry. It seemed an amazing and incomprehensible thing.

From the deck of the *Mariposa*, at the sailing hour,

he saw Lizzie Connolly hiding on the skirts of the crowd on the wharf. Take her with you, came the thought. It is easy to be kind. She will be supremely happy. It was almost a temptation one moment, and the succeeding moment it became a terror. He was in a panic at the thought of it. His tired soul cried out in protest. He turned away from the rail with a groan, muttering, "Man, you are too sick, you are too sick."

He fled to his stateroom, where he lurked until the steamer was clear of the dock. In the dining saloon, at luncheon, he found himself in the place of honor, at the captain's right; and he was not long in discovering that he was the great man on board. But no more unsatisfactory great man ever sailed on a ship. He spent the afternoon in a deck-chair, with closed eyes, dozing brokenly most of the time, and in the evening went early to bed.

After the second day, recovered from seasickness, the full passenger list was in evidence, and the more he saw of the passengers the more he disliked them. Yet he knew that he did them injustice. They were good and kindly people, he forced himself to acknowledge, and in the moment of acknowledgment he qualified—good and kindly like all the bourgeoisie, with all the psychological cramp and intellectual futility of their kind. They bored him when they talked with him, their little superficial minds were so filled with emptiness; while the boisterous high spirits and the excessive energy of the younger people shocked him. They were never quiet, ceaselessly playing deck-quoits, tossing rings, promenading, or rushing to the rail with loud cries to watch the leaping porpoises and the first schools of flying fish.

He slept much. After breakfast he sought his deck-chair with a magazine he never finished. The printed pages tired him. He puzzled that men found so much to write about, and, puzzling, dozed in his chair. When the gong awoke him for luncheon, he was irritated that he must awaken. There was no satisfaction in being awake.

Once, he tried to arouse himself from his lethargy, and went forward into the forecastle with the sailors. But the breed of sailors seemed to have changed since the days he had lived in the forecastle. He could find no kinship with these stolid-faced, ox-minded bestial creatures. He was in despair. Up above nobody had wanted Martin Eden for his own sake, and he could not go back to those of his own class who had wanted him in the past. He did not want them. He could not stand them any more than he could stand the stupid first-cabin passengers and the riotous young people.

Life was to him like strong, white light that hurts the tired eyes of a sick person. During every conscious moment life blazed in a raw glare around him and upon him. It hurt. It hurt intolerably. It was the first time in his life that Martin had traveled first class. On ships at sea he had always been in the forecastle, the steerage, or in the black depths of the coal-hold, passing coal. In those days, climbing up the iron ladders from out the pit of stifling heat, he had often caught glimpses of the passengers, in cool white, doing nothing but enjoy themselves, under awnings spread to keep the sun and wind away from them, with subservient stewards taking care of their every want and whim, and it had seemed to him that the realm in which they moved and had their being was nothing else than paradise. Well, here he was, the great man on board, in the midmost center of it, sitting at the captain's right hand, and yet vainly harking back to forecastle and stoke-hole in quest of the Paradise he had lost. He had found no new one, and now he could not find the old one.

He strove to stir himself and find something to interest him. He ventured the petty officers' mess, and was glad to get away. He talked with a quartermaster off duty, an intelligent man who promptly prodded him with the socialist propaganda and forced into his hands a bunch of leaflets and pamphlets. He listened to the man expounding the slave-morality, and as he listened, he thought languidly of his own Nietzsche philosophy. But what was it worth, after all? He remembered one of Nietzsche's mad utterances wherein that madman had doubted truth. And who was to say? Perhaps Nietzsche had been right. Perhaps there was no truth in anything, no truth in truth—no such thing as truth. But his mind wearied quickly, and he was content to go back to his chair and doze.

Miserable as he was on the steamer, a new misery came upon him. What when the steamer reached Tahiti? He would have to go ashore. He would have to order his trade-goods, to find a passage on a schooner to the Marquesas, to do a thousand and one things that were awful to contemplate. Whenever he steeled himself deliberately to think, he could see the desperate peril in which he stood. In all truth, he was in the Valley of the Shadow, and his danger lay in that he was not afraid. If he were only afraid, he would make toward life. Being unafraid, he was drifting deeper into the shadow. He found no delight in the old familiar things of life. The *Mariposa* was now in the northeast trades, and this wine of wind, surging against him, irritated him. He had his chair moved to escape the embrace of this lusty comrade of old days and nights.

The day the *Mariposa* entered the doldrums, Martin

was more miserable than ever. He could no longer sleep. He was soaked with sleep, and perforce he must now stay awake and endure the white glare of life. He moved about restlessly. The air was sticky and humid, and the rain-squalls were unrefreshing. He ached with life. He walked around the deck until that hurt too much, then sat in his chair until he was compelled to walk again. He forced himself at last to finish the magazine, and from the steamer library he culled several volumes of poetry. But they could not hold him, and once more he took to walking.

He stayed late on deck, after dinner, but that did not help him, for when he went below, he could not sleep. This surcease from life had failed him. It was too much. He turned on the electric light and tried to read. One of the volumes was a Swinburne. He lay in bed, glancing through its pages, until suddenly he became aware that he was reading with interest. He finished the stanza, attempted to read on, then came back to it. He rested the book face downward on his breast and fell to thinking. That was it. The very thing. Strange that it had never come to him before. That was the meaning of it all; he had been drifting that way all the time, and now Swinburne showed him that it was the happy way out. He wanted rest, and here was rest awaiting him. He glanced at the open port-hole. Yes, it was large enough. For the first time in weeks he felt happy. At last he had discovered the cure of his ill. He picked up the book and read the stanza slowly aloud:—

" 'From too much love of living,
    From hope and fear set free,
We thank with brief thanksgiving
    Whatever gods may be

That no life lives forever;
That dead men rise up never;
   That even the weariest river
Winds somewhere safe to sea.' "

He looked again at the open port. Swinburne had
furnished the key. Life was ill, or, rather, it had become ill—an unbearable thing. "That dead men rise
up never!" That line stirred him with a profound feeling of gratitude. It was the one beneficent thing in the
universe. When life became an aching weariness, death
was ready to soothe away to everlasting sleep. But
what was he waiting for? It was time to go.

He arose and thrust his head out the port-hole, looking down into the milky wash. The *Mariposa* was deeply
loaded, and, hanging by his hands, his feet would be
in the water. He could slip in noiselessly. No one
would hear. A smother of spray dashed up, wetting
his face. It tasted salt on his lips, and the taste was
good. He wondered if he ought to write a swan-song,
but laughed the thought away. There was no time.
He was too impatient to be gone.

Turning off the light in his room so that it might
not betray him, he went out the port-hole feet first.
His shoulders stuck, and he forced himself back so as
to try it with one arm down by his side. A roll of the
steamer aided him, and he was through, hanging by
his hands. When his feet touched the sea, he let go
He was in a milky froth of water. The side of the
Mariposa rushed past him like a dark wall, broken here
and there by lighted ports. She was certainly making
time. Almost before he knew it, he was astern, swimming gently on the foam-crackling surface.

A bonita struck at his white body, and he laughed
aloud It had taken a piece out, and the sting of it

reminded him of why he was there. In the work to do he had forgotten the purpose of it. The lights of the *Mariposa* were growing dim in the distance, and there he was, swimming confidently, as though it were his intention to make for the nearest land a thousand miles or so away.

It was the automatic instinct to live. He ceased swimming, but the moment he felt the water rising above his mouth the hands struck out sharply with a lifting movement. The will to live, was his thought, and the thought was accompanied by a sneer. Well, he had will,—ay, will strong enough that with one last exertion it could destroy itself and cease to be.

He changed his position to a vertical one. He glanced up at the quiet stars, at the same time emptying his lungs of air. With swift, vigorous propulsion of hands and feet, he lifted his shoulders and half his chest out of water. This was to gain impetus for the descent. Then he let himself go and sank without movement, a white statue, into the sea. He breathed in the water deeply, deliberately, after the manner of a man taking an anesthetic. When he strangled, quite involuntarily his arms and legs clawed the water and drove him up to the surface and into the clear sight of the stars.

The will to live, he thought disdainfully, vainly endeavoring not to breathe the air into his bursting lungs. Well, he would have to try a new way. He filled his lungs with air, filled them full. This supply would take him far down. He turned over and went down head first, swimming with all his strength and all his will. Deeper and deeper he went. His eyes were open, and he watched the ghostly, phosphorescent trails of the darting bonita. As he swam, he hoped that they would not strike at him, for it might snap the tension of his will. But they did not strike, and he found time to be grateful for this last kindness of life.

Down, down, he swam till his arms and legs grew tired and hardly moved. He knew that he was deep. The pressure on his ear-drums was a pain, and there was a buzzing in his head. His endurance was faltering, but he compelled his arms and legs to drive him deeper until his will snapped and the air drove from his lungs in a great explosive rush. The bubbles rubbed and bounded like tiny balloons against his cheeks and eyes as they took their upward flight. Then came pain and strangulation. This hurt was not death, was the thought that oscillated through his reeling consciousness. Death did not hurt. It was life, the pangs of life, this awful, suffocating feeling; it was the last blow life could deal him.

His willful hands and feet began to beat and churn about, spasmodically and feebly. But he had fooled them and the will to live that made them beat and churn. He was too deep down. They could never bring him to the surface. He seemed floating languidly in a sea of dreamy vision. Colors and radiances surrounded him and bathed him and pervaded him. What was that? It seemed a lighthouse; but it was inside his brain—a flashing, bright white light. It flashed swifter and swifter. There was a long rumble of sound, and it seemed to him that he was falling down a vast and interminable stairway. And somewhere at the bottom he fell into darkness. That much he knew. He had fallen into darkness. And at the instant he knew, he ceased to know